KISS THE GIRL

Susan Sey

Copyright © 2012 Susan Seyfarth
All rights reserved
ISBN 10: 1938580001
ISBN 13: 978-1-938580-00-0

Other titles by Susan Sey

MONEY, HONEY

MONEY SHOT

Dedication

For Inara Scott, who's been with me every step of the way.

For Ann and Katrina, who know how to keep calm and carry on.

For Claudia and Greta, who do like to see their names in my books.

And for Bryan, whose faith in me is big enough for the both of us. And because he has never once suggested that we eat out too much.

CHAPTER ONE

Nixie Leighton-Brace wasn't afraid to die. She'd been in the humanitarian business long enough to know that death was hardly the worst thing that could happen to a girl. She just didn't want to go before knocking Dr. James Harper--her soon-to-be-ex-boyfriend--on his cheating ass.

The hard blue sky wheeled around the bubble window of her helicopter. A yellow line of drought-stricken horizon veered crazily into view every so often while the pilot fought the controls, the wind, and the bucking helicopter. He kept up a terse commentary over his headset to whatever authority governed Kenya's air traffic.

Well, that caps it, Nixie thought as a bubble of hysterical laughter lodged in her throat. Every single second of her life had been documented by some form of media, and now this. Somebody was going to narrate her death via radio.

But it wouldn't end here. She knew that. If she died today, James would sell exclusive photo rights to the funeral to *Chat Magazine* for millions. He'd cry crocodile tears for the cameras then continue to fuck his way through the entire Peace Corps. She and God had had their differences over the years, but Nixie refused to believe He'd stoop so low.

As if in direct response to this inner conviction, the shearing cross-wind died. The helicopter wobbled, spun, then steadied. The pilot's grin broke like dawn over his dark, sweat-sheened face, and he gave Nixie the thumbs up. Nixie thought *hey, both hands on the stick there, pal*, but smiled back anyway. She was going to live. Long enough to deliver James' beat-down, anyway. Nixie's faith, such as it was, remained intact.

The pilot lowered the chopper lightly to the ground. Nixie watched from her protective glass bubble as the rotor wash blasted the thirsty earth, stripping away yet another layer of Kenya's precious topsoil. She unbuckled her harness and pulled the headset gingerly out of the wild bramble of her hair. The desert was not kind to the naturally curly. She muscled open the door of the chopper just as Karl Dettreich, Leighton-Brace Charitable Giving's long time political advisor and Nixie's de facto parental figure, rolled up in a white Land Rover.

Nixie hopped out, and turned to catch the canvas bag the pilot tossed her. "*Asante*," Nixie thanked him. "I wasn't looking to die today."

"God is good," the pilot said, grinning. He adjusted his headset and waited for Nixie to duck-walk her way out of the danger zone, then lifted off. He executed a neat little pivot and bulleted into the sharp blue dome of the cloudless sky. Nixie trotted over to the Land Rover.

"Hey, Nixie," Karl bellowed. He was the only person Nixie knew who habitually spoke at a roar. The top of his head rose bald and sweaty from a bushy ring of salt and pepper hair. He swabbed it with a red bandana, which he then stuffed into the drooping pocket of his cargo shorts. "How was Nairobi?"

"Huge. Hot. Crowded." Nixie patted the canvas duffel at her side. "Successful."

"You got them signed?" Karl's eyes were black and bright behind his glasses. "All of them?"

Kiss the Girl

"Our clinic is now fully accredited by the Minister of Public Health, and our standards of care will be posted in every rural hospital in the country."

Karl shook his shaggy head. "How do you do that voodoo you do so well?"

Nixie smiled. Karl liked his Frank Sinatra. "I bribe quite lavishly. It's Leighton-Brace policy."

"I know. I wrote the guidelines. You must bribe exceptionally well, even by our standards."

"I was in a hurry to get back." Nixie handed over the canvas bag with the documents and wrenched open the Land Rover's passenger door. Hot air blasted out of the cab and she tossed a towel from the floorboards over the blistered vinyl seat so it wouldn't barbecue her thighs. Karl rounded the hood, squeezed his bulk into the cab and took the wheel.

He fired up the Land Rover and laid the accelerator on the floor. The truck leapt forward, and they both sighed in relief at the air circulation.

"Listen, Nixie," he said. He cut his eyes at her, but the lenses of his glasses went opaque in the sun. Nixie's chest tightened. "There's something we need to talk about."

"Okay."

"You're not going to like this."

"Okay." She put her hands together, tucked them between her knees. "What is it?"

"You're *really* not going to like this."

"Karl, *what*?" This was the man who'd unflinchingly delivered every piece of bad news in her life, from boarding school to her father's death. The fact that he hesitated told her it was beyond bad. "Did the clinic burn down while I was away? Did Mom drop the f-bomb on a live mic again?"

"No, nothing like that." Karl patted Nixie's knee with one of those big, avuncular paws. He put his hand back on the wheel and stared straight out the windshield while they rocketed past a collection of slip-shod huts and plywood buildings on the outskirts of town. "It's about James," he finally said.

Nixie sighed, both relieved and resigned. "You know already?" she asked.

"*You* know?"

"That my boyfriend is a faithless bastard? Yeah, I know." Nixie's hands fisted between her knees and she stared out the window at the tents and shacks zipping by, built closer and closer together as they approached city center. "Don't worry about it, okay? I'll take care of it. I have a plan."

Karl slowed in deference to foot traffic and the occasional chicken but his volume went the other direction. "Don't worry about it? Don't *worry* about it? How can I not worry about it? It's my job to worry about this shit, Nixie." He shifted his bulk, rolling up onto one cheek so he could fish out his bandana again. He mopped his crown and said, "Jesus. What a day. And what's this about a plan?"

Nixie smiled. She felt evil, and she kind of liked it. She never got to be evil. "I found a pair of panties--not mine--in my pocket this morning," she said. "In James's pocket, really. I must've accidentally packed his shorts instead of mine. Anyway, you can imagine my surprise."

"Nice." Karl threaded the Land Rover through what passed for rush hour traffic in rural Kenya. Mostly goats and kids. He shot her a look, then boomed, "Jesus, you fit into your boyfriend's shorts?"

"I'm tall." Nixie shrugged. "Still, I probably should've listened to Mom. She always says, if he *fits* in your pants, he shouldn't *get* in your pants. Who would have thought I'd ever look back on my dating life and wish I'd paid more attention to Sloan Leighton?"

Kiss the Girl

Karl's mouth was a grim line inside his silver-streaked beard as he parked outside the abandoned Red Cross building Nixie had co-opted as project HQ.

"Ironic," he said. "Now about this plan?"

"The press is going to eat this up, you know. They love messy break ups. People will be wearing t-shirts taking sides. I'm going to have to turn the other cheek in public. A lot."

Karl nodded tersely. "I know, Nixie. I'm sorry."

He cut the engine and Nixie leapt onto the hard-baked earth, slamming the door behind her like a rifle-shot. She stalked through the corrugated tin doors of the white stucco building, Karl huffing at her heels.

A handful of journalists were gathered in the foyer, leaning on the front desk, telling each other lies and smoking. It was a nice assortment, Nixie noted with satisfaction as she mowed a path through them without so much as a greeting.

They lifted their heads, sniffed the air, and came to attention with the collective intelligence of their species. Nixie had been raised in front of a camera lens. She knew these men and women by name, asked after their kids, their spouses, their pets. She respected their work, and understood that without them she didn't have a job. She never failed to greet them, or stop for a picture or a quote. Her failure to do so now was tantamount to running a red flag up the pole and announcing, "I am bent on homicide. Be ready with the cameras."

Nixie knew exactly what she was doing.

"Don't be sorry for me, Karl," she said. She didn't have to look behind her to know she was now leading a small parade. "Before I start turning the other cheek, I'm going to make sure Team Nixie has adequate ammo."

"Oh God." Karl broke into a trot as Nixie took the stairs two at a time toward the living quarters on the second floor. The journalists fumbled for notebooks, cell phones, cameras, anything that would record the delicious disaster Nixie was about to serve up.

As she barreled down the narrow, dimly lit hall, a savage joy welled up in Nixie. She was too honest with herself to believe she was heart broken. She hadn't loved James, but she *had* expected him to be faithful. If she had to live through the public humiliation of his infidelity--and she would; some secrets never kept--at least she could strike the first blow. In the endless retellings of the Nixie-James break-up the press was sure to provide in the coming months, there would be irrefutable proof that she'd been the one to end the relationship. She'd make sure of it. She was about to toss his cheating ass out in front of a dozen witnesses with cameras and a direct line to public opinion.

She paused outside the room she'd shared with James these past months and Karl caught her elbow. "Nixie, Jesus, slow down and think! James is a shit, I know, but he's a well-connected shit. His father's about to run for president, for Christ's sake. You do this, and Team James is going to come back at you with some serious firepower. Are you sure you want to do this?"

She just smiled at the journalists hovering behind him like vultures waiting for the lions to clear out. "Get ready with those cameras, kids."

"James!" she shouted through the door. "Get out here! I want to talk to you, you lying sack of..."

She threw the door open, and the words died in her throat. She stared in paralyzed horror at the bed. At James's naked ass, specifically, as it diligently humped some faceless woman in a similar state of undress. The woman's moans crescendoed toward triumph, but Nixie was stuck on her legs. Long, toned and golden, they poked out of the tangled sheets on either side of James' busy butt, feet to the ceiling, bouncing to the beat of the bedsprings.

Kiss the Girl

Nixie's vision wavered and grayed, and she sucked at the thin air. She knew those legs. Everybody knew those legs. They were famous. Legendary. Insured in the mid-seven figures each.

"Mom?"

James's butt lunged heroically once more, shuddered, then went still. He groaned and dropped his head to the pillow, giving the room a clear view of her mother's equally famous face--her head thrown back on a cloud of amber curls, her full lips parted in ecstasy, her eyes squeezed shut as she milked the moment for every ounce of pleasure. The cameras clicked and whirred like a plague of locusts at Nixie's back, the strobing flashes burning into Nixie's brain forever the image of her mother's airborne feet, flexed and striving, as she finished up what must have been one humdinger of an orgasm.

"Well, Nixie?" Karl said, resigned. "I assume you wanted to say something?"

Nixie's throat worked, her mouth opened, but no words presented themselves. She thought about the past twenty-eight years, the entirety of her life, spent trailing after her gorgeous, needy mother. Her childhood washed pale with the explosion of flashbulbs, overlaid with shouting paparazzi. Boarding schools interspliced with refugee camps, Red Cross outposts, and war zone after war zone. Her mother always holding an orphan, a victim, a widow while her father, then later Karl, held her. Then nobody holding her. Just her holding a clipboard while she slowly learned to run the show that revolved around Sloan Leighton and her fame.

"Nixie?" Karl's hand touched her shoulder. "Honey?"

Nixie walked into the room, pulled the panties from her pocket and hooked them over her mother's toes. Sloan's knees slowly folded, and the panties descended like the flag of a defeated army. Her eyes stayed closed, though, as if not acknowledging the situation would somehow erase it.

Nixie finally found her voice.

"Hey, Mom. I quit."

CHAPTER TWO

Six weeks later

Nixie stood in the echoing kitchen of Leighton-Brace Charitable Giving's DC apartment and eyed the stove. It was a hulking beast, a couple cubic yards of gleaming chrome, cast iron and bad attitude. Nixie was almost sure it was French. She'd already assigned it a snooty Parisian accent in her head. *Ouf! Always wit zee tiresome attempts at zee cookeeng, zees woman. I must put her in her proper place, non?* Last night's attempt at dinner had actually caught fire before Nixie admitted defeat.

So her stove hated her. Big deal. She was no stranger to being disliked for arbitrary reasons. Nixie currently occupied the moral high ground in the battle for public sympathy but Sloan was way hotter and had mastered the art of indulging her self-destructive streak for the greater good. With six lavish weddings, one harrowing widowhood, five bitter divorces, and countless well-documented scenes under her belt, Nixie's mom was a perennial tabloid favorite. But she'd also spent the past twenty-odd years pitching her fits in corners of the world most people wanted to forget, sharing the spotlight with the kind of unspeakable suffering people *couldn't* forget once they'd seen it. And *that* made her an American institution. The kind of bad girl her country loved. So no matter what she did to her only daughter, Sloan's fame was at this point a self-propelled mower.

Which was exactly why Nixie needed to figure out this damned stove.

She cooked competently over a campfire, and she knew how to handle herself with grace at a state dinner. The gray area--admittedly large--between those two extremes had been handled by chefs in her mother's homes and take out in all other circumstances. But since her bitter break up with Leighton-Brace Charitable Giving, even the take-out guys had sold her out. Every time she ordered in, they showed up at the door with the paparazzi in tow. Photos of Nixie with startled eyes, bad hair and a steaming bag of Chinese food appeared in the tabloids with dismaying regularity.

She poured herself a large glass of wine for courage. There was a great deal in her life she couldn't fix. Not knowing how to feed herself in plugged-in, urban America wasn't one of them. Nixie cracked open *The Passionate Vegetarian* — all thousand plus pages of it--and applied herself to the business of producing a pumpkin and bean lasagna.

The phone rang just as she slid the diced onions into a pan of sizzling canola oil.

"Hello?" She had to shout a bit, as the onions were cooking with enthusiasm. So far, so good.

"Nixie, it's Karl."

She gave the onions a good sharp poke with the wooden spoon and turned away from the stove. She was a little lonely, sure. But not lonely enough to welcome another stop-being-ridiculous phone call from Karl.

"What do you want, Karl?"

"I want you to come home. We have work to do."

She stepped out of the kitchen and sighed. "I am home."

Kiss the Girl

"You're not home. You're camping out in the corporation's DC apartment, hiding from the world and eating a lot of take out, if the tabloids have it right. Come on, Nixie. Sloan dumped James weeks ago. That big scene in Prague? You must've read about it. Why don't you come home now?"

She realized she was trying to choke the spoon to death and consciously relaxed her grip. "Because I *quit*, remember?"

"I can't believe you're this upset about an asshole like James Harper." He sighed. "Didn't I tell you he was a dirt bag? Didn't I say he wasn't good enough for you?"

"This isn't about James. This is about Sloan."

"Oh, please." Karl snorted. "Sloan's no different than usual."

"Yeah," Nixie said grimly. "I know."

"Then don't pretend to be all shocked and injured. Sloan being Sloan is the reason what we do works, and you know it. She's like the Angelina Jolie to your Princess Diana, and people eat you guys up. Which is why you need to come home. There's work to do and without you we've only got half a schtick."

"Schtick?" Nixie slapped the spoon against her thigh. "My fifty-year-old mother screws my boyfriend on You Tube eight hundred times a day, Karl. That's not a schtick, that's a deeply dysfunctional family finally falling apart."

"No, that's Sloan burning herself to the ground in a new and novel way. Your job is to rise up from the ashes and take her with you so we can keep building hospitals and schools and orphanages. You're named Phoenix for a reason, you know."

"I thought it was because I was conceived at a Rolling Stones show in Arizona."

"Cute." Karl cleared his throat. "Come on, Nixie. You've been sulking for nearly two months now. Lives are at stake. It's time to get back to work. Come home."

Nixie squeezed her eyes shut against the rush of guilt and rage. Her suffering was so small compared to what she'd seen. But at least she could still hurt. At least she wasn't stone-cold and numb yet, like Sloan, forced to act out more and more wildly to feel anything at all. She hadn't lost herself entirely. Not yet.

"Come home?" Nixie laughed bitterly. "You keep saying that like I have a home to come back to, Karl."

"We're your home," he said. "Me and your mom."

Tears filled Nixie's eyes and she brushed them away impatiently. Okay, so she was lonely. But not lonely enough to hang around while her beautiful, brittle mother destroyed herself over and over again in the name of charity.

"I'm sorry, Karl. I need more than that."

"More? More what? Jesus, Nixie, you're a ridiculously gifted young woman. You're beautiful, famous, and wealthy beyond imagining." There was a pause and Nixie closed her eyes, waiting for it. The inevitable punch line to every argument she'd ever had with Karl. "You have a responsibility toward those who haven't been so lucky, Nixie."

Nixie thought about the Kenyan clinic she'd built with Karl, her mom and the man who'd screwed her mother halfway across Europe after treating Nixie to an avalanche of public humiliation. She thought about the clinic's first patient, a little girl with huge, trusting eyes in a head that was entirely too big for her withered, failing body. She'd asked if Nixie was an angel, come to take her home to God. Nixie had lied without hesitation, and been rewarded with a smile so pure it made her eyes sting even now to think of it.

Kiss the Girl

"Give me one more month," Nixie said. "One more month to be...away. I promise, if I haven't found some way to live up to my responsibilities by then, I'll come back to work."

"One more month. Christ, Nixie, you're killing me." She could hear him scratching at his beard.

"I know. I'm sorry."

He sighed. "Okay, okay. One month, and not a day more. I'll be coming for you."

She smiled into the phone. "I know you will."

"All right then." There was an awkward pause, then Karl said, "You eating okay? I don't like all this Chinese food I'm seeing in the papers."

Nixie smiled, warmed by the concern in his voice. "Don't worry about it, okay?"

"You pay me to worry. You're a brand, Nixie. Little girls look up to you, and if you eat like crap--"

The warmth faded abruptly and Nixie cut him off. "I'm actually learning to cook."

"Seriously?"

She bristled at the deep skepticism in his voice. "Seriously. In fact, I'm making a lasagna right now, so--" Nixie broke off in horror. "The onions! Damn it! I have to go."

"What?"

She hung up on him, threw the phone toward the couch and raced into the kitchen. She seized up the smoking pan and dumped its crispy black contents into the sink. She flipped on the faucet and the gush of water vaporized the instant it hit the million-degree pan. The smell of damp, incinerated onions wafted through the entire apartment.

At least the smoke alarms didn't go off this time, Nixie thought. That was something, right?

The stove smirked at her. *Take zat, you eensolent dog! You eensult to zee noble art of cookery!*

"That was rude and unnecessary," she told it. "My last onion, too."

Maybe she should run out and get another. It was early yet. She could still have lasagna on the table by nightfall. She glanced at the window. An ugly drizzly snow pelted against the pane, obscuring her view of the Potomac. She shivered just looking at it. She wasn't going out again.

She supposed she could run upstairs and ask Elizabeth Dole for a loaner onion. Surely, all the work she and her mother had done for the Red Cross was worth an onion? But no, that would mean explaining to the former president of the Red Cross that she'd abandoned humanitarian work in favor of murdering innocent onions on a nightly basis.

Yeah, that conversation could wait. Maybe the woman across the hall had an extra onion. That was a nice, normal thing to do, wasn't it? Borrow an onion from a neighbor? So what if that neighbor happened to be the most senior female Senator in DC. It was still normal.

Nixie wandered toward the front door. Even her bare feet sounded loud in the generic emptiness. Aside from the cathedral ceilings and the mean stove, she could easily imagine herself in a hotel room. Nixie was across the hall and knocking on the door before she realized it, sucking air into her lungs like she'd just been released from prison.

The Senator herself opened the door, an earring in one hand, cell phone in the other. She barely glanced at Nixie, just waved her in and went back to the phone call.

"I want six more votes in my pocket by morning, Jack. I don't care who you have to sleep with to make it happen. You've never been fussy. Enjoy yourself, darling."

Nixie pushed the door shut behind her and followed the woman's back through the foyer and into the living room. It was a mirror image of her own apartment, structurally, but where hers could have been furnished by Beige Incorporated, the Senator's place breathed like a living thing.

The walls were such a rich café au lait that Nixie was tempted to taste them, and plump cushions roosted on the leather couch like funky velvet birds. Chunky sculptures and draped tapestries in the same jewel tones as the Senator's signature suits added just the right note of sophistication. The collection of spindly houseplants at the window made Nixie smile. They were gasping almost audibly for water. She'd bet anything they had been gifts, plunked in front of the window to expire quietly.

She followed her into the kitchen, noting the normal, serviceable range. No gigantic, temperamental beast of a stove for the Senator from Indiana. Nixie's respect for the woman grew. Nixie watched her drop her phone onto the desk and clip her earring back into place.

"So, Nixie Leighton-Brace," she said with a smile. "I'd heard you were squatting next door."

Nixie smiled back. "I hadn't thought of it that way until I saw this place, but yeah. I think I have been."

"Brenda Larsen," she said, extending a delicate hand. Nixie tried not to crush it. "What can I do for you?"

"I'm hoping to borrow an onion."

The Senator's perfectly drawn brows lifted. "Is that code for something?"

"No, ma'am." Nixie laid one bare foot on top of the other and admired the older woman's ability to carry off her trim suit the color of ripe eggplants and the matching three inch heels. "I actually need an onion. I burned the last one. My stove doesn't care for me."

The Senator pursed her lips and walked back out into the living room. "Is that why this place smells like a bad Indian restaurant every night?"

"Probably." Nixie trailed after her, enveloped in the cloud of expensive perfume she left in her wake. "Sorry about that. Did I mention my stove hates me?"

The Senator disappeared into what Nixie presumed was the bedroom. Surely she didn't keep her produce in there? "Your stove?" the Senator asked, her voice muffled. "Why are you cooking? Don't you make have your hands full enough fronting Leighton-Brace's Charitable Giving branch?"

"I used to." Nixie wandered over to the window, drawn by a particularly crisp ivy. It shot a handful of brown, star-shaped leaves to the floor at her approach, an SOS from a desperate plant. "I quit."

The Senator emerged from the bedroom in a rustling sapphire-blue ball gown. "Why?"

"I'm exploring a new direction." Nixie eased closer to the ivy. "Wow, are you *trying* to kill these plants? I've seen wetter soil in the Sahara."

The Senator frowned. "What? Oh, those. I'm not trying to kill them, no." She thought a moment. "Though I can't say I've been trying to keep them alive, either." She turned, presenting the half-done zipper at her back to Nixie. "A little help?"

Nixie stared at the woman's back. It wasn't the first time a total stranger had asked her to perform an oddly intimate service. People Nixie had never seen before often viewed her as an old friend after having read about her in newspapers and magazines her whole life. She didn't think this was the case with the Senator, though. The Senator was as much a public figure as Nixie was, but where Nixie still had the occasional twinge of claustrophobia, the Senator had apparently embraced her lack of personal space to the point of asking near-strangers to zip her dresses.

Nixie pulled up the zipper with two fingertips. She had no doubt the woman was a formidable opponent on the Senate floor, but lord she was tiny. Nixie could probably pick her up and throw her a couple yards if necessary.

"Fancy," Nixie said as she threaded the hook and eye at the top of the zipper. "Dolce and Gabbana?"

The Senator smiled over her shoulder. "Alexander McQueen." She clipped a twisty bracelet studded with what looked like genuine sapphires to her wrist. It matched the glitter peeking through the perfect wings of honey-blonde hair over her ears. She studied her reflection in the giant framed mirror on the wall and her mouth curved in satisfaction.

"No necklace?" Nixie asked.

The Senator turned to check her rear view. "Oh, heavens, no. My neck still has a few good years left. Let them see it." Her smile went sly. "A woman's bare throat can be very alluring. Don't over decorate, dear." She turned away from the mirror and focused on Nixie. "Now, what's this nonsense about an onion?"

"I was making lasagna and got distracted by a phone call. The onion didn't make it. I was hoping you'd spot me a new one." She gave her a winning smile.

"Do I look like a woman who keeps onions on hand?"

Nixie squinted at her. She looked sleek, powerful, vibrant. "Um, no. You don't."

"Good. Because I'm not. And neither are you."

"Excuse me?"

The Senator advanced on her and Nixie edged closer to the ivies. "Do you want to know what you look like to me? You look like a second generation activist with a world-class publicity machine and an approval rating my colleagues and I would kill for. You look like a young woman sitting on one of the most famous faces and fortunes in the world and suddenly doing nothing with it. If this is an identity crisis, let me clear it up for you.

You're Nixie Leighton-Brace. You don't need a new direction. You need to get back to work."

Nixie picked at the ivy. "I just wanted to come home."

"And this is it?" The Senator studied her. Nixie tried not to squirm. "You feel at home here?"

She thought of the echoing, empty apartment across the hall. "I will," she said, but her eyes slid away from the Senator's skeptical gaze. "Do you even own a watering can?" she asked. "These poor plants are killing me."

"In the kitchen, I think. Under the sink."

Nixie was filling the watering can when the Senator appeared in the doorway. "My cab is here. There's a key in the basket by the front door. Lock up when you're finished with the plants, hmmm?"

"Oh, are you sure? I can always come back later--"

"Are you kidding me? Your tender little heart would be torn to shreds imagining my plants gasping their last all night. Weed and feed all you like. Just remember to lock up. And think about what I said. We'll talk again. Soon, I think."

Then she was gone, leaving Nixie with nothing but some dying plants and a vague dissatisfaction. And no onion, damn it.

She filled the brass watering pot at the sink, then wandered back into the main room. She'd spent a happy twenty minutes drenching the parched plants when the front door opened. It wasn't the Senator, she knew immediately. No perfume, no greeting, no clickety-clack of pencil-thin heels.

Nixie's heart thudded into her throat. Karl had tried to warn her about DC – the murder rate, the muggings in broad day light. But for crying out loud, she was living in the *Watergate*. That hadn't been a hotbed of crime since the Nixon era.

Kiss the Girl

But as she stood there, watering can hovering over the ivies, she was willing to concede this one to Karl. Footsteps clomped purposefully across the foyer, and Nixie knew she would be eyeball to eyeball with the intruder--oh God, the possibly *armed* intruder--any second. She set down the watering can before her trembling hands made a sprinkler of it, breathed deep and prepared to face down the enemy.

CHAPTER THREE

Dr. Erik Larsen shook his head, scattering tiny droplets of melted snow all over his mother's smooth, polished foyer. He smiled grimly. Served her right. He didn't have time for this. The snow had snarled traffic until it was practically moving backward through the space-time continuum, and now, thanks to his mother's mysterious summons, he would surely be late to the clinic.

Erik hated being late. It was one of the many reasons he and Mary Jane got along so well. She was as pathologically punctual as he was, and would not look kindly upon his failure to show up on time for a meeting regarding their jointly run clinic. Especially not an emergency meeting of the how-are-we-going-to-pay-the-rent variety.

He raked a hand through the crust of slush melting on his hair--damn, it was coming down out there--and rounded the corner.

He moved through the living room at a near jog. His mother's little *surprises* were almost always time-sucking disasters, and he was already late enough. She'd promised this one was a no-brainer--*You'll know it when you see it, dear*--and Erik prayed she was telling the truth.

Kiss the Girl

He gave the living room a cursory glance, then headed for the kitchen. He was halfway there when his brain registered what he'd seen, and he froze mid-stride.

He turned and looked again at the window. His stomach sank. Yep, there she was. A woman, standing absolutely still in his mother's miserable collection of dying plants, hands knit together, mouth pursed, an expression on her face that wavered between friendly interest and I-have-911-on-speed-dial.

Oh, Christ. His mother had left him a *woman*? She'd thrown any number of horse-faced debutantes at him over the years, but she'd never booby-trapped her apartment with one before.

He stared her. She was taller than usual, but thin to the point of near-transparency in her well-worn jeans and the sort of loose, gypsyish top only found at third world bazaars and Goodwill. She stepped away from the window, a mop of red curls bobbing around sharp cheekbones and enormous eyes the color of pasture land. Her feet were bare.

She was no horse-faced debutante, but he made a mental note to kill his mother anyway.

"One of us probably doesn't belong here," the woman said with an oddly familiar half-smile. "Is it you or me?"

"Since this is my mother's apartment, I'm going to say you," he said.

"Senator Larsen didn't tell me she had a son in town."

"Should she have? Who are you?"

"Oh, sorry. I'm in 616. Across the hall?" She wiggled one finger toward the door. "I came over to borrow an onion and ended up rescuing the plants your mother seems determined to starve to death. She said I should just lock up when I was done." She tipped her head and studied him. "You have the look of her, don't you? Your mother."

He frowned. The Senator was approximately five feet nothing and built like a bird. "Nobody's ever said so."

"It's not a physical resemblance so much as a similar energy." She pursed up her lips and nodded slowly. "You *feel* like her."

"Right. Similar energy." Erik glanced around the room in the rapidly dwindling hope that his mother had left him something other than this woman. "Listen, did my mother happen to mention that she was leaving something here for me?"

"Like what?"

"I don't know. She said I'd know it when I saw it."

"Oh. Mysterious."

"That's my mom." *Subtle as a sledge hammer.* He checked his watch, barely suppressed a wince. He stalked into the kitchen, hoping the woman would leave while he was in there, and thus spare him the duty of explaining his mother's fixation with his marital status. He jumped half a foot when her voice sounded at his shoulder. God, she was quiet in those bare feet.

"Does she do this often?" the woman asked. "Send you on scavenger hunts?"

"No." He gave the empty counters a desperate look. Nothing. Not that he expected anything. He turned to her and found that oddly familiar smile still on her lips. He frowned.

"Do I know you?" he asked. "Who are you again?"

"Apartment 616," she said. "The plant savior?" Her smile widened cheerfully, and it made the freckles on her nose stand out like nutmeg sprinkled on cream. That smile wasn't just weirdly familiar, he realized. It was famous.

"Like hell," he said, staring. "You're Nixie Leighton-Brace."

She lifted one of those sharp, bony shoulders in a half-shrug. "That, too."

Kiss the Girl

"Of course you are." He closed his eyes, just a little longer than a blink. "You're it, aren't you?"

"I'm what?" Her mossy eyes went wide, and one hand crept to her throat.

"You're what my mother left me."

Okay, now Nixie was a little alarmed. At first she'd been strangely comforted by him. He looked like nothing so much as a Norwegian farm hand--large, blonde, perpetually sunburned--but he radiated energy in big, fat, buzzy waves. She'd spent her life in the company of men and women like this, people whose ambitions were too large to be contained in a single body and spilled over into the air around them.

She'd been tempted to move closer and warm herself, like he was a cozy fire on a cold night. It was a weakness, she knew. Back sliding. Not on her Normal Life Game Plan. The next guy she fell for was going to be an accountant with a thing for minivans and tuna noodle casserole. The kind of guy who'd pass out cold if Sloan ever flashed him the come-hither.

But Nixie didn't have anything right now in terms of a life, normal or otherwise. It was grey and nasty out, she'd been thoroughly chastised by the closest thing she had to a father, and she'd just turned her last onion into charcoal. Surely she could be forgiven for clinging to the familiar?

But now she wasn't so sure. He wasn't radiating that beautiful energy any more. Now he was looking at her with a familiar speculation, the kind she'd seen on strangers' faces her whole life. He wanted something from her.

"Listen," she said, "I don't know what you and your mom have cooked up here, but whatever it is, forget it. I'm retired."

"Hey, don't look at me. My mom works alone. I just get caught in the cross fire every now and then. But for once, I don't mind."

"Well, I do."

"Yeah? Mind what?" He flashed her a grin, and she immediately revised her initial impression. This man wasn't a farm hand. He was a Viking. Big, blonde, wide enough to sack entire villages without breaking a sweat.

"What?"

"You said you minded. Mind what?"

Nixie frowned. "Being manipulated."

"Have you been?"

"I..." She broke off. "I don't know. All I know so far is that I've been co-opted as the grand prize of a scavenger hunt my new neighbor set up for her adult son. Does that strike you as weird, or is it just me?"

"No, it's weird."

"Yeah, that's what I thought."

"She's hoping we'll fall in love, marry, and produce gorgeous children that will be an asset to our good name when I run for president."

Nixie's hand rose to her throat. "Oh."

"Yeah, but don't worry. I have no intention of reproducing at my mother's behest, nor in running for public office. You're safe with me."

"Well that's a relief."

"Yeah." He tucked big hands into his pockets and studied her. "Listen, are you interested in a job?"

"A job?"

"I know you said you were retired, and from what I've seen on the news, it's for good reason."

Nixie closed her eyes and pushed a thumb into the headache starting to burrow between her brows. "Glad you approve."

"So here you are, hunkered down in DC, trying to put a life back together, am I right?"

Kiss the Girl

Nixie opened her eyes and gazed at him. He was a train wreck. Pitching was not this man's strong suit. But what he lacked in finesse, he clearly made up for in tenacity, because he was still going.

"I have just the project to get you back on your feet, philanthropically speaking." He grinned broadly, and that beautiful, buzzy energy was back. It filled the air around him, reached out and wrapped itself around Nixie, pulling at her in spite of her efforts to resist.

"I volunteer at a little clinic in Anacostia," he said. "We provide free medical care for anybody who can't afford it, of course, but our focus is on poor kids. We're managing to keep the lights on, but barely. Nobody in this city wants to acknowledge kids going without basic medical care barely three miles from the Capitol Building. We need to raise our profile, really put our kids on the map, but it's political suicide for an incumbent to touch something like this in an election year, even midterms."

Nixie stared at him, her skin going abruptly cold. "You're a doctor?" she asked. "Cripes."

He frowned. "Is that a bad thing?"

"No." What was *wrong* with her? Hadn't James taught her anything about being seduced by doctors with political ambitions? Maybe James had been a smoother talker, and maybe he'd been a little more generically handsome, but he was the same *type*.

"Oh. I was just checking, because it sounded like you were kind of down on doctors."

"No," Nixie said again. "It's just..." *It's just that I recently built a clinic with a hot doctor who had a crush on my mom. I'm not interested in an instant replay.* She said, "My last project was very similar. A children's clinic in Kenya. I'm not really looking to do another medical thing so soon. If you had an orphanage or something, maybe I'd be your girl. It sounds like a worthy project, though. Isn't your mother interested?"

His face went stony. "I prefer to keep the personal and the professional separate."

"Oh." Nixie would bet her trust fund there was a story worth hearing behind that small, terse answer. Not her business, she reminded herself. "Well surely somebody will come along--"

"Yeah, I doubt that. We're looking at a financial crisis in the next month, if not the next week. What do you think the chances are that another superstar humanitarian with a little time on her hands will drop into the neighborhood in time to do us any good?"

Guilt rushed over her like high tide. "Not so hot, huh?"

"Not so hot." He shrugged. "But listen, I understand. This is small potatoes compared to what you usually deal with. These kids aren't *starving* or anything. Not for food, at least."

"Poverty is poverty," Nixie said, stung. "It comes in all shapes and sizes. I don't judge whose need is greater."

"No? Somebody has to. Who does it for you?"

Nixie blinked. She'd never thought of it just that way before. "I guess that would be Karl. He's our...my... He's Leighton-Brace's COO of Charitable Giving."

"I see. And now that you're on your own?"

On her own. Loneliness crept up and tightened her throat. "I don't know. I haven't thought about it."

"Well think about it now." He stepped toward her, stopped barely short of crowding her. "Just come see the place. Our clinic. Come see what you're saying no to. Give us at least that much."

She thought about another long weekend in her anonymous apartment and she heard herself say, "Fine. I'll have a look."

He smiled at her, and it transformed his face. The hard edges and sharp bones disappeared into a delighted grin that warmed something in her Nixie hadn't even realized was cold. He checked his watch and winced. "We have to go. You'll want shoes."

"You want me to come with you? Right now?"

"Sure. Time is of the essence and all that."

Nixie thought of her empty apartment. She didn't have to go back there tonight. Not yet. That cold space in her soul warmed a few more degrees. "Okay. Your call, Dr. Larsen," she said.

"Erik." He stuck out his hand.

"Nixie," she said and gave his hand a quick shake. It was like squeezing a brick. His patients must love that. "Pleased to meet you. I'll go get my shoes."

CHAPTER FOUR

Erik inched his way east on Constitution until the White House was a pale, rectangular smear through the slush on his window. The Washington Monument speared up into the hovering clouds on Nixie's side, and she turned to him.

"So where's this clinic of yours again?" she asked, her eyes large and green and interested.

"Anacostia."

"Oh. Tough neighborhood?"

"One of the worst in the country. Almost half the adults don't have jobs and more kids get shot or killed than graduate from high school. Three miles from the Capitol Building, if you can believe it."

"And Karl thinks I have to fly around the world to do my job." She turned back to the view out her window. "My old job, I mean."

She shook her head as if to reorder her thoughts and the scent of her hair crept across the car to him. He pressed his lips together. He didn't want Nixie Leighton-Brace to smell so good. So real. So vibrant and tangy and sweet. Like lemons or something, with a little bit of char thrown in, as if she'd burned something recently. It made her far too human for his comfort. He'd rather she stayed two-dimensional, the answer to a pressing problem, nothing more.

Kiss the Girl

"Your old job," he said. "Yeah, what happened there? I mean besides what played out in the press."

"I quit." She stared out her window, treating him to a profile that had probably inspired sculptors the world over.

"Why? Seems like that asshole you were dating should have gone first."

She was quiet for a minute, and Erik's hands fisted on the wheel. He'd gone too far, as usual. He'd wanted to dial her down a little in his head, get some distance from that unsettling surge of physical awareness. He hadn't meant to needle her into quitting before she'd even signed on. Now she'd probably get out at the next red light, catch a cab home and tell his mother that he was pushy and rude and that she'd rather not see him again.

Which would be great in one sense, because God knew he didn't want to date a woman like Nixie Leighton-Brace. That was the Senator's dream come true, not his. But he didn't want to kiss the clinic goodbye, either. He was going to have to walk a very fine line here, he realized. He'd have to balance on the knife edge between providing the fawning attention she required as a celebrity without encouraging her on a more personal level. At least until she was hooked on their mission. On their kids. Then he could relax.

In the meantime, he'd have to be very careful. For a woman who'd been to every armpit the world had to offer, she had the most improbable air of innocence about her. It was like she'd been hermetically sealed and inserted into pictures of horrible suffering, so she could emerge fresh and clean and smelling like lemons. He doubted she'd ever been without a team of handlers in her life, and here he was, ready to take her across the Anacostia River and into the kind of poverty and hopelessness she'd probably only ever viewed from inside the sterile bubble of her fame.

"Why did I quit?" she asked.

"Yeah."

"I was tired," she said, and her eyes were a clear, mossy green. "I wanted to come home."

Erik understood the impulse better than he wanted to admit. "And home is DC?"

"It's wherever I want." She didn't look away from the window.

"Just that easy, huh?"

"It's never easy. But it can be done. I'm good at building things. Why not home?"

"Because it's more complicated than building an orphanage."

"Have you ever built one?"

"What, an orphanage? Or a home?"

"Are they that different?"

"Yeah." Erik shook his head. "And if I have to explain why, you wouldn't understand."

"If you say so."

And with that, they hurtled across the bridge and into a whole new world.

Nixie sat in the waiting room while Erik swiped his ID badge through the reader and let himself into the receptionist's pen. There was an enormous woman working the front desk, and even through three inches of bullet-proof glass, Nixie could see her giving him crap. She smiled. Dr. Erik probably didn't get enough crap.

She settled into her molded plastic chair. It was profoundly ugly, the exact color of puke. Nixie looked up when a man at the end of the row started heaving with exhausted resignation into a pink plastic bucket. That, Nixie thought, explains the vomit-colored décor. A stack of paper cups sat next to the rust-streaked sink in the bathroom so she filled one with water and delivered it to the puker.

Kiss the Girl

"Ah, fuck," he mumbled. Nixie took it as thanks. She patted his shoulder and returned to her seat.

She sat down again and turned her attention to the drama unfolding in the receptionist's pen. The woman was a full foot shorter than Erik, but she looked mean, and meanness counted more than anything in a fight. A Colombian farmer had explained this to her years ago and the ensuing cockfight had proven it. Nixie hoped she wasn't about to see the principle in action again. Maybe he was pushy and opinionated, but Erik seemed like a decent enough human being. It would be a shame if the receptionist killed him.

But Erik had raised his palms in a gesture of surrender and backed away slowly. He said something that seemed to mollify the woman, accompanied it with a winning smile. Then he pointed toward Nixie. The woman swiveled to stare at Nixie. Nixie gave her a little finger wave. The woman's eyes narrowed, her mouth bunched to the side with suspicion. She turned back to Dr. Erik and served up another helping of crap with renewed vigor. Nixie grinned.

She ducked her head so Erik wouldn't see her laughing at him and caught the eye of the toddler at her feet. The kid was maybe two and a half feet tall, of indeterminate gender, with an intricate spiral of tight braids snaking over its shiny brown scalp. It was one of perhaps five kids of varying sizes and colors orbiting a thin woman in the puke-colored chair opposite her own. Nixie had seen enough really sick kids to know that this one wasn't at death's door, so she leaned forward, elbows on knees and smiled into the kid's giant brown eyes.

"What are you in for?" she asked.

"Breathing machine."

"Seriously?" Nixie lifted a skeptical brow. "A machine that breathes for you?"

The child giggled. "No, I gots to breathe into it."

"Huh. Why?"

"Asthma. We all gots it."

Nixie looked at the brood of children sprawled across the chairs. "All of you?"

"Yeah. Mama Mel say it the cockroach shit."

Nixie blinked. "Really?"

"Yeah, that and the cheap-ass carpet the super put in."

"La Toya Kennedy?" The receptionist called through a small grouping of holes drilled through the glass at mouth level.

The woman across from Nixie didn't open her eyes, but prodded the kid with a slippered foot. "That you, child. Go on, now. We don't gots all day."

"Okay, Mama Mel." La Toya bounded to her feet and barreled toward the door the receptionist was holding open.

Mama Mel cracked open one eye. "Don't run, neither. You want to give yourself the asthma before you even gets your turn on the machine?" She settled her bony frame back into the chair, muttering, "I ain't talking just to hear myself talk, neither. Dang."

"All these kids yours?" Nixie asked.

"Lord, I collects them," the woman sighed. "I don't stand for nobody raising their hand to no child."

"Your landlord's okay with all the kids?"

"He gots to be, don't he? Government gave 'em all to me right and proper. I gots the court papers to prove it, and the social worker coming by every month to make sure they's all taken care of."

"How'd they all get asthma?"

She fanned a thin hand in front of her face, like the question was a pesky fly. "All the kids in our building gots it. We supposed to be in the good project, the *new* project. Tell you something, that place ain't nothing but a rat trap. The paint stink, the carpet stink, the rats eat all the insulation out and fill up the walls with shit, then the cockroaches come and eat that. It ain't no wonder my babies don't breathe right."

She closed her eyes again and dropped her head back against the seat. "But it worse outside. Between the shooting and the mugging and the drugs and lord knows what all, I don't dare let them out of the apartment. They come straight home from school and stay where I can keep my eye on them. My kids is going to graduate if it's the last thing I do." She blew out a weary breath. "Some days I think it might be."

The receptionist leaned toward the glass and called, "Nixie Leighton-Brace? Girl, if your famous self is gracing our building, please step forward."

Nixie smiled at Mama Mel. "That's my cue. Nice talking to you."

Mama Mel finally opened both eyes and gave her a thorough once over. "You ain't Nixie Leighton-Brace," she finally said. "You too skinny."

Nixie laughed. "Camera adds ten pounds, even in Somalia. Think about that." She headed toward the startled receptionist, who bounded from her swivel chair in a blur of skin-tight white polyester. She buzzed open the door and Nixie sailed through it like she was walking the red carpet. She knew how to be *Nixie Leighton-Brace* when it suited her.

She had to give the woman credit--she pulled it together quickly. She drew back her chin and eyed Nixie from head to toe. "Are you really Nixie Leighton-Brace?" she asked.

Nixie relaxed the take-my-picture pose and smiled at her. "That's what it says on my passport."

"Girl, what are you doing here?" The woman's wattle jiggled in reproof. "Shouldn't you be in Darfur or something?"

Nixie gave her an apologetic shrug. "Probably." She checked the ID badge proffered up by the woman's impressive bosom. "Wanda?"

"Yeah, that's me."

Nixie grinned. The woman was about five feet tall and nearly as wide, with hair an improbable shade of check-me-out red and a mouth painted to match. "You look like a Wanda. Do people tell you that all the time?"

The mouth that had been nearly hidden between fleshy cheeks widened now into a smile that changed her face like the sunrise changed the sky. "Time or two."

"So Dr. Erik tells me times are tough here at the clinic. What's the situation?"

Wanda's smile died and she wagged her head. "Dr. Erik and Dr. Mary Jane, they're doing their best, but don't nobody care about us folks down here. Up there on the Hill, they like to pretend we don't exist so they can pat each other on the back and take each other out to lunch. Pretend they're all *good* and *noble*." Her mouth twisted into a flaming curve of derision. "Dr. Erik gives 'em new hearts, but he can't put no love in 'em."

"He's a surgeon?" Nixie asked.

"At George Washington University Hospital," Wanda said. She nudged Nixie with an elbow. "They don't just give them jobs away, neither. Our boy's mad skilled."

Nixie pictured Erik's hands in her mind--large, square, strong. She'd imagined him as an ER doc, or maybe an orthopedic man. Something that required his farm-hand build and Viking attitude. But apparently, he was fully capable of delicacy and grace. No, not just capable. He must be incredibly skilled. Called. Gifted.

She asked, "What's he doing here if he works up at GW?"

Wanda rolled her eyes, and it made her look like nothing so much as a startled pony. "He's saving the world, honey. One poor black kid at a time. Sound familiar?"

"It used to." Nixie tried a smile.

"His mama makes laws, and Dr. Erik catches the kids who fall through the cracks. But don't tell him I said so. He's dead-set on not growing up to be his mama."

Nixie lifted her brows. "Why's that? I'd be pretty damn happy if I grew up to be the Senator."

"With your mama, no wonder."

"Ouch."

"Oh, honey. I'm sorry. I shouldn't have said that."

Nixie forced a reassuring smile. "Don't worry about it. The truth hurts sometimes. But what does Erik have against politics?" She thought about those summer sky eyes and the fast, flashing smile that struck like lightning. Then she thought about the way he moved, in a straight line and utterly without hesitation. Not fast, necessarily, but inexorable. Like a steam roller. "Seems to me like politics would be a nice fit with his personality."

"I know." Wanda chuckled. "You should ask him about it. I'd like to hear that answer myself. Here he comes now. You gonna ask?"

Nixie followed her gaze and found Erik striding toward her, a white-coated woman at his side. She was no more than shoulder high on him, but matched his pace with an ease that suggested perhaps he was keeping up with her rather than the other way around.

Nixie frowned. She knew that walk. Determined, purposeful, way faster than those short little legs ought to be able to go. She knew that face, too. Soft and round on the surface, solid steel resolve underneath.

"Hi," the woman said, sticking out a hand. "I'm--"

Nixie laughed, bypassed the hand and threw her arms around the woman. "Mary Jane Riley! Oh my God, is that really you? You're a doctor?"

Mary Jane patted gingerly at Nixie's shoulders. "I can't believe you remember me."

"Of course I remember you!" Nixie pulled back and grinned into the shorter woman's face. "I wouldn't have survived chemistry without you. Sister Charbonneau *hated* me."

"Sister Charbonneau hated everybody."

"Everybody but you." Nixie hugged her again, then let her go. "God, I'm sorry. We haven't seen each other for fifteen years and I'm squeezing you like a tube of toothpaste. It's just so good to see you." Nixie knew she was beaming at the woman like an idiot, but she couldn't get hold of her cool. Friends--real friends--had been so few and far between in her life. Stumbling across one now, when she needed one so badly, was a gift.

No, Nixie realized in a moment of clarity. It was more than a gift. It was a sign. Nixie hadn't previously thought of God as the *quid pro quo* type, but there was an unmistakable whiff of karma to this meeting. This was destiny.

She was going to save Mary Jane's clinic, a cosmic reward for the chubby little blonde who'd braved hoards of pencil-thin, designer-dressed harpies to befriend a girl too rich, too well-traveled, and too notorious to be anything but a target.

And maybe, Nixie thought, maybe, if she was very good and very lucky, she might cement an old friendship at the same time. Put down a few tentative roots in her new home town. She glanced at Erik, at the skeptical set of that super-hero jaw. Her stomach lightened with a bolt of involuntary feminine appreciation, which she promptly squashed. No, she told herself sternly. No more falling for the clients. This one's for Mary Jane.

"You two know each other?" Erik looked back and forth between the women, one golden brow arched. "You could've mentioned something, Mary Jane."

Kiss the Girl

"How was I supposed to know she'd remember me? We were freshman together for like two minutes at the Holy Sisters of Unmerciful Discipline and haven't spoken since."

"Every time my mom filmed a movie, I got dropped off at a new boarding school for a couple months," Nixie told Erik. "I don't know if you remember what teenage girls are like, but let me tell you, it was like being thrown to the lions. Only worse, 'cause lions just want to eat you. Girls want you to bleed."

Nixie smiled warmly at Mary Jane. "You were one of the few people to show me any genuine kindness during those years. I'm in your debt for that."

Mary Jane shook her head, an uncomfortable flush climbing her cheeks. "Oh for God's sake. You are not."

"I am." Nixie clasped her hands and looked around the clinic while a lovely, familiar sense of purpose washed over her. "Being my friend in high school was like painting a huge bull's eye on your backside--"

Mary Jane snorted. "Plenty of real estate back there."

"--and just to prove to you that being brave and good always pays, I'm going to raise your clinic a boatload of money."

Mary Jane stared. "What?"

"What's your funding like?" Nixie asked.

"Private," Erik said.

"Private?" Nixie lifted a skeptical brow. "What does that mean?"

Erik shook his head. "It means we have a few loans and grants, but Mary Jane mostly operates out of her trust fund. Or did, until she blew through it."

"You spent your trust fund?" Nixie asked, shocked.

"Don't look at me like that," Mary Jane said, shoving her hands into her lab coat pockets. "What was I going to do with it? Buy another Benz?"

"Well, no," Erik said. "But you could have kept a *little* back for the occasional luxury item. Like rent and groceries."

Nixie shook her head and said, "Never spend your principle, Mary Jane. That's rule number one of the charity game. People don't give money to people who can't manage it."

Mary Jane's brows came down ominously. "I didn't mismanage my money. I spent it exactly as I saw fit."

"I believe you. But this isn't about what you did, it's about what it looks like. See, poor people are poor because they can't manage money and don't make good decisions," Nixie said. "Conversely, rich people are rich because they can and they do."

She held up a hand to stave off the heated protest she could see on Mary Jane's face. "Of course it isn't true. You and I both know that. But it looks pretty darn true to Joe Average, trying not to waste his charity dollars. He wants to give his money to people who know how to use it, and use it well."

"Ergo, he gives it to the people who already have money," Erik said to Mary Jane. "I told you that."

Mary Jane frowned mutinously and Nixie spread her hands. "It sucks, I know. But I don't make the rules."

"And I don't have to play by them," Mary Jane said. "Listen, I appreciate the offer but I don't play the appearances game. I don't have the looks for it." She smiled grimly and Nixie exchanged a worried glance with the Viking doctor. "I don't have the stomach for it, either. I never have."

"Mary Jane," Erik said, touching her elbow. "This is an incredible opportunity--"

"To what?" she asked. "Pimp an old friendship for the cash? The work should speak for itself, Erik. If it takes a celebrity endorsement to keep the doors open, maybe they shouldn't be open."

"You don't mean that," Erik said.

Mary Jane made a strangled noise and shoved at the pale wisps of hair escaping from her smooth ponytail. "I don't know what I mean," she said. "I know what we do here is important, I just can't understand why nobody else thinks so."

"I think so," Nixie said. "If you're willing to let me, I'd love to--"

"I'm sorry, Nixie, but it's not going to work, okay? You know what your two months with the Sisters were like? My whole life used to be like that."

Nixie blew out a breath. "Ouch."

"Right." Mary Jane smiled tightly. "Getting rid of the trust fund was kind of a relief, to tell you the truth. So, no offense, but as glad as I am to see you, I don't want what you do in my life. Present company excepted, of course, I don't like rich people. I didn't like rich people when I *was* rich and I don't like them now. I won't pander to them any more, not even for this place. It costs too much."

"I see."

Mary Jane shoved her hands back into her pockets. "God, now I've hurt your feelings."

"No, of course not." Nixie thought about Mama Mel and her babies who didn't breathe right. She thought about a waiting room full of pukers. She thought about orphans and homes and kids the laws didn't provide for. About her cold, generic apartment and the dazzling promise of a life rich with connections and purpose she'd glimpsed just a few moments before. God forgive her, she wasn't going to give up so easily. Not even for Mary Jane.

"I was just trying to think of some way to ask you for a favor," she said.

"*You* want a favor from *me*?" Mary Jane's eyes were wide and blue and disbelieving.

"Yeah. I recently broke up with Leighton-Brace Charitable Giving. You might've read about it in the papers?"

"I think everybody in the free world read about it in the papers, Nixie."

She nodded. "Yeah. So I've got some time on my hands. Turns out I suck at being lazy. I need something to do. I don't suppose you have anything here that would keep me busy while I'm reinventing myself?"

Mary Jane stared at her, mouth open. "You want a job?"

"I don't want you to pay me," she said quickly. "I just need something to do. To stay busy." *To work on you until you see reason about this fundraising thing.*

Erik nodded slowly, as if he could see the wheels turning inside her head and liked her direction. He turned to Mary Jane and said, "We *are* looking for an evening receptionist."

Mary Jane looked doubtfully at Nixie. "I don't think--"

"Yeah, you're probably right," he said, cutting her off and sliding Nixie a dismissive look. "I'm sure Nixie Leighton-Brace is way too important to pull desk duty at a free clinic. Isn't she?"

CHAPTER FIVE

As Erik expected, Nixie's cheeks pinked and those green eyes went sharp. "If I take the job, will you stop speaking about me in the third person?"

"Sure thing." He smiled at her, and she glared back. Perfect. She was pissed at him, but not enough to reject the job. He was going to save the clinic without sacrificing himself on the altar of his mother's ambition.

"Super," Mary Jane said. "You're hired. Wait here, okay?" She turned to Erik. "Can I see you a moment?" Erik followed her to her tiny office, pulling the door shut behind them.

"What was that all about, there at the end?" she asked, her shiny head bent over the desk. She was double and triple tasking, as usual. Scanning patient files, signing off on forms, talking to him. "Nixie tried to do us a favor--a big one--and I threw it back in her face. She has every right to be pissed, but she offered to man the desk instead. Why on earth are you antagonizing her?"

"It's kind of a long story."

"Bottom line it for me. What's the deal?"

"Nixie Leighton-Brace is my mom's latest pick for my First Lady."

Mary Jane glanced up, gave him a mischievous grin. "She's right, you know."

"My mom?"

"No, Nixie. You do sound snotty when you say her name like that."

"Good. I don't want her to get any ideas. Can you imagine her and my mom on the same team?"

"I'd rather not." Mary Jane shuddered, then went back to her forms. He smiled at her impeccably straight part. The Senator was Mary Jane's worst nightmare. Monied *and* powerful, with a taste for publicity. And unless he missed his guess, Nixie caused her some anxiety, too.

"She was right about you, too," he said.

"Who, Nixie?"

"Yeah. You get hives just thinking about celebrities. Being Nixie Leighton-Brace's best friend must've been an act of supreme courage. Especially in high school."

"You saw her out there. You think she gave me a choice?"

Erik rolled his eyes. "Yeah, right. You don't do anything you don't want to."

"So I'm a sucker for the underdog." She scribbled her name across one last sheet. "Why do you think I gave her the receptionist job?"

"Because you want her to raise you that boatload of money she offered and save this clinic."

Her pen froze for an instant before continuing. "I do not," she said without looking up.

Erik leaned forward, hands on the desk. "Come on, Mary Jane. That woman is nobody's receptionist and you know it. You let her squeeze one pretty foot in the door and she's going to do whatever the hell she pleases. Thank Christ it seems to please her to throw us a fundraiser." He plucked the pen from her fingers, forcing her to meet his gaze. "A badly needed fundraiser."

Mary Jane snatched her pen back. "Oh, all right. So I might've overstated my objections a few minutes back. But that doesn't mean they weren't true. If there's any way to get the money without all the hoopla, she'll find it now." She smiled. "She owes me, remember?"

Erik snorted. "Good luck with that. I don't care what she owes you. Nixie Leighton-Brace *is* hoopla."

Mary Jane gazed at him shrewdly. "You really don't like her, do you?"

"It doesn't matter if I like her or not," he said, as much to himself as to Mary Jane. "She's going to raise us that money. Then she'll make up with her crazy mom and fly off to save the world. If I'm lucky it'll be before my mom convinces her I'm some kind of JFK Jr./Prince Charming hybrid."

Mary Jane winced on his behalf. "Yeah, that would be bad. Your mom's kind of...intense."

"I know. Believe me, I know. And the fact that we're in harmony on that point makes me love you even more. When are you going to give in and admit we were meant for each other?"

She shook her head. "You've been going on about that for five years," she said. "Isn't it time to admit that I'm out of your league? Too much woman for you?"

He laughed. "Never. Determination is the hallmark of my personality."

"Tell you what." She scooped up a sheaf of papers and dropped the pen into her lab coat pocket. "If I'm still single at, say, forty, I'll think it over." She squinted at him. "Better make it fifty."

"Sweet talker."

"You know it, bro. Now go introduce Wanda to her new receptionist."

Wanda plunked Nixie into the receptionist's chair. Nixie sank so far into the divot Wanda's butt had left there that her feet dangled like a little kid's.

"Ninety-nine percent of the folks who drag their sorry asses here on a Friday or Saturday night will be one of the five Ds," Wanda said. She counted them off on long red nails. "Drunk, drugged, disturbed, dinged up or diseased. There's a pending file for each one on the back counter. All you have to do is fill out a registration form for each patient, stick it in the right file. The docs will take it from there."

Nixie eyed the pile of blank registration forms on the desk. "Sounds doable."

"Mmm-hmmm." Wanda's tone made it clear she was reserving judgment. "Keep an eye on the waiting room, too. You don't want people fighting or puking in there. Flu's going around. Barf buckets are in the closet, right beside the mop. Get 'em one, or you'll be using the other. I am not going to clean up your mess in the morning, you understand?"

She gave Nixie a steely look. Nixie nodded. "I understand."

"All right then. Have fun." She sashayed toward the door with a two-packs-a-day chuckle that had Nixie frowning suspiciously at her back.

Then she was gone and for the next two hours, Nixie didn't have time to think about it. She was too busy handing out buckets and figuring out which D each patient most closely resembled.

She'd just handed out her fourth puke bucket when a woman staggered up to the receptionist's station. Her plaid shirt was buttoned crookedly and flapped around skinny thighs. She gripped the desk with fingers like wires and slumped into a folding chair. Nixie gave her a professionally concerned smile and said, "Welcome to the Anacostia Health Center. What can we help you with tonight?"

"Oh, honey, I got me the flu, bad."

Nixie nodded. "It's going around." She drew a registration form out of the pile. "Let's get you signed in."

"I don't need signing in. I need a doctor. I'm dying."

"The doctor will see you as soon as I get you into the system. So I'll just--"

"Oh lord, the room's moving." She leaned in, propped an elbow on the counter and frowned at Nixie. "Is the room moving, sugar?"

"No, ma'am."

She closed her eyes and laid her cheek on the counter. Nixie could see a single pink curler dangling behind her ear. "Lord Baby Jesus, just take me on home," she moaned. "I done suffered enough."

From the waiting room came a single, muttered, "Amen."

Nixie clicked open her pen. "Name?"

The woman opened one eye. "Regina Wilks, baby."

"Have you been here before, Regina?"

"No. But I ain't never been dying before neither. Oh, lordy, it's getting worse. I'm all cold now." Sweat beaded on the woman's forehead. She crossed herself and started to hum Swing Low, Sweet Chariot.

"Any insurance?"

Regina groaned and lifted one butt cheek. She squeaked off a delicate fart. Nixie took that as a no.

"When did your symptoms start?" Nixie looked up from the form. The woman was staring at her, but the focus was clearly internal. Uh oh. Nixie scrambled for a pink bucket but it was too late. Regina leaned over and barfed between her knees onto the floor.

Nixie sighed, then hauled herself out of the chair and dropped the registration form into the box labeled *Diseased*.

Regina sat up and wiped at the corners of her mouth with the hem of her shirt. "Well what do you know? I feel better. Thank you, Merciful Jesus!"

"Praise be," Nixie said. She grabbed a pink bucket and let herself into the waiting room. "Okay, let's get you comfortable, Ms. Wilks."

She planted the woman in the row of chairs she'd mentally designated Upchuck Alley, handed her the bucket and a Dixie cup of water. She was filling the mop pail when Erik came into the reception area and fished a form out of the pending files. He got halfway to the door before his nose twitched and his eyes went unfocused.

"Whoa, that's ripe. One got away from you, huh, princess?"

"Princess?"

"You said I couldn't speak of you in the third person anymore."

"So I get a patronizing nickname?"

"Until you start catching the pukers ahead of time, yeah."

Nixie shrugged. "Beware the sudden blank look."

"Tell me something I don't know." He held open the door and she aimed the mop bucket and its three functional wheels toward it. "How do you like the job so far?"

She thought of Regina Wilks humming Swing Low, Sweet Chariot and imploring the good lord for release from gastrointestinal distress. "It has its moments."

Erik shook his head and called his patient. Nixie attacked the remains of Regina's last meal with a stringy mop, but stopped when a car jammed on its brakes in the street outside. She saw it through the glass front doors, something from the bygone era of vehicles the size of ocean liners. It laid waste to a stubby tree and landed on the sidewalk, two wheels on the curb, two in the street. The back door opened and two bodies bounced onto the sidewalk. The car fish-tailed away from the curb before they'd even stopped rolling.

"Oh Christ," she heard Erik say. "Not another one." He flew past her, and Nixie followed without thought. A wail rose on the cold night air, brittle with grief and rage. Nixie had heard women make that cry over their wounded men in more countries and more languages than she'd care to count. It always sounded exactly the same.

She shoved through the doors. A woman was on her knees on the pavement, struggling to pull a man into her lap. It was hard to tell at first who was bleeding. Blood was everywhere, a bright, vivid red against their white t-shirts, the metallic scent of it heavy on air already laced with panic. The woman rocked on her knees. The man's arms dangled limply to the bloody concrete.

"What happened?" Erik asked, his voice brisk and utterly calm as he plucked the man from the girl's arms and laid him out on the sidewalk.

"He's shot, oh my God, oh my God, he's shot!" The woman lunged for the man again, tried to drag him back into her arms. Nixie hooked both hands through the woman's elbow and yanked back hard. They both went down on their butts on the frozen sidewalk.

"Let the doctor work, okay?" Nixie said, wrapping both arms around the woman. The girl, really. She couldn't be more than sixteen, Nixie thought as she rocked her, the embrace as much about restraint as comfort. The girl thrashed for a moment or two, then crumpled into Nixie's arms.

Erik took the man's blood-soaked t-shirt in both hands and ripped it in two right down the center. The girl made a low, keening cry at the sight of two ugly holes in her boyfriend's chest, each pulsing a dark rivulet of blood down his ribs. Snow floated down, touched the man's face, his hands

"What happened, honey?" Nixie asked her.

"He's fucking shot is what happened!" She rocked back and forth in Nixie's arms, shaking so hard Nixie could feel it in her teeth. "They just drove around and around, waiting for him to fucking die. They finally shoved us out here. Oh God, oh God, is he dead?"

"No." Erik rolled the man carefully to his side. "No exit wounds," he said, his face grim. He tore the T-shirt into two pieces, fashioned them into pads and pressed them hard against the bullet holes.

Mary Jane crashed through the door and stopped short. "What happened?"

"Homeboy ambulance," Erik said.

"911?" she asked.

"Not yet," Erik replied.

"I'll do it."

"Double GSW to the chest," he told her. "No exit wounds, thready pulse. Lost a lot of blood." He glanced at the pad of t-shirt under his hand. It was already black with blood. "Damn it. Bring me a pressure wrap and a shitload of five by nines when you come back."

"Right." She disappeared into the clinic.

"What's his name?" Nixie asked the girl in her arms.

"DeShawn." She wiped a sleeve across her face, smearing away the blood and tears and snot.

"Is he your boyfriend?"

"Yeah. We're having a baby."

Nixie's heart didn't break. She'd heard this story too many times for that. It took a hard hit, though. Nice dent. "Congratulations. When?"

"Summer, I think."

"You'll want to be seen by the doctors here as soon as you can," Nixie said. "Find out for sure."

The young man's eyelids twitched and he coughed up some pink foam.

"Oh my God, oh Jesus, is he dying?" The girl shrank against Nixie's chest and they both held their breath. Mary Jane and one of the nurses burst through the door. The nurse flapped open a blanket over the man's legs while Mary Jane snapped on a pair of rubber gloves. She handed a second pair to Erik and went to her knees beside the bleeding man. "CPR?"

He shook his head once. The look he gave Mary Jane said *don't bother*. "Still breathing on his own for the moment."

The girl shuddered in Nixie's arms. "Is he going to die?" she whispered.

"I don't know, honey." Nixie held the girl tighter. She strained her ears for the wail of a siren, heard nothing but the whisper of falling snow.

Erik accepted a wad of gauze from the nurse. He laid it on top of the soaked t-shirt bandage and pressed hard. The bleeding man coughed again, bringing up more pink foam. This time his eyelids cracked open and he said, "Jass."

The girl shrank against Nixie. "Oh God oh God oh God," she said.

"Jass?" One hand twitched, seeking.

"Is that you?" Nixie asked the girl. "You're Jass?"

She nodded, but pushed her heels against the sidewalk to put more distance between herself and death. Nixie had seen that before, too. *If I don't look, it's not happening. If I don't see it, it can't be real, right?*

Nixie grabbed a handful of Jass' collar and hauled her to the man's side. "She's here, DeShawn. Jass is right here."

She took his hand and put it in Jass'. Jass tried to pull away, her eyes rolling with terror. Nixie took the girl's face in both hands and brought it to hers. She didn't want her to see the blood, the doctors, the limp hand searching for her own. She wanted Jass to look only at her.

"Listen to me," she said, her voice fierce. "Listen, right now. Are you listening?"

Jass blinked, focused.

"Tell him you love him," Nixie told her. "Tell him he's fine."

"He is?"

"No. He's dying."

Jass jerked as if Nixie had slapped her. Her hands came up to claw at Nixie's, but Nixie wouldn't let go. She kept Jass' face between her bloody hands and kept talking.

"Tell him you love him. Tell him it's all going to be all right. You tell him everything he needs to know if you never talk to him again, you understand? Right now. Do this now or you'll regret it for the rest of your life. This is the father of your baby. If you love him, tell him."

Jass stared at her, her cheeks wet. She was shaking so hard her teeth chattered.

"Tell him!" Nixie roared the words and it seemed to shatter Jass' paralysis. She bobbed her head and didn't resist when Nixie turned her toward her dying boyfriend and put his weakly seeking hand in hers. This time, the girl gripped it hard in both her own and brought it to her cheek.

"DeShawn, baby, I love you. You're going to be okay. The doctors are taking care of you. It's all going to be okay."

Nixie sat back on her heels behind the girl, her dirty hands splayed on the knees of her jeans. DeShawn tried to smile, but it wavered and became a choked sob.

"I'm sorry, baby," he whispered. "So sorry." His eyes closed, two tears slipped down cheeks that were still so young and soft that Nixie's heart took another dent.

"Don't you leave me," Jass said, bending to put her face against his. "Don't you dare die. I need you. I can't do this. Not without you. Come on, baby." She was sobbing, great, wracking, open-mouthed sobs, but DeShawn didn't open his eyes again.

"Nixie?"

She shifted her eyes to Erik, found him looking at her with something new in his face. "We need to do CPR now."

Nixie nodded. The shriek of a distant siren finally sounded as Nixie pulled Jass away from DeShawn. His hand fell to the frozen sidewalk and laid there, as if already dead. Jass stumbled at the sight of it, a moan of terrified anguish escaping her. Nixie opened her arms. Jass went into them and crumpled. Mary Jane and Erik worked together with wordless efficiency, breathing for DeShawn until the ambulance arrived.

After DeShawn had been loaded, Jass followed his gurney into the rear doors of the ambulance. She was silent, her eyes wide and blank. Nixie, Erik and Mary Jane all stayed on the sidewalk until it was out of sight. Nixie looked down. There was blood on her jeans, on her shirt. Erik and Mary Jane had it on their hands, on their knees, on their white coats.

Nobody said anything. Mary Jane finally turned and walked back inside the building. Nixie shoved her hands into her pockets.

"I'm sorry," Erik said.

"For what?" Nixie didn't look at him.

"I'm sorry this happened." He went to push his hands through his hair, but even when he snapped off his gloves, his hands were still bloody. He shook his head and slipped them into the pockets of his ruined coat instead. "I wanted you to get a good taste of what we do here, but I didn't mean this."

Nixie smiled, though she still didn't look at him. "You think that was my first gun shot wound? You think that's the first time I've walked a woman through saying goodbye to the father of her babies?"

"No," he said. "No, I guess not."

She blew out a breath and it hung like smoke in the cold air. "At least nobody took pictures," she said. "That's a step in the right direction."

"You did good work tonight, Nixie."

She finally looked at him. He was staring down into the street, snow flakes on his hair and shoulders. "And that was a big surprise to you." She waited for a response but none came. "I'm not quitting, Erik."

He glanced at her, his eyes very blue and searching in the glare of the street light. "Why not?"

"I find mopping unexpectedly fulfilling."

"Come on, Nixie."

I like surprising you. Nixie didn't know how much of it was him and how much was finally impressing somebody after years of having her work taken as the least she could do. But she'd earned his respect tonight and she had a feeling it wasn't an easy thing to do.

"It fits. This place and what I know how to do. They go unexpectedly well together." She lifted one hand, let it drop. She knew she wasn't explaining very well but she didn't entirely understand it herself. "Plus, I do like the mopping. See you inside."

CHAPTER SIX

It was too quiet, and Nixie didn't like it. She'd perched on the edge of the Wanda divot most of the next afternoon and aside from a few reporters who'd disappeared after Nixie gave them a couple snaps, she'd seen a whopping total of three people come through the doors. Something wasn't right. It felt unnaturally hushed, like when a predator's shadow falls over a field and all the small, furry things go silent.

Nixie wasn't the only one feeling that way, either. Not from what she could gather. Mary Jane walked through the deserted waiting room for the hundredth time and peered out into the street. Nixie got to her feet and went to stand behind her shoulder. She looked where the doctor looked, seeing over the woman easily. Maybe Mary Jane had been short and round in high school, but now she was just curvy and petite. With perfectly behaved blonde hair and everything. She was the ideal complement to Erik's large Nordic Vikingness. Throw in a common cause and the easy affection Nixie saw in every exchange between them and Nixie couldn't help a twinge of curiosity.

Exactly how close were Mary Jane and Erik?

None of my business, Nixie reminded herself. And not what she'd come over to ask about.

"What's going on tonight?" she asked. Mary Jane didn't turn away from the falling night. "I have snacks, hand sanitizer and an extra change of clothes right down to the underwear in my back pack. I'm wearing shoes I can hose down."

She stuck out a foot. Her clogs were, indeed, made out of recycled tires and looked like it. Not flattering, but waterproof, as advertised. And eco friendly. "I'm totally prepared for mayhem, but it's all *High Noon* out there."

"*High Noon?*"

Nixie shrugged. "I think so. I've never seen the movie myself, but I have this impression of silent streets and tumble weeds and the locals hiding out under their kitchen tables while waiting for the gunslingers to open fire."

Mary Jane stared at her. "You got this from having *not* seen a movie?"

Nixie smiled. "I'm imaginative. I didn't have a TV growing up. So, really, what's the deal? Did the flu cure itself since yesterday? Was there a toxic spill last night? Was there a comet? Is everybody a zombie?"

"I would never have guessed you didn't have TV."

Nixie leaned around her to peer into the empty street. "What are you looking for out there?"

"You know that boy who died last night?"

"DeShawn?"

"Yeah. He was a well-placed member of the Yard crew."

Nixie frowned. "He was a lawn mower?"

"No." Mary Jane rubbed her forehead and laughed. "No, the Yard is a gang. They call them crews here, and they're very neighborhood specific. The Yard is from up on the River, near the Naval Ship Yard. DeShawn was a pretty influential member. His girlfriend was from down here. And by down here, I mean all of a mile and a half south."

Kiss the Girl

Nixie nodded. "Oh. A Montague-Capulet thing."

"Right. Star crossed lovers. Anyway, word on the street is that the Dog Crew--that would be our local crew--took exception to DeShawn poaching their women."

"So they shot him," Nixie finished for her. "And now all the Capulets are hot to kill the Montagues and cover themselves with bloody glory?"

"In a manner of speaking." Mary Jane turned back to the rapidly darkening street. "You'll probably be glad for those shoes later. I keep telling him we're not an ER, but the kids come anyway."

Nixie frowned. "Him?"

"What?"

"You said you keep telling *him*. Who's him?"

"Oh." She fluttered a hand then stuck it in the pocket of her white coat. "Sorry. I meant them. I keep telling *them*, all the kids who roll their buddies out of the cars on the sidewalk for us to patch up. We're not an ER and bringing them to us when they need one is the next thing to letting them bleed out in the back seat. Every time we treat one of them without reporting it we're putting our funding, meager though it is, on the line. It's like they don't hear me. They just keep coming."

"Why don't you report it?"

"Sometimes I do. Whenever I have to call an ambulance or the morgue. But I'd rather lose the clinic than let a kid die because his buddies are worried about the consequences of dropping him off here."

Nixie nodded. "I can understand that." She looked at the skinny tree lying on the sidewalk, all that was left of last night's violence. She didn't like seeing it there. It reminded her how indelible chance was. Sometimes things happened and there was no fixing them. You could only go forward.

Mary Jane seemed to read her thoughts. "I liked that tree. I planted it myself."

"I'm sorry," Nixie said, touching the woman's shoulder. Mary Jane shrugged, whether to brush off the sympathy or Nixie's hand she didn't know. Nixie let her hand fall away. Mary Jane turned and walked back to the treatment rooms. Nixie stood a few minutes more, while the sky deepened from periwinkle to slate. Nobody was coming. The street was empty. Nixie made a decision.

Within ten minutes, she was outside under the yellow glow of the street light with a shovel she'd found in the mop closet. She attacked the dingy patch of dirt where the tree had been trying to grow, but it was frozen solid. This was a job for a jack hammer. Possibly dynamite.

"Now I've seen everything."

Nixie turned and found Erik strolling up the sidewalk toward the clinic, hands in pockets, his jacket open to the snapping wind. He looked large and completely at home in the cold that had Nixie's eyes watering and her hands close to frozen. He was smiling at her. No, laughing. His blue eyes were alight with merriment and he made a show of looking over both shoulders.

"No press in sight, but the princess is digging a hole. What's this all about? A new neighborhood well?"

He smiled at her and Nixie felt it all the way to the tips of her frozen fingers. Oh no, she told herself. She was *not* developing a crush on her potential best friend's potential boyfriend. She jabbed her shovel at the dirt again. It bounced off.

"I'm trying to get this tree out of here." She put all her weight on the handle of the shovel and tried to force it into the ground. She didn't make a dent.

"Why?"

Nixie stuck her hands into her armpits and looked at him. "You're huge," she said. "You try."

Erik took the shovel. "I ask again. Why?"

She watched with a glimmer of resentment as he sank the shovel into the impenetrable earth, wiggled the handle and freed up a pitiful root ball without so much as a grunt of effort.

"Why are you huge? Damned if I know. Your mom's tiny."

Erik handed back the shovel. "Most people think I look like my dad."

"Most people don't look very closely."

Erik sighed. "Can we please not talk about my mother?"

"Why? I like your mom. Don't you?"

"It's complicated. Just please tell me why we're out here holding a memorial service for dead tree."

"Mary Jane seemed sad."

Erik's gaze sharpened on her face. "Did you make her come to your tree funeral?"

"Again with the effort to be funny. It's not your strong suit. You should stick to stoic."

"Nixie."

She shrugged. "She just seemed sad, okay? About the tree."

"What makes you say that?"

"She said so."

Erik lifted a brow. "She said so."

Nixie nodded. "It's a little out of character, isn't it? I mean, even in high school she wasn't an emoter."

"Emoter. Is that a word?"

Nixie shrugged. "We'll call her reserved. So anyway, we're standing by the door discussing *High Noon*, and suddenly she starts talking about the tree, how it was too bad, how she'd always kind of liked it. She was clearly very sad about it."

Nixie nudged the tree with her toe. She couldn't really feel it, though. Her clogs might be waterproof, but they were more practical indoors. "She must have really, *really* loved this tree. So I decided to get the remains off the sidewalk so she wouldn't have to see it every time she walked through the doors."

Erik sucked his teeth. "What did she say again? Her exact words, this time. Not your interpretation."

"Her exact words?"

"Yeah."

Nixie frowned. *"I liked that tree. I planted it myself."*

"And from this you diagnosed a raging case of grief?" He shook his head and smiled at her. "That's...very you."

"Hey, I just listen. It's amazing what you hear when you stop pushing your own agenda for a minute and actually listen to people." She gave him a sweet smile and started rocking from foot to foot. Maybe she should reconsider her decision to work so far from the equator. "You ought to try it sometime."

Erik took a step closer. Nixie was tall enough that she didn't look up to many people. At least not this far up. He was radiating energy, as usual, and Nixie's smile went from saccharine sweet to genuine. It was so nice to be with edgy, energetic people again. People who weren't worried about either offending her or ingratiating themselves with her. Or proving their importance by dismissing her. People she could provoke and needle and who would provoke and needle her in return. This man's ego was like flint. He was safe.

"What's that supposed to mean?" He spoke softly, dangerously. The hot rush of pleasure about thawed her toes.

"I know your type, that's all," she said. "Guys like you are a dime a dozen where I'm from."

He took another step. Nixie didn't back up. He'd left six inches at best between their bodies. She could smell coffee on his clothes, on his breath and the heat from that big body reached out to envelop her.

Kiss the Girl

"Guys like me?" he asked. His mouth was very near hers, and Nixie let herself glance at it. For a guy with a face carved out of stone, his mouth was amazing. Perfect without being pretty.

"Sure." Nixie smiled up at him. The warmth pumping off him made her want to stretch like a well-fed cat. "Big ideas, teeny-tiny…budget."

He stepped closer, close enough that she felt as much as heard the low rumble of his voice. "My *budget* is fine."

I'll bet it is, she thought but made herself nod doubtfully. "Then what am I doing here?" she asked.

"Hell if I know. Looks like you're reading minds and holding memorial services for trees."

She gave his arm a bracing pat. "Just because you can't see something doesn't mean it isn't real."

"And just because you feel something doesn't mean it is."

She blinked at him, surprised. "That's the saddest thing I've ever heard."

"Real life is like that, princess. You should get inside before you freeze to death."

"As soon as I'm done here."

"Up to you."

He stepped around her and disappeared into the clinic. Nixie looked after him for a moment, nonplussed. Then she grabbed the poor, mowed-down tree with both hands. It was heavier than it looked, still attached to the frozen earth by a couple stringy roots. She'd just set her heels for some serious yanking when a white coat whistled through the air and thwapped against her head.

"For God's sake, put that on," Erik called from the doorway. He stood there, frowning at her.

"What, you're dressing me now? That's cool. I sort of miss my entourage," she shouted back.

"I bet they don't miss you. Not with your twenty dollar wardrobe budget and your Goodwill habit." He made a disgusted noise and moved away from the door. "You're the worst dressed rich woman I've ever met in my life."

Nixie laughed and shoved her arms into the sleeves of his white physician's coat. She had to roll them up four times before her hands emerged, but the coat was still deliciously warm, probably from his body. Against her better judgment, she sniffed the collar. God, it smelled good. Like soap and shaving cream and hard work. Like him.

Lucky, lucky Mary Jane.

She swiped a sleeve under her nose as if to erase the scent and reached again for the tree. She didn't need any distractions. Particularly not in the form of a too-ambitious, too-handsome, too-stubborn doctor. She'd had her fill of those. Plus, she had a tree to bury.

A few more ferocious yanks and she was suddenly on her butt on the frozen concrete with the sad little tree in her lap.

"Ha!" She scrambled to her feet and did a quick victory boogie. She was mid-butt-wiggle when she heard it. The distinctive growl of a big American-made engine, gulping gas and pouring out performance. It occurred to Nixie as she watched headlights sail toward her through the night that the only places she heard those engines anymore was in third world countries and here in Anacostia.

The car beached itself on the sidewalk inches from her frozen feet and Nixie dropped the tree. Another bleeding kid was about to roll out of that car and he'd need help. She raced to the car's back passenger door and yanked it open.

CHAPTER SEVEN

Nixie saw only one person in the backseat. He was fully grown, but had the outsized bravado of a teenager only pretending to be a man. He was dressed identically to the kid in the driver's seat--enormous jeans, white t-shirt and a blue bandana around his head. Nixie patted at him with frantic hands, looking for the injury.

"Easy now," she said, keeping her voice smooth and low even while her heart thumped around in her chest like a crazy thing. "We'll take care of you."

The kid scrambled away from her touch. "What the hell?" He glanced toward the driver, then back to Nixie. "I ain't hurt, bitch."

Nixie frowned, the first glimmer of alarm surfacing through her impulse to tend. "You don't seem to be. What's going on?"

"Jesus," the driver said. "Will you just grab her?"

Nixie eased toward the open door at her back, keeping her eyes carefully blank and uncomprehending. "What? Grab who?"

The driver rolled his eyes in the rearview mirror. "I ain't talking to you, bitch. Damn, dawg, grab her."

Nixie's stomach went hot and tight as the kid in the back seat snatched at her wrist with one hand. With the other, he yanked up his t-shirt and showed her the ugly black gun in the waist band of his boxer shorts.

"Get in the car, bitch."

She shook her head slowly. Carefully. No disrespect, even though her impulse was to grab the gun out of the kid's shorts and at least engage the safety before he blew his baby maker off.

But she'd seen too many boy soldiers in her line of work to underestimate the danger of her situation. Just because kids didn't understand death didn't mean they couldn't deal it out. She'd often thought that was precisely the reason children *were* such effective killers. After all, how hard is it to pull the trigger when you don't fully understand what it means?

She raised her free hand slowly into the air--*See? I'm harmless*--but kept moving toward the open door at her back. Toward safety.

The kid yanked at Nixie's wrist again. "Get in here, doc. You got work to do."

Nixie yanked back. "I'm not going anywhere with you."

The driver slouched into his seat. "Just hit her, dawg. Or you'll be telling Ty how the girl doctor kicked your ass."

The kid balled his free hand into a fist. Nixie squeezed her eyes shut, sucked in a breath, and released a scream of such startling volume that the kid released her wrist and dropped back against the vinyl seat, his eyes crossed. Nixie snatched back her wrist, satisfied. She'd been the victim of more haphazard kidnappings than she could count, and in her experience, a good, healthy scream derailed a would-be kidnapper far more effectively than pepper spray or some fancy martial arts.

"Jesus!" The driver turned around and grabbed Nixie by the hair. She doubled her volume and poked stiffened fingers toward his windpipe.

"Aaaack," he said. A surge of victory had her flipping her hair out of his lax fingers and scuttling out of the car like a demented crab. The gun man recovered enough to throw himself after her, and since she was already on her butt on the sidewalk, Nixie pistoned out with both feet to slam the door. He took it square in the face, the window a perfect frame for his stunned, squished expression before he sank out of view onto the floor boards. Nixie wondered for one hysterical moment what the back door of a '79 Ford LTD must weigh to ring a kid's bell like that.

The driver cursed--Nixie read his lips; it was an easy one--and opened his own door. Nixie scrambled up to sprint for the building, only to find Mary Jane at her shoulder, an emergency kit in her hand and fury in her face.

"What the hell is this?" she said.

"I'll explain later," Nixie said, grabbing for her elbow. "For now, let's run." She dragged at the smaller woman's arm, but it was like trying to haul cinder blocks.

The driver looked back and forth between Nixie and Mary Jane, a hint of uncertainty under the bravado and scorn. "What the hell? There ain't supposed to be two of them."

"Two of what?" Mary Jane asked.

Nixie hauled desperately at her arm. "They have a *gun*, Mary Jane. This is not a good time for conversation."

"Two lady doctors," the driver said. "Ty said there was only one."

Mary Jane's face went stony. "Ty sent you?"

Nixie frowned. "Who's Ty?"

The driver gave Nixie a sullen stare and rubbed at his throat while the gun man emerged from the back seat, a little shaky but upright. His gun wavered between Nixie's liver and Mary Jane's.

The driver said, "He wants the lady doctor. Now."

"Fine." Mary Jane walked to the passenger door, opened it and slid onto the giant bench seat. She drew her seatbelt down, buckled it. "Let's go."

"Um, Mary Jane?" Nixie tapped the window as the kids scrambled back into the car. Mary Jane rolled it down.

"I'll be fine," she said. "Some poor kid probably needs stitching up. At least they didn't toss him out on the sidewalk this time. Tell Erik to cover for me. I'll be back later."

The driver stomped the accelerator and the car bucked to life. It jumped the curb and laid a perfect *S* of rubber on the street as it peeled away. Nixie stumbled back and watched it roar off into the night, taking Mary Jane with it.

"So she got into the car voluntarily?" the cop asked, his uniform starched, a sharpened pencil poised over his flip pad. The four of them were crowded into Mary Jane's tiny office, Erik, Nixie, and the two cops who'd answered his 911 call. Erik gulped at the Styrofoam cup of coffee he'd brewed. It went down like boiling hot rocket fuel, but what the hell. He doubted he had any stomach lining left anyway. Nixie was killing him.

"They didn't drag her into the car, if that's what you're asking," she said.

"It's not," Erik told her. "They're trying to make it sound like Mary Jane went off with her boyfriend so they don't have to investigate."

A second cop turned toward Erik. This one was older, had the bulbous nose of a heavy drinker and the spare tire to match. The comb-over was gratis. "Did you witness the event?"

Erik pinched the bridge of his nose. "No," he said, weariness and nerves burning in his gut. "Only Nixie did. And she just told you these guys pulled a gun on her and Mary Jane."

"That's true," Nixie put it. "They definitely pointed a gun at us."

"Did they threaten to shoot you or Ms. Riley?"

"Dr. Riley," Erik said, his eyes closed.

"Did they threaten to shoot you or *Dr.* Riley?" the first cop asked, his voice mechanical.

"They never actually *said* they were going to use the gun, no," Nixie said.

"And Dr. Riley got into the car of her own free will?" the second cop asked.

Nixie gave Erik an apologetic look that put another cramp in his stomach before turning back to the cop. "Well, yeah," Nixie said. "She did."

Pressed Cop looked at Paunchy Cop. "This doesn't sound like an abduction to me," he said. Erik could almost see him slam the lid shut on the case and mentally wander into a doughnut shop

"The hell it doesn't." Erik was on his feet, his hands fisted by his sides. Both cops touched their firearms in warning.

"You'll want to take it easy, sir," said Pressed Cop.

"How the hell am I supposed to take it easy when the woman I--" He broke off when the cops exchanged a smug look. "A woman I work with gets snatched off the street in front of her own clinic by a couple of gang bangers and the cops refuse to classify it as an abduction?"

Paunchy Cop smoothed a hand over his scalp. "Dr. Riley got into the car without coercion after she was told that somebody named Ty had sent for her. She then told Ms. Leighton-Brace that she would be back. I frankly don't see how we can justify using departmental resources to track down a woman who seems to have simply accepted an invitation from an...um, acquaintance."

"Accepted an invitation?" Erik shoved his hands into his hair. "I don't believe this."

"It sounds to me like you're having trouble accepting the nature of your relationship with Dr. Riley."

Erik stared at him. "What?"

Paunchy Cop gave him a greasy smile. "It's not a crime to choose the gang banger over the doctor, sir. Call us if something illegal happens or if she's not back within twenty-four hours."

Erik had never in his life been more tempted to play the do-you-know-who-my-mother-is card. But he'd never played it yet and he wasn't going to tonight. On the slim possibility that Mary Jane had taken off of her own accord, she would never forgive him for bringing his mother into the situation.

The cops filed out the door, and Erik watched them, his hands clenched into impotent fists. Anger and frustration boiled up inside him and he rounded on the only person left to yell at.

"What the hell, Nixie?" He didn't bother to disguise his rage. He wanted her to feel it, wanted her as afraid as he was. "What the hell was that? Are you trying to get Mary Jane killed?"

He caught her mid-yawn. She tried to bite it off, but was apparently too far into it. She finished up with a jaw-cracking *yah!* and pushed one of those long, elegant hands into her hair.

"Oh, sorry, am I keeping you awake?" he asked. "Is Mary Jane's abduction interfering with your beauty rest?"

"Sorry. It's a stress thing. The body trying to get extra oxygen to boost performance." She tried a smile. "Like dogs do?"

"Dogs. Right." He shook his head. "What's the matter with you, Nixie? You deliberately let the police assume Mary Jane went with those kids voluntarily."

Nixie frowned at him. "She did."

He shoved his fists into his pockets. It was either that or strangle her. "She's a doctor. Of course she went. She thought there was an injured kid somewhere. But that doesn't mean she didn't go at gunpoint. That doesn't mean she isn't in danger."

"It sounded to me like she knew this Ty person." Nixie hiked herself up onto the reception desk, let those ugly clogs dangle from her toes.

Erik rolled his head side to side, trying work out the headache. "Everybody knows Ty. Of him, at least."

"Why? Does he run the...what is it? The Dog crew?"

"No. That would be Marcus P. Ty is the money man." He smiled at this, though he wasn't amused. "Legend has it he's a homeboy made good. Had an MBA and a closet full of two thousand dollar suits until he took a knuckle-rapping courtesy of a little post-Enron crackdown. Got lucky, you ask me. Martha Stewart went to jail."

"Martha Stewart went to Camp Cupcake," Nixie said.

"Ty didn't even get that. They just suspended his broker's license."

"Ah." Nixie nodded slowly. "Legitimate employment was off the table, so he went under the table instead?"

"Right. Gangs are businesses, after all. Even a drug lord needs profit and loss reports. And then, of course, he'd need some sage advice on where to launder--oh, excuse me, *invest*--said profits. So maybe Marcus P runs the gang, but Tyrese Jones runs the money. And that, Nixie, makes him the most powerful man in this neighborhood. An invitation from him isn't exactly a request."

Nixie frowned, her brows coming together in a perfect little furrow that should have had a cartoon caption: *thinking!*

"Well how was I supposed to know that?" She slid off the desk and started pacing.

"Everybody knows that." Erik dropped into the receptionist's chair, somewhat mollified by Nixie's pacing. The more anxious she got, the better he felt. Getting her head on straight might be the only thing of any consequence he did tonight. "Everybody with half a brain, anyway."

"Hey!" She stalked up to him, poked a finger into his deltoid hard enough to hurt. "That's not fair. I'm new, not stupid."

"No?" He closed his eyes and hoped she'd back off but she didn't. He could still smell her, fresh and lemony. How the hell could she smell so good after a full shift, a tree burial and a near abduction? And why on earth would he even notice what she smelled like when his best friend had just been snatched by gang bangers? "Then stop acting like it."

She hissed in a breath and he braced himself. That had been over the line, and he knew it. She was going to tell him to screw himself and his stupid clinic now, and he deserved it. But she didn't. He opened his eyes, and found her staring down at him. Her eyes were hazel, he saw. Copper-flecked green and very, very steady.

"Why didn't you tell the police who your mother is?" she asked softly. "You could've had the mayor, the chief of police and the police commissioner down here with one phone call. Why didn't you do it?"

"I'm a grown man, Nixie. I don't call in the mom squad to fix my problems."

"I see. So Mary Jane's safety ranks lower than preserving your ego?"

He stood up. "What, you're a psychoanalyst now?"

"I know mommy issues when I see them. What exactly did your mom do to you that was so awful, anyway?" He walked away from her, but she was right at his elbow, nipping like a herding dog. "Are you really going to let your hang ups put your girlfriend at risk?"

Kiss the Girl

"Me?" He huffed out an incredulous laugh. "I put Mary Jane at risk? Jesus, princess, that's great. Let me run this down for you one more time, okay? *You* witnessed the abduction. *You* gave a statement to the police that made it look like Mary Jane ran off for a little fling with Tyrese 'CPA-to-the-Dark-Side' Jones while I called the cops like a jealous boyfriend. And suddenly she's in trouble because I have mommy issues?"

Her pretty mouth snapped shut. She threaded a finger through one of those shiny curls of hers and frowned into the middle distance. "Okay, so there's enough blame to go around."

Erik dropped his head. "Jesus."

"The question is, what are we going to do now?"

"*We* aren't going to do anything. You're going home. I'll come back in the morning, do some door knocking. Somebody's bound to know what's going on."

She swished her elbow away from his grip. "I want to go with you."

"Like hell," he said. "This isn't exactly Mr. Roger's Neighborhood."

"No kidding?"

"You'd be a liability, Nixie. You'd just slow me down."

"I might surprise you."

"Yeah, you're just full of surprises. But no, it's too dangerous." He grabbed at her elbow again, got it this time. Damn, it felt fragile. He gentled his grip until he wasn't worried about her bones. The urge to tuck her away safely was strange and overpowering. She was much taller than Mary Jane, and clearly had some skill in the art of self-defense or else she'd have been the one riding off with a couple of under-aged felons. So why did he want to wrap her in cotton batting and lock her away? Mary Jane traipsed through this neighborhood twice a day and it had never put this kind of knot in his gut.

"I'm a big girl, Erik." Her eyes were huge and intense, and she was still wearing his extra lab coat. It made her look small, breakable. "I feel responsible. I need to do something."

"Let me take you home, Nixie. We'll talk in the morning, okay? Maybe you can go to the police station, revise your statement. That'll help more than anything."

"You'll go with me?"

"Sure," he lied. He would be back here by first light, and without Nixie in tow. "I'll call you after we've both gotten some sleep."

He forced himself to meet that steady gaze. She finally nodded. "Okay," she said. "Okay."

It was nearly midnight when Nixie climbed out of Erik's beat up Jeep Cherokee.

"I'll walk you up," he said, but Nixie waved him off.

"There's a doorman," she said, pointing to the brightly lit awning protecting the entrance to the Watergate. "I'll be fine."

The uniformed doorman swept open the doors as she spoke and Erik frowned, but nodded. "Okay."

"You'll call me first thing?"

"Yeah, sure."

Nixie gave him a skeptical look, but he didn't catch it. He was too busy looking innocent and studying the steering wheel. The man was a terrible liar. She shook her head.

"See you tomorrow, then." She wanted to leave but worried guilt hung in the air around him like a miasma. She reached over and touched his arm. "She's fine, Erik. I really think she is."

"Yeah." He gave her a crooked smile that clearly cost him an effort. "Of course she is." Nixie shored up the crumbling walls around her heart. God, she was a sucker for the stiff upper lip.

She squeezed his arm, and it felt so solid and strong under her hand that she took an extra second to bask in the unexpected sense of safety. She was used to giving comfort, not taking it. Funny how she could do both with this man.

"I'll see you tomorrow," she said again.

He waited until she was safely inside the building before pulling away and Nixie smiled. Wouldn't his mother be pleased to see her boy showing such a decent set of manners? She glanced toward the Senator's door as she was fitting her own key into the lock. It was silent and dark. Either nobody was home or nobody was up.

She hesitated a moment, then made a decision.

She rapped smartly on the Senator's door. It took a few minutes, but eventually a light flipped on and the Senator herself appeared, wrapped in a brilliant blue silk robe.

"This had better be good," she said.

"It is." Nixie studied the Senator. "Your son is a terrible liar."

"You didn't have to wake me in the middle of the night to tell me that."

"He's trying to cut me out of something I need to do. I want you to help me get around him."

The Senator stepped back, opened the door. "Come in."

CHAPTER EIGHT

Mary Jane hefted the emergency kit onto her shoulder and swallowed a huge lump of terrified rage. She didn't look at the adolescent goons flanking her, just kept her eyes on her shoes. She didn't need to look up to know they were marching her deep into the bowels of the Wash.

Washburn Towers was one of the newer projects and as such, its stairwells stank of cheap paint and exposed insulation along with the usual stew of grease, pot smoke and abandoned bodily fluids. Mary Jane was no snob. She handled the rawer elements of the human body all the time. A little puke and piss on the landing didn't normally faze her. Neither did blood, but they were following fat black blobs of it like it was a trail of bread crumbs and Mary Jane couldn't deny the little darts of panic streaking through her stomach.

Embrace it, she told herself. Use it. Let it make you stronger, not weaker. But her imagination loaded up horrifying images of Ty sprawled somewhere at the top of the stairs in a pool of his own blood, far beyond her ability to help him.

They turned a corner, started up another flight of stairs. Still following the trail of blood.

"Is it Ty?" she finally asked.

No answer.

Kiss the Girl

She picked up the pace. If he wasn't dead, she was going to kill him herself. Hippocrates would surely understand. Though at this point, breaking her oath would be the least of her transgressions.

The goon on her left knocked on the door, a specific-sounding combination of raps and pauses. Mary Jane closed her eyes. Boys and their secret codes. God.

The door opened just wide enough for her and the goon squad to be yanked through.

"All right," she said, digging into her bag for a pair of rubber gloves. "Where's the bleeder?" She snapped them on and looked around the circle of painfully young faces gazing at her with such open hostility. They hated her, she realized with a sinking certainty. No, not her. Just her face, her hair, her skin. Her privilege. Her refusal to show fear to a group of heavily armed teenagers. She hardly knew which.

"The bleeder?" she asked again, this time putting a little more authority into her voice. She glanced around the room like she was taking it in, but in reality, she was just avoiding eye contact. It was one thing to be authoritative. It was quite another to issue a direct challenge.

The apartment was small and generic, but clean. There were more bookshelves than anything, each one stuffed to overflowing with everything from economic and political theory to John Grisham's latest. A laptop hummed gently on a table by the window, another blinked from the kitchen counter. She could see it from the door.

The floors were a dull grey linoleum, but clean except for the blood. There was less here, she saw with a surge of relief. He must have either clotted on his own or done a little first aid. Temper skated in hot after the relief, and she flipped her bag back onto her shoulder.

"Never mind. I'll just follow the trail."

The bodies parted silently for her and she didn't bother to knock. She stepped up to the closed door that presumably led to the bedroom--Ty's bedroom, God help her--and let herself in. She closed the door against the blank, hateful eyes that followed her, then turned and found him there. Perfectly alive if a little dinged up. Relief was a choking pressure in her throat, so she glared at him.

He smiled back at her from the bed where he sprawled, shirtless, a bloody bandage swathing his left shoulder. In spite of the chilly air, his chest was sheened with sweat and Mary Jane tried not to notice the way his dark skin gleamed. How it threw all those long, lean muscles into gorgeous, touchable relief.

"Dr. Riley," he said, his voice was as smooth as aged whiskey even if his smile was a little pinched around the edges. "How good of you to come."

"Did I have a choice?"

He lifted his good shoulder in a lopsided shrug. "I've been drilling the boys on their manners but they were a little worked up when they left."

"First time they'd seen a gunshot?" Mary Jane dropped her bag on the bed next to his shoulder. She smiled when he winced.

"In this neighborhood?" He gave her an amused look. "We see more blood than this before breakfast most days. Nah. They were just worried Marcus P was going to kick their asses."

"For what?"

"For shooting his money man."

Mary Jane froze. "Those were the boys who *shot* you?"

"Accidentally." He shrugged. "Occupational hazard."

"Sure. I guess you should expect to get shot when you *arm children* for a living."

"Hey, I didn't give them guns. I just crunch the numbers."

"So they can make more money to buy more guns."

"So they can run their business as efficiently as possible, which, yes, results in more money. A great deal of which goes back into the neighborhood." He slanted her a look, formidable even sprawled across the bed. "I don't see anybody else lining up to give these folks money or jobs, do you, Mary Jane?"

She glared at him, a familiar helplessness already curling into her belly. "I'm not having this argument again," she said. They'd had it too many times already and Mary Jane never won. "Just...show me your shoulder, all right?"

He waved a casual hand toward his bandage. "Help yourself, doc."

She snipped through the gauze wrapping, peeled it back and inspected the wound. If her stomach twisted at the sight of his elegantly powerful shoulder ripped open by a bullet, she didn't let it show on her face. She eased him forward to have a look at his shoulder blade.

"No exit wound," she said.

He grinned at her. "If there was, you wouldn't be here."

She dropped his shoulder back to the bed without ceremony, took savage satisfaction in his grunt of pain. "You're lucky I'm here at all. Your boys almost brought you Nixie Leighton-Brace by mistake."

His dark eyes went wide, then he laughed. "Not that I don't think you're beautiful, doc, but how would my boys have mistaken you for a rich, famous celebrity?"

"She was wearing a lab coat, standing outside the clinic. They had instructions to grab the lady doctor, so they were trying to grab her when I happened by."

"What the hell is Nixie Leighton-Brace doing in Anacostia? I didn't think we were third world enough for her."

"She's on hiatus. She's experiencing the real world via my receptionist's desk. It's a long story. Don't ask."

Mary Jane doused a square of gauze with alcohol and dabbed gently at the wound. Ty hissed and she frowned at him. "Serves you right, you jerk."

"Come on, MJ," he said, a trace of weariness under his trademark smoothness. "Don't be like that."

"Don't be like what?" She adjusted the latex gloves on hands that wanted to tremble. "Don't be pissed at you for choosing a life that gets you *shot at* on a daily basis? Or don't be pissed because you chose it over me?"

He didn't answer. Not that she'd expected him to. That was another argument they'd worn out.

Mary Jane ripped open a sterile pair of forceps and went after the bullet. Ty closed his eyes. She could see the muscle in his jaw working and she forced back the tears that wanted to well up. She needed clear eyes if she wanted to work. If she wanted to make right choices. Ty had a way of screwing with her vision.

She finally pulled out the mangled slug and showed it to him. "Nice. You want me to sew it up pretty or do you want a nice scar for the street cred?"

She didn't expect an answer, nor did she get one. "I'm making it pretty," she said, threading her needle. "God knows you don't need any more idol worship."

He sat up and caught her wrist before she could take the first stitch. "Mary Jane. Look at me."

She focused on the bedspread between his knees. He took her chin, brought her gaze to his. "I know you don't understand."

"Then make me," she said, her voice fierce and jagged. "*Make* me understand."

Kiss the Girl

"I can't. I wish I could. But you need to know I never meant for this to happen. I never meant to break your heart."

"God." She wrenched her chin from his fingers, hating the way every inch of her skin warmed at his touch. "It was years ago, Ty. *We* were years ago. Back when you wanted to be an executive and I wanted to be a doctor. Back when we both thought we could be more than where we were from."

"And here we are, working within half a mile of each other."

Mary Jane made her voice cold. "We're working worlds apart, Ty. Worlds and worlds."

He eased his grip on her wrist, slid his fingers through hers. "I tried to live in your world, babe. God knows I tried. You saw how that turned out."

"I saw you get caught up in the rush of playing with other people's money. I saw you get sucked into a culture of greed and risk and I saw how it screwed with your moral compass."

"My moral compass?" He shook his head. "Business is war, babe. Soldiers follow orders, not a moral compass."

"So, what, you weren't guilty of anything? You were just a casualty of war?"

"Hell yes."

"And you think that makes it okay to *join a gang*?"

"I didn't join anything. Maybe I'm a mercenary, but I'm an independent mercenary. I don't do anything but the books." He pressed her hand between his when she tried to pull it away. "Seriously, MJ. I know you don't like the people I work for, but how different are they really from the assholes I used to work for when I was legit? You can shoot a man, or you can strip him of his dreams and ambition. He's dead either way, so what difference does it make how he got wounded?"

She stared at him. "You can ask me that with the bullet hole in your shoulder still bleeding?"

"Yeah, I can. I've been hit both ways now. I preferred the bullet."

She jerked her hand free of his and applied herself to stitching him up. It cost her to put even one more hole in his beautiful, stubborn hide, but she didn't let him see that. She focused on her work to the exclusion of all else. It was what she always did.

She snipped off the thread. "I'm not giving you any painkillers."

"I wouldn't take them even if you did." He laid back, closed his eyes. "I may work for pushers, but I don't sample the merchandise."

Mary Jane frowned. She didn't like the way sweat had beaded on his forehead, or the way he'd gone ashen under the rich cocoa of his skin. She shook a couple antibiotics out of a vial and knelt down beside the bed.

"Hey," she said, tapping a fingernail against his cheek. "Take these."

He rolled his head to the side, opened clear dark eyes. "What will you give me if I do?"

She recognized that look, that tone. It pulled at her with a traitorous warmth, tempted her to ante up a really excellent bribe. Something that involved lots of skin and heat and rumpled sheets. He must've seen it in her face, the wanting that never fully died, because he reached out to finger a lock of her hair.

"Stay with me, MJ. Just tonight."

She shook her head. She was pretty sure that *no* wasn't the first thing she'd say if she risked opening her mouth. He tugged gently on her hair and she bowed under the silent request. God she missed his touch. He leaned forward, as if to whisper something, but it wasn't words that hit her ear. It was his mouth. His hot, magical, seeking mouth. Time flipped, twisted, stretched, until she couldn't remember if he'd ever been away. If they'd ever been apart. Had she really denied herself this? Had she really convinced herself she didn't want it? Didn't want him?

He nipped at the shell of her ear until she heard herself sigh, half resignation, half desire. She could feel him smiling as he dragged that talented mouth lower, ran a chain of tiny kisses along her throat, her collar bone.

When he pulled her onto the bed, she went. But she didn't speak. She never said a single word until she pulled her rumpled clothes back on and caught the first train out of Anacostia the next morning.

Coffee. Oh sweet baby Jesus, somebody was making coffee. Erik pulled the smell into his lungs like it was pure oxygen. Then he remembered.

He lived alone and his coffee maker was broken. Had been for months. What the hell?

He checked the bed side clock. 7:12. He scrubbed a hand over thirty-six hours of stubble and forced himself upright. He doubted a thief would hang out for a little coffee, and the only person who had a key to his apartment was his mother. He took a moment to weigh his options.

He wanted that coffee. He didn't want to talk to his mother. He needed to tear a strip off her for trying to fix him up with Nixie, and he didn't have time. He needed to be in Anacostia knocking on doors before Nixie attached herself to him like a pretty, long-legged barnacle. He decided it was a draw. He'd face his mother but the coffee would make it bearable.

He yanked on a pair of flannel pajama pants and ambled toward the kitchen.

"That better be the good stuff, Mom," he said. "Because after the Nixie Leighton-Brace thing, you owe me."

"Why do you insist on using my name like a title?" Nixie asked. "You know it drives me nuts."

Erik froze. He laid both hands on the doorframe for support and squinted into the kitchen. "Nixie?"

"That's better." She was perched on one of the stools beside the counter, grinning at him. She looked impossibly clean and fresh. Rested. He wanted to sniff her, to see if she smelled like she looked.

She slid off the stool and offered him a steaming paper cup of coffee. He took a cautious sip. "How did you get in here?"

"Your mom let me in."

"My mom."

"Yeah."

"I'm going to kill her."

"Yeah, she mentioned that. It doesn't bother her the way you'd think it might."

Erik swallowed some more coffee, willed the caffeine into his bloodstream. "What are you doing here, Nixie?"

"I'm going with you."

"Going with me where?"

"To rescue Mary Jane." She gave him a sunny smile.

"What makes you think I'm going to rescue Mary Jane?"

"Oh please." She rolled her eyes. "Your girlfriend was quasi-kidnapped last night, probably to patch up some gun-shot drug lord, and hasn't answered her cell phone or home phone since. And yes, I've been dialing her all night. So forgive me for making assumptions on short acquaintance, but I don't believe you're planning to do nothing but wring your hands until she turns up again." She folded her hands serenely in her lap. "You're going after her and I'm going with you."

"No." Erik gulped down some more coffee. God, where was the caffeine?

"See? You *are* going after her."

Kiss the Girl

"And I have no intention of taking you with me."

Her lips went thin and she crossed her arms over a sweater the color of ripe pumpkins. It was soft-looking and a little clingy and Erik had to force himself not to look south of her collar bones. "Why not?"

"Because you're Nixie Leighton-Brace. That's why. Jesus." He scratched at his scruffy cheek and watched her try to wipe the hurt off her face. "Don't look at me like that. I'm not trying to be a jerk. It's not my fault you're...you."

"It isn't mine either. Get over it. I'm going with you."

He crossed the room and plunked himself down on the stool next to hers. The scent of lemons mixed pleasantly with his coffee and he shook his head to clear it. She was confusing him. Confusing everything. Mary Jane was in danger and all he could think about was how soft her sweater looked. How soft *she* looked. He was sorely tempted to touch her just to satisfy his curiosity, and that was unacceptable.

He'd spent his childhood swimming in and out of the fishbowl his mother called a life. His test scores, his baseball stats, even his first date for God's sake--they were all a matter of public record, thanks to the press's insatiable appetite for details and his mother's insatiable appetite for publicity. As a child, Erik had dreamed of privacy the way hungry kids dreamed of food, and as an adult he'd worked hard to achieve it. So what kind of bizarre, self-destructive impulse had him jonsing after a crazy-famous second-generation celebrity? It was that soft sweater and her stupid lemon soap, he thought. They were screwing with his judgment.

"Come on, Nixie. I'm not going to wander into the worst neighborhood in the country with America's princess on my arm. It's asking for trouble and we've got enough of that, don't you think? We're already in deep shit over last night. If Mary Jane did treat somebody without reporting it, there's no way we'll be able to keep it quiet. Not with you in the picture. Best case scenario, we lose what little funding we have."

"And worst case?"

"Mary Jane loses her license. Is that what you want?"

"Mary Jane is a big girl. She knew what the risks were when she got into that car."

"For herself. I don't think she counted on running that decision through the meat grinder of your celebrity." She flinched at that. He felt like he'd kicked a puppy. "God, don't *look* like that. I'm not making things up to make you feel bad, Nixie. But you have to understand. At this point, you're more liability than asset."

Her smile faded, and those giant eyes went very serious. "You have no idea what kind of asset I can be. If I've done something wrong, I'll fix it. But don't freeze me out because of who I am. I'm working like hell to be more than just my name, Erik. Surely you of all people can understand what that's like."

Erik bowed his head until it nearly touched the plastic lid of his coffee cup. He'd spent so much of his own life fighting against a larger-than-life parent to forge his own path. Screwing with Nixie's shot at forging her own just because she smelled good and distracted him suddenly seemed incredibly petty.

"Fine," he said. "You can come. But can you dial down the Nixie Leighton-Brace factor a little? It's bad enough that you're coming. I don't want anybody to recognize you."

"Thank you, Erik." She didn't hug him exactly. It was more sort of squeezing herself up against his shoulder, but the feel of her body burned itself into his brain. The subtle curve of her waist against his elbow, the cool swish of her hair against his chin. It was her shampoo, he knew now, that smelled like lemons. Christ.

Kiss the Girl

"Well, what are we waiting for?" she asked, her eyes shining like he'd just served her up a hunk of birthday cake instead of a grudging invitation. She wriggled like a frisky puppy and Erik smiled in spite of himself. "Let's go get Mary Jane back from the Dog crew."

CHAPTER NINE

The sky was a cold and unforgiving blue as Nixie and Erik crossed the bridge into Anacostia. They turned onto Kingston, passed the clinic and parked on the street outside a row of lopsided, grayish houses. The yards were stingy patches of reluctant weeds, separated by bow-legged chain link fences. The occasional window had been replaced with plywood, giving the whole street the vaguely menacing air of someone who'd lost an eye under questionable circumstances.

Nixie tried Mary Jane's cell phone one last time. She watched the wind sweep a fistful of dirty snow into a mini-cyclone in the gutter while Mary Jane's voicemail picked up yet again. She shook her head at Erik and flipped shut the phone. "Well?" she said. "Where do we start?"

He switched off the Jeep's ignition. "What would you say if I asked you to stay here and guard the car against marauding bands of teenagers?"

"I'd say teenagers don't maraud at eight a.m. on Sunday mornings. Now quit trying to get rid of me."

"Right." He sighed. "Let's start with the south side of the street and work our way down to the Wash."

"The Wash?"

"Washburn Towers. It's one of the newer projects. The Dog Crew is supposed to have a serious presence there. If Mary Jane's disappearance has anything to do

Kiss the Girl

with the Dog Crew, somebody on this street saw something."

"And we're just going to knock at their doors bright and early on a Sunday morning and ask them to tell us what it was?"

"Yep."

Nixie looked at him doubtfully. "That's going to piss some people off."

"I think you're discounting my immense personal charm." He smiled at her, and Nixie rolled her eyes.

"I don't know if anybody's mentioned this before, but charm isn't exactly your strong suit."

His smile widened. "I haven't been trying to charm you. You'd feel differently if I had."

She didn't doubt it. Still, he didn't know that.

"Right," she said. "Maybe you should let me do the talking."

"Yeah, I don't think so." He stepped out and rounded the hood. She pushed open her own door and joined him on the curb.

"Where to?" she asked.

"We'll start with Otto Lyndale's place." He waved his arm toward the nearest tip-tilted house. The fence looked a little firmer than the others.

"You know Otto?" she asked.

"Know of him is more like it," Erik said. He strode to the center of the fence where a crooked gate hung. He rattled the gate on its hinges and waited. Nixie frowned. The yard was small but they were still a good twenty feet from the house.

"You don't think the doorbell would be--"

She was going to say *more effective* but the words died in her throat when what looked like a small pony with fangs rounded the corner of the house. It streaked across the yard toward them, picking up speed as if the fence between them didn't exist. Nixie stumbled back until her butt hit the Jeep and she sighed in deep gratitude when the fence not only withstood impact but boomeranged the thing back into the yard a good couple feet.

"Yikes. Is that a dog?"

"Yeah." Erik took a careful step back from the fence himself. The dog scrambled to its feet, gave itself an almighty shake, then stood there blinking owlishly around the yard. Maybe looking for something that would explain the massive concussion, Nixie thought. It spotted them again and lunged at the long suffering fence, headache apparently forgotten. It barked fiercely--big, deep, sonic booms of noise accompanied by the occasional streamer of spittle.

"That dog can only eat one of us at a time," Nixie said, watching sharp white teeth gnash against the chain links. "No offense, but if it comes down to running for it, I *will* be faster than you."

"Thanks for the heads up."

The front door of the house opened, and a man stepped out. He was as old a human being as Nixie had ever seen, bent practically half, his neck permanently craned upward like a vulture's so he could train his one remaining eye on the world. He had a shotgun in one hand and what looked like a remote control in the other.

"Lady! Chissakes, Lady, shut it!"

Nixie blinked. "That dog's a girl? And he calls her *Lady*?"

Erik waved at the man. "Hey, Otto. Have a minute?"

"Lady! Shut the hell up!"

The dog continued her frenzied barking until Otto shook his head and pointed the remote at her. Lady gave a short yip, twitched and fell over. Nixie felt the impact in the concrete under her feet. Ooh, she thought. Shock collar. No wonder the dog took concussions in stride. Otto leveled the shotgun at them.

"Who the hell are you?"

Kiss the Girl

Erik held up both hands in the classic we-come-in-peace position. "I'm Erik Larsen. I'm a doctor at the clinic next door."

"Who's your friend?"

"Our receptionist."

Nixie gave him a respectful nod. She'd met plenty of people at gun-point in her life. The key was to look wary of the gun, but interested in the person. Definitely don't smile. A guy with a gun is never funny. She glanced down at the dog, who'd dragged herself to a sitting position. Her eyes were a little unfocused, but her lip curled around a rumbling, death-threat of a growl. Nixie groped behind her back for the door handle of the Jeep, just in case.

"What do you want?" Otto asked. His brows were so big and bushy that from the sidewalk they looked like some kind of grey caterpillar marching across his forehead. Nixie had no reference in nature for the matching tufts of hair sprouting from either ear.

"We're wondering if you've seen a friend of ours. She's about yea big--" Erik leveled a hand around his shoulder "--blonde, blue-eyed. She works at the clinic."

Otto considered this as he stumped down the porch steps. Lady trotted to his side, her head chest-high on the old man. Nixie wondered if it had ever occurred to the dog that she could just step over the fence whenever she felt like eating somebody.

"The lady doctor?" Otto asked. He pulled at his ear hair and sucked his teeth as he thought it over. "I seen her around here and there. Don't say much, but she got a world class ass. Just the way I like 'em. Quiet and curvy. You lose her?"

"I'm not sure." Erik gave the old man a wide smile. The shotgun came back up to chest level and Nixie winced. *Never smile at the gun man.* Erik poked his hands back into the air.

"If you ain't sure, what are you bothering me for?"

"I heard Tyrese asked for her, that's all." Erik didn't smile this time. "You know where we might go looking for her?"

Otto studied them. "You kin of hers?"

Nixie shook her head, and Otto said, "I know *you* ain't. Damn, I got eyes, don't I? You ain't got no ass whatsoever."

"Hey!" Nixie said. "You have *one* eye, and I have a very nice ass." At least according to *Chat Magazine* she did.

"Pah. Seen better curves on an ironing board," Otto said. "Got yourself a smart-alecky mouth, though." Nixie bit her tongue while he turned to Erik. "What about you? You related to the lady doctor?"

"No," Erik said. "But she's important to me."

"Huh." Otto cracked a wide smile. "Tyrese done stole your girl."

Erik frowned. "He didn't steal my girl."

"You don't got her. Ty does. Sound like girl-stealing to me." He bent suddenly, whacked at his filthy trousers and started making an awful hacking noise. Nixie hesitated. If he collapsed, they'd have to go in there to help him. Lady would eat them, but Erik had probably taken some kind of doctor oath that mandated it.

Then Otto straightened and from the gleam in his eye, Nixie deduced he'd been laughing. She pressed a hand to her stomach. Geez.

"Have you seen her, Otto?" Erik looked less than amused himself.

"Nope." Otto grinned and thumped Lady on the head. She blinked appreciatively. "You got a problem with Tyrese, you going to have to take it to him. I ain't your snitch. Come on, Lady."

He disappeared into the house with his assault vehicle of a dog trotting behind him.

"Nice work, Colombo."

Erik sneered at her. "This from the woman who spent the last ten minutes with one foot in the car."

"Somebody had to go for help if Cujo decided to eat you."

"You'll never know how that eases my mind."

"No problem. And hey, word of advice? Don't smile at the gun man."

"What?"

"It makes them feel like you're not taking them seriously. So next time you're questioning the gun man, even if he cracks a joke, don't smile. You're going to get your caps blown off."

"My caps?"

"Oh, sorry. Are those your real teeth?"

He glowered at her. "Yes."

"They're very...white."

He stalked past her toward the next house on the block. "Thanks."

"No problem," Nixie said again, hiding a smile.

"I had no idea you were such an expert on human nature," Erik said. Nixie shrugged modestly. "You want to take this next one?"

Nixie eyed the house. It was identical to Otto's except that the fence was a little more ramshackle and the yard a little more over-grown. Garbage was heaped along the fence, and a narrow alley ran between the two yards. "No dogs?"

"Not that I'm aware of."

"Who lives here?"

"Mattie Getz-Strunk."

"Mattie gets drunk?"

"No. Mattie. Getz. Strunk. Hyphenated."

"Tell me she's not a drinker."

"Not as far as I know."

"Okay. Watch and learn, doc."

Nixie let herself into the yard and picked her way over the heaved-up front walk to the porch, Erik trailing behind. She rapped her knuckles on the stingy window in the door.

"Mattie?" she called. She was *not* going to call her Ms. Getz-Strunk. She gave Erik a suspicious look. He wasn't above making that up just to pay her back for making him take her along. "Mattie? Are you at home?"

Something moved across the hallway beyond the living room. Nixie couldn't tell what it was, only that it was approximately human sized, ambulatory and very fast.

"I think somebody's in there." She put her face to the window, framed it with her hands for a better look. She rapped again on the glass. "Mattie? We just have a couple questions for you."

"Ooooh, I wouldn't have said that." Erik stood behind her, hands tucked into his pockets, jacket open to the biting wind. He looked perfectly comfortable in the forty degree air, his cheeks reddened, his eyes very blue. He wagged his head at her.

"Why not?" Nixie went back to the glass. "Damn, she *is* in there! Or somebody is."

"Was." Erik tipped his head toward the sound of the back door slamming.

"What?" Nixie hopped off the porch into the alley that separated the houses and headed back. "Where's she going?"

"Jesus, Nixie, don't--"

The door to the detached garage flew open and an El Camino rocketed into the alley. The woman at the wheel had tortured red hair that stood up and waved around her head like she was underwater. She was addict-thin and between that and the hair she looked like a lit fuse. She stomped on the accelerator and the car lurched forward, eating up the distance between Nixie and her fender with alarming speed. Nixie dove over the fence into a pile of garbage and slimy leaves that must have been rotting away since last fall. The El Camino screamed by and sailed sideways into the street on two tires, taking out Otto's garbage can on its way.

"Fuck you, pigs!" Mattie's laugh was like gravel in a can, and she stuck one skinny arm out the window, middle finger extended as she blew through the stop sign at the corner. "Kiss my white ass!"

Nixie sat up and blinked at Erik. He came down the porch steps to squat beside her.

"Nice reflexes, princess." He picked a leaf off her cheek with two fingers. "You ever want to play softball, you let me know. The hospital team could use a girl who's not afraid to get her shirt dirty. Who would have thought an ironing board could move so fast?"

"Ironing board," Nixie muttered in disgust. She rolled to her hands and knees, mentally cataloguing her injuries--scraped palms, banged knee, filthy clothes, and yes, bruised ass. She patted at it and winced.

Something hot and elusive shifted in those calm blue eyes. "Don't take it so hard, Nixie. Some men like their women, ah, subtle."

She snorted. "Okay, that guy was at least six hundred years old and he only had *one eye*. I'm pretty sure he was talking about you with the ironing board thing."

"Those fabled people skills of yours could use a little work, though," he mused as if she hadn't spoken. "Hold still now. There's a little bit of slime right--" He took her chin in his hand, used his thumb to rub gently at her cheek bone. Her heart took a funny little tumble in her chest and she slapped at his hand. It was probably just a delayed reaction to having nearly been Mattie Getz-Strunk's hood ornament, she told herself.

"You knew that was going to happen." She got to her feet, brushing at the frozen slime coating her jeans. A Big Gulp lid and straw had somehow adhered to her butt. She flicked it off. Erik picked at the leaves in her hair. She slapped at him again and he tucked his hands into his pockets with a shrug.

"I certainly did not."

She treated him to a nice, long look.

"I figured she'd bolt. I didn't figure she'd try to run you over."

"Why would she bolt?"

"Funny story there." Nixie glared at him and he hurried to continue. "While Mattie doesn't get drunk, she does get stoned. And when she's high, she's paranoid and a little, um, violent."

"A *little* violent?" Nixie gaped at him. "She tried to run me over with her truck!"

"Well, you did threaten to question her. She probably thought we were the cops. And to be fair, an El Camino is really only half a truck." She gave him a shot to the shoulder and Erik winced. "Nice arm. You could maybe get into the batting line up, too."

"I am *not* playing softball for your stupid league." Nixie kicked her way free of the knee-high trash heap, and stomped toward the front gate.

"Up to you, of course." He swished the gate open in time for her to blaze through. "What now?"

"What do you mean, what now? Let's hit the next house."

"You don't want to go home to change?"

"And let you ditch me while I'm in the shower? I don't think so, ace. I'm good to go." She tucked a slimy lock of hair behind her ear and folded her arms over her chest. "The smell will wear off in a few minutes, I'm sure. And if it doesn't, I'm going to smear myself all over your passenger seat on the way home."

Erik nodded grimly. "Right."

"Look on the bright side. Who would believe I'm Nixie Leighton-Brace now?" She looked around the deserted street. "Not that there's a pack of roving tabloid reporters hanging around or anything. Guess I'm not quite the catalyst for disastrous publicity you thought."

"It's early yet. We'll see what happens when the clinic opens this afternoon."

"Fine. So we have the next four hours to find Mary Jane in relative peace and quiet. Let's get busy. Who's next on the to-be-questioned list?"

Erik jerked his head toward a house down the street, crouching in the squat shadow of The Wash. "Daryl Johnson. He's the reason McDonald's puts pictures instead of words on their cash registers. Flips burgers, lives with his mom, buys beer for the under aged. Smokes a lot of dope. Loves the ladies, thinks they love him back. If he saw anything, he'll tell us."

"Why didn't we start with him?"

"Oh, I think you'll see for yourself."

CHAPTER TEN

Erik fell in behind Nixie as she marched down the ancient concrete toward Daryl Johnson's house. Rotten leaves and litter fluttered in her wake like she was a one-woman ticker tape parade. She didn't have Mary Jane's curves, it was true. But there was a very pleasing swing to what ass she did have. He had to admit it was a nice view.

There was a half-chewed stick of beef jerky dangling from one curl and he smiled into his collar. Damn, he liked this girl. He didn't know a single woman who would slap at her jeans and declare herself good to go after a head-first dive into a trash heap. The women he generally dated would be in tears by now, both the ones he picked out and the ones his mother threw at him. This girl was something else. He'd miss her when she went back to being Nixie Leighton-Brace.

His smile died. God, what was he thinking? He wouldn't miss her. Maybe the women he dated didn't have quite her...panache, but at least they weren't tabloid bait. And they certainly didn't intimate that he had game-show-host teeth or bad people skills. Caps, indeed. He sucked on his perfectly natural teeth and frowned at Nixie's back.

Still, he couldn't deny she was interesting company. He'd go to his grave savoring the sight of her rising up from the leaves like some white-trash version of her namesake, pissed and righteous. Unfortunately, he'd probably go to bed tonight savoring the sight of her elegant hands running over the curves of her own butt, searching for injury while Erik's mind made a beeline for the gutter. He sighed. And that was the downside to being a normal man with two eyes and a healthy sexual appetite. But it didn't mean anything. As soon as he had the clinic back on solid financial footing, he could forget Nixie Leighton-Brace *and* her world-class backside.

He stopped on the sidewalk and watched Nixie stare at Daryl Johnson's house. It was neater than most--no graffiti and a newer fence. Still, it sidled up to the side of the Wash like a submissive dog approaching the alpha. Which was appropriate when Erik considered Daryl's relationship with the Dog crew.

Nixie rattled the gate. No snarling hounds materialized. She opened the gate and waved Erik through. "You first."

"You're sure you don't want to wait in the car?"

"I'm sure."

"Did I mention that Daryl likes the ladies?"

"Yep. And I'm pretty sure that, given my current condition, he's not going to get out of hand."

Erik shook his head. "Daryl doesn't mind dirty. I think he might actually like dirty."

Nixie stepped closer. "The aroma is my second line of defense."

Erik's nose twitched. "Right. Well, don't say I didn't warn you."

She waved him through the gate and trailed him to the front door. Not that he could see her, but she had a point about the aroma. It was pretty stiff. He knocked on the door. Nothing. He knocked again.

Something crashed inside the house, followed by some cursing, a heart-felt moan and a little more crashing. The door opened a sliver and one sleepy eye appeared.

"What the fuck, homes?"

"Hey, Daryl," Erik said, nudging Nixie a little farther to his left. "I'm looking for a woman--"

"Sheee-it, homes, she yours?" The eye opened fully. "Damn, she bounced on me *all* night. Fucking ride 'em cowgirl, you know what I'm saying? Lucky ass motherfucker." The door opened wider and Daryl beamed at Erik, in perfect charity with the universe for having created a woman who would fuck his brains out, even if she was just on loan from the guy at the door.

Erik lifted his eyebrows. "Unless she's about this tall--" he waved a hand at shoulder-height "--blonde, blue-eyed and qualified to crack your chest, I don't think so."

Daryl's smile didn't falter. He just stood there, a chubby dimwit in droopy boxers and sweat socks. "Damn, G, she cracked *everything* last night, you know what I mean? But she wasn't no blonde. You looking for a white bitch?"

"Yeah," Erik said. "You seen one lately?"

"Shit, dawg. I seen lots of white bitches. They're all *this ain't no Diet Coke!* and *I asked for the dressing on the side!*" He turned from the door and treated them both to a couple inches of hairy ass cleavage. Nixie made some kind of strangled noise in the back of her throat as Daryl ambled to the ancient floral-print couch.

Erik gave Nixie another little nudge toward the side of the porch and whispered, "Stay here."

"Not on your life," she whispered back. "I want to meet the cowgirl. Do you think she's still in there?"

"I need a smoke," Daryl said. Nixie poked at Erik and made get-going eyes at him until he sighed and followed Daryl into the house, Nixie at his heels.

"Well, damn, bro. There's your white girl right there!" Daryl looked up from the joint he was rolling and gave Nixie a big smile. "'Sup, home girl." He reached up the leg of his boxers and produced a flabby, wrinkled dick.

"You want a taste of ol' D, too? I got enough to go around."

Erik sighed. He'd tried to warn her.

"Oh, wow," Nixie said. She waved a hand through the air. "That's...flattering, really, but--" Daryl waited, jiggled his equipment. Erik watched the emotions race across Nixie's mobile face. She was going to laugh any minute now, and the last thing they needed was to wound Daryl's pride. Especially when he was holding it in his hand. Erik searched for anything that might change the subject.

"Your mom lets you smoke in the house?" Erik asked, nodding toward the half-rolled joint.

Daryl tucked his dick back into his shorts. "No, I ain't allowed to light up in here. But it ain't no thing. Mama's at church all morning and I got me a Bounce blower."

"A bounce blower?" Nixie edged closer, curiosity clearly winning out over prudence. You'd think she *wanted* to get flashed again. "What's that?"

Daryl held up a paper towel tube. "It's stuffed with Bounce. You know, like from the dryer? You suck in the weed--" He demonstrated, taking an enormous hit from the joint. "Then you blow it through the tube," he croaked. He lifted the tube to his mouth and exhaled a mighty stream of smoke into the end. The smell of extremely high laundry filled the room.

Erik sighed but Nixie pressed her hands against her chest and treated Erik to a brilliant smile, the kind that sold magazines by the stack. She was filthy, leaves still tucked into those coppery curls of hers, dirt caked on both knees, but when she looked at Erik, her face was pure delight.

This was why she was Nixie Leighton-Brace, he thought suddenly. This was why people ran for their checkbooks every time she smiled. Nixie didn't care about race or class or intellect. You could plop her down with anybody on the planet and within minutes, she would be charmed with them about something. Here was a man who'd just reached up his shorts and flopped out his penis for her admiration, and two minutes later, Nixie was laughing with him.

She looked up and caught Erik's eye, a personal invitation to join her, to share the joke, to be with her in the moment. Erik smiled back, and her approval spilled over him like warm honey. Daryl squinted at her through the smoke.

"Dang, do I know you?" he asked Nixie.

Erik watched her clamp down on that famous smile. "Could be. It's a small world."

"You ever come into the Chow Down? On Berkley?"

"Is that where you work?" Nixie asked.

"Yeah. You come on in, I'll fix you up with some free grub." He stared at her, grinning foolishly. Erik imagined she got that quite a lot. Still, she grinned back with every sign of genuine pleasure.

"You know what I'd really like?" she asked.

Daryl's hand went for the leg hole of his boxers again.

"Um, no, not that." Nixie perched on the edge of the coffee table, carefully keeping her filth off Mrs. Johnson's furniture and her distance from Daryl's underwear. "I'd really like to find my friend Mary Jane. Tyrese sent a car for her last night, to the clinic. I haven't seen her since and I'm a little worried." She put wide-eyed concern all over her face and leaned forward just enough to keep Daryl interested. "Do you know Tyrese?"

Daryl sucked down another lungful of smoke and leaned back. The fly of his boxers gaped open. Erik looked away. He couldn't take it. "Yeah, baby, I know Ty." He exhaled into the paper towel tube. Meadow fresh pot smoke poured into the room. "Mad smart, that boy. Got all kinda diplomas and shit."

"Do you think he'll see us?" Nixie asked. "Can you take us to him? I mean, if your girlfriend wouldn't mind?" She glanced around the room as if the woman were hiding under a sofa cushion, and Erik suppressed a snort. Nixie's face was all sincerity, but there was a wicked flash in those mossy eyes. She still wanted to meet Daryl's cowgirl. Yeehaw.

"Ain't no bitch gonna tell me what to do," Daryl said, giving Nixie a narrow stare he'd probably seen on MTV. Then he broke into a sunny smile and said, "She gots to roll 'fore Mama get home from church anyhow. Yo! Babe!" He scooped up his stash, hiked up his boxers and ambled toward the back of the house. "Time to jet, home girl!"

Nixie waited, her eyes trained on the doorway, an expectant look on her face. Erik waited, too, for the inevitable discovery of a missing woman and a missing wallet.

"Hey, she done took off already." Daryl was back and clearly nonplussed. "Forgot to leave her digits, too. Shit."

Nixie gave a soothing little cluck. "Shy, maybe."

Daryl brightened. "Yeah." He scrubbed a hand over his head and shrugged. Short attention span. Erik figured it was a blessing. Probably kept him from noticing anything amiss with his life, or dwelling on it when he did. "You wanna get some chow?"

"We'd like to visit Ty," Nixie told him gently. "You were going to take us?"

"Right!" Daryl snapped his fingers and nodded. "Right." He stood there, a bit uncertain. "Now?"

Nixie nodded slowly. "Yes."

Daryl lifted his shoulders. "Okay. Let's roll."

Nixie had seen far worse than the Wash as far as ghettos went. Refugee camps, shack cities, whole communities living on garbage dumps. Comparatively, the Wash was the lap of luxury. But there was a feel here, an energy that Nixie recognized. It was a toxic stew of poverty, hopelessness and fury, and it hung in the air, as real to Nixie as the stench of urine and old grease.

Daryl heaved himself up the last flight of stairs, then bent at the waist and sucked wind. "Damn, I got to switch to Diet Coke."

"I think it's more the fries," Erik told him. He joined Nixie on the landing where she delivered a sharp hip check. Erik gave her a *what?* face.

"Try not to antagonize the guy who's taking us to Mary Jane, huh?" she whispered.

He shrugged. "Kid's on a collision course with angina."

"So tell him *after* we get Mary Jane back."

"Right."

Daryl straightened and swiped a sleeve over his shiny forehead. "Shit. Okay, I'm good. Let's roll."

He led them down a dim hallway that smelled of cigarettes and ammonia. The occasional fluorescent bulb gave off a soft hum, and TVs chattered away in the apartments they passed. Daryl stopped at the end of the hall, rapped on a door.

"Tyrese? Yo, Tyrese! It's me, Daryl Johnson. Yo, homes, got some folks want to talk with you. It's about that lady doctor down at the clinic. You know, the one with the onion butt?"

Nixie leaned toward Erik. "Onion butt?"

He didn't look at her, just shook his head.

Daryl knocked again. "Tyrese? Come on, man, open up."

Nixie frowned at Erik. "Onion butt? What the heck does that even mean?"

He sighed and ignored her. Nixie poked Daryl. "Onion butt?"

Kiss the Girl

"Booty. Big, round, scrumptious, poppin'-ass booty. Kind so good it can make a brotha cry, know what I'm saying?" He gave her a quick inspection. "You ain't got one, sister girl. Sorry."

Nixie sighed and Erik hid a grin in his collar. "You're not the first one to mention that to me today."

Daryl knocked on the door again. "Hey, man, you in there? I got a doc out here, if you need sewing up or some shit like that. You being all shot up and whatnot."

There was the sudden rattle of locks being worked-- several locks, if Nixie heard correctly--and the door swung open. Standing there in the doorway was the most beautiful creature Nixie had ever seen. His skin was the color of really high-quality baking chocolate--dark and sweet and pure--and it was stretched over a lean, elegant set of bones that made even the white bandages at his shoulder look haute. Nixie blinked at him, a little stunned. His mouth, even set as it was in irritation, was full and lush, the cheekbones high and sharp under deep brown eyes.

"Keep it down, huh, Daryl?" Tyrese said. He was shirtless in deference to the shoulder wound, and while his chest was certainly beautiful to look at, it wasn't his physique that hit Nixie. It was the energy. This man was born to command. Nixie had felt this same power vibrating off heads of state, CEOs of multinational corporations, and warlords of all stripes. It was the same energy that hung in the air around Erik, and had surrounded her parents like a familiar perfume.

Daryl seemed oblivious. He just grinned at Tyrese like an overgrown toddler. "'Sup, Ty?"

"'Sup, Daryl." Tyrese returned the greeting wearily. "Who're your friends?"

"They're from the clinic down the street."

"I'm Dr. Erik Larsen, and this is our receptionist." Erik stepped forward, offered his hand to Tyrese. Tyrese took it. Somehow, both men made it clear that it wasn't a friendly greeting. Nixie had no idea how men did such things.

"Come in," he said, and stepped back from the door. He put a hand on Daryl's chest. "Not you, Daryl."

The kid's face fell. "Aw, man."

"Go home and open some windows. You smell like the Laundromat started selling pot. Your mama's going to have your ass."

"Later, dawg."

"Later."

Tyrese closed the door and turned to them, his face a blank. Erik stood next to one of the overflowing bookshelves, glaring at Tyrese, but Nixie took in the tiny apartment with interest. It looked like somebody with an addiction to both books and computers was squatting there. No photos on the walls, no posters or pictures, no stash of grocery bags, no clutter. Not even a piece of mail or a newspaper or a take-out carton. Just a breathtakingly vast collection of books and a laptop humming on every flat surface.

"Have you lived here long?" Nixie asked.

"A few years, Ms. Leighton-Brace."

"You recognized me?" She patted at her filthy hair. "Erik assured me I was incognito like this."

Tyrese smiled, and it made him look seriously angelic. "I'll admit, Mary Jane tipped me off."

"Where is she?" Erik put himself between Nixie and Tyrese. If possible, he looked bigger, squarer, than usual. Nixie sighed. Again with the nonverbals.

Tyrese gave Erik an assessing look. "Is she late for work or something?"

"She's off today," Nixie said, putting herself between the two men. It was like stepping between a couple of growling dogs. "Erik's just worried about her."

Kiss the Girl

"Why?" Tyrese didn't look at Nixie. Neither did Erik. They just glared at each other over her head. "She something special to you?"

"Yeah." Erik's hands were fists, and Nixie wanted to seize them in her own hands and gentle them. "She is."

Tyrese's dark eyes went hot, then utterly cool. "Does she know that?" he asked, an edge of mockery in his melted butter voice. "Because she didn't mention you last night."

"My relationship with Mary Jane is none of your business," Erik said. "The only thing you need to know is that she's under my protection."

"Oh? Is that supposed to mean something to me?"

"Listen, Tyrese. I don't give a shit who you are, what you think you need or who's dying. Mary Jane isn't yours to snatch off the street whenever you feel like it. That happens again, I'll make sure you're sorry. You understand?"

Tyrese was silent long enough to be insulting. Nixie sighed. Please God let us get out of here without anybody taking a swing, she thought. Because as ripped as Tyrese was, Erik was taller, more muscled and probably had a fist like a wrecking ball. If these two were going to tangle, Nixie didn't want to see it.

"Mary Jane didn't get snatched, cuz," Tyrese drawled. "I asked her to come, she came. Simple as that." He smiled at Erik, and it was full of malice. "You ain't been getting so lucky with her, huh?"

Nixie could see the white of Erik's knuckles through his skin. Any minute now he was going to try to put them through Tyrese's perfect white teeth and then she'd have to break up the War of the Alpha Dogs. God help her.

She took a deep breath and threw herself into the fray. "Listen, Tyrese, do you know where we can find Mary Jane? We're both worried about her. The kids who came to collect her last night were armed, and it didn't sit so well with Erik. We both care about her, though. All we want to know is that she's safe. Is she?"

"Safe." Tyrese seemed to think that one over. "Yeah, I guess she is. Safe and sound in her little apartment on the other side of the river." He showed his teeth in a twisted parody of a smile. "Far, far away from the stink of people like me. Good enough for you, doc?"

Nixie caught her breath at the depth of pain in his face, and even Erik looked taken aback. "How do you know Mary Jane?" he asked abruptly.

"Me? I don't." Tyrese shook his head. "I never did. That's where the trouble started."

Nixie chewed her lip. This was bad. Tyrese was in love with Mary Jane. How did Mary Jane feel about that, she wondered. And how did Erik feel about how Mary Jane felt?

"Well, okay. That's what we needed to know," Nixie said brightly. She tucked her hand into Erik's elbow and started hauling him toward the door. "We'll just swing by her place on the way home and make sure that everything's, you know, okay." Erik's arm was like a steel cable in her hands but she ignored that and kept pulling. Tyrese opened the door and she flashed him a grateful smile as she steered Erik through it.

"Thanks, Tyrese. See you around."

The door closed in her face and Nixie turned to Erik. He was staring thoughtfully at the door. "Huh," he said. "You think Mary Jane actually knows that guy?"

"You'll have to ask her that." Nixie scratched at something disgusting in her hair. "Oh, ick. I think there's beef jerky on my head."

Erik surprised her by laughing. "Yeah, I think there is. Come on, princess. I'll get you home, then swing by Mary Jane's."

Good luck with that conversation, Nixie thought. But she kept her mouth shut. His heart wasn't any of her business, now was it?

CHAPTER ELEVEN

Erik frowned at his cell phone while Nixie gazed studiously out the windshield. I am deaf, she thought to herself, as if she could make it so by concentrating hard enough.

"What the hell does that mean?" Erik said into the phone as they cruised down Constitution. "Jesus, Mary Jane, you were abducted last night at gun point--"

Nixie couldn't hear Mary Jane's response to that, but the fact that she worded it strongly enough to derail Erik mid-sentence pointed to serious irritation

"Can I at least swing by and see for myself that you're--"

Uh-oh, Nixie thought. Another interruption. This did not bode well for Erik's courtship. She resisted the urge to pat his knee. She didn't dare risk a look at him, because she knew her own face would betray all sorts of sympathy, and that was probably the last thing he wanted.

"Because I care about you, Mary Jane." He pushed the words through gritted teeth. He sounded more terminally pissed than caring, but Nixie figured he'd had a hard twelve hours. The object of his affection had been snatched away, first by armed teenagers, then by a renegade CPA. And she didn't seem at all interested in soothing Erik's bruised ego.

He glanced toward Nixie and lowered his voice. "I was hoping I could take you out to lunch. We need to talk."

Deaf, Nixie chanted in her head. I am deaf. La la la la la.

"Oh. No, sure. I understand. I'll call you later." Erik flipped the phone shut and tossed it onto the console between them. Nixie didn't speak, and neither did he. They drove in tenuous silence until Erik turned into the Watergate complex.

He angled the Jeep into a spot near the front doors and cut the engine.

"Are you coming in?" Nixie asked, unaccountably cheered by the prospect. For years, she'd dreamed of what it might be like to be completely alone. No advisors, no press, no assistants, no directors, managers, or foreign dignitaries. Nobody but herself and her thoughts.

As it turned out, she and her thoughts weren't such good company. Her life had always been packed with people who orbited her mother like planets spinning around the sun. Nixie had never learned to make friends, at least not lasting ones. She'd never had to. What was the point? People were always leaving, but there were always new ones coming, too. Love the one you're with, right?

She thought of another long, solitary Sunday afternoon with nothing to do but plan her next culinary disaster and suddenly she was regarding Erik with naked hope in her face.

"Are you hungry? I was going to try an eggplant roulade this afternoon."

"Eggplant what?"

"Eggplant roulade. Big slices of eggplant smeared with filling and rolled up?" Nixie frowned. "At least I think that's what it is. The recipe is a little complicated, but I like a challenge." She realized with a start that she was pretty hungry herself, but not for eggplant. What she really wanted was a taste of the Viking doctor's lovely, firm mouth. Geez. She must be lonelier than she thought.

"Eggplant," Erik said slowly. "Smeared with something and rolled up."

"Forget I offered, okay?" His lack of enthusiasm made her feel suddenly needy and pathetic, so she threw a little exasperation into her voice. "You make it sound like I'm trying to poison you."

"Are you? I'm trying to decide."

Nixie sighed and shook off the moment. His mouth was still appealing, even curled up as it was in disdain for all things vegetable. "I was trying to be nice, Erik. You just got dumped. I thought maybe you wouldn't want to be alone with your misery all afternoon."

He patted her knee. Zingy little shock waves rolled up her thigh and on into parts better left unmentioned. "That's sweet. But I didn't get dumped."

"No? Then why did your girlfriend ditch you for an ultra-hot criminal accountant, then refuse to let you take her out for brunch?"

Erik smiled. "See there's the problem right there. You think Mary Jane's my girlfriend."

"She's not?"

"No, of course not. She's my best friend. Has been for years."

"I see."

"Which is not to say that I wouldn't snap her up in a heartbeat if she showed the slightest interest. The older I get, the more I'm convinced that she's exactly what I want."

"And that is?"

"Somebody smart, funny, driven and absolutely unfamous. Somebody *normal*." He glanced at Nixie. "No offense."

Kiss the Girl

"None taken. But what are you going to do about her being... How to put this delicately?" She tapped her lips and pretended to think. "Not into you." She gave him a sweetly concerned and patently false smile. "No offense."

He shrugged. "Nothing really valuable in life is free, Nixie. I'm not afraid to wait for it. Or work for it."

She had one hand on the door. She needed to end this conversation, get back to her apartment, clean up and start on the eggplant. She did *not* need to sit here any longer, contemplating his beautiful mouth, and the prospect of a man--any man--thinking *she* was everything he'd ever wanted. Wanting her enough to work for her. Lucky, lucky Mary Jane.

"Well, as long as you're okay." She opened the door and slid out. A small flurry of leaves and straw wrappers fell out at her feet. "I'm not on till Tuesday," she said. "See you then." But she was talking to an empty truck. He'd opened his door and was rounding the hood, fingers tucked into pockets, a smug grin on that mouth.

"What's this now?" Nixie smacked at her jeans and gave him a dismissive look. "There's no eggplant for you, mister. That was a pity invitation, and I've decided you need psychotherapy more than pity."

"Why? Because I'm goal-oriented and not afraid of a little rejection?"

"Ha. Tell it to the judge when she issues Mary Jane's restraining order."

"Besides, I wouldn't eat eggplant on pain of death."

"No? Then why are you coming up?"

"Because my mom needs a little talking to about how she uses my spare key."

"Ah." Nixie's enthusiasm deflated. She'd been enjoying their little spat, and thought he had been too. As it turned out, he was just keeping up his end of the conversation. All he wanted to do was drop her politely at her door and go yell at his mom. How...lowering.

"Well, let's get going," she said, starting for the lobby at a brisk trot. "I stand still in all this dirt much longer and something's bound to start sprouting."

Erik kept pace easily. "Your head was made for a flower garden." He reached over and plucked out a leaf. "Looks good on you."

Nixie hardened her heart as she strode through the posh lobby. She avoided the mirrored panels on the walls. She knew what she must look like. No wonder Erik didn't want to have lunch with her. She'd gotten used to the smell herself, but boy was she turning heads here at the Watergate. She punched the elevator button and gave a face-lifted socialite and her pocket-dog a nod.

"I'm not a flower garden sort of girl," she told Erik. "I always figured I'd have a Victory Garden someday, though."

"Hell, no. You'd just grow eggplant. Nobody eats eggplant."

"I do."

"You're...unusual."

She caught sight of her dirty face in the polished metal elevator doors. "Tell me about it," she muttered.

The doors opened with a discreet *bing*, and Nixie stepped into the lift. Erik followed, put a hand across the door and looked a question at the socialite. She shook her head and firmed up her grip on her dog, who squirmed desperately to get on the elevator. Nixie smiled at them.

"Sorry. I almost got run over by a truck."

"Half a truck," Erik said.

The door swished shut on the socialite's frozen brow.

"I think she was trying to register sympathy," Nixie said.

"I think she was trying to frown," Erik said. "Hard to tell with Botox."

"Her dog liked me."

Kiss the Girl

"Her dog wanted to roll in whatever's on your jeans. Plus you have jerky in your hair. And you smell."

Nixie frowned at her blackened knees. "Right. Thanks so much for reminding me."

The elevator rose, and they were silent. Nixie glanced at Erik.

"Are you breathing through your mouth?"

He gave her big, innocent eyes. "What?"

"Jerk."

He was still laughing when the doors parted again. Nixie sailed out of the elevator like she was the Queen of England. "Tell your mom thanks for me."

"I'll do that.

She could feel his eyes on her back as she marched down the hallway to her apartment. She didn't look back, just opened her door and let it bang satisfactorily behind her.

Erik rapped on his mother's door. He checked his watch. Eleven twenty-five. Perfect. The Senator worked insane hours--much like his own now that he thought about it--but Sunday mornings were sacred. She reserved them for coffee, the New York Times, the Washington Post, and a single sticky bun from Heller's Bakery.

The door swept open and the Senator appeared, wrapped up in a silky red robe that matched her polished toenails.

"Ah, yes. I'd recognize that hammering anywhere. Good morning, beloved child, oh my favorite son."

"I'm your only son," Erik told her as he stepped into the foyer. She presented her perfumed cheek and he deposited the ritual peck on it.

"Indeed. Which is why my hopes for you are so high."

"Yeah. We need to talk about that."

She turned her back on him and swished toward the kitchen. He followed. "Coffee?"

"No, thanks. I won't be here that long."

"Suit yourself." She seated herself at a pretty little café table near the window and raised a china cup to her lips. Her dark eyes danced merrily over the rim. "So, what are you angry with me about this time?"

"Let me count the ways."

"Oh dear." She set the cup down and broke off a piece of sticky bun. "That bad? I thought you'd like Nixie. She's not your usual fare." Her mouth twitched. "Or mine, for that matter. You've got to admit, she's a refreshing change of pace from the debutante parade."

Images of Nixie flashed through his mind like a slide show on speed. Nixie diving into a pile of rotten garbage. Nixie laughing delightedly at Daryl's home made pot smoke filter. Nixie, her hands wet with a dying man's blood, guiding a hysterical teenager through goodbye.

"You have no idea." Erik sat down in the chair facing his mother and pushed aside the *Times*. "But that's not the point, Mom. You need to stop this."

"Stop what?"

"Stop *steering* me." He resisted the urge to shake like a wet dog. His mother always made him feel this way. Like he was too huge, too clumsy, like he required a gentle nudge in the right direction at every crossroads life handed him.

"I beg your pardon." The Senator sipped her coffee. "I have never steered you a moment in your life. I suggested American History, you insisted on science. I suggested law school, you went to medical school. I've introduced you to dozens upon dozens of well-bred, highly educated young ladies and you date..." She lifted her brows and waved an airy hand. "Nobody."

"I date, Mom."

"Who? Certainly nobody recently. At least not that you've deigned to introduce to your mother. Or--" She blinked, her coffee cup frozen halfway to her mouth. "Oh my God, Erik. Are you gay?"

Erik laughed. "No, Mom. I like girls just fine."

She set down her cup and patted her chest. "Good heavens. My heart."

"Your heart." Erik smiled. "Your heart is made of stainless steel."

She leveled the gaze on him that had mowed down countless uppity men who'd mistaken her gender for a weakness. "My heart is committed to seeing you settled with the right woman."

"And by the right woman, I assume you mean somebody who can trace her ancestors back to the Mayflower and would be a political asset should I ever do you proud and run for office?"

"Well." She sipped delicately at her coffee. "It *is* a dream of mine. I'm not going to work forever, you know. I'd hate to turn this office over to some brash young person with no vision."

"Mom, I'm a doctor. When are you going to accept that?"

"Edward Harper's son is a doctor and *he's* serving on his father's presidential campaign."

"You really want me to be more like James Harper? The guy who ditched Nixie so he could screw Sloan Leighton across Europe?"

The Senator lifted her chin. "Howard Dean's a doctor, too."

"I like the job I have, Mom."

"You're giving fat diplomats new hearts and stitching up drug dealers in your off hours." She looked thoughtful. "No wonder you don't date."

Erik rubbed his eyes. "I date, Mom."

"Not successfully. If you did, I'd have grandchildren right now."

"You don't want me to have kids. You want me to have a First Lady."

"Ideally, you could have both. Children can be a political asset."

"Sure, but at what cost?"

She leveled a look at him and said, "Is that a dig?"

He gazed at her in silence. She sighed and said, "I'm just trying to help you, Erik." She leaned forward and took his hand. "You are something special, you know. And I'm not speaking as your mother now. You have a world-class brain, a stellar education, and a social conscience a mile wide. One day your ambition's going to kick in, and I don't want to see you chained to an inappropriate family situation when it does."

Old bitterness washed over him like sour coffee. "Is that how you thought of us? Of me and Dad? Your inappropriate family situation?"

She let go of his hand, ran a finger around the rim of her coffee cup. "Do you want me to be honest, or do you want me to be your mom?"

"Honest."

"I loved your father, Erik. He's been gone over ten years and I still do. But we were never made to live together. We wanted different things from life." She gave him a crooked smile. "The only thing we ever agreed on is you."

"That's not exactly an answer."

"It's the best you're going to get, young man."

"Right. Fine." Erik sat back, blew out the bitterness with his pent up breath. "Just quit catapulting women at me, Mom. And for that matter, quit letting Nixie Leighton-Brace into my apartment. She nearly gave me a heart attack."

The Senator's smile went sly. "Did she now?"

Kiss the Girl

"God, Mom. Not like that."

"Hmmm." She went back to her sticky bun. "But you're not gay?"

"Not gay."

"Okay. Sorry. She was just so lost and lonely."

"Lost and lonely?" Erik snorted. "Aside from maybe her mother, she's the most recognizable humanitarian on the planet. I don't think she's lonely."

"Famous and lonely go hand in hand, dear. Try to listen a little, hmmm?"

"What's that supposed to mean?"

"Just that. I love you more than anything, darling boy, but sometimes, you're all send and no receive."

Erik frowned. He thought of Nixie's bright, cheerful effort to feed him eggplant and his casual rejection. She was so...easy and flip. She was the most approachable woman he'd ever met, for all that she was ridiculously rich and famous. Naïve and kind and warm and smart-mouthed. How could she be lonely?

"Just try not to leave any more women in my kitchen, okay?" He leaned down and kissed her cheek.

"Okay, okay." She tapped a polished nail on the *Post* and sipped her coffee. "What are you going to do?" she asked as he headed for the door.

"About what?"

"Nixie."

"I already gave her a job."

"She needs a friend."

"I'm sure she'll be fine."

"Of course."

Erik let himself out of his mother's apartment and stood breathing the fresh air for a moment. He always wondered what was in that perfume of hers. He couldn't think straight when it got into his brain. He looked at Nixie's door and shook his head.

Lonely. Ha. His mother must think he was a fool. How lonely could the country's favorite do-gooder be?

He strode toward the elevator, but stopped halfway there. He sighed, called himself six kinds of idiot, then turned around and walked back to Nixie's door. He gave a few quick raps.

She answered the door wearing clean jeans and a simple white shirt, her feet bare, her hair wet. The scent of lemons wafted out into the hallway.

"No eggplant," she said. "I mean it."

"Me, too. Nobody should eat that crap. Come on. I'm taking you out to lunch."

CHAPTER TWELVE

She spotted the diner half a block away.
"Is that where we're going?" she asked Erik.
"Yep."
Nixie's eyes watered, but she couldn't tell if it was from the wind blasting down the street or all that neon lighting in one place. They reached the plate glass door, and Erik yanked it open. With one hand at the small of her back, he thrust her into a world she'd only ever read about.

It was a shoebox of a place, longer than it was wide, with black and white tiled floors. Everything that wasn't tiled was either stainless steel or covered with neon lights. Vats of smoking hot oil filled the air with the promise of artery-clogging goodness, and Nixie stood just inside the door, gaping at it all.

She allowed Erik to peel off her scarf and coat and hang them next to his own on a coat rack as a tiny train raced around a track near the hammered tin ceiling. A juke box--the old fashioned kind that played honest-to-goodness vinyl records--squatted in the corner, resplendent with zipping lights. She started toward it automatically. She wanted to play some Patsy Cline. This place *demanded* Patsy Cline, but Erik took her elbow.

"Couple counter seats just opened up," he said, then muscled his way through a sea of coats and purses and elbows, towing Nixie behind him. He deposited her on an industrial strength stool. It was bolted to the floor and shiny from the countless behinds that had surely been plunked on it over the years. She was delighted to find that it spun beneath her like it had been greased. Judging from the amount of oil hanging in the air, it probably had. She laughed and grabbed the counter for balance as she slowed. Erik shook his head, but he looked more amused than irritated.

"This place is great!" Nixie beamed at him. "How did you find it?"

Erik handed her a crumpled paper menu. "Steve-O's has been around since time immemorial. It's a DC institution."

Nixie laid the menu open on the counter in front of her. "Wow."

"Yeah." Erik smiled at the waitress who'd appeared in front of them. She was at least sixty, with a Jackie O flip dyed ruthlessly black and shellacked into place. She wore a pink uniform, white sneakers, a cardigan and frosted orange lipstick. Nixie couldn't have loved her more if she'd been popping a big wad of chewing gum.

"What can I get you two?" she asked, pen to a little spiral bound tablet.

"Coffee," Erik said.

"Two?"

"Um, no." Nixie looked at her menu. "Do you have herbal tea?"

The waitress looked blankly at her, then at Erik.

"Two coffees," he said. "Make hers a decaf."

"Right." She gave Nixie a suspicious look, then thumped their white mugs right side up on the stainless steel counter. She seized two coffee pots from the burner behind her and filled the mugs. "Y'all eating today?"

"You bet," Erik said. "I'll have the American burger with fries."

"How you want that done, honey?"

"Rare. Lettuce and tomato."

She nodded her approval, then turned to Nixie.

"Oh, gosh." Nixie looked at the menu still laid out on the counter.

"No eggplant," Erik said. "I mean it."

"Um, okay. But..." She gave the waitress tentative smile. "What can you recommend for a vegetarian?"

The waitress' penciled on brows came together. "We have chicken salad," she said doubtfully.

"Oh." Nixie bit her lip and went back to scanning the menu. Now she'd disappointed the waitress. She sighed and soldiered on. "I was looking for something without meat."

"Chicken's not meat, hon."

"Right. Well, I'm more looking for something that never had a face. I try not to eat anything that once had a face."

The waitress' doubt faded into irritation. "We got fries. But hey, potatoes have eyes. Is that going to be a problem?"

"She'll have the American burger, too," Erik said quickly. "Well done, lettuce and tomato, with fries. And hey, give the lady a chocolate shake, too."

Nixie frowned at him. "I don't eat--"

"--enough. No, you certainly don't." Erik gave her knee a warning squeeze and smiled pleasantly at the waitress. "She's too skinny."

The waitress smiled back at Erik, clearly pleased to be working with somebody who knew how to order. She scribbled on her pad, then turned to the stainless steel partition at her back, behind which bobbed a sea of paper-capped line cooks. She bellowed, "Burn two, one hockey puck, one on the hoof, and walk 'em through the garden! Frog sticks and one cow, muddy!"

Nixie found the American burger on the menu. "No mayo on mine, please."

"High and dry on the hockey puck!" She gave Nixie one last look that said *I'll be watching you, missy* and swished away to take care of more deserving customers. Nixie turned on Erik.

"I'm not eating cow."

He smiled at her, and it was a smug little grin that said *I should have known*. "So, you're a vegetarian?"

"Yes."

"Why?"

"Eating meat is incredibly wasteful. It takes something like fifty times more natural resources to raise cattle rather than crops. Given the rate our rainforests are disappearing and our aquifers are drying out, eating meat borders on immoral. Plus it's bad for you. Aren't you a heart surgeon? Don't you know this?"

"I know the facts, Nixie. I asked why *you're* a vegetarian. Tell me the story."

She frowned at him. "I just did."

"No, you spouted a party line. I was asking for your *a-ha* moment, the one where you suddenly looked at the hamburger in you hands and beheld evil instead of a tasty treat."

"Oh." Nixie picked up her coffee and took a tiny, scalding sip. It was slippery and burnt. "I don't have one. I've always been a vegetarian."

"What? Like your whole *life*?"

She plunked down her cup. "It's not a birth defect, Erik."

"I didn't say it was."

"You sure made it sound that way."

"Sorry," he said, rubbing a hand over the stubble on his jaw. "It's just sad."

"Sad?" Nixie swiveled her stool to face him, poked a finger into his chest. "You think it's sad that I was parented by long-sighted and compassionate people who taught me to be gentle on the planet? Do you have any idea how many of my peers are blowing their trust funds on oxycontin addictions and starring in their own reality shows? Turning out vegetarian isn't so bad."

"No, of course not. It's just..."

"It's just what?"

"It's just that you never chose it yourself. You inherited it."

"So what? If it fits, what's the problem?"

"You don't know if it fits. You've never tried anything else. I mean, here you are, finally making a break for it. Against the advice of everybody who knows and loves you, you've planted yourself in a random city, and are knocking yourself out trying to make your own way in spite of tripping over your face and name at every turn. You're doing desk duty at a free clinic in the worst neighborhood in the city, and you're actually liking it. Surprise, surprise. You're finding yourself, Nixie, and I can't believe I'm saying this, but I'm impressed. You've got guts."

She was prepared for the coffee this time, and managed to take a sip without grimacing. She wanted something warm in her stomach to blame the little glow on. He thought she had guts. "But? I'm sensing a but."

He lifted those big shoulders and said, "But you're still clinging to the old habits. If you're shooting for a revolution, don't skimp. You've never tasted red meat in your life. You have no idea if you like it or not."

"It doesn't matter if I like it," Nixie said. "I might like crack cocaine, too. I've heard it's a trip. But I'm not going to indulge in that."

"I don't think a burger at Steve-O's rings the sin bell quite like crack, Nixie."

The waitress stumped back and slid two enormous platters in front of them. "There you go, kids." She gave Nixie a hard look. "You treat that with the respect it deserves, you hear?"

"Yes, ma'am." Nixie spoke automatically. Her plate was the size of a hub cap. She stared in awe at a mountain of steaming fries nestled in the lee of a burger split in half and wrapped in waxed paper. Nixie swallowed. It hardly captured the moment to call this thing a burger. A juicy slab of beef reclined on a crusty sourdough roll, coyly covering itself with half a head of lettuce and a thick slice of tomato. Nixie could smell it, hot and greasy, slathered in ketchup, the mustard so yellow her taste buds were already singing in anticipation. It had to be six inches tall.

"Nixie? You all right?"

She didn't look away from the burger. "It's got to be a sin."

His chuckle rolled over her like the tide, inexorable and reassuring. "Maybe. But it's a small one."

"There is nothing small about this...thing."

"Hamburger. That thing is a hamburger. And a hamburger from Steve-Os on a crappy March day is one of the very best reasons to live in DC." Erik nudged her. "Go on. Try it."

Nixie frowned. "How? It's as big as my head."

"Watch and learn, grasshopper." He scooped up half of his burger, squeezed it until condiments squirted onto the plate and wedged a corner into his mouth. He closed his eyes and chewed with utter bliss. Nixie took a moment to envy anything that could put a look like that on the practical doctor's face. Then she turned her attention back to her own burger.

She hefted one half of it and peeled back the waxed paper, then looked at Erik. "I'm not doing this to prove anything to you," she said.

"Of course not." He looked solemn.

"You just happen to have a valid point. My rejection of meat will be even more meaningful once I've tasted it and made a more informed decision."

"Right."

Kiss the Girl

"Because then I'll know exactly what I'm saying no to."

"Yep."

She addressed the burger. "I'm sorry, buddy."

"Quit stalling, princess."

"It's just...I feel so guilty."

"I don't want to hear about the less fortunate, Nixie. Starving yourself doesn't help them. You're the richest woman I know and you look like one of those orphans you're always getting your picture taken with. Just this once, why don't you indulge yourself?"

"Indulge myself?"

"Yeah. It's okay, Nixie. The earth won't spin off its axis if you eat red meat."

She rolled her eyes at him, then turned back to the burger with renewed determination. She squeezed the bun until ketchup and mustard plopped onto the plate and took a bite. The flavors hit Nixie's defenseless system like an atom bomb and she closed her eyes to moan. She chewed slowly, to savor every last taste and texture before she swallowed.

"It *is* like taking drugs," she finally said, when she found her voice. "People tell you how wrong it is, how bad they are, and it makes you wonder why anybody would do them. Then you try them and realize they left out the part about how frickin' *awesome* they are."

She opened her eyes to find Erik staring at her, his blue eyes hot with something she didn't recognize. "Not that I've ever done drugs or anything. I haven't. I was just...What? Why are you looking at me like that? Do I have it all over me?" She reached for a napkin and wiped her mouth. "Sorry. I've never done this before."

"No, you're fine." He looked away from her, his face closed and cool again. "It's fine."

But it wasn't fine. The easiness between them had vanished, and Nixie was suddenly awkward and self-conscious. She set down the burger.

"I've disappointed you, haven't I?"

"What? Nixie, no."

"Of course I did." She pushed her plate away. "I disappointed myself. I just violated a principle I've held for twenty-eight years, and why? Because you baited me." She shook her head. "What were the chances I'd be corrupted into eating red meat by a heart surgeon?"

"Okay, now you're just being stupid."

"I beg your pardon?" She perched stiffly on the stool that had given her such pleasure a few minutes ago. "I am many things, but stupid is not one of them."

"Okay, you're not stupid," Erik said. He turned to face her, leaned forward until she had no choice but to look at him. "But it pisses me off to watch you sit there, skinny as a rake, wearing second-hand clothes, berating yourself over a bite of burger. You're so generous to other people. Why can't you be that kind to yourself every once in a while?"

She felt the beginnings of a smile tug at her mouth. "So it wasn't a test of my strength and willpower? I didn't fail?"

He stared at her. "Do people do that to you? Test you?"

She shrugged. "Comes with the territory. Every journalist in the world wants to be the one to report that Nixie Leighton-Brace is a big phony. Or so I've been told."

Erik pulled her plate back toward her. "Eat the damn burger. All of it." The waitress came back and plunked a tall silver canister, an empty glass and a long handled spoon at Nixie's elbow. "And here's your shake. I want that gone, too."

"Now I *know* that's a sin."

"No point in a half-assed revolution."

She tipped her head and looked at him. "Why are you doing this, Erik? What does it matter to you what I eat or don't eat?"

"No reason," he said. "Sometimes I do things just because they're fun."

"And feeding me is fun for you?"

"I can't explain it." He smiled at her, and there was something in it that had her mouth going dry. "It doesn't mean anything. It just feels nice. Isn't that reason enough to do something?"

"Um, no. Usually not."

"And that's why you're twenty-eight years old and having your first burger."

"Right." Nixie turned back to her food. She stuffed a fry in her mouth and concentrated on chewing, because she had the most inexplicable urge to crawl right up into his lap and curl there like a kitten. Just because it would feel nice and not have to mean anything.

"Eat up, princess." He got to his feet and reached into his pocket. "I'm going to hit the jukebox. This place needs some Patsy Cline."

Nixie was chewing her second bite of burger when the strings wound up for Patsy's honky-tonk heartbreak. All that crying, trying and loving inappropriately.

Tell me about it, Nixie thought.

CHAPTER THIRTEEN

Erik pulled into the Watergate complex an hour and a half later. He glanced over at Nixie. Her eyes were closed, her cheeks flushed, her hair a shiny, cinnamon tangle against the headrest. Those famous lips were curled into a contented almost-smile, and the pull they exerted over him was so constant he was almost used to it. Almost. And then, in quiet moments like this, it punched him in the gut all over again. He sighed. She could be a problem if he wasn't careful.

He angled the truck into a spot near the door and tapped her shoulder with one impersonal finger. She stirred, and her mossy eyes took a moment to flutter open and focus.

"Oh." She blinked around the parking lot. "Here already?"

"You conked out."

She gave him a sheepish grin that ended in an enormous yawn. "Sorry. Must be the tryptophan, or whatever."

"Yeah, that's turkey."

"Oh."

"What you're suffering from, Nixie Leighton-Brace, is a good old-fashioned red meat coma."

He reached over and gingerly unsnapped her seatbelt. Her hands remained curled loosely against her thighs, and his stomach went tight and hot. What else was she willing to let him do for her? Did she even realize how damn soft and inviting she looked with those curls rioting around her sleepy eyes?

He risked a glance at her face and had to chuckle at himself. She was half-snoozing again already. He got out of the Jeep, rounded the hood and opened her door.

"Come on, princess. Let's get you home."

Her eyes opened at that and the flash of hope in them surprised him. Then she looked at the building and again at him, and it died out.

"Right. Home." Her voice was curiously flat but Erik didn't ask. Hadn't he told her it wasn't so easy to build a home? It wasn't his fault she was disappointed. He took her elbow and helped her step down from the truck.

He started to guide her across the parking lot. She said, "You don't have to come in. I'm okay now, honest."

He looked down into that heart-breaker face of hers and saw that it was true. Her eyes were open and alert, and the wind had slapped away the sleepy flush and replaced it with the pinched bafflement of a complexion more accustomed to the tropics. He should relinquish her elbow, pat her on the head and say goodbye.

"It's no trouble," he heard himself say. "I fed you the burger. As your friend it's my duty to get you to your couch so you can sleep it off in peace."

She frowned at him. "Wait, we're friends now?"

"Any girl who can polish off one of Steve-O's burgers is a friend of mine. You nailed the fries and shake, too, so you get a Christmas card for life."

Her frown dissolved into a brilliant smile. "And I don't regret a single bite." She tucked her hand into his arm, gave it a companionable little squeeze. "You're a terrible influence."

"What are friends for?" *Friends*, he repeated silently. *Friends, friends friends.* It didn't do a lot to neutralize the lust in his heart, but it was a distraction. She kept her hand in his elbow as they got into the elevator, a small, warm connection between them. He wouldn't have been surprised if she nestled her head into his sleeve and took another quick nap. Something hot and wanting bubbled in his blood at the thought.

The doors swished open, and Erik all but sprinted down the hall toward Nixie's apartment. She was killing him. She was killing him and she had no idea. He stood there, tensed on the edge of either bolting or seizing her up in his arms while she rooted around in her purse for her key. She finally came up with it, and he breathed a sigh of relief. Almost done.

She inserted it into the lock, but didn't turn it. Instead she faced him.

"Thank you, Erik." She laid a hand on his arm and he closed his eyes against the vicious tide of wanting it created in him. "I know this was a pity lunch. I'm sure between the hospital and the clinic you don't have many free afternoons, and I can't tell you what it means to me that you were willing to part with one of them to keep me company."

He forced a smile. "Friends don't let friends eat eggplant, Nixie."

She shook her head. "We'll do it your way, then. No heartfelt speeches. Just know that I'm grateful, okay?"

She rose up on her toes and brushed a kiss onto his jaw. To be fair, it was a friendly kiss. The kind a friend gives another friend. A thank-you note of a kiss. But her hair slid over his chin, silky, sweet and lemony, and it issued an invitation all its own. It all but begged Erik to tangle his fingers in it, turn her face to his and address those lips properly.

Kiss the Girl

Erik tried, really tried, for the space of three endless heartbeats to ignore it. Then she backed up and gave him a chagrined half-smile. "And now I've made you uncomfortable. I'm really sorry, Erik. I can't seem to get the rhythm of making friends."

He could resist the elegant bones, the lost eyes, even that smart-alecky mouth. But when she went all endearingly, awkwardly self-conscious, she pushed him over the edge.

"Have I ruined everything?" she asked, her brows knit adorably.

"Nope. I'm going to do that." He buried one hand in those gorgeous soft curls and pulled her up onto her toes so he could finally, finally, *finally* kiss her.

The breath caught in Nixie's lungs, tangled there, and refused to come out. But that was okay with her. She would never breathe again and not mind as long as Erik kept kissing her. His mouth was everything she'd imagined it might be and he was kissing her like she was breath itself, like she was the center of the universe. Like he'd been starving for her.

One of those big hands speared into her hair, lifting her up, holding her steady, while his mouth moved over hers in a dance that was both fierce and seeking. He wanted something from her, she realized. Something besides the obvious. There was more than just desire here, and it was dark, needy and jagged. She wondered what it was at the same time she recognized it in herself.

She rose up, wound her arms around all the solid strength of him and offered up a matching need, a desire to know and explore and *have* that had been dogging her relentlessly and against her will since she'd met him. She opened her mouth under his and tasted him. He made some kind of noise that might have been approval, might have been anguish. Nixie smiled. She felt the same way.

His hand against her head shifted, brought her to a new angle under him and he slid his tongue along her lips. He tasted her slowly, and Nixie felt...savored. The thrill of it shot over her skin, settled in her stomach and glowed there. His thumb brushed over her cheek and she turned helplessly into it, like a cat begging to be petted. When he pulled back, it took her a moment to surface, to register that he was looking at her. Waiting for something.

She stepped back, cleared her throat and touched a finger to her lips. They were exquisitely sensitive. "What...um, what was that?" she asked.

"Nothing." His blue eyes still glowed with the embers of that kiss and Nixie's brows shot skyward. She might not be an old hand at casual kissing, but that didn't mean she was entirely naïve either.

"Nothing." She repeated it with patent disbelief.

He gave her a careless grin. "Well, obviously it was a kiss, Nixie. A nice one, too."

"Okay, but why?"

The grin broadened. "Why was it nice? You want a critique?"

"No, I want to know why you kissed me." Mortification burned in her gut, but she kept her face calm and assured.

"Friends don't kiss?"

"Some cultures more than others, but with tongue? Usually not."

He rolled his linebacker shoulders in an easy shrug and said, "No reason, really. Impulse. I thought it would feel good."

"Feel good?"

"Sure. Didn't you like it?"

Nixie considered the way she'd almost devoured him. "I guess."

"Listen, Nixie, just relax, okay? It was fun. That's all. Just like the burger. It doesn't have to mean anything."

She studied him, then said, "First the burger, now kissing. What's next? A little harmless tax fraud?"

"No. Tax fraud is boring."

She shook her head, but smiled in spite of herself.

Suddenly the door under Nixie's hand opened and she leaped back, startled. She landed on Erik's feet and he picked her up and set her behind him. She didn't know if he meant to save her or his toes, but it was strangely gratifying to have somebody who wasn't paid to do so put his big body between her and an unknown threat.

"Are you buying this crap, Nixie?" a voice boomed out. A familiar voice. Nixie peeked around Erik's shoulder and sighed. She knew only one person who habitually spoke at a shout.

"Hi, Karl," she said. He was a big man, but next to Erik's tough, Viking bulk, he looked soft. Almost huggable if you didn't know him.

"It just *feels good*? It was an *impulse*?" Karl shook his shaggy head at Erik in disapproval. Then he turned on Nixie again. "And you. You're *okay* with a quick grope in the hallway? Haven't I taught you anything?"

"It wasn't a moonlight and roses kind of moment." She shrugged. "My self esteem will survive."

He peered past them down the empty hall way. "Any asshole with a cell phone walks by and you and Romeo here are front page news. What were you *thinking*?"

She shut her mouth. This wasn't about her self esteem. Of course it wasn't. This was about her *brand*. She reached for a neutral tone of voice and said, "I wasn't expecting you for a few more weeks, Karl. What are you doing here?"

"Elementary PR, looks like." His round glasses had slid down an impressive beak, and he was glaring at her over the wire rims. "Get inside, both of you. Now, please."

Nixie looked at Erik.

"You don't have to stay," she told him.

"What? And miss all the fun?"

She walked into the apartment, Erik at her heels. Karl clicked the door shut behind them and leaned back against it, arms folded over his chest. He tucked his chin into his chest and drilled Nixie with his patented brand of disappointment-laced reproof.

"Don't look at me like that," Nixie said, though she sidled away from Erik like a guilty teenager. "He's not a reporter or anything."

"You could have called," Karl said. "I know we haven't been on the best of terms lately, but you could have at least called."

"Why? So you could do a background check on a guy I'm not dating?"

"So I wouldn't have to scramble for a spin when the pictures hit the tabloids."

"There are no pictures, Karl."

"There are always pictures." He shook his head. "You're a *brand*, Nixie. How many times do I have to tell you that? If we're going to be of service to anybody, the brand has to stay pristine."

Nixie rolled her shoulders under the sudden, familiar weight of guilt. "Tell it to Sloan."

"Sloan is her own brand. Very different."

"No kidding."

"Introduce me to your friend, Nixie," Karl said. His overly patient tone made her feel petulant and sulky so she plunked herself down on the beige couch. It was hard, as uncomfortable as it was expensive.

"Dr. Erik Larsen, meet Dr. Karl Dettreich." Nixie said. "Karl is my political advisor, and COO of Leighton-Brace Charitable Giving."

"Ah." Erik nodded. "Pleased to meet you."

"Erik is on the board of directors at the clinic where I'm working."

"You've associated yourself with a clinic?" Karl's grey eyes were aggrieved behind his glasses.

"I told you I was looking for a project."

"And I told you to keep me in the loop. For Christ's sake, Nixie." He stalked toward the laptop humming on the coffee table at Nixie's knees. "Sloan!"

Nixie covered her face with her hands. "Oh, God. Mom's here?"

"Sloan Leighton is here?" Erik asked in awed tones. Nixie ignored him. It was bad enough that her old life had just hijacked her new one. Did she really have to watch while the object of her raging and unrequited lust turned into a slack-jawed, starry-eyed fool over her mother?

Sloan strolled out of the kitchen, an iPhone in her hand, a wireless phone bud parked in her ear, only to find her daughter--whom she'd last seen from a prone position beneath their mutual lover--parked in the center of the sofa. She looked miserably unhappy. Sloan could have told her not to sit on that couch. It was desperately uncomfortable.

"We're booked on the eight o'clock flight out of Dulles," Sloan said to Karl, flipping her curls over one shoulder and smiling at the tall, broad stranger standing beside the coffee table. "Scheduled to touch down by nine tomorrow local time." She let her gaze drop to her daughter. "Hello, Nixie."

"Hey, Mom. How's James?" Nixie asked. "Or should I say how *was* James? I understand you dropped him somewhere in Prague."

Sloan fluttered a hand dismissively. "I did. He was such a bore, and a bit of a disappointment once the dirty wore off. Didn't you think so?"

Nixie stared at her. "I am *not* going to compare notes on men we've both slept with."

Sloan laughed lightly. "You *are* a paragon, aren't you? Note to self: Nixie doesn't mind a bad lay. Steer clear of her boyfriends in the future." She cut her eyes toward the silent stranger. "Though I may make an exception in this case." She draped herself over the arm of the couch, offered him a languid hand and said, "I'm Sloan Leighton."

He took Sloan's hand, gave her a smile that, had Sloan been a few years younger and several lifetimes more innocent, might have sparked an interest. As it was she only thought *Nixie's latched onto a live one this time. Careful, baby girl.*

"Erik Larsen," the man said. "It's a pleasure, Ms. Leighton. I'm a big fan."

Sloan dropped her lashes and gave him a little smolder. "The pleasure's all mine," she purred automatically, but her attention was fixed inward. She should feel something, shouldn't she? This was the first time she'd seen Nixie since seducing the poor girl's boyfriend, after all. Surely even she ought to suffer a twinge of nerves or guilt or...something.

She poked at the arid, barren place where her conscience used to live and a faint glimmer of feeling rose up inside her. Was it shame? How wonderfully novel. She hadn't had the self-respect to feel ashamed of herself in years. Had she finally gone too far? Had she finally been outrageous enough to shock even herself? To wake up the dead weight that was her heart?

She focused on the sensation curling in her stomach, willed it to strengthen, to grow, as if it were a tiny spark she could coax into a flame.

Shame, she told herself. For shame, Sloan.

But her heart was silent. Dead.

She felt nothing.

"Don't bother with the sex-kitten routine," Nixie said, rolling her eyes. "This one's spoken for, and not by me. His heart belongs to his best friend Mary Jane."

"How...sweet," Sloan said as Erik continued to hold her hand and grin at her with that slightly dazed look men so often wore around her.

"Isn't it?" Nixie said. She stood up and delivered a sharp slap to the back of Erik's head. "Pull it together, lover boy."

Erik frowned at Nixie and let go of Sloan's hand. "God. Cut me some slack." He rubbed the back of his head. "That was the fulfillment of a twenty year old fantasy."

Sloan gave a twinkling little chuckle. Nixie plunked herself back down on the unforgiving couch and said, "Eyes on the prize, doc. Moony idiots never won fair ladies. Think of Mary Jane."

Karl snapped shut his laptop and seated himself in the chair to Nixie's right. "Cancel the flights, Sloan."

"What? Why?"

"Nixie's aligned herself with a local clinic."

Sloan sighed and punched a few buttons on her cell. "Amelia? It's Sloan again. Cancel the tickets, will you? Nixie's giving us trouble. Thanks, darling. I'll be in touch. Soon, I hope."

She slid bonelessly into the square arm chair to Nixie's left. It was just as beige and hard as the couch, but Sloan worked hard to make every piece of furniture she touched look like a love nest. There were appearances to maintain, after all.

"So?" Karl leaned back in the matching chair on Nixie's right. "Tell us about this clinic."

She watched with interest as Nixie bit her lip, a sure sign her chronically honest little girl was about to play fast and loose with the truth. How entertaining. Sloan exchanged a glance with Karl and settled in for the show.

Nixie hesitated, gnawing her lip. *I'm a receptionist* didn't have quite the gravitas of *I'm fostering peace in the Middle East.* Karl was going to blow a gasket.

Erik said, "We're a medical clinic based in Anacostia. Nixie's been--"

"Named Director of Outreach!" She nodded vigorously. "I'm spearheading a project to build awareness around poverty-related diseases." She was silent for a moment, in awe of her own lie. Nobody spoke, so she cleared her throat and said, "The focus is on childhood asthma. It's practically an epidemic in the local projects."

Karl tapped thick fingers against his knees. He glanced at Erik, who stared at Nixie in bemusement. She shrugged. She was a desperate woman. She didn't care *what* global disaster Karl wanted her back for, she was not going to suck up her pride and trot after Sloan like a kicked puppy.

Besides, the more she thought about it, the more she liked the idea of tackling the asthma epidemic in Anacostia. Mama Mel would be a killer ambassador for the cause. She was making a mental list of reporters and legislators to contact when Karl finally spoke.

"Dr. Larsen, is there anything in your Personnel and Policy Handbook that would preclude a relationship between a board member and a benefactor of Nixie's stature?"

"Not that I'm aware of," Erik said, still frowning at Nixie.

"We're not having a relationship," Nixie put in. "It was just a kiss. Now about this asthma project--"

"Because if there were some kind of regulation against such a relationship, it would be easy enough to spin the photos into a severance of the clinic project."

"*There aren't any photos*," Nixie said.

Kiss the Girl

"There are always photos," Karl said without glancing her way. He stroked his beard and gazed into the middle distance. Sloan curled her legs into the chair and smiled at Erik, who cleared his throat and glanced warily at Nixie, one hand going to the back of his head.

"I don't want to sever the clinic project. Besides, there are no photos," Nixie said. Nobody responded, and a familiar sense of futility descended on her. "Hello? No photos. No relationship. No rule against one even if there were."

Nothing. Nixie looked at Erik. "Will you please tell them?"

He lifted his shoulders. "I can try." He leaned against the arm of the couch, made a face and straightened up again.

"Listen, Karl," he said. "There's nothing on the books that would preclude me from kissing Nixie into next week if I wanted to." Nixie closed her eyes. This was not going well. "But you can rest assured that I'm not going to do that. It was just lunch. A couple burgers and an impulsive kiss."

The silence that followed was long and grim.

"I don't believe this," Sloan said, a slow smile curving her lips.

Karl just stared. "Nixie, have you been eating *meat*?"

CHAPTER FOURTEEN

Erik blinked at Karl in fascination. "You say *meat* exactly like somebody else might say *toxic waste*," he said.

Nixie's advisor raked a paw through that wiry halo of hair and looked grim. Sloan smiled her sly, cat-like smile. Nixie looked like she was praying for deliverance.

"Oh, come on," Erik said, glancing from face to face. "It was just a burger."

"Did anybody see you?" Karl asked. Nixie sank into the couch and Karl turned accusing eyes on Erik.

"Everybody in Steve-O's, I imagine," Erik told him.

"Nixie, we're still under contract to PETA," Karl said. "Do you have any idea what kind of damage this could do your credibility? The credibility of your brand?"

"I know," she moaned, flopping back against the couch. She winced and sat up again. Erik sympathized. That couch was like a mirage. It only *looked* like a comfortable place to sit down. "I can't explain it. I don't know what I was thinking. I'm sorry."

"You're sorry." Karl shook his head. "I'm ashamed of you, Phoenix."

Nixie flinched and bowed her head. She looked small, defeated, and it was...wrong somehow. Nixie was never defeated. She was bold and charming and outrageous. She talked her way into unsuitable outings and mopped up puke and beat down teenaged punks who tried to snatch her off the street. Was she really going to let this self-satisfied talking head shame her?

"It was a *burger*," Erik said to Karl. "Not Armageddon."

"Have you ever pissed off the PETA people, Dr. Larsen?" Sloan asked. "It's a lot more like Armageddon than you'd imagine."

Erik turned back to Nixie. "And you. Where's your spine, huh? Where's the woman who sweet talked a Senator into a little breaking and entering, then spent the rest of the morning dodging killer dogs and El Caminos without turning a hair?"

Sloan's smile grew. "Yeah, she sounds like fun. Where are you keeping *her*, Nixie?"

"Breaking and entering?" Karl finally looked alarmed. "Which Senator?"

"Oh, calm down," Nixie said. "All of you." She stood up, clapped her hands together decisively and said, "Okay, here's the deal. Erik, you're right. I'm being a wimp. Thanks for the reminder." She smiled at him and Erik's stomach did a weird little flip. She turned to her advisor. "However, Karl's also right to be ashamed of me right now. But not for eating a stupid burger. He ought to be ashamed of me for letting other people--PETA included--tell me what I believe. What I want. What I am."

Sloan looped thin arms around her knees and said, "Hallelujah. There's some of me in the old girl after all. How *did* you like that burger, Nixie?"

Nixie shot her mother a poisonous look, and Erik suddenly realized that Nixie wasn't a vegetarian because of Sloan. Sloan probably ingested anything that landed in front of her, from a handful of rice to a couple lines of coke. No, Karl was the evangelical vegetarian.

"Nixie, come on." Karl stood up, put a hand on Nixie's arm. "I would never be so hard on you if I wasn't absolutely sure that we believed the same things. The same things we've been working and fighting for all your life."

"I know that, Karl," she said, and patted his hand. Erik sat on the arm of the couch and shook his head. He was losing track of the score. Was Karl winning? Was Nixie? Sloan seemed wearily amused by the whole thing, as if she'd been hearing the same argument for years. She probably had. He wondered who usually won.

Not that it mattered to him. The bottom line was that Nixie had baggage--big, heaping piles of it, excellent for squashing any lingering traces of an inconvenient lust. His stomach settled nicely at the thought.

"We do believe the same things," Nixie told Karl. "Fate smiled on me in a big way, in terms of wealth and fame. And that means I've got an enormous responsibility toward people who haven't been so lucky. But it's dishonest and patronizing to pretend I know what people need to rebuild their homes, their *lives*, when I've never had either one."

Karl took up her hands. "You're a good kid, Nixie. Truly."

"But?"

"But we don't have time for an existential crisis right now."

"I should have known." Nixie frowned at him. "You wouldn't show up a month early for nothing. What's happened?"

He squeezed her hands, a smile cracking the habitual soberness of his round face. "Aribi finally died."

"What?"

He spun her around in an impulsive little two-step. "We got word this morning. Aribi's dead, Nixie!"

Erik figured he spoke for ninety-eight percent of his countrymen when he said, "Who?"

Kiss the Girl

But Nixie knew. One look at her face told him that. She was like a wooden doll in Karl's big hands. He stopped dancing, took her by the shoulders and said, "We need to be in Bumani by morning if we're going to catch the best action. We're in talks with HBO to send a documentary film crew with us, and I've already sold the initial photography rights to *Chat Magazine*. Women and children are dancing in the streets, Nixie, and Sloan's going to lead the party. And then it'll be your turn. You can build a few schools, educate some little girls. You can have all the clinics you want after we bury this bastard."

He swung her back into that manic two-step, but Nixie jerked out of his arms.

"No," she said.

Sloan sighed. "Here we go again. Back on the pedestal."

Karl frowned. "What do you mean, no?"

"I mean no." Nixie's eyes were bright, her cheeks flushed. "I'm building something here."

"Nixie." Karl dipped his chin and watched her over the top of his glasses. "I appreciate your wanting to finish this clinic thing out, but be reasonable."

"I *am* being reasonable."

"You really think putting a bunch of fat American kids on TV and boo-hooing over their asthma is more important than helping build an infrastructure that will support the intellectual and economic development of an entire nation of disadvantaged women?"

Erik watched Nixie bear up under that one. Damn, this man was a master. Erik would bet good money at least one of his many degrees was in psychology.

"That's not the point," Nixie finally said.

"Then, please, Nixie. Enlighten us. What exactly is your point?"

She swallowed visibly, and Erik could see her hands trembling. She twisted them together and said, "I can't live that life anymore. It was bad for me."

Karl frowned at her. "What are you talking about?"

"I'm talking about this!" Nixie's arms wheeled around, taking in her mother, her advisor, the entire apartment. "What we do together. We're dysfunctional and sick, and I don't want to do it anymore."

Sloan propped her chin on one lacquered fingernail. "Don't you think you're being the teensiest bit dramatic, Nixie?"

"No, that's your job." Nixie turned to Erik. "How many times has my mom been married since my dad died?"

He blinked. "Um, six?" He turned to Sloan. "Did you ever marry that Italian guy?"

"Which one?"

"The one whose ring you tossed off a yacht into the Mediterranean?"

"No. His mother didn't care for me."

"Five, then," he said to Nixie.

"Which means five messy divorces and countless ugly public break ups. I used to think she was an incurable romantic, but now I know better. It's just business, isn't it, Mom? Karl IDs the world's next fashionable disaster, you self-destruct en route, I prop you up, the cameras eat it all up, and we sell a million magazines. Am I the only one who thinks this is unhealthy?"

Karl looked at Nixie, his face round and stern. "We reach an incredibly wide audience because of the particular dynamic between you and Sloan. Compared to most humanitarian organizations, our donor base is huge. We raise money they only dream of, and we use it to build orphanages, hospitals, and schools. We immunize children, we dig clean wells, we provide money for books, computers, medicines, farms and food. More importantly,

Kiss the Girl

we bring our issues to more people than the Red Cross, Amnesty International and The AIDS Project combined. So it costs us a little personal discomfort. What we buy with it is priceless."

"Easy for you to say. It doesn't cost *you* a thing." Nixie turned to her mother. "Mom. You don't have to do this anymore."

"Do what?" Sloan gave her a lazy smile.

"That," Nixie said flatly. "The whole sex-drenched, red-hot siren thing you do. It still works, don't get me wrong. But how long before it starts to get pathetic? You're not getting any younger, you know."

Sloan's smile froze. "I was young enough for your boyfriend, wasn't I?"

Nixie made a rude noise. "You didn't even like James. You were just ramping up the publicity for the Kenyan clinic's grand opening."

Sloan sat up like she'd been slapped. "I'm no angel, Nixie, but I am *not* a whore."

"Oh, God. I didn't mean that." Nixie's hands went to her mouth, her eyes giant and green above her fingertips. She reached for her mother, but Sloan turned away, her hands gripping her elbows until the knuckles showed through her skin. "I..." She broke off helplessly, turning to Karl in mute appeal.

"Okay, Nixie," he said gently. "That's enough. You've made your point."

He went to Sloan, patted her arm. "We'll take this one step at a time. Let's get Nixie's asthma project wrapped up, then we'll talk about Bumani." Sloan let him take her hand, and she nodded silently.

Karl turned to Nixie, who was still frozen with horror at her own ugly words. He dropped a paternal kiss on her forehead and Nixie leaned into him like she'd received a benediction.

"I'm sorry," she said. "I never meant..."

"I know, honey. Don't worry. We'll work it out. We always do. Isn't that right, Sloan?"

"Yeah. Sure." Erik watched with interest as Sloan obeyed Karl with the reluctant faith of a cynic in the presence of her own personal messiah. Erik wondered if she knew that Karl watched Nixie the same way.

And this, Erik thought, was why he didn't date women like Nixie. All women were complicated, but women like Nixie were complicated in ways he'd never figure out. She was trouble. And while he shouldn't want any part of it, he was afraid there were a few parts he wanted quite a lot.

He needed to get his head on straight. Right now.

Mary Jane watched the Home and Garden channel half-heartedly from the depths of a curvy Victorian sofa. She'd found it at a yard sale last summer and reupholstered it herself in a luxe cranberry microfiber. It was her favorite place in the world to lie down and take refuge from a crappy day, but it wasn't doing the trick this afternoon. She still had a stuffy, low-grade headache, courtesy of her all day crying jag.

She sat up and flipped over to the Food Network. Jamie Oliver was flirting his way through a Nicoise Salad. She tried to pay attention, but somewhere between the olives and the eggs her mind wandered back to Anacostia. To Ty.

She punched the power button on the remote with a frustrated little moan. She wanted to go to work. She needed the edgy rush of non-stop decisions and overpowering stress. She didn't want to think about why a clean, quiet apartment full of her favorite things felt so empty and sterile.

But she couldn't go back to Anacostia. Not today. It was too full of Ty and the way he'd had her body purring like a high-performance engine all night. It had stomped the living hell out of her heart when sun came up and she realized that she'd been a fool. Again.

Tears rushed into her eyes with a stinging vengeance and she blinked them back. God, how could she have any tears left? She'd cried a lifetime's worth when Ty had first walked out on her.

It was just sex, she reminded herself. Purely physical, purely over.

But when the doorbell rang, her heart leapt into her mouth and her pulse launched itself right into orbit. Oh God, she thought, looking down at herself. Did anything scream broken-hearted quite like a bathrobe and puffy eyes at four p.m.? Wads of Kleenex littered the carpet around the couch like new fallen snow. She scooped them up and stuffed them into her pockets. Great. Now she looked like her ass had finally conquered the thigh-territory it had been eying since high school.

The doorbell rang again, this time accompanied by a voice calling, "Mary Jane? Are you in there?"

Erik. Not Ty. Her heartbeat stuttered back to normal. "Idiot," she muttered to herself. Ty wasn't going to suddenly change his mind about his life's work. Why couldn't she wrap her stupid brain around the fact that he was never going to turn up on her doorstep with a dozen roses, a ring, and a more appropriate outlet for his business acumen? Particularly not if she kept fucking his brains out every six months or so. At least this time it hadn't been on her desk at the clinic. That was something.

"Mary Jane?" The bell rang again. "It's Erik."

"Just a sec," she called. She detoured into the kitchen, emptied the Kleenex into the trash can. She checked her reflection in the stainless steel toaster and sighed. Maybe she could claim allergies.

She snapped a few fresh tissues from the box on the counter and opened the door. Erik was there, square and solid and concerned. She tried a smile.

"Have you been crying?" he asked. He didn't wait for an invitation, just stepped into her apartment and took her hands in his. She faked a sneeze so she could turn away and have her hands back.

"Hay fever," she said.

He nodded slowly. "Okay."

Mary Jane fought the urge to roll her shoulders. She was a terrible liar, and they both knew it.

"What are you doing here, Erik?" she asked. "I thought I was pretty clear about not wanting company this afternoon."

He smiled. "You were. I'm persistent." He shut the door behind him and wandered farther into her apartment.

"Yeah, well, I'm rude. Go home."

"No." He helped himself to a seat on her girlie, curvy couch with a maddening self-assurance. "You have every right to kick me out. But I hope you'll hear me out first. I want to talk to you."

"You can have five minutes," she said. "Talk fast."

"I talked with Tyrese today."

She stared at him. "You what?"

"You were kidnapped last night, Mary Jane. I needed to make sure you were safe."

"I wasn't kidnapped. I told Nixie I was going, and that I'd be fine. She watched me get in the car and buckle myself in. Didn't she give you the message?"

"Well, of course, but I didn't think--"

"Didn't think what? That I knew what I was talking about? That I *was* fine? That anybody besides you could possibly be right?" Her hands were shaking with rage and humiliation. "How could you have done that?"

"Those kids had *guns*," he said calmly. "People say lots of things at gunpoint. How was I supposed to know you weren't just trying to protect Nixie?"

"Because Nixie would have said *gosh, Erik, Mary Jane just sacrificed herself to some gun-toting thugs so I could get away and bring help.* But I'm betting that's not what she said. I'm betting she said something more like *Mary Jane went with those kids. She said she was fine and would be back later.*" She glared at him. "She's not an idiot, you know. No matter what you seem to think of her."

He stood and pushed both hands through thick, wheat-colored hair. "This isn't about Nixie."

"No? Then what is it about?"

He studied her for a beat, just long enough for her nerves to start twitching, then he said, "You don't have hay fever, Mary Jane. You've been crying. All day, from the looks of it. Now I don't know what's going on between you and this Ty person, but it doesn't take a genius to see that it's not making you happy. I can't say I know what you're feeling, but I do know what it is to want somebody wrong for you."

"You have a thing for criminals, too? Now there's a coincidence."

Erik ignored her with his usual ease and went on. "For a long time, I kept thinking that life or the universe or something was going to put the right woman in my path eventually." He gave her a smile, a full on charmer. "Turns out that my mom is the only one interested in throwing women into my path."

Mary Jane was surprised to find herself unbending a little. That was some powerful smile. "Thus the debutante parade?"

"Exactly. I've thought a lot about the kind of life I want, Mary Jane, and the sort of woman who'd fit into that life. She's starting to look an awful lot like you."

Mary Jane stared. "Me?"

He laughed, a toothpaste commercial come to life and a tiny pang of regret tightened her throat. Erik was a good-looking, charismatic man. Normal women liked men like Erik. Hell, they loved him. Why couldn't she be normal? Why couldn't she fall in love with him?

"Oh come on, Mary Jane. It's not like we've never talked about it before."

"Yeah, but never seriously. I mean, if I was single at fifty and it was between dating you and getting a cat, I'd probably pick you, but I don't think I'm quite there yet."

"Why not? You know me. You know who I am, what I'm like. You know that I think the world of you. I know that you're smart, driven and principled. I know that you're honest, that money's not your biggest motivator and that if you ever appeared on the evening news, it would be completely unintentional. We both have careers that take up the bulk of our lives, and we both like it that way. Lots of successful marriages are based on less. Why shouldn't we go out a few times, see where it takes us?"

"Because I don't..." Mary Jane flapped a mortified hand between them. "We don't...you know. *Feel* that way about each other."

"Feel what way?"

Her cheeks burned. "*That* way."

"The way you feel about Tyrese, you mean?"

Mary Jane thought about all the hours she hadn't spent sleeping last night. She thought about all the delicious aches and twinges and abrasions she'd collected as a result. "Yes."

"And how's that working out for you?" he asked. "Following your libido into a relationship."

Mary Jane frowned, struck. "Not so well."

"There you go, then."

She stared at him, a curious lightness blooming in her chest. She thought it might be hope, but she wasn't sure. She hadn't hoped for anything in so long. "You really think this could work?"

"Think about it, Mary Jane. Our careers didn't just happen. We set goals. We researched schools, hospitals, specialties. Then we did what it took to get from there to here. We expect to work like hell for all the other good things in our lives. Why should love fall into our laps?"

"I don't know." She bit her lip. Surely it wasn't this simple. But she couldn't think at this particular moment of any reason not to at least try it. "I guess we could go out sometime."

His strong, square face lit up with that killer smile again. "Great," he said. "But there's one more thing I need to know."

"What is it?"

"Be honest now. A lot is riding on this answer." He paused, gave her a very serious look. "You don't want to be First Lady, do you?"

She snorted. "I can't even look your mom in the eye she scares me so bad. I'd chew off my own arm before I dated a guy running for office."

"Yeah, I thought so. But I had to make sure."

He tucked his fingers into his pockets and smiled at her. She smiled back, but it felt like wearing somebody else's jeans. Even if the size was right, it was still awkward. She forced herself to focus on this new idea, that she could choose a partner for the life she wanted rather than depend on her stupid heart.

It was actually kind of appealing. She'd wasted half of her adult life having sporadic sex with a guy who viewed money-laundering as a perfectly legitimate form of protest against institutionalized racism. Was she really going to waste the other half, too? Or was she going to get practical and stop expecting her wants and her needs to correspond so neatly?

Not that she had much of a choice. It was either that or resign herself to a future of conjugal visits.

She looked at Erik, standing a respectful distance away, those big hands tucked safely into the pockets of his jeans. She couldn't deny that it felt nice to have a guy like him thinking of her as wife material. She noticed that he hadn't spoken a single word about love or desire or need, though. It was an interesting omission from a guy as inherently passionate as Erik.

"It's Nixie, isn't it?" she asked.

"What's Nixie?"

"The woman you don't want to want."

He shook his head. "Why would I not want to want Nixie Leighton-Brace? She's hot. Everybody in the world wants Nixie."

"Yeah, but she's definitely First Lady material." Mary Jane's smile morphed into a smirk that felt much more natural. "Plus your mom picked her out for you."

"Okay, fine." Erik pinched the bridge of his nose. "I'll admit it. I lust inappropriately, same as you. But I grew up with a famous mom. I know what that's like, and I'm not going to do it to my own kids."

"Nixie's a whole different kind of famous than your mom." Mary Jane said. "It's not the same thing at all."

"Listen, how about this? You don't hassle me about Nixie, I won't ask you about Ty. Let's focus on each other for now, huh?"

Mary Jane considered this. "Fair enough," she said. There was a pause that stretched clumsily into a silence. Finally she said, "So, how do you see this working?" She moved her shoulders uncomfortably. "This dating business."

"Let's just go out." He made it sound so easy. "A couple dates. A movie. Dinner. Bowling."

"Bowling?"

"You like mini golf better?"

"Bowling's fine." She gave him a smile. It was small, but by far the most genuine of the day. An answering smile broke over his face, turning all those hard edges into something arresting and beautiful.

"Have you eaten today?" Erik asked.

She tried to remember when she'd last eaten and prayed her stomach wouldn't mortify her with an almighty rumble. "Um, no."

"Come on. I'll take you out to dinner and break my own rule about Nixie-talk."

Mary Jane frowned. "Uh-oh. Is she in trouble?"

"No, she *is* trouble. She seems to think she's our new Director of Outreach."

"Oh."

"Yeah. Get dressed. I'll fill you in."

CHAPTER FIFTEEN

"It's a pretty simple set up," Nixie said as she guided Karl through the clinic's waiting room on Monday. She badged them into the receptionist pen where Wanda frowned at a computer screen and poked at a keyboard with two-inch finger nails.

"This is Wanda," she told Karl. "She sees all, knows all and punishes without mercy. Try to stay on her good side."

"Pleased to meet you," Wanda said absently, then frowned at her computer. "What? What internal error? Oh no you didn't." She smacked the monitor with the heel of her hand. It whirred sadly and brought up the correct screen. "Yeah, that's what I thought," she said. "There's more where that came from, too."

Karl looked up from his cell phone and paused, momentarily arrested by the sight that was Wanda. "Right," he said. "I'll be careful."

Nixie smiled and led Karl back into a treatment room. "The clinic provides all your basic medical services but most of its patients present with diseases related to poverty. Obesity, substance abuse, diabetes, asthma."

She waved an arm toward the nebulizer station. "These machines mix asthma medication with oxygen and the kids breathe it in. They're not expensive but most of our families could never afford one of their own."

Kiss the Girl

"Mmmm hmmmm." Karl didn't look up from his phone. For all Nixie knew he was making a grocery list. He finally slipped it into his pocket, and cast his eyes around the cramped room. Nixie was suddenly conscious of how clean and spacious it looked compared to some of the hospitals they'd seen outside the U.S. Hell, compared to the ones they'd *built* outside the U. S.

"I know it's not our usual thing," she said. "I mean, nobody's going to turn up here with a machete injury or anything, but--"

Karl cut her off. "Why are we here, Nixie? With your bank balance you could've had a nebulizer in every house on the block last week."

"So I could be on a plane to Bumani by tonight?"

Karl didn't answer, just gave her a doleful look over the rims of his glasses.

"I don't want to buy them more nebulizers, Karl. I want to fund a full-time pediatrics position for somebody who specializes in asthma."

Karl shook his head. "I had a feeling you'd say something like that." He consulted his phone again. "I put together a list of potential invitees last night. I'll just--"

Nixie cut him off this time. "Invitees? To what?"

"To the fund raiser." Karl peered at his tiny computer. "I assume we'll be hosting one on site within the week."

"No."

Karl blinked and finally focused on her. "No?"

"Nope." Nixie gave him a sunny smile. "I've been thinking about this, and I've decided on a two-pronged approach."

Karl's mouth tightened into a skeptical line inside his beard. "A two-pronged approach."

"We do a photo op first," Nixie said. "Something small and exclusive to generate interest. Then we'll follow it up in a week or two with a gala. Off site, though.

I'm thinking down town, black tie. Something pretty for the social climbers, lots of press."

Karl frowned. "That's going to take time and planning, not to mention connections. The social climbers you have in mind don't turn out for any old cause."

"We have connections," Nixie said. "We've been making them for years. Let's use them."

"I don't mind that so much as the time. Come on, Nixie. Bumani isn't going to wait forever."

"I already told you," Nixie said. "I'm not going to Bumani."

Karl's brows came together in a disapproving line. "Tell me you're not in love with the doctor."

Nixie threw up her hands. "How many times am I going to have to tell you before you believe me?"

"I don't know," he said. "Maybe when you start the sentence with *I've come to my senses and am packing for Bumani because...*"

Nixie glared at him. "I'm not going to Bumani."

There was a rap on the door frame. Nixie turned to find Erik and Mary Jane watching her, Erik's hand in the small of Mary Jane's back. A tiny sliver of hurt wedged itself into her heart. Was there something about kissing her that sent men scuttling into the arms of other women? She supposed she should be grateful he hadn't turned to her mother.

"Hey, Nixie," Mary Jane said. "Or should I say Madame Director of Outreach."

Nixie shot Erik a look that said *tattletale*. Erik shrugged and Mary Jane stepped away from his hand. Nixie couldn't help but notice how much more comfortable she seemed with her personal space back.

"Erik," Nixie said with a saccharine smile. "What are you doing here?"

"I have a date with Mary Jane," he said.

Karl sent Nixie a meaningful look. Nixie ignored him. She turned to Mary Jane and said, "How nice."

"We're just grabbing a cup of coffee," Mary Jane said. Her face brightened. "Hey, you could join us! Do you have time?"

"Um, no, sorry," Nixie said, unaccountably cheerful all of a sudden. "Karl and I are hashing out plans to raise your clinic that boatload of money I promised you."

"Oh." A clear internal battle played out on Mary Jane's face--money for the clinic or company for her date? She sighed. "I guess you need to keep focus, huh?"

"Yeah." Nixie smirked at Erik. "Sorry."

"Should we stay here?" she asked Karl with wide-eyed appeal. "In case you need us?"

"Ah, no." Karl gave her a warm smile. "The beneficiary's job is usually quite simple. You'll just need to show up in a ball gown and chat up the reporters all night. Nixie and I will take care of the rest."

Mary Jane blanched and she turned to Nixie. "Reporters?"

A trickle of alarm snaked into Nixie's stomach. "Um, yeah. We need all the coverage we can get if we want to make the gala profitable. Is that a problem?"

Mary Jane turned accusing eyes on Erik. "Gala? Nobody said anything about a gala."

Erik looked at Nixie and said, "She's a little camera shy."

"How camera shy, exactly?"

Erik lifted a shoulder. Mary Jane said, "I would rather gouge out my own eyes than walk a red carpet. Even if Brad Pitt and George Clooney were both standing at the other end waiting for me."

"Oh," Nixie said faintly. "So no gala?"

"Please God no."

Erik watched Nixie's advisor pat Mary Jane's hand with one big paw. "Not what you bargained for when you hired a Director of Outreach?" he asked, a kind twinkle in those pale eyes. Erik didn't trust it for a second.

"I never..." Mary Jane said, then stopped. She was no dummy. She saw exactly what he saw--that Karl had never believed Nixie was anybody's Director of Outreach. He'd never thought he was really going to have to shill for childhood asthma. He'd been waiting patiently for Nixie's lie to bite her on the ass so he could shame her into coming back to Team Save The World.

Mary Jane cleared her throat. "I never expected a gala. That's all." She smiled weakly at Nixie. "Boy. We're getting our money's worth, huh?"

"I can scale back," Nixie said, glancing at her advisor whose smile had gone from kindly to smug. "It'll mean less money, of course, but if you're not happy with the plans as they stand--"

A sudden surge of anger caught Erik by the throat. "Not happy?" he heard himself say. "Of course she's happy. You're going to keep us afloat for another year, maybe even allow us to hire that dedicated pediatrics person we've been talking about. Why wouldn't she be happy?"

Mary Jane nodded reluctantly. "I *do* want a dedicated pediatrics person, and I'm thrilled you might be able to get me one. Even if it's just for the winter. Flu season is a killer for kids with asthma."

"But you just said..." Nixie trailed off and frowned.

"Listen, Nixie, here's the deal. I don't like crowds, I don't like media types and I hate parties of all kinds." She grimaced. "Small talk. Eeeesh. It's like the ninth circle of hell."

"Um, okay. But in order to pull this off, we kind of need crowds. And media types. And it's pretty traditional to cap off the campaign with, you know, a fundraiser. A gala. Black tie. Red carpet. Speeches and interviews. The works."

"Oh, God. Really?" Mary Jane looked pained, and turned to Erik. "You'll have to do it."

Erik blinked. "Me?"

"Him?" Nixie asked.

"Well it can't be me." Mary Jane shook her head. "I get hives when I talk to reporters. And you can stop looking at me like that," she told Erik. "You know it's true."

Erik laced his fingers together on top of his head and blew out a breath. "Yeah, I know."

Karl leaned forward. "We don't need to do something so elaborate, Dr. Riley," he said. "If it suits you better, we can certainly do something less intense."

"Less intense means less money," Nixie said again.

"It also means less time and less press," Karl said, smiling at Mary Jane. "Nixie's a pretty potent donor draw. I'm sure we'll keep manage to keep the lights on for you."

Nixie's pleading eyes met Erik's, and he sighed. If it was just a matter of disappointing Nixie, that would be one thing. But this advisor of hers was steamrolling her with an efficiency and precision that suggested years of practice, and Erik didn't like it. He gave Karl an oily smile and said, "I'll handle the press for Mary Jane."

"You will?" Nixie's head shot up and she gazed at him with such radiant gratitude that Erik smiled at her. He couldn't help it. She smiled back and something hard and twisted in his gut smoothed out. He'd done the right thing. Now it was just a matter of keeping his hands as virtuous as his intentions.

"Yeah," he said. "I will. But don't abuse it. I'm not a huge fan of the media myself."

"You're strictly 911," Nixie assured him, beaming. "I'll do as much as I can myself."

"You'd better," he said. He turned to Karl. "Looking forward to working with you."

"Likewise," Karl said, but his eyes were sharp and hostile behind his glasses. Erik's skin went a little tight. Jesus, he thought. Who *is* this guy? Karl reached out for a handshake. Erik was startled to see a tattoo running along his inner forearm, just below his rolled back sleeve. Two rows of tiny numbers and letters. He forced his eyes back to Karl's, took the older man's hand and shook it briefly.

"You're working tomorrow?" he asked Nixie.

"Yeah."

"I am, too. Give me an update then." He turned and headed for the door, suddenly desperate to get out of the clinic. There was something so strangling, so claustrophobic in the air between Nixie and her advisor. He couldn't breathe.

He had one foot on the sidewalk before he stopped. He closed his eyes and ran a weary palm down his face.

He'd forgotten Mary Jane.

Nixie watched Erik stalk silently back into the room, take Mary Jane's arm and shepherd her out the door. Nixie shook her head. She would never lie again. Not if punishment was always this swift and unflinching. Not that it was the first time a guy had gone right from kissing her to another woman's arms, especially not after he'd seen the people she kept company with. But still.

She turned back to Karl who was watching her in silent approbation.

"You heard the man," she said. "Let's have something for him by tomorrow." She picked up her cell phone and started to scroll through the stored numbers.

Karl stilled her hands with one of his and ran a critical eye over her. "Maybe you should start with a haircut and a facial first," he said. "You look a little...rough."

"Oh, come on. It's not *that* bad." Nixie put a stealthy hand to her hair to assess the mayhem. She flattened a particularly wild curl. It sproinged back into place with a happy bounce. "Is it?"

"You could use a little trim."

Nixie folded her arms. "I don't want a hair cut. I want to work."

"A haircut *is* work, Nixie. You're a brand, remember? If people don't admire you, they don't give us the money to change the world. You want to change the world, don't you?"

"Not all of it," Nixie said. "Just this little corner."

"Start with your hair."

She sighed. "Okay, fine. But tonight we work."

"Tonight we work."

CHAPTER SIXTEEN

By Friday, Nixie's hair looked great. DC had transformed itself, too. Gone was the punishing wind, the half-frozen raindrops, the steely sky. Suddenly, the sun beamed and the breeze bounced by, full of the scent of cherry blossoms. Even the graffiti looked cheerful, Nixie thought as she stood in the alley behind the clinic. Kind of bright and festive and exuberant.

"Nixie!" Wanda stuck her head out the door. "What are you doing out here? Missy Jensen from Channel Four is standing in the waiting room!"

"Did you know that your hair matches this graffiti exactly?"

Wanda touched her hair and glanced at the wall. "That says Fuck Da Police."

"I meant in color, not in spirit."

"Mmmm-hmmm." Wanda gave her a skeptical look. "Well, listen, unless you want Mama Mel going on about cheap-ass carpet and cockroach shit to Missy Jensen, you'll get moving."

"I just wanted a minute to gather myself," she said. But she got moving. "I figured you could handle Mama Mel," she said, as she trotted behind Wanda's rolling behind. "She's about as big around as a chop stick."

"She's wiry. You've got to respect that. Besides, I'm not dressed to wrestle on national TV."

Kiss the Girl

"I'm sure it's just local." Nixie eyed the straining seams of her uniform pants. "And I think you're dressed to wrestle just fine."

Wanda shot her a warning look over her shoulder. "Girl, you are wasting my time. Now get your skinny butt into that waiting room and do your thing."

"Right."

Nixie paused at the door to the waiting room, scanned the scene as if it were a field of landmines. She made her living walking into crowds of strangers who knew everything about her. Maybe they hated her, maybe they loved her. She never knew until it was too late to do anything about it. As far as stressful occupations went, she supposed jumping blindfolded out of airplanes might be worse. But not by much.

Nixie spotted a petite blonde woman in front of a camera reviewing notes while her camera man checked the light levels. Missy Jensen, Nixie assumed, as nobody else in the room came equipped with her own camera man. Expertly streaked hair kicked around her Miss Kansas face in a cute, choppy shag as she licked her teeth behind glossy lips. Probably prepping for a long stint of professional smiling. The camera man made a comment and the woman rewarded him with what looked like a genuinely amused grin. So either she wasn't a cut-throat shrew, or she was too smart to alienate the help. No way to tell from here. She'd have to wing it.

Nixie slid through the waiting room doors, sticking to the perimeter of the room until she'd circled around behind the camera man. She watched as Missy Jensen ran through several intros. The woman radiated an unusual combination of ambition and compassion, brains and sex appeal. She was young, probably Nixie's age, give or take a few years, but she was going places. The question was, what would she do or who would she screw to get there?

The million-watt light from the camera snapped off, and Missy Jensen blinked at Nixie. "Nixie Leighton-Brace?" she asked.

"Missy Jensen?"

Missy strode forward on ice-pick heels that matched her peacock-blue suit. "It's an honor to meet you in person, Ms. Leighton-Brace," she said. "I've followed your work since I was a little girl."

"Since *I* was a little girl, then."

"That's right. I was thrilled to get your call. This is a wonderful cause, of course, but I'd be lying if I didn't admit how much I appreciate the exclusive."

"I have faith in the power of personal connection," Nixie said. "From what I've seen so far, you're a good fit. Are you ready to take the next step?"

"Always." Missy's glossy mouth curved in anticipation.

Nixie couldn't help grinning back. "Great. I have somebody I'd like you to meet. Follow me."

Missy made *you're with me* eyes at her camera man and they fell in behind Nixie. She picked her way through the crowd. It was thicker than usual--word that the press was coming had spread through the neighborhood faster than the flu.

"Hey, white lady!"

Nixie turned and found Darryl the Flasher grinning at her. He'd put on basketball shorts in deference to the summery weather, and though he looked sober, Nixie couldn't see him resisting the opportunity to offer Missy Jensen some good loving.

"Darryl!" she said, grabbing both his hands in hers as a pre-emptive strike. "I was hoping you'd be here." She turned to Missy. "I want you to talk to Mama Mel first, but Darryl here is one of Anacostia's success stories. In a neighborhood where more than half the adults are out of work, and young black men have a greater chance of being

Kiss the Girl

shot than graduating from high school, Darryl has both a diploma and a job."

Missy smiled warmly at him. "You must be an exceptional young man."

"Yeah, baby, I got it where it counts."

Nixie gripped his hands with a desperate strength. "Ow." He frowned at her. "You're crushing my hands, girl."

"Oh." Nixie didn't release her hold on him. "Sorry."

Missy said, "I'm looking forward to our chat."

Darryl's eyes went unfocused, as if Missy's dazzling charm were a sudden blow to the head.

Nixie put herself into his line of sight. "You're going to represent the neighborhood, Darryl. *On live TV.* Be...good. You understand?"

"I'm always good, baby." He beamed foolishly at Nixie. "I'll be right here," he told Missy.

Nixie sighed and started across the room again.

"What should I know about Darryl?" Missy asked. Nixie could hear the distinctive tippy-tap of the woman almost trotting in those punishingly high heels. She'd never understood how women did that.

"Good kid," Nixie said. "Not bright. Tendency to flash his junk."

"Seriously?"

"Unfortunately, yes."

"Okay." Missy turned to her camera man. "Run tape on the kid. Nothing live."

"Got it."

They arrived in front of Mama Mel who snoozed in her usual corner of the waiting room, her kids parked around in her various states of wakefulness. The older ones slouched in the puke-colored chairs, plugged into their cell phones and headsets and iPods. The younger ones tumbled on the floor at her slippered feet, where she could poke the appropriate one with a toe when his or her name was called.

"Mama Mel?" Nixie sat in the vacant seat across the row and tapped the woman's sharp knee through her house coat. Her eyes opened a slit and she humphed out a snort.

"I gots a bone to pick with you, Madame Rich and Famous."

"Yeah?" Nixie leaned forward, elbows on knees.

"Yeah." She slid her irritated gaze to Missy, then back to Nixie. "This place was enough of a zoo before your famous self started hosting parties for reporters. I got eight kids to get through their breathing treatments. That's a lot of time sitting here in this place. It *used* to be quiet enough for my babies to get some homework done." She sent Daryl, who was telling a loud, profane story two rows over, a killing look. "Ain't nobody getting no homework done today."

"I know," Nixie said. "I'm sorry, Mama Mel. I promise things will calm down soon. But it's for a good cause."

"Yeah? What cause is that? Getting our neighborhood idiots on TV?"

"No, ma'am." Nixie drew Missy forward. "I want you to talk to Missy Jensen. She's a reporter."

Mama Mel's slitty gaze moved back to Missy. "From Channel Four. I know. We may be poor, Nixie, but we got TV. How come?"

"We're going to raise some money for the clinic, Mama Mel. If we raise enough, we can pay for another doctor here. Somebody who'll focus only on kids, particularly kids with asthma."

"Sounds expensive." Mama Mel humphed again. "I ain't got no stories that good."

"I think you do," Nixie said. "But even if you don't, at the very least, we'll be able to buy more nebulizers."

Kiss the Girl

"More nebulizers?" Mama Mel's eyes finally opened all the way. "How many?"

"A lot. Enough to get your kids in and out of here in thirty minutes instead of four hours."

Mama Mel sat up, smiled at Missy. "What you want to know, girl?"

Missy motioned to her camera man, then perched on the very edge of the chair next to Nixie's, tucking her skirt carefully under her rear. "Are these kids all yours?" she asked.

"Some's mine, some I picked up here or there, but yeah. The courts gave 'em to me right and proper."

"They all have asthma," Nixie said. "To the degree that they need breathing treatments three to four times a week."

Missy frowned. "But they're not all biological relations?"

"Well, let's see." Mama Mel gazed into the middle distance and rubbed the single whisker that poked out of her chin. "I gots one brother-sister pair, and another two are cousins, but they ain't related to one another, no. I mean the cousins to the brother-sister set. Nor none of the others. They come to me through the foster system, see?"

"Is it unusual to see rates of asthma like this among unrelated children?" Missy asked. Her camera man crouched in the aisle between them, getting Nixie and Mama Mel in the frame. He'd shoot Missy's reaction shots later.

"Not if they living in the Wash, it ain't." Mama Mel's mouth worked like she was chewing something sour.

"The Wash?"

"Washburn Towers," Nixie said. "It's one of the low incoming housing facilities here in Anacostia."

"Is there a connection? What does Washburn Towers have to do with childhood asthma?"

A hand landed on Mama Mel's thin shoulder, and a hearty voice boomed out, "Nothing!" at the same time she said, "Everything."

Nixie knew that hearty boom. She knew that hand, too, its tan a calculated contrast against the white of the shirt. But it was the cuffs that gave him away. Senator Edward Harper--James Harper's father--always wore his cuffs rolled back exactly once. More than once, and you worked with your hands for a living. Closed cuffs--or cuff links, God forbid--and you might as well tattoo Ivy League Intellectual on your forehead and kiss the red states goodbye. Cuffs rolled back only once said *I am educated but I am not unmanned. I could clear brush if necessary*.

Edward stood in the aisle between Nixie and Mama Mel, his good side toward the camera, his serious smile trained on Missy. She leaped to her feet, pleasure at an unexpected ratings bump flaring in her wide brown eyes.

"Senator Harper! What are your thoughts on the idea that living conditions in Washburn Towers are contributing to childhood asthma?"

Edward smiled at Missy, but reached for Nixie. He leaned down and planted a smacking kiss on her cheek.

"Nixie, it's been months! How have you been?"

"Okay." She smiled grimly. *Better since your son stopped screwing my mother across Europe*.

"Never thought I'd see you stirring up trouble in my neck of the woods." He smiled at her, but they both knew he wasn't being funny.

"It's a living." She smiled sweetly.

"Now what's this about Washburn Towers giving kids asthma? You know that's not true. The government goes through a rigorous bidding process that weeds out unscrupulous contractors. There's not a fiber of asbestos in that building, and it's inspected regularly."

"Asbestos causes cancer, Edward, not asthma."

Kiss the Girl

He went on as if she hadn't spoken. "And it was freshly carpeted and painted last summer."

"With materials so cheap they're outgassing enough chemicals to keep these kids on nebulizers through college."

"Cheap-ass carpet," Mama Mel muttered, sticking her fists into her armpits.

Edward put on his concerned face. "I had no idea such a thing was even possible."

Missy stuck her microphone in Edward's face and said, "Environmental toxins have long been suspected in the link between poverty and childhood asthma. How do you address the accusation that the government itself is responsible for poisoning these children?"

Nixie smothered a smirk. She decided she liked Missy Jensen after all.

"That's a very serious charge, Ms. Johnson."

Missy smiled. "Jensen."

"And I give you my word as an elected representative of the people that I will get to the bottom of it. Children are our most precious resource, and deserve all the protection we can provide. I believe the children are our future."

"Teach them well, and let them lead the way," Nixie muttered, disgusted.

Mama Mel snickered. "Show them all the beauty they possess insiiiiide," she warbled.

Missy turned her back on a baffled Edward to give the camera a serious face. "Whitney Houston couldn't have said it better. From Anacostia's Free Health Clinic, this is Channel Four's Melissa Jensen, reporting."

The camera man lowered his camera. "That's a good feed, Missy."

She beamed at him. "Thanks, Mike. You were totally on top of it, as always. You're going to have to wear a tux when we win our Emmy." He shuddered theatrically, and Missy turned to Mama Mel. "Thanks for the interview, ma'am. I'll see that Mike sends you a tape."

"That would be real nice."

Missy shook Edward's hand, then Nixie's. "Thanks again for the opportunity," she told Nixie, then turned to Edward. "I'll be following up with your office about the carpet at the Wash."

"I hope you do."

"I'll look forward to it." Her smile this time was less shark, more heat. Edward's own smile went sleek and self-satisfied as he watched Missy stride off on those killer heels.

"She looks a lot bigger on TV," Mama Mel said.

Nixie nodded. "The camera really does add weight. You think all those women in Hollywood are anorexic because it's fun?"

"Huh."

"Nice work, though, Mama Mel. You were perfect."

"Anything for my babies," she said, patting her hair net. "I wish you'd told me we was expecting company, though." She cut her eyes to Edward. "I'd have worn my better dress."

"I wish somebody had warned me, too. What are you doing here, Edward?"

"Karl called me." His dark eyes warmed with the sincerity Nixie suspected he could summon up at will. James had to have learned it somewhere. "He said you were stumping for childhood asthma in my backyard and could use some high-profile backers."

Nixie grabbed his elbow. "Will you excuse us, Mama Mel?" Mama Mel waved them away and settled back into her chair. Nixie led Edward to the corner by the bathroom, dropping his elbow the instant they left the crowd.

"Let's be honest, Edward," she said, her voice low and tense. "James didn't come off well in his tangle with the women of Leighton-Brace."

Kiss the Girl

"He looked like an ass." Edward smiled pleasantly.

"I'd think you'd want to distance yourself from us and anything associated with us, given your presidential ambitions. Why would you risk dragging the scandal back into the papers by turning up here?"

He smiled. "Your mother--a fifty-year-old woman--stole your boyfriend. She humiliated you with the whole world looking on, and you're worried about me? Come on, Nixie. Where's your pride? Aren't you angry?"

Nixie opened her mouth. To say what, she didn't know because it wasn't like the guy was lying. Edward shook his head, cut her off before she could speak. "Don't deny it, Nixie. We both know what Sloan is. She sacrificed you to her need to be outrageous, sexually provocative. Desired. Don't you want to get even?"

Nixie studied him wearily. "Edward, please. Don't insult my intelligence. You wouldn't be here if you didn't want something. What is it?"

He gave her a blinding campaign-poster of a smile. "I want you to take James to the gala you're planning."

She stared. "Why on earth would I do that?"

He smiled, but it was flat and joyless. "Sloan's always been terrified of getting old. I can't think of anything that would gall her more than thinking you were finally coming into your own. Your stealing back the man she stole from you tells the world that you're finally eclipsing her sexually."

"Oh my lord." Nixie waved both hands in the air between them, as if erasing the words. "Let me rephrase. Why on earth would *you* want me to do that? It'll be a tabloid blood bath."

"That's the point, Nixie. James has been off the rails for some time now. I thought indulging him with this African hospital project would bring him back on line, but--" He shrugged. "You saw how that went."

"Yeah. The whole world saw."

"Damn internet." He spread his hands helplessly but his eyes went dark and hard. "The boy's a liability right now. If I'm going to keep him on staff his image needs a serious overhaul. I want the world to see him do the right thing."

"And that is?"

"Ask forgiveness from Nixie Leighton-Brace."

"Ah." Nixie nodded, finally seeing the angle. "And receive it. Be judged sincere and worthy of forgiveness in a nice, high-profile venue."

Edward stretched his lips in a parody of a smile. "You're a bright girl, Nixie. James is an idiot for screwing you this way."

"I've always thought so."

"Listen, if you agree to this, I'll pack your ball with influential people and their checkbooks. But I want James on your arm, and I want you smiling at him."

"And if I say no?"

"My influence works the other direction, too. This is a pretty risky cause for an incumbent to endorse so close to mid-term elections, you know."

Nixie's eyes narrowed. "You'd keep a bunch of kids from *breathing* so strangers will think better of your son?"

He shrugged. "I'll bend over backward for these kids, Nixie. You're the one putting them at risk so you can indulge a personal grudge."

Rage swelled up inside her, but she squashed it down. Losing her temper would only dig this hole deeper. "Okay, fine," she said. "I'm willing to let Sloan squirm for a few hours if it means raising money for these kids. Tell James he's got a date. But if he makes one move I don't like--on me *or* Sloan-- I'll knock his front teeth out just in time for the campaign trail. Are we clear?"

"Crystal." Edward squeezed her shoulder. "You're a good girl, Nixie. I don't know how you managed to stay so good all these years."

Kiss the Girl

"Yeah, me neither."

CHAPTER SEVENTEEN

Darryl Johnson spoke to the pretty reporter while Erik stood by, ready to slap some sense into the kid if he showed the slightest sign of veering into exhibitionism. So far, so good, but Erik stopped watching when he spotted a man with a conservative haircut and an expensive shirt standing near the bathroom with Nixie.

He'd clearly cut her off from the herd and Erik didn't care for the way his thick white fingers squeezed her shoulder, like she was a melon at the market.

Mary Jane arrived at his elbow. "Hey," she said. "Who's the hair do feeling up Nixie?"

"That would be Senator Edward Harper."

"Oooh." Mary Jane's eyes went wide and she peeked around Erik's arm to get a better look. "As in the father of James Harper? The guy who--"

"--cheated on her with her own mom? Yeah."

"Nixie should have accidentally stomped on the guy's foot half a dozen times by now. If not for feeling her up then certainly for fathering such an asshole." Mary Jane looked up at him. "You should go say hello."

Erik watched the Gentleman from Virginia knead Nixie's shoulder with those soft white fingers. "Yeah, I might do that."

He waded through the crowd, making liberal use of his elbows. He planted himself at Nixie's side, close enough that she had to tilt her head back to look him in the face.

"Nice work today, Nixie," he said, wrapping an arm around her shoulders. He gave her a squeeze that forced Harper to release her. "You've worked a miracle. Mama Mel is now a celebrity in her own right."

"She was great, wasn't she?" She patted Erik's lapel and leaned in confidentially. "She only said cheap-ass once."

"I know. You did good work, Nixie."

"Thanks." Nixie gave him a smile so dazzling and generous that he blinked, momentarily stunned.

The Senator took advantage of his inattention to step forward and offer a hand. "I'm Edward Harper," he said. "My son is an old friend of Nixie's." He gave Nixie an intimate smile.

"Old is right," Erik said cheerfully. He turned to Nixie. "Didn't you kick that guy to the curb in Kenya a couple months back?"

Nixie made some kind of noise.

"Sort of," she said, her eyes locked studiously on his lapel. She patted it again then stepped back so Erik could shake the man's hand.

"This is Dr. Erik Larsen," she said to the Senator. "He's a volunteer here at the clinic, as well as a board member. In his other life, he's a cardio-thoracic surgeon at GW."

"Senator Larsen's boy?" James asked, his eyes going bright with interest. Suddenly, Erik felt a lot like a melon up for inspection himself. "Impressive."

Erik didn't think he was talking about his medical credentials as much as his bloodlines. The old claustrophobia crept up on him, a cloud of doubt covering the sun.

"So." The man released Erik's hand and put his hand on Nixie's elbow. "I'll give James the message, will I?"

Erik frowned again at the easy way he laid his hands on Nixie's person. "Message?"

Harper gave him a professional smile, this time with an ugly edge. "Nixie's agreed to be James's date to the gala."

"You did?" he asked Nixie.

She edged away from the Senator. "Yes. It's work."

"Every day is play if you pick your job right," Harper said with a booming laugh. He gave Nixie a little squeeze. She took another step away from him.

"I see." Erik clapped the guy on the shoulder just a shade harder than necessary. "Well, I'll be sure to say hello to James if I see him at the gala. As a board member, I'm required to put in an appearance, too." He glanced at his watch. "But speaking of work, I'm about to cut out for the day. Are you almost done here, Nixie? Why don't we get a cup of coffee and debrief?"

She gave him a grateful smile and said, "That would be great. I'll just alert the crew." She broke Harper's grip on her elbow with more tact than Erik thought strictly necessary, saying, "I'll be in contact regarding the logistics for the fundraiser appearance, Edward."

She disappeared into the crowd, leaving Erik and Harper exchanging hostile smiles. "She's a firecracker," Harper said at last. "Always has been. My boy screwed the pooch when he ditched that one."

"Yeah."

Harper leaned in and lowered his voice to the *just us guys* register. "Though, seriously, you can't really blame him, can you? I mean, if Nixie and her mom were both knocking at your tent flap, which one would you let in?"

Erik's hand curled into a fist at his side and he let the pause linger just a beat or two beyond comfortable.

"I'm sure I didn't hear you properly," he said. "Say that again, please?"

Kiss the Girl

Harper's eyes darted to Erik's fist, then back to the crowd. He shrugged. "I was just saying that Nixie's a firecracker."

Erik nodded. "That she is."

Harper cleared his throat. "Well, I should get back to the office. Nice meeting you."

"Same."

Erik watched him gladhand his way to the door, slapping people on the back, barking out his jolly laugh and asking after wives, children, and pets with no obvious interest in the answers.

Mary Jane appeared at his shoulder. "Well?"

"Nixie's taking James Harper to the fundraiser."

She nodded, unsurprised. "No publicity is bad publicity." She patted Erik's arm. "Hold on tight, baby. This clinic's about to go *high* profile."

Erik stared. "She's doing this for *us*?"

"You think she'd smile for the cameras with James Harper for fun?"

The thought of Nixie selling her self-respect to the highest bidder--even for a good cause--sent a savage anger licking through his veins. He squashed it with precise care. "Like mother, like daughter, I guess," he said. *Remember that*, he told himself sternly.

She lifted a brow. "That's a bit harsh, isn't it?"

Erik jerked a shoulder. "Hey, you pimp your private life for the cameras, you forfeit sympathy."

Nixie reappeared, with Karl in tow. "Oh good, you found Mary Jane," she said. "Where to?"

Erik glanced at Karl. "How about Steve-O's?"

"So you can feed Nixie another hamburger?" he asked. "I don't think so."

"I know a place," Mary Jane said. "You'll like it. All of you. Let's go."

Cuppa Joe's squatted on a busy corner of South West, somewhere between the touristy bustle of the Fish Wharf and the self-importance of Capitol Hill. Nixie figured the place for a two-story row house that had been chopped into several smaller commercial spaces. Cuppa Joe's anchored the ground floor corner space.

Lavender trim and a funky, hand-painted sign gave the sober architecture a jaunty, carnival flair. Window boxes ran the length of plate-glass windows on either side of the building, clearly tended by somebody, Nixie decided, with a serious gift for gardening. Geraniums and poppies leapt out of them in a riot of mismatched enthusiasm.

Karl expertly slid the hybrid SUV he'd rented into a street spot and Nixie stepped out onto the cracked concrete. Karl herded her toward the building while he remoted the locks and pocketed the keys.

"This looks like a great place," Nixie said as she opened the door. She stepped back so Karl could precede her, but he put a hand in the small of her back and propelled her through ahead of him. Nixie landed inside with an awkward hop. "Geez, Karl. Would it kill you to let me hold a door for you once in a while?"

He frowned at her, confused. "Why would you want to hold a door for me?"

"It's symbolic. An outward demonstration of an inward respect?"

"That's sweet," he said, patting her arm. "But taking care of you is my job. You want to do something nice for me, we could be on a plane to Bumani in an hour."

Nixie rolled her eyes. "I'd rather get the door."

Erik waved at them from a tall wooden booth in the corner. A giant fern dangled by a wire from the wood-beamed ceiling above his head, dipping into the booth and all but eclipsing Mary Jane across from him. Karl put his hand under Nixie's elbow and steered her toward them.

Kiss the Girl

Nixie didn't bother mentioning that she was perfectly capable of walking twenty feet without guidance.

She hesitated at the booth's edge, then slid in next to Erik. It was either that or let the two largest people in their party squash into one side of a small booth together.

It was just a kiss, she told herself. Nothing to get all weird about.

"Wow," she said, doing her best to ignore the long stretch of hard thigh pressed against hers. "Cozy." She reached forward and fingered the fern frond that hung at eye level.

Mary Jane, sandwiched between the plaster wall and Karl's considerable bulk, gave her a stiff smile. "That's one way to put it."

Karl reached out and snapped off the offending frond.

Mary Jane said, "I wouldn't have done that."

A scandalized gasp had them all turning toward the aisle where a thin man with a white apron and accusing eyes stood covering his mouth with his hands.

"That fern is a delicate living creature," he said with great dignity. "Please refrain from doing it further violence."

Erik covered his face with a cloth napkin and hacked into it suspiciously. Nixie whisked the amputated frond off the table.

"We're so sorry," she said. "It won't happen again."

"I should say not."

Nixie handed the waiter the frond. He tucked it into his apron pocket with a stern look for Karl.

"The flower boxes are lovely," Nixie said. "Are they your work?"

He nodded, breaking into a pleased smile. "Aren't the poppies a smash?"

"I'll say. And I haven't seen a trailing geranium like that outside Bavaria. Where did you find them?"

"I smuggled a seedling through customs."

"Pre-9/11, I assume?"

He threw a glance over either thin shoulder. "Post. Sister, you have no *idea* what I went through."

"If you're half as committed to coffee as you are to your flowers, you must do pretty well."

"We brew the finest fair trade coffee in DC."

"And here I am, about to order tea. Is that a terrible faux pas?" Nixie asked.

"I have a Lapsang Souchong that'll put hair on your chest."

"Just what every girl needs," Mary Jane muttered.

"I'll take it," Nixie said.

The rest ordered coffee--black, hot, unimaginative. The waiter sailed off to the counter, and Mary Jane said, "Well, I can never come here again. Thanks a lot, Fern Killer."

"I've been a vegetarian for thirty years," Karl said. "I have great respect for life. But plants are food."

"Tell it to Cuppa Joe."

"Yeah, I don't think so."

A few minutes later, Nixie was sipping something that tasted like it had recently put out a campfire while outlining the highlights of her plan to save the clinic.

"Today laid the groundwork for the gala we're putting on two weeks from tomorrow," she said. "It's short notice, but I've called in a few favors and it looks like we'll have a decent turnout among DC's taste makers."

"Including Edward Harper and son," Erik added with an edge to his voice that had her setting down her cup with exaggerated care.

"You can thank Karl for that one," she said, giving Karl a pointed look.

Karl consulted his phone, dragged a few things around the touch screen. "Edward talked to you about making nice with James, then?"

"He asked me to take him to the gala," she said, her lip curled in distaste.

Karl shrugged his massive shoulders, pasting Mary Jane even more firmly against the wall. "I figured."

"Sloan's going to have kittens," Nixie said. "There's no way she'll show up for the gala if she knows about this."

Karl didn't look up. "Are you kidding? Sloan's a pro. Of course she'll show up."

Erik leaned forward. "Show up, make a scene and stomp off?"

"In full view of the press, yes." Karl nodded absently, then set down his phone. "Like I said, she's a pro."

Erik leaned back, his face dark and closed. Nixie's stomach twisted. "She knows already? About my taking James to the gala?"

"What does it matter? It'll play the same in the press either way."

Nixie stared, stunned at this breathtaking bit of insouciance.

Karl put his elbows on the table. "I have to admit, I wasn't so hip on this childhood asthma thing, but it's paying off. You can't buy publicity like this. It'll make a great jumping off point for Bumani."

"Good for you," Nixie said. But her face was so tight with rage she didn't know if she'd managed to move her lips. She'd walked away from all this, hadn't she? Her mother's endless publicity stunts? Her own frantic efforts to calm the waters and get something done while Karl milked it for every last charitable cent? She'd *quit* for heaven's sake. How were they still using her to create this sick dynamic?

"I've spoken to *Chat Magazine*, and they've agreed to give us a photographer starting this Monday," Karl said.

"Sloan's agent is opening an auction for the documentary film rights tomorrow morning."

The furious pressure in Nixie's head died and guilt rushed in to fill the vaccuum. "Wow. That's fantastic."

"Just doing my job, kid."

"How did you get *Chat Magazine* interested in asthma?"

"Asthma? No, Nixie, they're coming with us to Bumani. The documentary crew, too. We'll have to fly out first thing in the morning, but don't worry. We'll get you back in time for your gala."

"Bumani?" Nixie asked. The photographer, the documentary crew, the mock date with her asshole ex-boyfriend--none of it was for the clinic. Of course it wasn't for the clinic. Karl's agenda had only one item on it: putting Nixie where he thought she could do the most good, whether or not she wanted to be there.

"We can hardly skip the gala," Karl said. "Poor Edward's gone to a lot of trouble to set up James's redemption. Let's not disappoint the guy. We can land in the afternoon, do the gala and let the publicity follow us right back to Bumani, where it belongs."

"I'm not going to Bumani, Karl." Nixie locked her hands together and placed them on the table. "I told you that already. Several times, in fact."

He poked absently at his phone. "Hmmm?"

"I'm not going to Bumani with you and Mom. I have work to do here."

He finally looked up. "What are you talking about?"

"The gala is in two weeks, Karl. I have lunches, brunches, coffees, drinks, walk-and-talks. I'm meeting with anybody who'll see me. Edward's agreed to put me in touch."

"Nixie, I already put you in touch. With Bumani. Don't tell me you're seriously thinking about ignoring an entire nation of abused and impoverished women so you can buy asthma meds for fat kids?"

Mary Jane sat up. "So our poor aren't deserving of help because they're American?"

Karl glanced at her. "Poor kids in the rest of the world make soccer balls out of rags. Poor kids in America stuff their faces and play video games. Forgive me if I don't see the comparison."

Erik smiled genially. "You want to make a ball out of rags and kick it around Anacostia, Karl? I'm sure it's perfectly safe."

"Obesity is as much a consequence of poverty in America as asthma is, Dr. Dettreich," Mary Jane said.

"I recognize that," Karl said, his eyes on Nixie. "But poverty in the Middle East kills children. Poverty in America makes them unhealthy. Not ideal, I understand. But it's not as urgent a situation. A woman of Nixie's means has to consider her responsibilities on a global scale. She can't just follow her heart, she has to prioritize. You're medical professionals; surely you understand?"

"I'm not saying you should ignore Bumani," Nixie said. "You've got Sloan. All you need now is a straight man, because I'm not doing it anymore." A lightness rose up in her, fragile but gloriously buoyant. "I quit, Karl. I quit almost two months ago now. I promised you I'd find something worthwhile to do with myself, and I have. Now it's time for you to hold up your end of the bargain. Take Sloan and go save the world. I'm staying right here. At home."

CHAPTER EIGHTEEN

"This isn't your home, Nixie, and Sloan's not you," Karl said. "She's beautiful and she's well-intentioned, but she's also brittle, shallow and self-destructive. People tune in to watch her implode. They tune in to watch you endure it all with grace and serenity. They see something special in you."

"There's nothing special in me," Nixie said quickly.

"Except for, what, your face, your figure and your trust fund?" Mary Jane asked.

"Nixie's more than her face," Karl said.

"Please, don't start with this," Nixie said, putting her fingers to her forehead.

"With what?" Erik asked.

"People identify with Nixie," Karl told Erik and Mary Jane. "They all have crazy mothers, rotten jobs, difficult relationships. But Nixie has all that crap in spades and look what she manages to accomplish anyway. She's proof that good *works* in the world. She gives people hope."

Nixie grabbed Erik's forearm. "He's not reasonable about this. Don't listen to him."

"But it's more than that," Karl went on. "In this business, you get a lot of people with the face and the money to do some good. Sometimes they even have an education. But Nixie? Nixie *connects*. You give her a

Kiss the Girl

one on one with anybody from a sultan on down to a goat herder, and within five minutes, they're dying to build her an orphanage or write her a personal check. Money rains out of the sky wherever she lands. But more importantly, people listen to her. They follow her. They *learn* from her. Nixie makes a difference."

Mary Jane stared at Karl in silence. Erik glanced between him and Nixie, his golden brows drawn together in some unreadable line. Nixie sighed.

"So now you know," she said. "The secret is out--I'm the Messiah. The one the Red Cross has been praying for lo these many generations."

"Don't be flip, Nixie. Six million Jews died in the Holocaust because the world didn't know what was happening to them. Because of you, the world knows what's happening in Darfur. In Afghanistan. In Kosovo. Deliberately withholding the same aid from Bumani because it's *inconvenient* for you is tantamount to abuse and it's beneath you. Now get your head out of the clouds and get back to work."

"No." The word skidded into the taut silence between her and Karl like a stone skipped on a frozen pond. "You want too much from me, Karl. I can't save the world. I tried. God knows I tried, but I can't. Whatever you think you see in me just isn't there."

"You're wrong."

"I'm not. You want proof? How's this? I like *hamburgers*."

He sighed but Nixie nodded furiously. "That's right, Karl. I like hamburgers and flush toilets and long showers and that bright yellow cheese that comes in a squirt can. It's awesome on potato chips. You can't recycle those cans, either. What do you think of that, huh?"

"Come on, Nixie. Be serious."

"I am being serious. You've been feeding me this chosen one business my whole life and I tried for so long to make it true. To make you happy. But I can't do it anymore."

Karl leaned back and gazed at her for a long moment. Nixie swallowed and twisted her shaking fingers together, hoping to look strong and confident instead of terrified. He said, "So what *do* you want, Nixie? If not Bumani, then what?"

"What everybody wants, I guess." Her voice came out pitifully small and Nixie cleared her throat. "A home of my own, a job I like. Friends. Not the kind that come and go with the cause of the day, either. Real friends." She glanced at Mary Jane, who gave her an encouraging smile. She studiously avoided looking at Erik when she said, "Maybe even a family of my own someday." She shrugged casually. "I like kids."

"Kids." Karl snorted and glared at Erik. "With him, I presume?"

"If I feel like it. So what if I do?" Erik jolted in the seat beside her and Nixie glanced over at him. Great. The very suggestion of having kids with her had the fearless Viking doctor all vacant-eyed and startled. She patted his elbow. "Hypothetically speaking, of course."

"Of course," he murmured.

Nixie turned back to Karl. "It's none of your business, Karl. That's the point I'm trying to make here. If I want to throw myself at Erik's feet and beg him to bang me six ways from Sunday, it's nobody's business but mine. Why is it such a crime to want a nice, normal personal life?"

"I'm not sure that qualifies as normal," Mary Jane said, looking doubtfully at Erik.

"Hey, women beg me to bang them all the time," he told her. "*All* the time."

"Oh." Mary Jane nodded. "Of course."

Karl slapped his palm on the table and Nixie jumped. "For Christ's sake," he snapped. "You don't have a

Kiss the Girl

normal life because you're *not normal*. When God was handing out gifts, you got the money, the face and the fame instead. You also got the responsibilities that go with them, so let's not waste any more time on this fairy tale bullshit, okay? It's time to get back to work."

Nixie glanced at Mary Jane and Erik. Erik watched her, his face stoic and grave. Mary Jane bit her lip and avoided Nixie's gaze, as if to say *you know, the guy makes a good point*. Nixie's chest filled with searing frustration and hurt disappointment. Why couldn't she make anybody understand? She wasn't asking for anything special. Just what everybody else seemed to have automatically. Why was it so hard for her?

"I can't do it anymore," she said to Karl, her voice low and distinct. "Maybe it's not what you want for me, but I'm building something here. Something I believe in, and won't walk away from. I'm not going to Bumani with you. I quit."

She moved to stand up but Karl grabbed her wrist, pinned it to the table. "Don't do this, Nixie. You'll be sorry."

"Are you threatening her?" Erik asked. His voice was mild, but something hard and cold ran just under the surface.

"What? Of course not." Karl gave him a startled frown. "But I know Nixie. I know her better than she'll ever know herself, and this isn't her. She needs to just settle down and remember who she is."

"Let me go," Nixie said slowly. She looked into his round, genial face, the face of the man who'd been her father, her teacher, her mentor for so many years, and saw a stranger. "Please, Karl. You've got to let me go."

"You're upset about James," he said.

"No, I'm not."

"It's okay. We'll talk when you've had time to cool down."

Karl opened his hand and Nixie scooted out of the booth, rubbing her wrist. She turned to Erik. "Will you take me home, please? I'm done here."

"Yep." He slid out of the booth and Nixie marched to the door, her knees watery with adrenaline. She climbed into Erik's Jeep parked at the curb, but her hands were shaking too badly to manage the seat belt. She folded into herself, arms banded over her stomach, forehead to knees, and wheezed a few breaths in and out until she felt a little less like passing out.

She heard Erik get in on the driver's side. Then his hand was on the back of her neck, his strong fingers digging through the mess of her hair to press lightly against her skin.

"Nice work, princess," he said. "First time you've told off an authority figure?"

Nixie tried a shaky laugh. "You could tell?"

His fingers drew slow circles on the corded muscles of her neck, gentling the tension there in tiny increments. Nixie closed her eyes and finally filled her lungs. She felt like she hadn't breathed in twenty minutes.

"Better?" he asked.

"Yeah. Thanks." She sat up slowly, his fingers still threaded through her hair. She gave him a shaky smile, and he sighed.

"Liar," he said, and his hand curled around the back of her neck, drawing her forward until his mouth touched hers. Panic zipped along her skin, but she couldn't make herself pull away. She was already awash in adrenaline from the fight with Karl. Another blast like this and her heart was going to explode. Then she thought about all the times she'd faced death before and gave a mental shrug. If she had to go, she'd go kissing Erik. It was definitely better than a chopper crash.

But as his mouth moved over hers--warm, firm, coffee-flavored--an unexpected peace settled over her.

Kiss the Girl

This, she realized dimly, was a whole different kind of kiss. Sweet, uncomplicated and infinitely more dangerous. The first kiss had been all shock and awe, a kind of sexual pyrotechnics she'd been completely unprepared for, and it had sent her entire system into orbit. But this, this was different.

This kiss was...gentle. It took nothing and offered everything--comfort, support, safety. The harsh buzz of adrenaline leaked away, replaced by a warm honey glow. Her very bones softened under the undemanding press of his mouth, and when he drew one knuckle down the edge of her cheek, Nixie's lips curved under his. God, she could love this man.

He drew back and let his hands fall away. "That's more like it," he said.

"Like what?" Nixie blinked slowly at him, still smiling like an idiot.

"Like you. That other smile was awful. I couldn't stand it."

"Oh." Nixie gave herself a brisk mental shake and made an effort to reconnect the synapses that had clearly come unglued under the delicious heat of his kiss. "You kissed the boo-boo better, is that it?"

He shrugged. "Did it work?"

She took a quick inventory of her injuries. The fight with Karl was history, yes, but now her heart was dangerously exposed. Good lord. "I guess," she said. "Yeah."

"Is he always like that?" Erik glanced into the side view mirror and pulled into traffic, cool as you please. Nixie, hot, flushed and unhappy, wanted to kick his shins in. "I mean, my mom's no slouch when it comes to planning futures for her offspring, but even I thought that was a little disturbing."

She pulled her focus back to the conversation at hand. She could berate herself later. "Karl's not a bad guy. He's just a believer."

"In what?"

"In the idea that people are honor-bound to give back to the universe in equal measure to what they take," she said. "Or in my case, what they've been given."

"And he's what, the universe's enforcer?"

"Not exactly," she said. "It's just that his particular gift is for direction. He's like a chess master. He can see to the end of every game, right? All those moves, counter-moves, back up plans? They're all in his head at once and he can access any one of them at any moment, no sweat."

"Scary."

"No kidding. Sometimes when I feel like arguing with him I just go and slam my hand in a car door instead. Easier."

Erik was silent for a moment, then said, "What's the deal with his tattoo?"

"The one on his inner arm?"

"Yeah."

"Those are the coordinates for Auschwitz, along with the words *never again*."

"Auschwitz, the concentration camp?"

"Yep. There's a movement that pops up every couple of years to dismiss the Holocaust as an urban legend, and with the survivors dying and physical evidence disappearing, Karl felt the need to put the evidence on his body. His own personal mission statement, I guess." Nixie clicked her seatbelt into place. "I have the face, the money and the fame to be a big part of making sure *never again* holds but Karl has the vision to use my gifts--and me--to the maximum possible potential. For him, nagging me into doing my duty is fulfilling a sacred responsibility."

Kiss the Girl

"I don't know, Nixie. He sounded a little unhinged there toward the end."

"He's not. He's just--" She broke off as Erik stomped the brakes and sent her flying into her seatbelt's strangle hold.

"What?" she yelped, hands on the dash, hair in her mouth. She spit out a curl looked around wildly. "What?"

Erik gripped the wheel and stared straight out the windshield.

"I forgot Mary Jane." He closed his eyes, laid his forehead on the wheel. "Again."

"I'm so sorry," Erik said for the third time, peering into the rearview mirror. Mary Jane lay across his backseat, one arm dramatically over her eyes. "Will you please sit up front now?"

"No. I'm punishing you. Plus I need to lie down. My nerves are shot. You abandoned me with the holy roller fern killer. I thought I was a goner."

"Nixie said he wasn't dangerous."

"Nixie thinks Cheez Whiz is yummy." She peeked out from under her elbow, caught Erik's eye in the rear view. "You're totally into her."

"What?"

"You are." She sat up, leaned her chin over the bench front seat. "You tried to play it cool, I'll give you that. You were all *oh everybody's hot for Nixie. So what?* But you're totally into her. She did her wounded princess routine and you about killed yourself getting to the door so she could sweep through without missing a beat."

"I don't like seeing anybody bullied, Mary Jane. It wasn't personal."

"Oh, please." Mary Jane flopped back against the seat. "She had an emotional tiff with her father figure and you *forgot your girlfriend*. For the record, that's me."

"I didn't forget you," Erik said. "I just got caught up in the moment." *In kissing Nixie*, he thought. *Again.*

She threw her arm back over her eyes. "I don't think this is working out, Erik."

"What?"

"This. Us."

"We've been dating a week, Mary Jane. Give it time."

"We've had five years, Erik. That's plenty of time."

He pulled to a halt in front of her apartment building and hooked his elbow over the seat. "So what, you want to break up? Because I forgot you at a coffee shop?"

Mary Jane shook her head and got out of the Jeep.

"Hey, wait!"

Mary Jane yanked open the front door and slid onto the passenger seat.

"Kiss me," she said.

He stared. "What?"

"Kiss me. Right now." She leaned toward him, eyes closed and offered him her mouth. The interior light glared down on her nose, illuminating skin as white and soft as Wonder Bread. She smelled like the soap they scrubbed with at the hospital.

"Didn't you used to have freckles?" he asked.

Mary Jane's eyes opened and she gave him a puzzled look. "No."

"Never?"

"Nope."

"Oh." He frowned. "I could have sworn. Just a couple, right there, across the bridge of your nose."

"Nixie has freckles, Erik. Just a couple. Right there." She tapped her nose.

"Oh." Erik stared at her, horrified and embarrassed.

"Yeah." She folded her arms and gazed at him with sympathy. "You're in deeper than you thought, huh? I'm

Kiss the Girl

sorry, Erik. It sucks. Trust me, I know." She shook her head. "Can we call it quits now?"

"No. I just need more time."

"You're only delaying the inevitable."

"No, I'm not. Nixie is absolutely wrong for me. She'll prove it if I just give her enough time. Bear with me, okay? I swear to God, I'm a better boyfriend than this."

Mary Jane pursed her mouth and studied him. "Yeah, okay. But only because I don't have anything better to do. And you'd better believe you're going to make it up to me."

"I will. I swear I will."

She opened her door and slid out. "Forgetting me at a coffee shop. God."

"I said I was sorry."

She slammed the door and waved over her shoulder as if to say *yeah, yeah*. Erik waited until she was safely in the building, then pulled out his cell phone and dialed his mother. She answered on the fourth ring.

"Hello, darling."

"Hey, Mom. You have a minute?"

"For you? Always." She covered the phone and said, "Whoever secures the Independent Party vote on this gets a summer intern. Move, people. Make it happen."

Erik smiled. "You know it isn't politically correct to bribe your staffers with *people*, right?"

"But it's the only treat they really like." She covered the phone again. "Gender of your choice," she called out. "Ivy Leaguers. Ambitious and of questionable moral fiber." Erik heard her smile. "Ah, there they go. I love it when they hop to like that. Now, then. What can I do for you?"

"Do you still have Grandma's ring?"

"Her wedding ring?"

"Yeah."

"Of course. Why?"

"I need it."

There was a long pause. "Oh, Erik. Honey. What's her name and how far along is she?"

"Jesus, Mom. I didn't get anybody pregnant."

"Thank God."

"I just...there's a girl."

"Somebody serious?"

"I'm hoping it'll get that way. That's why I need the ring."

"Who is it?"

"I'd rather not say right now."

"Ah." There was a significant pause. "I understand."

Erik frowned. "You do?"

"Of course, darling. You're a grown man. I respect your privacy."

"You never have in the past. Why start now?"

"For a start, we're on cell phones, and are both in what I assume are public spaces. I'm not interested in reading about your engagement in the paper before I even give you the ring. Besides, I know you. I know who this is about."

"Yeah, I don't think you do, Mom."

"Honey, you are giving me zero credit for basic human perception. A blind woman could see the sparks you two throw when you're together."

"It isn't Nixie, Mom."

"Did I say it was? But how interesting that she was the first person you thought of." Her voice was arch, knowing. "It's enough for me to know that your... girlfriend has issues with the press. You do, too. I completely understand that you two would want to stay low profile until you've come to an understanding."

"We do. But Mom, I'm serious. It's not Nixie."

"Of course not, dear. So who is it?"

"I can't say yet. I...need time."

Kiss the Girl

I need to kiss Mary Jane, he thought. Why the hell didn't he do it when she offered? He'd managed to kiss Nixie easily enough without an engraved invitation. The blood drained from his head and rushed south at the memory. God. He was in trouble.

"Mmm hmmm."

"I need to get my head on straight, and I think this will help. Can I have the ring?"

"Oh, sweetheart. Of course you can. I'll have it cleaned and you can pick it up whenever you like." She sniffed once, delicately.

"Are you crying, Mom?"

"Of course not." She sniffed again, a little less delicately. "Okay, maybe I am. But I've wanted this for you for so long. All those years, all those girls. I was running out of ways to sneak them under your radar, but I knew if I just kept..."

Erik's brows drew together and he said, "If you just kept what?"

"My patience." She gave a watery chuckle. "If I just kept my patience, you'd find one you liked. And you have. Haven't you?"

"I hope so." Nixie's million-dollar smile flashed through his mind, popped there like a flashbulb. He pinched the bridge of his nose and pushed the image away. He thought of Mary Jane's pale, soft skin, clear and freckle-free under the dome light of his Jeep. "I really, really hope so."

CHAPTER NINETEEN

Sloan Leighton peeked through her lashes at the man--the boy, really--leading her into Senator Larsen's private office the following Monday. He was painfully young, all Adam's apple and wrists.

"Thanks so much for this," she said, wrapping a hand around his arm and leaning in. "I can't believe I got the time wrong. I'm such an air head sometimes. You're sure it's okay if I just wait here?" She opened her eyes wide. *And now I am sincere.*

A flush stained the kid's soft cheeks as he gazed helplessly down at her. "Sure. Senator Larsen's due back any minute. I'm sure she'll want to see you."

Sloan gave his arm a little squeeze. His eyes about rolled back in his head and she hastily let him go. There was such a thing as over playing her hand. "Well, thanks. I owe you one."

She tucked her tailored skirt under her knees and sat primly on the edge of the Senator's soft leather loveseat. The kid shook himself out of the reverie he'd lapsed into at the idea of Sloan Leighton owing him and promptly backed into the door frame. His flush deepened alarmingly as he renegotiated his exit and disappeared. Sloan glanced around the room. It wasn't quite what she'd expected. The outer office was the usual fluorescent business space, but this room was something else entirely.

Kiss the Girl

The walls were a lush, smoky gray the exact shade of twilight, paired with a thick cocoa-colored carpet and this creamy sofa that made Sloan want to slip off her shoes and stretch out.

Framed photos lined the walls--the usual shots of the Senator shaking hands with other powerful politicians. A closer inspection revealed some unexpected black and whites mixed in, though. They all showed a younger version of the Senator with her arm around various incarnations of Nixie's new boyfriend. Sloan smiled reluctantly. Dr. Erik Larsen was a radically charismatic man, but he'd been a sweet and lost-looking child. There was something so elusive and familiar in the way he stared into the camera. Stared through the camera, really. Like it wasn't even there, like he was searching beyond it for something.

Just like Nixie, she realized with an unpleasant jolt. For a long time, she'd thought Nixie wasn't focusing on the camera when she had her picture taken. It had been years before she'd realized that Nixie was actually focusing on the camera too hard. Like she expected something from it. And why wouldn't she? She'd watched her mother debase herself for the cameras for years. Why wouldn't she expect there to be a reason?

"Sloan Leighton," the Senator said, pushing open her office door. "This is unexpected." She closed the door behind her with a soft click.

"I lied quite outrageously to your office boy," Sloan said, putting on her most charming smile. She was amused to find her palms a little damp.

"I gathered." The Senator folded her arms and leaned a sharp hip against the polished Victorian desk. "Why?"

"I wanted to chat with you," she said. "Girl to girl."

A single blonde brow arched, and it was the only movement the woman made. "Oh?"

"About our children." Sloan tried out a maternal mien. "They seem rather...taken with each other."

The Senator waited silently for her to continue, her face a study in barely masked skepticism. Sloan shrugged, but a flame of temper licked up inside her. Who was this woman to judge her? Were they really so different? They'd both used their God-given gifts to force a reluctant world to cough up their due. The Senator had gotten to use her brains, good for her. Sloan's gifts had been decidedly more earthy and she wouldn't apologize for using what she had.

"You can rest easy, Madame Senator. I'm not out to seduce your son. I do have standards. Low and twisted, yes, but standards nonetheless. Maybe you don't approve of me, but I've only ever done what--or who--was necessary."

"I'm biting my tongue, Ms. Leighton," the Senator said. "I've been following your career for years, and you've done quite a number of interesting things. And people. I'm desperately curious about a few of them. But you're not here to dish with me. Not about our children, and much to my regret, not about that delicious Italian prince you spurned. I know a woman on a mission when I see one. What do you want?"

A reluctant smile tugged at the corners of Sloan's mouth. "I don't like you," she said. "You're clever and hard and you see too much."

"I'm also on a schedule." The Senator glanced at her watch. "Could you possibly get to the point?"

Sloan's smile died. "I want Nixie to be happy," she said.

"I like Nixie very much," the Senator said. "But her happiness isn't under my control. Or yours."

"I know." Sloan spread her hands. "But her unhappiness has been very much under my control, and that's something I want to change."

Kiss the Girl

"And you think I can help you?"

"Well, yes. You see, we're at what you might call a crossroads at Leighton-Brace Charitable Giving. There's an important opportunity for Nixie in the Middle East right now, but she's digging in here in DC. Because of your son."

"Ah."

"She and our advisor are at each other's throats over it, and for once in my life, I want to do the right thing," Sloan said. "If your son is as serious about Nixie as she seems about him, I'll call off the dogs. But if he's toying with her, if she passes up the opportunity of a lifetime because he thinks he's lucked into the golden goose, well... I'd find that unacceptable."

"You're the only one allowed to hurt your daughter, is that it?"

"If you like." A small dart of pain landed somewhere in the vicinity of Sloan's heart, but she lifted a languid shoulder. "Let's just say that if Erik's intentions are less than honorable, I'll find myself compelled to drive a wedge between them." She smiled, finally on familiar ground. "And please remember how low and twisted my standards are. I'll do whatever it takes to protect my child."

The Senator gazed impassively at her. "Are you threatening me?"

Sloan gave a delicate chuckle. "Threatening you! The very idea." She slipped her purse over her shoulder and stood. "I was just hoping to keep this low profile, that's all. Things always get so...messy when the press is involved, and this being an election year, well, I'd hoped to avoid bloodshed." She paused. "Figuratively speaking, of course. But a mother must do what a mother must do."

"Or who she must do?" The Senator threw Sloan's words back at her with the calm assurance of the seasoned debater she was.

"Now that's up to you, isn't it?" Sloan smiled. "It was lovely meeting you. Good luck with the election." She walked toward the door, deliberately putting a lot of slink into her hips. She turned, one hand on the knob. "You *are* running again, aren't you?"

The Senator gazed at her shrewdly, and Sloan held her breath. *Come on*, she thought. *Give me something. Please God, give me something.* She didn't think she could bear to follow through on the threat she'd just made. Not again.

"If this ends up in the papers, I'll know where to rain down the fury," the Senator said finally.

"Understood." Sloan took her hand off the knob.

"Erik called me last Friday. He wanted his grandmother's ring. Her wedding ring."

"Ah." Sloan was shocked to feel an exquisite bittersweet joy rise up in her chest. Her baby. Her and Archer's baby, taking that foolish, ill-fated leap into something as ridiculous and fundamentally flawed as marriage. She blinked against a shaming flood of tears. "So he's serious about her."

"Looks that way."

"We'll have to learn to get along, then, won't we?"

"I wouldn't mind hearing about that Italian prince."

"He was just a duke. And something of a disappointment."

"Ah."

Sloan opened the door and slipped out.

Twenty minutes and one astonishing cab ride later-- Sloan hadn't experienced that kind of out-of-body terror since the last time she'd driven in Cairo--she stepped into the Presidential Suite at the Four Seasons. Karl lay on the couch, his stocking feet propped on the arm, his fingers laced together over his bald scalp while a laptop hummed happily on his stomach. He looked up from the screen when she opened the door.

Kiss the Girl

"Hey, Sloan. How did it go?"

"Depends." She stepped out of her shoes and let her arches weep with relief as she padded into the kitchenette. She retrieved a cold bottle of water from the fridge--God, she loved America--before wandering into the sitting area and lowering herself into the square arm chair facing the couch.

"Depends on what?" Karl's eyes were already back on his computer screen.

"On your point of view, I guess." Sloan folded her arms and propped her breasts on them, waiting for his full attention. To his credit, when he finally set aside the computer and looked at her, he didn't so much as glance at the cleavage straining against her shirt. She smiled. Karl's interest in her body was purely professional. She performed for him this way just to stay in practice.

"Screw my point of view, Sloan. Is this doctor going to be a problem or not?"

"He wants to marry her."

"*What?*" Karl sat up so fast he nearly bobbled the laptop.

"He's asked his mother for the heirloom ring and everything."

"Oh my God." Karl scrubbed big hands over his face. "This is a nightmare."

"It can be." It had been nearly twenty years since Archer had died, and grief still hijacked her with vicious regularity. But Sloan didn't fool herself. Karl wasn't thinking of Nixie's heart. He was thinking of Bumani. "What are we going to do?"

Karl's gaze dropped speculatively to her cleavage. "Do you think you could attract the good doctor's attention?"

Sloan had excised her conscience years ago, so she was surprised to feel it twitch in protest at that. But she forced her mouth to curve into the most knowing of smiles.

"Nixie had to slap him to his senses the first time we met, and I wasn't even trying." *Very hard.* "Of course I can get his attention. Do you think I should?"

Karl frowned and rubbed thoughtfully at his beard. "I don't know. It's probably too soon to go that route again. If we have to fly solo on Bumani, we might want to rehabilitate your public image a little."

"True." A sneaky rip tide of relief rippled in her veins, so Sloan lifted the bottle of water to her lips and took a tiny sip. She'd spent her morning committing all manner of minor sins in the hopes of avoiding a truly ugly one. In spite of her best efforts, it was still a very real possibility that she'd have to steal yet another of Nixie's boyfriends, and her stomach went sour with shame. "Karl? Do we really need Nixie for this one? If she's dead set on staying here, can't we--"

"Nixie's the key, Sloan. You know that. We need her."

She shrugged her acquiescence. Karl was rarely wrong. If he said they needed Nixie, they needed Nixie.

"So what are we going to do?" she asked.

"I have an idea," he said, reaching for his cell phone. "Let me take it from here." He ran a critical eye over her face. "Why don't you go rest or something? You look tired."

I feel dirty, she wanted to say, but she only smoothed her skirt and stood. A small twinge of panic tightened her stomach, and she touched the lines between her brows that formed whenever she frowned. She had to be more careful. She wasn't young anymore, and she needed to take scrupulous care of herself if she wanted to maintain the fiction that age hadn't touched her. That none of the cruel, countless sacrifices she'd made over the years had touched her.

Kiss the Girl

"Maybe I'll go have a shower."

Half an hour later, she rifled through the explosion of lingerie that had taken over half her suitcase. White satin, black silk, jade green lace. Filmy, slinky, expensive. She shoved it all aside and dug deeper. She didn't want any of it. Not today.

Her curls, carefully conditioned and combed, stuck wetly to her cheeks as she cursed and shoved both arms into the suitcase to lift away the mountain of underthings.

"Ha!" She reached into the last corner and fished out a pair of white cotton bikinis. The elastic was warped, the material worn and soft, and an improbable herd of ladybugs formed a heart on the derriere. They were the last thing Archer had ever given her and she lived in fear that one day she would wear them out.

She stepped carefully into them, smoothed the simple, serviceable cotton against her skin. For an instant, it seemed to smooth something inside her as well. Something raw and broken and dirty.

She shook her head and dropped her towel to clip on the matching bra. She yanked on a white t-shirt from BCBG. God, she was morose today. What did she have to whine about? Fate had been obscenely good to her. It had granted her the face and figure to earn everything she needed in the world, and then, for eight precious years--an administrative mistake on God's part most likely--it had given her Archer Brace as well.

It was an embarrassment of riches by any standard, one she'd gobbled up with her trademark appetite. By the time the mistake was sorted out and Archer whisked away--private plane crash, so sad, world in mourning--she was already irretrievably spoiled.

She'd gotten used to being loved.

She'd had a man who snapped photos of her with two weeks of camp dirt cementing her hair to her head, insisting she'd never been more beautiful. He'd worshipped her body, of course, but what she remembered most was his hand on her belly as Nixie moved--serene, purposeful and determined--inside her, a foreshadowing of the woman their child would become. She remembered his fingers stroking Nixie's fuzzy head as she nursed, remembered the astonishing fact that her exposed breast never even registered. Archer had loved her. *Her*.

She would never have that again, and she didn't want it. She'd barely survived the first time. What she wanted now was something comfortable, routine and expected. It didn't have to touch her heart. She didn't have one left to touch anyway. She'd buried it with Archer.

What she had was a face that, with proper care and excellent lighting, could still sell magazines. She had a figure that, with the right foundational garments, could wear couture for another few years yet. And she had Karl, Archer's best friend and fellow dreamer, who'd loved Archer as much as she had, who'd dedicated his life to the same causes and who valued most in her what Archer had valued least--her face, her figure and her willingness to exploit them both. She figured she owed the universe a whopping tab for those eight precious years, and God had left her Karl to make sure she paid.

"Sloan?" Karl knocked on her door. "You about finished in there?"

"Almost." She shimmied into a butter-soft pair of Versace capris. The ragged cotton underwear was a secret for her alone. An admission of weakness too shaming and destructive to claim.

"I want you to see something out here."

She caught sight of herself in the mirror and stuck out her tongue. God, she might as well just rent a mini van and go pick some kids up from soccer practice.

"Be right there."

She pulled off the t-shirt and yanked on a tank top instead. It ended just below her navel, leaving an expanse of smooth skin exposed above the low-slung waist of her capris. The word *lucky* stretched across her breasts, spelled out in tacky green rhinestones.

Better. She curled her mouth into its habitual surprise-me-baby-I-dare-you smile and padded barefoot into the common space to see what Karl needed from her now.

CHAPTER TWENTY

Erik left his mother's apartment the following Sunday with his grandmother's diamond in his pocket. He tried not to wonder if Nixie was at home across the hall. He didn't want to see her, he told himself. He didn't want to talk to her, or say something funny just to watch her laugh.

The next thing he said to her probably wouldn't be very funny anyway. It would most likely be about his and Mary Jane's surprise engagement. He punched the elevator call button and frowned at the doors. She'd congratulate him, of course. Tell him she'd seen it coming. But she wouldn't have. Why would she when he'd been kissing her instead of his fiancée?

He pushed the call button again. Somebody else would probably tell her. News traveled fast in Anacostia. Surely he wouldn't be the one to break the story? Not that she'd be disappointed or anything. A woman like Nixie didn't have her romantic hopes pinned on a doctor. But they were friends, weren't they? Good friends. And if any friend of his got engaged without even mentioning the possibility, wouldn't Erik be a little hurt?

The elevator binged and the doors slid open, but Erik cursed softly and let them close again. He turned and headed toward Nixie's door.

He had to tell her. It was the right thing to do. He punched her doorbell before he could think better of it.

Kiss the Girl

The door swung open and Nixie was there, holding a newspaper.

"Hey, Nixie. I was in the neighborhood, and I thought I'd stop by. I wanted to talk to you about something."

"Yeah?" A smile curved her lips and she pressed the newspaper to her chest. "Be still my heart. I didn't believe for an instant it could be true, but feel free to drop to one knee."

He automatically clapped a hand to the ring in his pocket. "Um, what?"

"You're here to propose marriage, right? To seal our families into a political dynasty for the ages so you can run for president and I can finally retire that ghastly china they trot out for state dinners?"

He felt his mouth open, but no words came out. He stared at her, speechless, until she laughed and tossed him the newspaper. It was the Sunday Post--all twenty or so pounds of it--and it hit his chest with a dull thunk. He scrambled to catch it before it did in his toes as well as his sternum. Nixie stood back and opened the door. "Come on in and read all about it."

Erik followed her into the kitchen. He didn't blame her for bypassing the living room. The kitchen, with a chain of garlic bulbs dangling from the pot rack and a cheerful assembly of little clay pots on the window sill, looked more like a Nixie-inhabited space. He couldn't tell a daisy from a dandelion himself, but he'd bet good money that everything on that sill was edible rather than ornamental.

"Go on," she said, leaning back against a mammoth stove, her arms folded across her chest. "Read."

He found the evidence of his mother's perfidy in bold face type at the top of the page. *Senator's Doctor Son Gears up for Political Career with Proposal to Nixie*

Leighton-Brace--Will Grandma's Ring Measure up for Heiress?

He closed his eyes and pushed a thumb against his eye brow. Mary Jane was going to laugh her ass off. Not the best way to start off a lifelong partnership. "I'm going to kill my mother."

Nixie laughed. "Oh, come on. Where's your sense of humor?"

"My personal life isn't a laughing matter."

"Of course it is. Everything is a laughing matter. You stop laughing at life, you stop living it. People *like* your mom. They're interested in her life, and you're a big part of that. So what? You'll go nuts trying to stomp on every little gossip columnist who mentions your name, and if you'll forgive my saying so, you don't have a lot of leeway in that arena."

"You think I'm nuts?"

"Maybe a little tightly wrapped." He frowned at her, but she went on without pause. "Take it from me, okay? One child of fame to another? If you can't control it--and you can't--you have to have fun with it."

He lifted one brow, folded his arms and leaned against a corner of the stove. "How exactly do you propose having fun with newspapers turning my social life into fan fiction?"

"First of all, you can't deny it. They love that." She pursed up that gorgeous apricot mouth of hers and gazed at him speculatively. "You want to make out?"

All the blood rushed out of Erik's head and into his lap. "Excuse me?"

Her eyes laughed at him. "I don't mean right now, champ. I mean in public. For the cameras."

He swallowed, hoping it would open his throat enough to speak. He couldn't quite tear his eyes away from the wicked curve of her lips. "I'm not sure how that's going to keep me out of the papers, Nixie."

Kiss the Girl

"Oh, it's not. But you're there already, aren't you? You're in for an arc of publicity now, and the only thing you can do is control the curve." She put a hand on the stove between their bodies and slid forward until he smelled lemons. He blinked, and tried to focus. "I say we hit the town. Make out in all the clubs, dance til four a.m. We could have a big, drunken fight on the sidewalk, I'd throw your ring at you, and that would be that. A few more weeks of he said/she said in the press and you can give that ring to the heiress of your choice."

Erik thought of the ring in his pocket, a pang of regret catching him by surprise. What kind of self-destructive streak had him half-ready to drop to one knee in front of Nixie? Hadn't he learned anything from his parents' disastrous marriage?

He forced a smile and said, "What? No couples rehab?"

She thought about that, then shook her head. "Not if you're looking for a short arc. You develop a taste for publicity, we could maybe go that route."

"Thanks for the offer, but no," he said. "I'd had enough publicity to last a lifetime before I turned ten. The last thing I want is to go clubbing with Nixie Leighton-Brace."

She shrugged and eased back, folding her arms over her chest again. "Your call." But there was something small and hurt in her eyes, and guilt tugged at him with relentless little hands. Why did being true to himself have to mean hurting her?

"Nixie, come on." He reached for her, but she shrugged away from his touch.

"No, really. It's fine. I just...I guess I thought we were past that."

"Past what?"

"The Nixie Leighton-Brace thing. I thought we were friends."

"We are." He bumped his fist lightly against her shoulder. So what if his entire body was screaming for him to pull her into his arms and kiss her until the hurt in her eyes went up in flames? He was sticking with the fist bump. It was neutral. Friendly. Better for everybody. "But that doesn't mean you're not still Nixie Leighton-Brace."

She made a disgusted noise, and Erik soldiered on. "Seriously. It's who you are. It's not like you can just walk away from the job and *poof* you're not insanely famous."

After a long moment of silence, she said, "Can I ask you a question?"

"Sure."

"Why did you kiss me? Was it all about the clinic?"

"*What*?" He stared at her in horrified disbelief, but there was nothing in her face but calm curiosity and a certain distance he didn't like one bit.

"It's a fair question," she said. "You claim to hate fame, but as you so adroitly pointed out, I *am* famous. You must hate me by extension, so why would a guy like you kiss a girl like me?"

"Besides the usual reasons?"

"All I can figure is you were after something worth more to you than your scruples."

"Something like funding for the clinic?" Fury pulsed in his head like a jackhammer. "You honestly think I'd kiss you--hell, kiss anyone--for the *money*?"

"You wouldn't be the first," she said, her voice cool and detached. Her face was a perfect oval, devoid of anything but a clinical curiosity. Anger still bubbled hotly in his veins, but a little riptide of pain swirled under it. He hardly recognized her. Who was this contained, condemning stranger who'd hijacked his laughing, easy Nixie? Okay, so maybe he couldn't have all of her, but

Kiss the Girl

did that mean he couldn't have any of her? Was she going to punish him with this absolute absence?

"I never lied to you." He shoved his fists into his elbows and glared at her. "I told you the clinic needed money, and I told you I wasn't in the market for a girl like you. And now you're acting all wounded because I'm *not* in love with you? What the hell, Nixie? What did I do to deserve that?"

"You *kissed* me!" Her reserve suddenly snapped, and the Nixie he knew came pouring through the cracks. Her eyes were blazingly green as she glared at him with a fury that leapt and danced like his own. "You kissed me like you couldn't help it. Like you shouldn't but couldn't stop yourself. And me, being an *idiot*, I let myself believe you. I actually believed you felt what I did."

"Yeah?" His anger took an abrupt left turn into an entirely less appropriate neighborhood. Probably a dangerous neighborhood. He took a step closer anyway. "What *did* you feel?"

"Don't make me hit you."

He reached for her anyway. "Nixie."

"Don't you Nixie me." She spun away from the stove and marched to the dish strainer where she started banging clean silverware into drawers. "I want the truth, damn it. Has it all been for the clinic?"

"Has what all been for the clinic?" He wanted to hear her say it. Was desperately curious, in fact, to hear her describe the bizarre way his libido short-circuited his common sense whenever he was within three feet of her.

She threw him a scorching look over her shoulder. "*This*," she said through her teeth, waving a fork between them. "This *thing* that happens whenever you touch me."

He smiled. He couldn't help it. This was turning into a very interesting conversation. "What happens when I touch you, Nixie?" he asked.

She pressed her lips together and snatched up a colander and a dish towel. "You know what happens."

He moved closer to her, close enough to smell lemons again. He was starting to like lemons. A lot.

"When I kiss you, you mean?" he said.

She kept her eyes firmly on the colander she was scrubbing to death.

"You melt in my mouth like chocolate, Nixie. Sweet and hot and rich. It makes me want to lick and taste and savor, to make you last and last. But at the same time I'm so damn greedy for you that I'm two steps from uncivilized behavior every time I smell your shampoo. I don't like it, but there it is."

Her eyes flew to meet his, green and startled, her lips open on a soft *oh* of surprise. "My shampoo?"

He reached for the auburn curl bobbing above her ear in blatant defiance of gravity. He pulled gently on it until she took a tiny half step forward, leaving them separated by inches. He could almost feel the heat of her body, but he didn't touch her. He just pressed the curl to his lips. "Lemons," he said softly. "Drives me nuts. And if you think I'm happy about it, think again."

She made a small noise. He couldn't tell whether it was a yes-noise or a no-noise, but everything in him said *kiss the girl*, and he wasn't one to ignore his gut. He kissed her.

The colander clattered to the stone tiles as her arms twined around his neck and her lips parted under his. Time strung out and his focus narrowed until nothing existed but Nixie's mouth and the slow, pulsing beats of his heart. Sensation lapped over him in a fractured wash of impressions. The subtle curve of her hip under his hand, the fragile weight of her skull as it fit into his palm. The sweetness of her breath against his cheek.

He turned her into the counter, pressed himself into her. Every line of her body matched up with his, and she felt so damn good. His hands streaked over her in equal parts desperation and disbelief. He wanted more at the same time he couldn't quite believe how much he already had.

The inner curve of her thigh slid up to cradle his hip, and he realized with a dizzying rush of desire that he'd boosted her onto the granite countertop. He rocked himself into all that welcoming heat between her knees, and took her mouth with a frantic appetite. She tasted dark and sweet and feminine, and he wondered for one panicky moment if he'd ever get enough of her. Every mouthful he took just made the hunger sharper.

He left one hand on the curve of her behind while the other walked up the delicate ladder of her ribcage to her breast. She arched into his hand like a cat demanding attention, and he lost track of his thoughts.

"Jesus, Nixie, you're killing me."

She smiled against his mouth. "You deserve it."

"I know." He traced the seam of her lips with his tongue and she opened for him. He sank into her like the desperate man he was, and she scooted herself forward on the counter until all her glorious heat was pressed right up against the pulsing evidence of his desire. She gave a satisfied little sigh and crossed her ankles behind his thighs. A clawing need rose up in him, roughening the edges until desire became something altogether different. Something consuming and primal and raw. Something less controlled and more controlling.

Erik broke away, jerked back from the silken cage of her hair, her arms, her scent. This was wrong. *She* was wrong. God, what was he doing?

Her eyes fluttered open, the gorgeous hazy green of still water. Her lips were parted, a little swollen from his kiss, and so goddamn inviting. His palms itched to reach for her again, to take up exactly where he'd left off and drive that churning engine straight home.

"How do you *do* that?" He glared at her. "One second we're talking like civilized people, the next second we're..." He trailed off, unable to find words that quite described what they'd just been doing.

"This is exactly what I was talking about," she said, remarkably composed for a women who'd just kissed him brainless. "*This* is that thing that happens when you touch me."

He smiled at her grimly. "I don't know what it is either, but believe me, it's genuine and it's dangerous and it's definitely not part of some dastardly plan to get you to stump for the clinic. As God is my witness, I do *not* want to prove it again. Don't push me on this."

She glanced at the front of his pants, and Erik didn't make any effort to hide the evidence of his sincerity. "Right. Okay. I won't."

"Good." He blew out a breath. "Great."

She slipped down from the counter and crossed her arms over her chest. Another pang of regret. Her t-shirt was old and soft and she wasn't wearing a bra. The memory of her pert little nipple pressing into his palm sent a giant crack snaking along the surface of his new resolve and he turned away from her.

"I'm going to kill my mother," he said.

Nixie shook her head doubtfully. "About the thing in the paper? Why would she make up a story about an heirloom ring and an impending proposal? Maybe she wants you to be president, but I assume she wants to be on speaking terms with you when you get there."

"Who else would plant a story like that?"

"Karl."

"What?" He turned back to stare at her.

"Oh, yeah. This has Karl's fingerprints all over it. Unless I miss my guess, he doesn't care for you." She gave him a crooked smile. "He thinks you're holding me back from my destiny, and figures painting you as a gold digger looking to pave your way to the White House with the Leighton-Brace fortune will deep-six any starry-eyed notions I had of eternal love."

She bent to retrieve the colander from the floor. Her jeans stretched over the curve of her backside in a way that made his mouth go dry. "Did it work?" he asked.

"You nailed that coffin shut yourself, buster." She smiled at him. Maybe it was still a degree or two left of true Nixie but it was better than nothing. "Though I'm sure you'll rue the day."

"I'm sure I will," he said, and feared he actually meant it. "Are you going to tear him up over it?"

"Oh, of course," Nixie said. "Now that I've had a taste of rejecting authority, I'm mad for it. I'm actually looking forward."

He tipped up her chin with one finger. "Liar," he said. "Call me when it's over. I'll buy you a cup of coffee and let you cry on my shoulder."

"Friends, then?"

"Friends."

"No more kissing?"

"God willing and the creek don't rise."

"What does that even mean?"

"It means I like you, Nixie." He forced himself to step back rather than forward. "I didn't expect to like you this much, and frankly I didn't really want to. But I do, and now I'm stuck. Real friends are hard to come by when money, fame and politics are on the table, and I'm not in the habit of throwing them away on an inconvenient lust."

A brilliant smile bloomed on her face, and Erik had to take another step back or risk making a liar of himself. "That was almost sweet," she said. "In a weird sort of way. I'll call you."

She walked him to the front door, and as he stepped into the hallway, she leaned out and said, "Hey, didn't you want to tell me something?"

"What?"

"When you stopped by, you said you wanted to talk to me about something. It clearly wasn't the article, so what was it?"

Erik's heart stopped for three endless seconds, then jerked to life again with a nauseating thud. How could he tell her about Mary Jane *now*? Maybe they'd established a *just-friends* policy, but that didn't mean it was appropriate to kiss Nixie one minute then propose to somebody else the next. She'd come to mean a lot to him, this sweet, half-cracked, absolutely true Nixie. Maybe he couldn't have all of her, but he'd be damned if he'd give up her friendship on a technicality of timing.

"It was nothing," he heard himself say. "I was in the neighborhood and felt like getting smacked in the chest with the Sunday Post."

She rolled her eyes and shut the door on him. He walked slowly to the elevator, his grandmother's ring a lead weight in his pocket, the path he'd chosen a lead weight in his heart. He'd tell her, he promised himself. Just not today.

CHAPTER TWENTY-ONE

Nixie didn't bother to knock. Karl had given her a key card weeks ago, so she let herself into his and Sloan's adjoining suites at the Four Seasons silently. Maybe she was going to hold this showdown on his turf, but at least she'd have the element of surprise on her side.

She stepped into the foyer, onto marble tile posh enough to make even her cheap sandals sound expensive.

"Karl?"

"Not here," her mother said. The room was so huge it took Nixie a moment to locate Sloan in the depths of an overstuffed white leather arm chair, a lavish view of the DC skyline behind her. She was curled in one corner of the chair in a pair of silky blue lounging pants and the kind of white t-shirt that cost ninety bucks and begged for an ink stain.

Nixie blinked at her in surprise. "Are you wearing *glasses*?"

Sloan touched the stylish square frames on the end of her nose. "Just for reading," she said, pushing them into the jumble of glossy curls on top of her head. She waved a hand toward the coffee table where a few dozen slim folios lay in neat piles. "I'm looking for my next film."

Nixie wandered closer, drawn by the scripts. In better days, picking Sloan's next project had been a family affair. Nixie would curl up at her mother's feet and they would spend hours digging through the piles, laughing at some, reading lines from others, imagining the locations, the costumes, the co-stars. "Anything look good?"

An irritable line appeared between Sloan's brows, and Nixie tried to keep the shock off her face. Sloan hadn't frowned for ten years. She hadn't laughed much either. Extremes of emotion were wearing, she claimed.

"No," she said, tossing a folder onto the table. "It's all junk."

Nixie picked up the discarded script. "This one's from Lars Von Heller," she said.

"I know who it's from, Nixie."

"He directed you to an Oscar nomination, Mom. I doubt he's sending you junk." She picked up the slim binder and flipped it open. She scanned a page or two, then said, "Oh."

"*Oh* is right," Sloan said, sinking deeper into her chair. She crossed her arms, making a shelf on which to prop her boobs. Nixie doubted she did it consciously. It was probably just a habit at this point, like not smiling, frowning or eating. Nixie cruised through another fifteen, twenty pages, enough to get a sense for the part's depth and scope, enough to know Lars had offered her mother another Oscar contending role. Still...

"He wants you to play a grandmother." Nixie bit down on a smile.

"Do I look like a *grandmother* to you?"

"Well, no. Not like any grandmother I've ever met. To be fair, though, you've never looked much like a mother, either."

Sloan narrowed her eyes. "Is that a crack?"

"Mom, you're fifty. Grandkids are on the way."

Sloan spread one hand over her cleavage and stared at Nixie. "Tell me you're not pregnant."

"What? Of course I'm not pregnant. You stole the last guy who could've made that happen, remember?"

Kiss the Girl

"Did I?" Sloan gave her that naughty kitty smirk she'd been playing off as a smile for the last decade. "What was his name again? Jonathon? Jeffrey?"

"James, Mom. His name was James. And I'm not here to talk to you about that."

"No? Then why are you here, Nixie? You haven't exactly been in the habit of dropping by lately."

"I need Karl. Is he around?"

"I'm afraid not. It's just your old mom here today. Want to leave a message? I'm sure Karl can parent you when he gets back."

Nixie's anger, already at a simmer over Karl's high-handed attempts to manipulate her love life, shot straight to a rolling boil. "I'm sorry, did you want a crack at parenting? You should've said something. Karl and I have established kind of a thing these past twenty years, but you can step up to the plate any time. It might damage your image as an international slut, though. Just so you know."

Nixie's heart tumbled as she heard the ugly words fall out of her mouth, but Sloan didn't flinch. She actually smiled. Better a slut than a mother, apparently. Nixie wished her conscience would embrace the idea and quit ordering up the tidal waves of guilt that were currently crashing over her head.

"I think I can afford a little motherly beneficence in the privacy of my own hotel room." She sent the script in Nixie's hand a poisonous look. "I'll ask you to keep it quiet, however, out of deference to my career." She put her feet on the floor, folded her hands and channeled the Mona Lisa. "Come now. Tell Mummy all about it. What's got our level-headed Nixie pissy enough to use an ugly word like slut?"

"You really want to know?"

Sloan just looked at her, amber brows cocked expectantly, all attentive patience.

"Fine." Nixie flopped onto the couch across from her mother, twisted the script in her hands into a tube and said, "There's a guy."

Sloan waved a hand. "There's always a guy, Nixie."

"Well, I like this one. I really like him." She frowned. "I think I might even love him. He's being kind of stupid right now so it's hard to tell."

"Stupid in what way?"

"He's got a problem with fame, money, politics and the press. Childhood incident, I guess. I didn't ask."

"I see." Sloan nibbled one glossy lip. "Are we talking in code or can we say Erik?"

Nixie slid sideways until she was lying down on the couch, the script over her face.

"Code it is," Sloan said. "Go on."

The script smelled like toner and her own breath and Nixie liked the feel of it over her face. It provided a sort of anonymity that made it easier to talk. To her mother, of all people. "He thinks he wants somebody ordinary. Somebody normal. Somebody who doesn't end up in the tabloids every other day. But I don't think he's absolutely sure about that."

"Why not?"

"Because every time we're alone together, he kisses me into next week."

"Ah."

Nixie pulled the script off her face and sat up. "So what do I do? I can't just hang around hoping he'll eventually take a chance on me. But what if I leave? He'll probably propose to the first pretty introvert he meets and then it'll all be over."

"Darling, listen to yourself," Sloan said. "It's all *he wants, he'll do, he says*. What about what you want?"

"What I want?"

"Yes, you."

Kiss the Girl

She twisted the script in her hands. "I...I don't know."

"Of course you do. Don't think, just answer. What do you *want*, Nixie?"

"Him." Nixie's heart bloomed as she finally said the words out loud. Finally admitted what was in her heart. "I want him."

"Go get him, then."

Nixie laughed, and it sounded startlingly sharp and bitter, even to her own ear. "I'm not sure it works like that."

"Of course it does."

"He doesn't want me, Mom."

"Of course he does. If he didn't, he wouldn't be kissing you all the time."

Nixie thought about that for a second. "Okay, so maybe he wants my body but he's not happy about it. In fact, I'd say he's pretty pissed about it. And now I'm supposed to convince him to not only want the rest of me but to be happy about it?"

"My darling, naïve little Nixie." Sloan gave a chuckle that was pure sexual knowledge. "Men are very primitive creatures when it comes down to it. Keep them fucked, keep them fed, and they'll do about any ridiculous thing you ask. Even marry you."

Nixie sighed, stung by Sloan's retreat into sex pot mode. "God, when am I going to stop being such an idiot? Every time I think you're going to actually parent me, you come through with a quote from *Cosmo*." Nixie shook her head slowly and tossed the script onto the pile. "It's a wonder Lars sent you this role at all. He must really believe in your talent if he thinks you can be the heart of a family. Even a make-believe family."

Sloan rolled her eyes at the script on the table, and Nixie rose to go. But halfway to the door, she stopped.

"It's a good part, Mom. It'll win you that Oscar if you're not too scared to do the work."

"Scared?" Sloan arranged herself on the white leather. "Please. I'm insulted, not afraid."

"Okay." Nixie shrugged. "Tell Karl I'm still not going to Bumani," she said. "He'll know what that means." She turned and walked out the door.

Sloan watched Nixie walk away with equal parts relief and regret. She was so brave and strong, her girl. So much braver and stronger than her mother. She'd go home and tackle her doctor with the straightforward openness that took Sloan's breath away every time she witnessed it. Nobody worked without a net like Nixie. Sloan had fallen in love with Archer's courage, and adored it beyond measure in their only child.

But when she'd opened her mouth to say so, it all fell apart in a rush of cowardice. She'd wanted to tell Nixie about Archer, about how loving him had been all breathless passion, unreasoning joy and utter terror. It was crazy to love like that. Sheer madness. And it didn't get better when the relationship got older and children fell into the mix. God, then it just got worse. She loved Nixie with parts of her soul even Archer had never touched.

But she'd been too afraid to say the words. It made her feel too...naked. Too exposed and awkward and uncertain. She'd made her living being every person's fantasy. The perfect fuck, the embodiment of beauty, of sex, of mystery. They all wanted her face and her body, and those she could give them without turning a hair.

Only Nixie didn't want her face or her body. She wanted what was inside Sloan. She wanted a mother, and Sloan was a long way from Betty fucking Crocker. Pleasing the world had been infinitely easier than searching her heart for the courage to love somebody who didn't care what she looked like.

Kiss the Girl

But hell, it wasn't the first time she'd failed as a parent. She'd failed much more spectacularly in the past and Nixie seemed to be okay. Better than okay, really. Archer's genes were that strong. Sloan took some comfort in that.

She put it aside just like she always did and focused on the path she'd chosen. She reached for the script Nixie had tossed down and cursed Lars for having the balls to even send it to her.

It *was* good. Really good. Nixie had always been able to spot them. But she'd be damned to hell and back before she let anybody strap her into a padded girdle and grey wig. She was Sloan Leighton, for God's sake. People didn't pay for ugly. Not from her. She knew what people paid her for, and she gave them their money's worth. She wasn't playing anybody's goddamn granny.

But she didn't put the script down.

Mary Jane looked up to find Nixie standing in the doorway of her tiny office, a mug in her hand, worry on her face. She held out the mug to Mary Jane and said, "Jass missed her prenatal appointment again today."

Mary Jane took a slug from the steaming mug then said, "Gah. What *is* this?"

"Coffee. I made it myself."

"I can tell."

She set the mug aside and pulled Jass' patient file from the pile on her desk. "That makes three missed appointments."

"I know." Nixie twisted her fingers together. "I keep leaving messages on her home phone, but she's either not getting them or ignoring me. I know it's none of my business, but what with DeShawn's dying..." She didn't say *right here on the sidewalk* but the words hung out there nonetheless. She trailed off, spread her hands. "I just really want that baby born fat and happy."

"I'll see what I can do, Nixie." An incandescent smile spread over Nixie's face and Mary Jane shook her head. "No promises, though."

"I know." Her smile didn't dim one degree as she backed out the door. "Thanks, Mary Jane. I really appreciate this."

Mary Jane sat down at her desk with a sigh and flipped open Jass' file to check her home address. Ah, crap. The Wash. Nobody in their right mind wandered into the Wash uninvited, let alone a woman. But what was she going to do? Call up Ty to ask for the pleasure of his company while she made a house call?

A hot shock ripped through her at the memory of those clever hands, that gorgeous mouth. Yep, his company was definitely a pleasure. While it lasted anyway. She could do without the aftermath.

Screw it, she thought. She was a doctor. If those kids were soldiers, she was a medic. And she was going after her patient.

Mary Jane flipped up the collar of her lab coat against the chill of early evening. She didn't normally wear her lab coat outside the clinic, but she was walking into hostile territory unarmed and figured it could double as a white flag.

She climbed the stone steps of the Wash and entered a filthy, poorly-lit lobby that stank of piss and mold. Tumbleweeds of discarded newspapers and candy wrappers squatted in the corners mingling with the occasional cigarette butt and beer can, but otherwise the place was deserted. Thank God.

She checked the address she'd scrawled on her palm. 6th floor. She glanced at the elevator, found an empty shaft. Okay. Stairs, then. She could use the exercise anyway. She pushed through a warped steel door and headed up.

Kiss the Girl

If she hadn't been in such miserable shape, she'd have heard them before she stumbled onto them. She could have stopped, crept back down to the lobby and regrouped. But three flights had her wheezing like a steam engine and she never heard a thing. She just staggered around the corner, red-cheeked and miserable at the prospect of climbing three more flights, and found herself smack in the middle of a hostile knot of dead-eyed boys and their junkie customers.

The junkies scattered like cockroaches, but the boys didn't budge. They cut disbelieving glances at one another until the kid in the center said, "Who the fuck are you?"

Shit. "I'm Dr. Riley," she said, amazed at the level calm of her tone. Her knees were like water, but damn, she sounded all right. "I'm looking for Jessica Pendergass. Jass. Sixth floor, I believe, so if you'll excuse me--"

She made as if to step through them, but the kid--the talker--got right in her face.

"What you think this is? Disney?" He shoved her back a step. "You think we let white folk just toddle on through for a look-see? This ain't no tourist attraction. This is Dog crew territory. You want to walk through my landing, you need permission, you got that, bitch?" He pushed his face right into hers. "Or is that Dr. Bitch?"

Mary Jane's heart threatened to pound out of her chest but she held her ground. "Permission from whom?"

The leader smiled, and his left front tooth glittered gold in the dying light. "From me, Dr. Bitch." He ran a lingering glance down her body and said, "But you look tasty enough. Maybe we can work something out."

"I'm a doctor," Mary Jane said again. She hoped she sounded exasperated rather than terrified. "I'm here to visit a patient, not sight see. You can take me right to Jass' door if you like--"

"I'll tell you what I'd like. I'd like a physical." He stepped closer, until his breath wafted hot and alcoholic against her cheek. "You want to examine me, doc?"

He rubbed himself against her thigh. Disgust and fear clutched at her gut. The rest of the boys stood between her and the stairs heading up, their eyes like black holes. A thin, stained mattress lay to the side, conveniently placed for women willing to work off their tabs, Mary Jane knew. Panic skittered along her skin, but she pushed it back. Think, she commanded herself. Stay calm and think.

"Yeah, I'm feeling real sick," the kid breathed against her neck. "But I bet you can fix me up right quick." He closed a hand over her breast and Mary Jane stopped thinking. On a bright spurt of terror, she drove an elbow into his gut, stomped on his instep, and spun back toward the stairs she'd just come up.

Pain sent shockwaves through her head as he twisted a fist in her hair and yanked her off her feet. She landed on her butt with a cry and he jerked her to her knees. She came up clawing but went utterly still at the kiss of gun metal against her temple.

"That was very, very stupid, Dr. Bitch. Now are you going to play nice, or do I get rough?"

Humiliation rose in her throat but she shoved it back to speak the bitter truth.

"I belong to Tyrese Jones," she said. "Touch me and he'll kill you."

CHAPTER TWENTY-TWO

Ten minutes later, Mary Jane folded herself still trembling into a chair in Ty's immaculate kitchen. He leaned back against the stove and glowered at her, hands fisted into his own elbows, a taut rage simmering in his eyes.

"Do you have some kind of death wish, Mary Jane? Or are you just stupid?" He bit the words off, threw them at her like hand grenades, and the fear and shame still knotted in her stomach went up like dry tinder. Five years worth of rejection and heartbreak roared instantly into a cold, consuming fury, and God forgive her she welcomed it. Anything was better than the chronic ache of missing what she couldn't have.

"You're blaming me?" she said. "The people you work for give teenagers drugs and guns. They make them mini-gods and let them run their little kingdoms like Machiavelli as long as the money rolls in. You take that money and multiply it, which means more kids, more drugs, more guns. A cycle of endless, exponential cruelty. And there you are with that righteous outrage you've been nursing all these years, throwing fuel on the fire until a woman can get raped for walking up the stairs." She met his gaze without flinching. "How is that my fault?"

Something shifted in his dark eyes, something elusive and achingly familiar. Something of the Ty she used to know before anger twisted him into somebody she didn't recognize. Hope leapt inside her, twisted with the raging cold and had her leaning forward for a better look.

But then it was gone. His face was all smooth perfection again, every trace of genuine emotion carefully erased. No anger, no remorse, no...anything. She didn't know if she was relieved or dismayed.

"What were you trying to do, MJ?" he asked, a weariness in his voice that blunted the leading edge of her anger.

"I was looking for a girl," she said. "A patient of mine. Jass. Jessica Pendergass. You know her?"

"Yeah, I know Jass. Everybody knows Jass. Plenty of nice boys right here at home but she had to fall in love with a Yard crew and touch off World War Fucking Three in my backyard."

"She's pregnant."

He pinched the bridge of his nose and closed his eyes. "Yeah, so?"

"She's missed three appointments for prenatal care." She made sure her voice was crisp, without inflection. "The girl's lost enough. I don't want her to lose that baby, too."

He opened his eyes to stare at her. "You waltzed into the Wash to pay a *house call*?"

"Something like that."

"You could have called me, MJ."

"No," she said flatly. "I couldn't."

He went still. "You'd rather risk your life than ask for my help? You hate me that much?"

"I don't hate you, Ty." She sucked in a breath and prayed for courage. "I just don't love you anymore."

He went still, his gaze searching. "This is about that doctor from the clinic, isn't it?" he said finally. "The one who dragged Nixie Leighton-Brace all over the neighborhood?"

Kiss the Girl

"It's none of your business," Mary Jane said.

"Like hell it's not." He pushed away from the stove and advanced on her until nothing but the tiny kitchen table separated them. He spread his hand on it and leaned in. The heat of his want pulled at her dangerously. "You don't turn your heart off and on like a faucet, MJ. You're not that kind of girl. You loved me last month, you loved me last week, and you love me today. That makes it very much my business who you're dating."

"I'll rephrase," she said. "Maybe I do still love the man you used to be. But you're not him. Not anymore. You're somebody different, somebody angry and wounded and too dangerous to love." She forced herself to keep her eyes steady on his, her face clear and impassive. "I wasted years waiting for you to get over this, Ty. To come back to me. To yourself. But I'm done now. I'm moving on." She rose to her feet. "I've *moved* on."

She headed for the door on trembling knees. He let her pass but the heat from his body reached out and wrapped itself around her, made her want to weep with the dear familiarity of it.

"So that's it," he said. "You're done with me."

"No, there's one more thing." She put one hand on the door knob. She waited until she knew her eyes were clear and dry, then turned to face him. "Get Jass into the clinic, Ty. You had a hand in making this place what it is for these kids. You owe her that much. You owe them all."

She closed the door behind her with a brisk *snick*, and though she wanted nothing more than to drop to her knees and howl with anguish and loss, she forced herself to march down the hall without looking back.

Erik exchanged nods with the tabloid photographer parked outside the clinic--Nixie's version of an entourage--and hung up on Mary Jane's voice mail for the fifth time that afternoon. Nixie wasn't supposed to be on for another hour, but there she was as he pushed through the doors, her auburn hair glowing under the fluorescent lights of the receptionist's pen. She had a pencil in her teeth as she pecked two-fingered at a keyboard and wiggled to some Top Forty trash playing on a boom box in the corner.

Energy bounced off her in happy waves, reached out to Erik and pulled at him even through three inches of bullet-proof plexiglass. He touched the ring in his pocket and sighed. Why the hell did he keep running into Nixie when all he wanted to do was propose to Mary Jane?

She looked up and smiled at him, warm and open and radiantly friendly. *Friends*, he cautioned himself as she buzzed him into the pen. *Just friends*.

"Where'd you hide the body?" he asked, sitting on the counter by her elbow.

"What?"

"I know the only way you'd be working days is if you killed Wanda and hid the body. So? Where is she?"

"You think I could take out Wanda? I'm flattered." She paused and squinted at him. "I think."

"No body, then?"

"Nope. Just a routine shift swap. Wanda's nephew graduated from kindergarten this morning. We switched so she could be there."

"Ah." Erik checked his watch. "Is Mary Jane around? I haven't been able to reach her on her cell, and thought I'd swing by."

Nixie shook her head. "No. She actually took off on time today."

"Seriously?" He frowned. "That's not like her. She say where she was going?"

"Nope. She looked distracted so I didn't ask. I think she's tracking down Jass, though."

"Jass?"

Kiss the Girl

"The girlfriend of the kid who died. Homeboy ambulance arrival my first night?"

"Oh, her. Right. What about her?"

"She's been missing prenatal visits, and I'm a little concerned. I asked Mary Jane to check into it." Nixie nibbled at her pencil. Erik tried not to think about her mouth. "I wonder if I should ask around the neighborhood, too. Mary Jane is so busy. I hate putting one more thing on her plate."

"No!" Erik paused, modulated his voice into something less horrified. "No, that's not a good idea. Remember what happened last time you insisted on poking around the neighborhood?"

Nixie shrugged. "Nothing a shower couldn't cure."

Erik sighed. "You almost got mowed down by an El Camino, Nixie."

"Which apparently is way less dangerous than a whole truck. Or so you've informed me."

"And then you got flashed."

"By a kid about as threatening as a stoned hamster."

She made it sound so benign. What really stood out for him about that day was trying like hell not to kiss her. And failing miserably.

"Just let Mary Jane handle it, okay? You'll only cause a riot."

She turned up her nose and sniffed. "That's very unkind."

"And very true."

A new voice boomed, "Boy, what's your behind doing on my counter?"

Erik jumped guiltily to his feet. "Sorry, Wanda."

"My daddy always said counters was for glasses, not for asses."

"Amen," Nixie said sweetly, with a superior look for Erik. She reached under the desk and retrieved a slouchy, colorful bag that was probably hand-woven by Nigerian orphans. "We're all caught up here, Wanda. It's been slow. How was the graduation?"

Wanda plunked herself into the chair which creaked forlornly. "You'd think the kid was going off to war the way his mama threw down for this party. Girl, they had a live band. A live band! For a five year old!" She shook her head and the beads in her braids clicked merrily. "Still, pretty good music. My dogs are barking."

A vision of Wanda shaking her groove thing wandered into his subconscious and Erik blinked. Nixie smiled at him as if she could read his mind. He smoothed out his face and cleared his throat.

"Well, I guess I'm off," Nixie said. "See you Wanda."

"Later, girl."

Erik propped open the door to the waiting room and motioned Nixie through as he hung up on Mary Jane's voicemail again.

"You heading home?" he asked.

"Yep. I have a hot date with a large pizza and some mindless TV." She grinned at him. "You want in?"

He touched the ring in his pocket and eyed her speculatively. Maybe fate wouldn't let him propose to Mary Jane until he confessed to Nixie. It was worth a shot. At the very least, he could make sure she went straight home without a pit stop at the Wash to ask after Jass and get herself shot.

"Pizza, huh? I could eat."

Nixie eyed the couch beside Erik, then folded herself cross-legged on the floor across the coffee table. Not that she was chickening out. Sloan's advice had some merit--it was time to be bold. And she had been. She'd invited him over for dinner, hadn't she? She just couldn't figure out how to go from splitting a greasy pizza to seducing the guy.

Kiss the Girl

She picked the mushrooms off her own slice of pizza and plopped them onto Erik's plate. What had Sloan said? About keeping them fucked and keeping them fed? She'd start out with the feeding, she decided. Maybe later with the...rest of it.

She waited for him to dig in, but he stared at his plate, still and silent.

"Oh, sorry," she said, reaching hastily for her discarded fungi. "Do you not like mushrooms either?"

"I like mushrooms fine. It's not that. It's just...I have to tell you something."

Her heart skipped into an anxious patter. "What is it?"

"I've been trying to tell you for a while now, but I just couldn't find the right time or place."

"Oh my God." Nixie's mouth went dry and her mind leaped to the worst possible scenario. "You're married?"

"What? No, of course not."

"Thank God."

"I mean, not yet."

"You're *engaged*?"

"That's what I've been trying to tell you."

"You have? When? Before, during or after all the kissing?"

He rubbed both hands down his face. "You're angry."

She jumped to her feet and started pacing the length of the room. "Oh, no. Of *course* not. I'm *thrilled* for you." She crushed her napkin into a tight ball in her fist. "Who is she? This fiancée of yours?"

He paused, as if weighing his words. "Mary Jane."

Nixie stopped mid-stride. She knew laughter was inappropriate, but she was so relieved she couldn't stop the chuckle from bubbling up. "Mary Jane? Our Mary Jane?"

He nodded silently.

"I know you said..." She shook her head. "You are *not* engaged to Mary Jane."

"Not technically, no. But I will be."

She crossed back to the coffee table, dropped to the floor and gazed at him over the greasy cardboard pizza box. "Have you even asked her?"

His eyes slid away. "Not exactly. I needed to talk to you first."

A tiny trickle of joy welled up in her heart. "Really? Why?"

"Hell if I know," he said, his eyes snapping back to hers. Irritation danced in them like blue lightning. "All I know is every time I put the damn ring in my pocket and go looking for Mary Jane, I find you instead."

"And here I am again." Nixie's heart gamboled around her chest like a new puppy. "You're one lucky guy."

"I am?"

"Sure. Fate doesn't give two shits about most people. There are whole countries fate forgot about. Believe me, I've seen them. But you try to marry the wrong woman and fate intervenes. It must have big plans for you."

He stared at her. "I don't know which part of that to scoff at first."

"You don't believe in fate?"

"Do I look like Karl to you?"

She laughed. "Point taken. But doesn't it seem like life is pushing you in a certain direction?"

"Toward magazine covers and gossip columns and a complete lack of anything resembling a private life or personal freedom?"

She waved that away. "What, and you're so free right now?"

"Freer than the girl whose political advisor plots her every move for maximum press coverage."

Kiss the Girl

"Hey, at least I quit," said Nixie, stung. "You've spent your entire life doing the exact opposite of what your mother wants you to, right down to marrying the wrong girl. How does that make you any freer than I am?"

"You haven't quit." He shoved aside his pizza and stood.

"Excuse me?" She forced an even tone as temper snapped and simmered.

"You haven't quit," he said again. "You're doing exactly what you've always done."

She shot to her feet, rounded the coffee table and poked a finger into his shoulder. "That is *so* not true! Okay, so I'm throwing you a fundraiser but that hardly means I haven't--"

"Jesus, Nixie, take a look at yourself, will you?" He frowned at her and rubbed his shoulder. "You're taking James Harper to the gala next week so you can forgive him, your mother can slap his face and his father can call him rehabilitated. You're whoring your personal life for the cause of the week while your advisor calls a press conference, just like always. You haven't changed. You've had a change of venue, that's all."

She sucked in a sharp breath, hurt rolling over her in jagged waves. "That was a cheap shot. You think I *want* to make nice with James Harper?"

Erik shrugged. "I don't know what you want, Nixie. I thought you came here to take back your self-respect, but you sold that to James' daddy, didn't you?"

"It was for a good cause," she said slowly, an empty chill creeping into her chest. Had Sloan felt this way when she'd stolen James? "*Your* cause, wasn't it?"

He looked away and shoved both hands through that thick, wheat-colored hair. "I'm not judging you, Nixie, okay? You have every right to draw your own boundaries between what you owe the world and what you owe yourself. We don't agree on where they should be, that's all."

"I'm redrawing those lines every day," she said. "That's what this is all about, Erik. I've spent my life healing, sheltering, feeding. I need somebody to feed me, too. A like soul to shelter me. Heal me. Recognize me." She took a deep breath then met his eyes. "Somebody to love me like I love you."

CHAPTER TWENTY-THREE

Erik's chest went hollow, then filled with a rush of conflicting emotions. Chagrin, resignation, terror, and guilt, all glued together with a bolt of pure, shining joy. God forgive him, he was *joyful*. The rogue part of him that wanted her body apparently wanted her heart, too. Christ. He was a fool.

"Nixie." Her name came out more like a prayer than a reproach, and she reached out to put a hand on his wrist.

"I know you don't want this, Erik. At least you don't want to want it. But love isn't like that. We don't get to pick and choose. It happens, and maybe it comes with some trouble, but it's always a gift."

He slid his wrist away from her fingers. "You don't love me, Nixie."

She watched him, grave and unsmiling. "You don't know what I feel."

"You can't love me." He paced to the window and watched the Potomac snaking its lazy way to the Atlantic. "You've known me, what, three weeks?"

"So? I'm not asking you to marry me. I'm just asking you to consider me."

"For what?"

"For your lover." She crossed the thick carpet on silent feet. He could feel more than hear her coming, and when she wrapped her arms around him from behind and pressed her warm cheek to his back, he had to close his eyes against a staggering wave of want. "For your love."

He drew in a breath, but it was dry and harsh. He stepped away from her and said, "This isn't going to work, Nixie."

"Why not?"

He forced himself to sigh as if it were his patience rather than his willpower wearing thin. God, she was beautiful. Skin like alabaster, hair like flame, and a heart so brave and courageous he ached for her. She had to break it every damn day.

"Your heart is like one of your orphans right now, all right? Banged around, beat up and half drowned. You told me once you were trying to build yourself a home here, but this is no home. It's an orphanage. A safe place for you to hole up and heal for a while. We've loved having you with us, and it'll be a sad day for us when you go, but you can't stay here forever. And I'm not going with you when you leave."

She smiled at him, and it was pure come-on. "Who's asking you to?"

Erik stared at her, half baffled, half aroused as she slinked toward him, that heart-stopping mouth all curved up in promise. He tried to backpedal but found himself already against her ugly drapes. She stopped a bare breath from touching him, planted her fists in the drapes on either side of his waist and leaned in. The scent of lemons floated up to him and he actually felt weak.

"You'll only hurt yourself," he said, but when she turned her face up to his, the surge of desire blanked out the rest of his planned speech. She studied him, her mouth pursed into a quizzical rosebud that made him yearn to take a bite.

"I won't get hurt, Erik."

Kiss the Girl

"Yes, you will." He leaned his head back, tried to get some air that wasn't full of her so he could think again. "You deserve somebody who'll belong to you."

"You could belong to me." She pressed her mouth to the column of his throat. "We could belong to each other."

He swallowed convulsively. "You're America's goddamn princess, Nixie. You already belong to them."

Her mouth went still. "If you start in with the *Nixie Leighton-Brace* thing, I swear to God, I'm going to bite you."

Everything in him flashed hot for an incinerating second and he said, "But you *are* N--"

He broke off as her teeth, sharp and just short of savage, nipped into his neck under his ear. She laved the sting with her tongue and for one wild moment, he thought about saying it again.

"It won't work," he said instead. "I can't give you what you want."

Her delicate fingers slipped his top button free and widened the V of his shirt. Her mouth landed on his collar bone, warm and sweet, and a groan rose up in his throat.

"You don't know what I want," she said, but he was beyond listening. He was caught in the haze of a blinding desire.

"I think I have a pretty good idea," he said, but his hands had found the delicate indent of her waist. "I'm nobody's Prince Charming, Nixie. You have to understand that."

"I don't want Prince Charming. I want you." Another button slipped free and she pressed a kiss directly over his heart.

His hands blazed up her back and he dug his fingers fiercely into the tumble of her hair. Some dim corner of his mind registered that it was silky cool. It ought to burn, he thought.

"Do you?" he asked, turning her face up to his.

She nodded solemnly and pressed her next kiss to his lips, sweet and gentle. "Not forever," she said. "Just for now."

"For now." Lust kicked off its chains and he fell into her with something perilously close to desperation.

"Now, I can give you."

Nixie's entire body sang as his arms came around her like steel bands, and her knees sagged with a weird combination of desire and relief. Not relief that he'd finally given in, though that was part of it. Being bold wasn't the piece of cake Sloan made it look like. But relief that the choice had finally been made.

Erik turned her into the wall, pressed her back against it, and took her mouth with a glorious air of purpose. She nearly smiled under his single-minded carnal assault. She'd forced him--forced them both--to confront this thing between them, knowing that once Erik made a decision, it was full-steam-ahead, damn-the-torpedoes. She gloried in the risky thrill of it, the thread of uncertainty and desperation that ran just under the surface. Maybe they were doing the right thing, maybe they weren't, but she was done waiting around for somebody else to make the call. She wanted him, and by God, she was going to have him. For once in her life, she was being selfish and it felt wonderful.

She wound her arms around his neck and plastered herself against him, reveling in the hard press of his chest, the possessive cage of his thighs. His hands were big and fast, one cradling her jaw, the other cupping her behind and pulling her ever deeper into him.

Then he moved lower, dragged a moist kiss up the side of her throat and conscious thought evaporated. He was so fierce, this Viking doctor of hers--aggressive and gentle, demanding and generous. He'd tried so valiantly to resist her but he wasn't resisting anything now. Now he

Kiss the Girl

was feasting on her, and her bones went to hot wax under his greedy, streaking hands.

She wound her fists into the crisp cotton of his shirt, inhaled the scent of hot man at his collar while his tongue did something knee-weakening and wicked to her ear. He nudged her knees apart and put himself there. He pressed against her, pulsed hard and demanding against the epicenter of her want. She sucked in a breath as he added these sharp notes of frantic need to the languid symphony of desire he was writing on her body.

His hands moved down her arms to encircle her wrists, to slide them slowly above her head. He pinned them there against the wall in one large hand and a draft of cool air shivered across her belly. She arched, and her t-shirt drifted away like magic. She yanked at his shirt until the tails came loose from his khakis, allowing her hands free access to the smooth muscled planes of his back.

His skin was warm and just slightly rough under her palms. He felt like a man, she realized. Not Hollywood's shaved, waxed and professionally sculpted version, but a real, live man. The kind with muscles and hair and unapologetic appetites. A fierce and answering hunger rose up in her and she tugged at his shirt until he stopped kissing her long enough to tear it off. She smiled at him, at them both, the way they were pulling and panting and snatching.

"You feel like a man," she told him.

"Yeah?" He gave her that lightning strike smile of his and she felt it all the way to the bottom of her belly. "You were expecting something else?"

"I've lived in a strange world."

"I'll bet." He reached for her, one hand warm on the curve of her waist, the other sliding up her ribs to cup her breast. He dipped a finger under the lacy edge of her bra and skimmed her nipple. She arched into his touch on a gasp.

"I like this," he said, rubbing the silky fabric between his fingers, while his knuckle brushed her aching nipple.

"Me, too," she managed, while hot showers of sparks danced down her entire body.

His chuckle was low and wicked. "I meant the bra. I never pictured you as the lace and silk type."

She opened her eyes and found him leaning into her, his mouth a whisper from her own. She let her lips curve into a knowing smile. "It's a special occasion. I usually don't bother."

"With silk?"

"At all."

He groaned and dropped his forehead to the wall beside her ear. "I didn't need to know that. How am I supposed to look you in the eye at the clinic now?"

She laughed and hooked a finger into his belt. "The same way you did before."

He pushed himself into her hand and she nearly purred at the surge of heat and wonder. He was gloriously hard, and large enough to give her a frisson of purely female anticipation. "Like I was two seconds from snatching you up and doing you on whatever flat surface was handy?"

She laughed, absurdly flattered. "Wow. I really *have* been dating the wrong guys."

He went still, and she looked up to find his eyes gone serious. "I'm not the right guy, Nixie. I thought you understood that."

She flipped open his belt and said, "I disagree." She dealt with the button fly with one smooth yank, and in seconds had him gloriously nude. She cupped him in both hands, and he sucked in a ragged breath. "Plus, I don't think you're entirely convinced yourself."

He strained against her hands, but his fists stayed rigid by his sides. "I'm convinced," he said. "I'm going to marry Mary Jane."

Kiss the Girl

Nixie stopped and looked at him. His jaw was clenched, a muscle jumping in his cheek. Every line of his body was taut, whip-tight and quivering for release. His eyes were the molten blue of fire, and she smiled. He wasn't going to marry anybody but her.

"Do you really think that's going to keep you safe?" she whispered, pressing a chain of tiny kisses along his cheek. "Do you really think giving another woman your ring is going to stop you from wanting me? From wanting this?"

She slipped out of her jeans, left the rest of her clothes in a tangle on the floor and pressed herself against him.

Home. The word passed through her mind, dissolved and ran through her veins like a life force. *Home.* She shuddered and Erik's arms came around her, fierce and strong.

"Jesus, Nixie," he said, his voice like a cat's tongue-- rough and somehow comforting. "You're killing me." He ran his hands up and down her goose-pimpled back, a curiously tender gesture.

She laughed, a sudden overflowing of joy. "You sure talk a lot for a guy with a naked woman in his arms."

He rolled his hips into hers and zingy little shock waves ran straight to her lower belly. "You want me to stop?"

"If I do, I'm sure I can render you speechless."

"Really?" He tugged her to the carpet and laid her there like a feast. "Me first." He eyed her head to toe, and her nipples tightened in anticipation. "Yeah, good thinking," he said. "I'll start there."

Nixie's entire body flashed hot as he closed his lips over her nipple, plucked lightly with his teeth and then soothed with his warm tongue. When she could breathe again, she grabbed a fistful of his hair and said, "Do that again."

"At your service, princess." He rolled her damp nipple between his fingers, and turned his attention to her other breast. The exquisite tug of his mouth had her arching up off the carpet and sliding a knee around his thigh in silent demand. He chuckled, though it sounded a little ragged to her.

"So impatient," he said, but his hands weren't precisely steady as they dealt with the condom he pulled from the tangle of clothes on the floor. He settled into her like she'd been custom designed to cradle his weight and a feline hiss of pleasure escaped her. She rocked under him, her hands greedy and urgent on his back, on his behind, pressing him forward.

"God," he said, as he slid into her, inch by glorious inch. "I swear, I'll do this right next time. I'll take my time. I'll make it up to you. But right now--"

"Are you still talking?" she panted, squirming with the urgent need to move, to rock, to lift up and bring him *home* to her. "This is the part where you shut up and just do me, okay?"

"Right," he said, and smiled down at her as he buried himself inside her. A dazzling fullness blurred the edges of her consciousness, mixed with an insatiable, driving hunger. "You can render me speechless next time."

She narrowed her eyes at him, clenched her internal muscles and twisted under him. He hissed out a breath.

"Do...What..." He shook himself like a wet dog. "Do that again."

"You stuttered." She smiled at him. "Does that count as speechless, or should I do it again?"

He didn't open his eyes. "Again."

"Are you talking through your teeth?"

"*Nixie*."

"Oh, fine." She flexed again, pulling at him, urging him deeper. He was still moaning when she poked a finger into his ribs. "Listen, Erik, you weigh about five hundred pounds, okay? If you want me to drive, you're going to have to roll over."

His eyes opened a crack, something dominant and edgy gleaming in the blue depths as he smiled down at her. Her heart stuttered ahead on a jet of pure anticipation. "Who said anything about you driving?"

He surged forward, and she felt it all the way to the soles of her feet. He made love exactly the way she'd hoped he would, exactly the way she'd *known* he would. Hard-driving, straight-forward, goal-oriented. And God bless him, his goal appeared to be shattering her into a million shards of twinkling light.

She wrapped her legs around him and took him with her when she went.

CHAPTER TWENTY-FOUR

"I have to go," Erik said.

"Hmmm?"

He lifted his face from the glorious tangle he and Nixie had made of her enormous four-poster bed. "I have to go." He dropped his head back into the sheets and closed his eyes.

"Right." Two warm fingers traced the indent of his spine to the crack of his ass. "Go ahead."

"I'll give you twenty minutes to cut that out," he said, an impossible stirring of lust pinning him to the bed. "Then I'll make you pay."

She laughed, slapped him smartly on the butt. "I'd call you on that, but I think it might kill one or both of us."

He caught himself smiling, and his heart flipped over and clenched with dread. He wasn't supposed to be smiling and laughing with her. He wasn't supposed to be seriously considering testing the limits of his endurance by taking her one last time. He was supposed to be walking away, physically satisfied, emotionally untouched, all lusty demons put to rest.

How had things gone so wrong?

He'd had his share of lost weekends, but he'd never experienced anything like what he'd just discovered with Nixie. She made love like nobody he knew, laughing, talking, teasing and playing the whole time, even during

Kiss the Girl

the parts he traditionally preferred not to chat through. But it was impossible to wall Nixie out of his heart. She was so ridiculously dear.

He needed space, he told himself firmly. A little distance to clear all the Nixie-dust out of his head so he could think straight. Surely this absurd feeling of connection, of contentment and bone-deep satisfaction was simply the by-product of too much sex, not enough sleep, and finally satisfying a month-long itch. Of *course* he was going to look at the woman responsible for easing it with some fondness. What guy wouldn't?

He rolled his head to the side and opened one eye. She lay on her side next to him, her long, slim body bowed into an easy C, her hair a rosy tumble around that perfect face. Her mouth tipped into a do-me-baby smile, but her eyes were still and shining with a depth of love and passion that had his heart grinding helplessly, looking for the right gear.

"I really do have to go," he said, sitting up abruptly.

She sat up as well, crossing her knees in front of her and resting her chin on them. "Why? What are you afraid will happen if you stay?"

He found his feet and stalked across her bedroom, following the trail of clothes toward the door. "I'm not afraid of anything, Nixie." He kept his back to her as he pulled up his pants and jammed his sockless feet into his loafers.

"You shouldn't be. I mean, come on. The dangerous stuff is already out of the way, right? The embarrassing declaration of unrequited love. The ill-advised leap into bed. There's no use panicking *now*."

"I'm not panicking." Much. He glanced back, found her flushed and rumpled in the middle of that giant bed they'd used every inch of, a happily fallen angel. He looked away, but the image was already burned in his brain, on his heart.

"Then stay." She leaned forward, her want tugging at him like a deadly and hypnotic undertow. "What harm could possibly come from hanging around and enjoying a little post-coital snack?"

He paused in the act of stuffing his arm into a wrinkled sleeve to stare at her. "Post-coital *snack*?"

She smiled. "I'm hungry. Aren't you?"

He checked in with his stomach. It was tight and hot with the desire to stay and the knowledge that he couldn't. "No."

"A little cold pizza isn't going to voodoo you into loving me back, you know."

He flinched. "Nixie, come on."

"No, seriously. This needs to be said. We had sex, Erik. Really great, wall-banging, mattress-on-fire sex. Enhanced, for me at least, by the fact that I'm in love with you."

He concentrated on buttoning his shirt, shaking off the silken strands she was spinning between them each time she said those words.

"But I understand that you don't feel the same way. I understand that you have a lifetime of experience telling you not to take a chance on me." She rose, pulling the sheet off the bed and twisting it around her like a toga. She scooped up one of his socks and handed it to him. "I get that. I respect that, okay? You don't need to love me back for us to enjoy this...whatever it is. For however long it lasts."

He stuffed the sock into his pocket and looked at her. "No."

She frowned. "No what?"

"No I'm not going to take advantage of how you feel about me to bang you into next week whenever the spirit moves me, all right? You love me. I don't love you back. That means the two consenting adults rule doesn't apply. Anything I take from you is stolen, and I don't want that."

Kiss the Girl

The laughing invitation went out of her eyes. "I see."

Erik hated himself. Whoever said the truth would set you free was a lying bastard. The truth was carving Nixie up like a Christmas ham, and it wasn't doing him any favors either. But what was the alternative? Handing over his heart on a silver platter so she could carve that up instead?

"For Christ's sake, don't look like that!" he said. "I'm not trying to hurt your feelings. But I spent my whole life watching what happens when two people who aren't equally in love try to make it work. My dad spent twenty five years loving my mom first, best, and always. I can't remember a time when we weren't waiting around for her to return the favor. Waiting for her to come home, to be a wife, a mother. To realize her family was worth at least as much as that vast, faceless constituency of hers. But she served at the pleasure of the people, and as it turned out, the people were damn possessive." He gave her a very steady look. "Sound familiar?"

Her eyes skated away. "Erik, please--"

"I was a sophomore in college when my dad had a massive heart attack. It was the Tuesday before Thanksgiving. I came home for the holiday and found him on the kitchen floor, two days dead."

Her face froze, her mouth gathered into a pink bud of sympathy. "I'm so sorry," she said softly.

"I was, too. Still am. A man that good should never have died alone." Erik lifted his shoulders, the memory a burden he'd never learned to carry comfortably. "He loved my mother exactly the way he promised: better, worse, richer, poorer, sickness, health. She's the one who broke her word."

"I'm not your mother. I wouldn't do that to you."

"No. I'd do it to you."

"What?"

He stuffed his shirt tails into his pants and walked back to her. God, he was making a hash of this. But she had to understand. She had to get it, once and for all, that he wasn't going to love her back. It was just too damn dangerous.

He took her hands in his and forced himself to look down into the bewildered hurt swimming under the bravado in her eyes.

"Nixie, I don't doubt your...feelings for me. And I'm humbled. I don't deserve that kind of gift."

"Why not?" She gazed up at him and he could see where his whiskers had marked the delicate skin of her throat. A thrill of possession shot through him, primitive and hot and unwelcome. He clamped down on the unruly tangle of emotions and forced himself to move forward.

To finish it.

"Because while I don't doubt you love me, I don't love you back. And I'm never going to."

She jerked back as if slapped, and Erik missed her hands like he'd miss his own.

"But I do like you, Nixie. Genuinely. And that's why I refuse to do to you what my mother did to my father, to me. I refuse to string you along with well-timed scraps of affection, just enough to keep you paralyzed with the false hope that one of these days I'm going to come to my senses and give you something I'm just not capable of. It would be criminally selfish, and while I'm a lot of things I'm not proud of, I'm not cruel."

She eased away from him, pain and wonder in her eyes. "You could have fooled me."

"Nixie, please. I know what it feels like to be where you are. I'm trying to do the right thing."

She gave a bitter, incredulous laugh. "Bullshit. You're scared. But it's easier to be Mr. Nobility and reject me than to look inside your heart and figure out what you're so damn afraid of."

Kiss the Girl

She turned to grab at her robe with shaking hands. She stuffed herself into it and when she spun back to him, he braced himself for the blast of rage and betrayal he knew he deserved. But her face was cool, composed.

Erik took it like a punch to the gut. He'd been prepared for her anger, her hurt. Anything but this perfectly polite *absence* he'd demanded. It was as if she'd imagined wonderful things behind the closed door of his head but when she'd finally pried it open had found it barren and empty. Everything about her, from the resigned set of that mischievous mouth to the sudden distance in those verdant eyes, spoke not of love betrayed but of love disappointed.

"I can't give you what you need," he said, and the words sounded pathetic even to himself.

"Of course you can. You choose not to."

He spread his hands. "I choose not to, then."

She sucked in a sharp breath, and something stirred in those unreadable eyes, something hot and hurt and furious. "You're a coward," she said, her words cracking through the confused brew of emotions hanging in the air between them. "You don't deserve me."

"No. I don't."

She strode to the bedroom door, pulled it open and turned on him with utter composure. "I want you to leave."

He nodded, misery clutching at his throat. God damn, why did doing the right thing always have to kick the shit out of him? The scent of lemons, sweet and hot, reached out to him as he passed her, and he stopped. He opened his mouth but whatever he'd planned to say evaporated in the face of her icy, magnificent disdain.

It was too late, he realized. Too late to save himself. Because maybe he could resist the laughing, smart-mouthed woman who charmed every human being she'd ever met. The lonely seeker who thought she could build a home out of volunteer work and disgusting eggplant-based casseroles. The broken woman-child who desperately wanted a family she could count on with him as the cornerstone.

But throw in this woman with the endlessly generous heart he'd just shattered, holding herself together with nothing but blazing courage and haughty determination? She destroyed him, and forced him to admit the truth, if only to himself.

Somehow, without his permission or even his consciousness, he'd fallen madly in love with Nixie Leighton-Brace. And not just with the famous face, the million dollar smile and the infectious easy charm, either. No, he'd gone and fallen in love with the whole complicated package.

Not that it changed anything. He could take that speech he'd just given her and give it to himself, because no amount of love could convince him to do this. To launch heedlessly into an affair with a woman whose first priority had always been--would always be--her endlessly demanding public.

He closed his mouth and walked out of Nixie's bedroom.

He grabbed his jacket from her awful couch and let himself out of the apartment, but stopped in the doorway. He hated himself, but knew he had to ask. There was more at stake here than his heart.

"The gala?" he asked, and her lack of surprise sliced at him. She'd expected him to ask. Had been waiting for it.

"Don't worry," she said, her voice distant and blank. "I'm a pro. Pimping my personal life is SOP, right? The gala's in five days. I'll do it to keep your clinic alive--I owe Mary Jane that much--but that's the last thing I'll ever give you."

She turned her back on him.

Kiss the Girl

He let himself out of her apartment. Out of her life. It was for the best, he told himself. For both of them. But he stood in the hallway outside her door for a long time before he could force his feet to move toward the elevator. Toward what he knew he had to do next. The only thing that could keep him safe from Nixie and her dangerous claim on his heart.

Mary Jane was numb. The kind of all-over dullness that made her think of Novocain, infomercials and the first time she'd broken up with Ty. How many times had she done that now, anyway? It was hard to keep track. Half a dozen? A dozen? Most of her twenties, certainly.

But this time felt real. Permanent. She poked around the fresh hole in her heart but only found that queer missing sensation. Not pain precisely. But something deep and grievous and serious. Something that was going to hurt like hell when her system realized the loss it had sustained. But right now? Nothing. Just the dread of what was coming.

The doorbell rang and she looked at the clock. Nearly midnight. She should be curious, shouldn't she? What if it was Ty? But she knew it wasn't. She'd seen his face when she'd walked out of his life. He understood the crushing finality of this decision, too.

Still, doorbells at midnight couldn't be ignored. She rose from the couch, muted the Home and Garden channel and looked through the peephole. Then she opened the door and let Erik in.

"Hey, Mary Jane."

"You look like hell," she said.

"Thanks. You, too."

"Thanks."

He stuffed his hands into the pockets of rumpled khakis and said, "I'm sorry it's so late. I just had something I wanted to ask you and it couldn't wait."

"Okay." Still, no curiosity. How very strange. Mary Jane in Wonderland. "What is it?"

He drew his hand from his pocket and held out a black velvet box. Small, square. The kind rings came in. "Will you marry me?"

She frowned at the box. "Why?"

He lifted his shoulders with a kind of bewildered helplessness. "I love you. I always have. You're my best friend."

"Right." She nodded. "I love you, too. But as my best friend."

"I know. That's what I want. I want to marry a woman I know and trust, a woman I respect and can be easy with. I don't want the rest of it."

"The rest of it?" Mary Jane eyed the little box and prodded herself to feel something.

"You know." He shoved a hand through hair as rumpled as his pants. "True love, soul mates, matches made in heaven? It's a field of fucking landmines, and I don't want to walk through it anymore. I want this." He took her hand, pulled her into his arms and rested his chin on top of her head.

"Ah." Mary Jane closed her eyes and let the simple comfort of a friendly hug seep into her aching bones. Relief washed through her, a balm on all the bruises and scrapes of the day. He wanted what she wanted. Just a friend to come home to. Somebody to care about, but not deeply enough or passionately enough to hurt.

He pulled back and looked down at her very seriously. "Will you, Mary Jane?"

"Yeah. I will."

He handed her the box and she flipped it open. It was a lovely ring--simple, tasteful, with a whopper of a diamond front and center. Probably antique. She wondered who he'd picked it out for. Still, she slid it onto her own finger and handed the box back. He pushed it into

Kiss the Girl

his pocket and smiled at her. If he looked unutterably weary and sad at the same time, she didn't let it worry her too much. She probably looked the same way.

He leaned down a pressed a kiss to her cheek. "Thanks."

"What are friends for, huh?"

"Do you want to make an announcement, or should I?"

She twisted the ring around her finger. It was a little big, so she held it in place with her thumb. "Why don't we give it a few days to sink it?" she asked. "Just keep it to ourselves for a little while?"

He shrugged. "Okay. Let me know."

"I will."

They stood in awkward silence for a moment. It occurred to Mary Jane that she should ask him to stay. He was her fiancé, after all. But relief was the only light glowing in her soul when Erik finally said, "I should go."

"All right." She opened the door for him, and even though all she wanted to do was crawl into bed and sleep for two years, she reached out and touched his shoulder as he passed.

"Hey," she said. "Do you want to talk about it?"

He looked at her, his blue eyes still and flat. "About what?"

"About whatever happened that's making you look like this. All dead and defeated. Because it's not very you."

He mustered up a smile and it was almost painful to watch. Or it would be if she were capable of feeling pain at the moment. "Um, no. No, thanks."

"Okay. See you tomorrow?"

"Yeah. Okay."

She closed the door behind him and went back to the couch, but she didn't turn up the volume on the TV. She twisted the ring around and around her finger and waited for it to start feeling like it belonged there.

    Waited to start feeling anything.

CHAPTER TWENTY-FIVE

Five days later, Nixie slipped her gala dress over her head and hauled up the zipper as far as she could. Crap. Unless she was willing to dislocate a shoulder, she was going to need help with the last two inches between her shoulder blades. She glanced toward the Senator's apartment before she could stop herself.

No. *He* wasn't there, of course. The separation of the private and the professional was the cornerstone of Erik's own personal constitution, mandating a gala guest list that conspicuously didn't include the Senator. So it wasn't like she'd risk running into him if she hopped over to his mother's for a little assistance dressing.

But his rejection had detonated in Nixie's heart like a dirty bomb, and the kill zone was still smoking. She was too raw to smile her way through the kind of sharp-eyed, well-meaning inquisition the Senator would surely deliver.

She twisted in the mirror, checking her rear view with a dispassionate eye. Bronze silk flowed from her shoulder blades to her ankles, glowed in the dying light of the day. The jeweled bandeau bodice caught the golden light and shattered it into jagged bits of color that played on her beige walls. She stepped away from the mirror and the tiered hemlines swirled from her knees to her strappy bronze sandals, whispering the expensive nonsense that had just a week ago sent a thrill of girlie vanity straight through her. She'd loved it. More than that, she'd loved that *Erik* would love it.

Now she couldn't work up even a glimmer of her former pleasure. The dress was haute enough to please the fashionistas who kept detailed track of her professional wardrobe but still reasonably comfortable to sit in. That was going to have to be enough, because even a cautious stirring of the embers that used to be her heart sent a wave of fresh, sparkling hurt dancing into the air.

She closed her eyes, pressed a thumb to the wrinkle between her brows and blew out a trembling breath. God, she'd been such a fool. All this time she thought that maybe her job was the problem. Maybe if she learned how to be something other than *Nixie Leighton-Brace*-- great, now he had her doing it; speaking her own name in italics--somebody would take a chance on the woman inside. Maybe some unlucky fool would fall in love with her. She herself managed to fall in love against steep odds all the time. Surely it wasn't a stretch to imagine that somebody else might, too. Somebody driven, talented, intense. Somebody intelligent, accomplished, dedicated. Somebody like Erik.

It had never occurred to her that, no matter which way she went, she was screwed. She could give up her name, her job, her place on the world stage, or she could use every gift she had in service of his dream. It didn't matter. He could still look at the heart she'd offered up and simply choose not to love her back.

The doorbell pealed, a solemn *bong*. James Harper. He'd insisted on picking her, and she'd agreed. It was going to be a long evening in his toxic company, but she'd made a bargain. At this point, she had nothing left to lose by keeping up her end of it. Let the press get a few good shots of them walking the red carpet together and maybe he'd be satisfied enough to leave early. If his daddy let him.

Kiss the Girl

She put on her most professional smile and opened the door.

"Karl!" She stood back, let him march into the apartment. "Wow. It always surprises me how good you look in a tux."

He pulled a hanky from his pocket and mopped at his glistening scalp. "I hate dressing up. Such a waste of money and resources."

"I know." In spite of everything unresolved between them, she smiled. He was just so...dependable. Maybe they didn't always agree but at least he never surprised her. "A necessary evil."

He looked at the hanky with disgust. "I don't know what the hell the hotel's washing these with, but it's like wiping my head with sandpaper."

Nixie rubbed a corner between her fingers. "Somebody starched the crap out of that."

"God, I miss Africa. Don't you?"

Nixie turned around, presented him with her back. "Can you get this zipper for me?" she asked. "I can't reach."

He yanked it up and Nixie gave an alarmed squeak. "Easy, Karl. This is a Badgley Mischka. And I have to give it back in the morning."

He frowned at her bare shoulders. "That's a lot of skin, Nixie. Is it going to stay up?"

Nixie crossed her arms over her chest. "Is that a crack at my figure?"

"What?" He colored slightly. "No. God. I'm just saying, it's kind of--"

"Hot?"

His flush deepened. "You didn't have to do this, you know. Taking Harper to the gala tonight was a good move, but nobody expects you to, um..." He waved a hand up and down toward her dress.

"To out-hot Sloan?"

Karl looked uncomfortable. "Yeah."

"Don't worry. I know my limits. Out-hotting Sloan isn't on the agenda."

She moved toward the mirror at the far end of the living room, leaned into the enormous mirror and slicked her mouth a deep bronze. She dropped the lipstick into her useless confection of a purse and turned to face him.

"Well? Will I do?"

He frowned at her. "As long as your dress stays up. I am *not* in the mood to smooth over a wardrobe malfunction."

She sighed. Had she really been expecting a compliment?

"So, we have a few minutes." She perched on the edge of the wretched sofa. She was going to burn it one of these days. "I know you too well to think you're just here to say hi. What's on your mind, Karl?"

He didn't sit, just watched her with those sharp pale eyes. "You know what's on my mind. Bumani."

She smoothed the silk over her knees while what was left of her heart twisted in her chest. "I'm not going to Bumani."

"Why not, Nixie? Jesus!" He flapped his arms and paced the length of the room. "I don't understand what's gotten into you! Is this still about that damn doctor?"

"This has nothing to do with Erik." She stood and clasped her hands calmly in front of her, as if speaking his name didn't make her stomach ache with regret and loss. She watched Karl stalk through the room, raking his hands through his hair until what little he had stood out like a frazzled halo. "This is purely my decision."

He shot her a narrow look. "Bullshit. Don't stand there with that martyred face and lie to me. I know he dropped you. Everybody knows."

"Lovely."

Kiss the Girl

Karl glared. "Nixie, come on. I don't begrudge you the detour, okay? You're young. You deserve a wild hair every now and then. But you had your fling and now it's over. The guy doesn't want you."

Nixie flinched and he relented with a great, gusty sigh.

"Listen, honey, I know you're hurting." He moved toward her, took her cold hands in his big warm paws. "For what it's worth, he doesn't deserve you. Never did, the asshole."

Tears came into her eyes in a wild rush and for a moment, she couldn't speak. A choked noise escaped her--a laugh? A sob?--and she shook her head. She let herself bask in the solid press of the hands that had picked her up from every fall she'd ever taken. And God knew she'd taken a doozy this time.

"Karl?"

"Yeah?"

"I've had a very bad week."

His laugh was a familiar rumble that eased the aching vacuum in her chest a degree or two. "I know, kid. What do you say we get out of here?"

"What? And stand up my date?"

He patted his chest pocket. "I have three first-class tickets to Bumani right here that say Harper can go stag tonight."

Nixie pulled her hands back, a sudden chill sweeping over her exposed skin. "You want me to go to Bumani tonight?"

"Of course." Impatience warred with warmth in Karl's eyes. "Where else? The doctor screwed you. Why don't we screw him right back? We'll go help some folks who'll appreciate you instead."

"You'd screw a bunch of kids to avenge my train wreck of a love life?"

Karl put both hands on her shoulders, and they bowed under the weight of the responsibility he placed there. "This isn't about your love life. It's about doing the right thing."

"The right thing."

"Listen to me, Nixie. What you're feeling right now? This whole dramatic life's-lost-all-meaning heart-break crap? It isn't real. Love is bullshit. Temporary at best." He bent until she had to meet his gaze. "You want to know what's real? Paying your debts. Recognizing what you've been given and giving back accordingly. People are dying--literally *dying*--because you're chasing a fairy tale. It's time to be the woman you were meant to be, the woman I raised you to be. And that means putting away these childish dreams and getting on the damn plane."

Nixie's eyes slid away from his while her stomach twisted inside her. "And if I don't?" she whispered.

He straightened, let his hands drop away from her shoulders. "Then you're nobody I care to know."

A panicked weightlessness shot through her limbs and for once she was glad for the couch. She sank onto the arm and tried to give him an ironic smile. "What does that mean, exactly? Nobody you'd care to know. Are we talking about a shunning? Disownment? Would I be dead to you, or would all be forgiven if I start behaving?"

He shook his shaggy head slowly, sorrowfully. "Don't joke about this, Nixie. I was there when you were born. When you were baptized. Phoenix Kasmira isn't just a name. It's a responsibility."

"To rise up from the ashes," she murmured, "and command peace." How many times had she heard that growing up? Hundreds? Thousands?

"A responsibility," he said again, "that I raised you to fulfill. I won't stand by and watch you deliberately sentence innocent people to poverty, disease and death just so you can chase rainbows. I love you, but I have to do what's right. I want to do it with you just like we always have, but if you refuse, I *will* replace you."

Nixie's heart fluttered like a wounded bird inside her chest. What was it with her and men with extreme ideas about the personal and professional? Maybe Erik was a little insane about keeping the two separate, but for Karl the distinction didn't even exist. The professional *was* his personal. Which meant, she realized now with another twist of her battered heart, that if Nixie wouldn't be his star, if she refused to be the face of his campaign to save the world, there was no room for her in his life. At all.

"I can't believe this, Karl. You've been my mentor, my guide, my father. You taught me what it means to be good. To *do* good."

"Then listen to me." He snatched up her hands in his and they were hot, urgent. "Come to Bumani."

She stared at him for an endless moment, her pulse bumping in confused circles. Then the intercom buzzed, shattering the stillness. Nixie jumped as if she'd been stung.

"That'll be James," she said slowly. "I have to go."

"Of course," Karl said, giving her hands one last squeeze before dropping them. "But we'll talk after the gala. You have a decision to make, Phoenix."

"I know." She gathered up her purse and keys with great care, as if the rapidly fraying fabric of her life might give at any moment. "I know I do."

"Oh dear God, is that a red carpet?" Mary Jane pasted herself to the tinted glass of the limo, dread clawing at her throat. "Is that *paparazzi*?"

Erik leaned past her, glanced out the window and said, "Yes and no."

"What does that mean, yes and no?" Mary Jane's chest felt tight, like she wasn't getting enough oxygen. "Either it is or it isn't."

"Yes, it's a red carpet. No, it's not paparazzi. That's a well-ordered, hand-picked press corps, led by Missy Jensen from Channel Four. Nixie asked her to do red carpet interviews, Oscar-style."

"Jesus." Mary Jane twisted the engagement ring around her finger. She watched a junior Senator from Texas exit a limo and stroll up the red carpet. The cameras went nuts and reporters shoved microphones into his face, into his date's face. They smiled shiny, professional smiles and hit their marks like Mr. and Mrs. America. Mary Jane's stomach tightened alarmingly. "I can't do this."

Erik gave her knee a distracted pat as the limo crept forward, easing them closer and closer to Mary Jane's personal vision of hell. "Sure you can."

"No, I can't. This is *not* what I signed up for. I'm a doctor, not a movie star." She yanked at the hem of the black cocktail dress that had been elegant and mysterious last week. Now, thanks to a stress-related doughnut habit, it hugged and snugged and blabbed everything. She checked one last time for powdered sugar on her skirt.

"You look fine."

"You know I hate crowds." She hauled at the dangerous V neckline as if she could make it swallow a few more inches of cleavage by sheer force of will.

They stopped again. Only two limos left to disgorge their passengers at the red carpet, then it would be Mary Jane's turn. Her breath came faster and shallower until black spots began to dance before her eyes. She grabbed Erik by the lapels of his tux and shook him with the strength of the truly terrified.

"What am I supposed to *do*?" she wailed. "Where do I walk? What do I do with my hands? What do I say?"

He gazed at her with wide, startled eyes, finally recognizing her as a woman in crisis. About goddamn time, she thought.

Kiss the Girl

"Jesus," he said, "you're hyperventilating."

He shoved her head toward her knees but she clawed at his hand. "Are you nuts? I can't bend over in this thing! It took two Spanx just to get the zipper up."

Erik paused. "I have no idea what that means, but you probably shouldn't mention it on TV."

"Spanx, Erik. You know, Gwyneth Paltrow's girdle of choice? Everybody wears them, even stick-skinny Missy Jensen, probably." She turned her attention to the window again, the red carpet exerting the same sick fascination over her as bloody car accidents exerted over people who hadn't seen enough of that sort of thing in med school.

She watched Nixie step out of the limo in front of them, and a queer shock of recognition but not-recognition shot through her.

"Whoa, except her. No girdle on her," she said, letting her breath whistle out through her teeth. "Hello, Hollywood Nixie. That's a little stunning, isn't it? When you're used to Reception Desk Nixie, I mean."

"She's not a Barbie, Mary Jane."

She ignored him and watched as Nixie's jeweled bodice--filled with exactly the correct amount of cleavage, Mary Jane noted with envy--shattered the flashbulbs and left them hanging in the air around her like diamond dust. "No Spanx on this girl. There can't be. It would be a crime to put anything between that material and your skin." She sighed. "It must be like wearing clouds."

She glanced at Erik but he gazed determinedly at his knees, and Mary Jane's brows inched up her forehead. No straight man in her acquaintance would ignore the sight of Nixie Leighton-Brace dressed up like the Greek goddess of sunsets and precious jewels, striding up the red carpet on those thoroughbred legs. Interesting.

"That guy she's with seems to like it, anyway. God, he's practically petting her."

"She's letting Harper *pet* her?" Erik sat up and looked out the window.

She smiled at the look of stunned wonderment on his face as he got a load of Nixie in all her glory. The girl had spent a lot of time these past weeks holding back, dressing down, *fitting in*. But Nixie wasn't holding back jack tonight. No, tonight she'd unleashed that whatever-it-was Nixie had, that full-tilt charisma and that, together with her perfect bones and her ability to wear couture like it was yesterday's pajamas, had the paparazzi on its knees before her, worshipping their own personal deity. Tonight, Nixie was burning the house down and knocking the oh-so-practical Erik on his ass in the process. Mary Jane was just evil enough to enjoy that.

"Nah," she said. "But giving you crap always takes my mind off my worries, and since I can't put my head between my knees..."

"Nice."

"Hey, I'm *this close* to a nervous breakdown and this is working for me."

"I hope so because we're up."

"Oh, dear God."

He smiled, but it was small and grim. "Let's go, doctor."

She crossed herself, said as much of the Hail Mary as she could remember and shoved open the door.

CHAPTER TWENTY-SIX

Sloan stood on the second story balcony outside the ballroom and watched Nixie stride up the red carpet, power and elegance in every step. Sloan's heart swelled with pride she knew she didn't deserve. She hadn't taught Nixie any of this, except maybe how to walk in heels. The rest--the composure, the serenity, the perfect knowledge of her own worth--Nixie had earned all by herself in the years when Sloan was too busy, too afraid to be a mother. Nixie had brought herself up and it showed.

God damn, her little girl had done a good job.

Nixie moved though the crowd, and every face followed her like flowers tracking the sun through the sky. She was so much like her father that Sloan had to close her eyes against an unruly rush of bittersweet love. She didn't spare a glance for the man she'd screwed for two pathetic weeks, the one now basking in Nixie's afterglow like some kind of parasite.

"Nixie's shaky tonight," Karl said. Sloan turned to find him in the darkness of the balcony behind her, swiping at his scalp with a hanky. She gave a light laugh, though she had to reach a little to pull it off. She didn't feel light tonight.

"She doesn't look shaky. She looks...powerful." Sloan narrowed her eyes and studied her daughter more closely. "Yes. Powerful and pissed." She cut her eyes to

Karl, who hovered just behind her shoulder. Always in the wings, always pulling strings. "You two had words?"

"She thinks she's in love with the damn doctor." He gazed down at Nixie who looked perfectly at home in the mayhem of strobing flashbulbs.

A waiter passed by the French doors separating them from the ballroom crowd and Karl took a couple glasses of champagne from his tray. He offered one to Sloan, who took it and helped herself to a healthy swallow. It went down like money, rich and ripe with possibility. He ignored his own glass, she noticed. Just like always.

Sloan followed his gaze to the red carpet, to Nixie's handsome Viking doctor handing a stiff blonde out of a limo.

"What if she is in love?" Sloan asked.

Karl paced the tiny balcony like a caged animal, his bulk and his energy pushing Sloan up against the railing. "Christ, Sloan, I'm sure she is. Nixie loves everybody. That's what she does. It's who she is. But he's not in love with her, okay?"

"He's not?"

"No. And he didn't deliver the news with any kind of finesse, either. Kid took a hard hit."

Sloan shook her head wonderingly. "How on earth do you find these things out?"

Karl ignored this. "She's reeling a little still. I don't trust her to follow through on the bargain we made with Senator Harper."

"To bring the prodigal son back into the fold?"

"Right." He stopped pacing and cut her a look. "You're going to have to help her, Sloan."

A wave of weariness washed over her. The last time Karl had said those words, she'd had to fuck her daughter's boyfriend across Europe. God she was tired. But she upended her glass of champagne and set it on the wide marble balustrade with a practical click. Time to shoulder her responsibilities. Again. "What do you want me to do?"

"Nothing like last time."

"Thank God for small favors." Sloan felt her mouth curve, but wouldn't have called it a smile.

"Senator Harper packed this gala with a lot of people who'll write big, fat checks on his say-so. He'll expect his money's worth from Nixie. And if she balks--" Karl spread his hands and smiled, his teeth very white in his beard.

"--I'll be there with the cattle prod, is that it?" Sloan reached for Karl's untouched glass of champagne, took a healthy slug. "And what about Bumani, Karl? Or the disaster after that? The next war? The next crisis? How long are we going to keep zapping her back into a place she doesn't want to be?"

"I'm dealing with that, Sloan. We had a good talk tonight, Nixie and I. I think she'll be okay. She's just--"

"Shaky. You said."

"Yeah. Shaky. So help her out tonight, all right? Keep her focused."

Sloan drained her glass. "Yes, all right," she said, but it chafed in a novel, unexpected way. Like a scratchy sweater or pants that were just a little too tight. Okay when you put them on, but irritating within the hour and unbearable by day's end.

Lucky for her, this wouldn't be a full day's work.

What was one more hour out of her life?

Erik waded into the sea of photographers and reporters, literally cutting a path for Mary Jane with his body. He took a certain pleasure in the violence of it, in using his bulk as a weapon against this writhing pack of cameras and microphones and blazing lights that had taken so much from him.

He looked up to get his bearings. He hadn't meant to look for Nixie, but the sight of her stopped him like a bullet. She was there, just there on the rise of the marble steps leading into the hotel, bathed in the incandescent glow of the spotlight.

Erik blinked, but the vision of her in that dress--oh dear God, that *dress*--was burned forever in his mind's eye. She was like a flame, long and slim and deadly hot from her tousled mass of coppery curls right down to her polished toenails. And yeah, he *had* noticed her toenails lacquered the same amazing sunset-on-speed color as her dress. He'd noticed everything, from the look of utter indifference on her face as her gaze skimmed over him without a hint of acknowledgement to the hand low and possessive on the curve of Nixie's hip. James Harper's hand.

Erik stood there, frozen, his gut clutched with rage until somebody squeaked behind him and jammed a fist into his lower back. He came back to himself with a startled blink. Oh lord. Mary Jane. He'd forgotten her. Again.

"Sorry," he said. "Come on. Let's get you inside."

Nixie had spent her entire life on red carpets and in war zones, and to her way of thinking, they weren't all that different. Both were crowded, hostile places full of shouting, confusion, and strangers with a violent desire for something. About the only way she could tell which was which anymore was the wardrobe.

She walked through the chaos as she'd been taught, smiling and serene, accessible yet apart. The queer weightlessness Karl's ultimatum had put in her middle helped. It kept her oddly untouched by the storm around her, like somebody had inflated a balloon around her heart. She ought to be feeling more than she was, but it was all

Kiss the Girl

trapped inside that straining bubble buried deep in her chest.

Just as well, she thought, moving through the jostling crowd. She didn't care to fully experience tonight anyhow.

James' hand lay heavily around her hip, low and possessive and uncomfortably hot through the thin material of her dress. He kept her close, intimately so, their bodies canted together, their smiles bright for the cameras. But even numb as she was, Nixie picked up the darker note swirling under his camera-ready smile. Resentment. Dislike. Maybe even malevolence. Was it for her? she wondered idly. His father? Himself?

She hit the top of the marble steps and struck the expected pose. Let James snuggle the curve of her hip into the line of his while the cameras snapped and whirred. All the while, his anger, his disdain lapped at her like an encroaching tide.

She ran her gaze over the crowd without curiosity, fixed on a point somewhere behind the paparazzi and their shouting, on something beyond the violence of their want.

And found Erik.

He helped Mary Jane, pale and trembling visibly, out of a limo and into the crook of his arm, but his eyes were on her. The void at her center gave a strange, searching quiver, but Nixie forced her gaze to skim over him, past him. She didn't want to see the judgment in his face. She knew exactly what he thought of her, of James, of this choice she'd made to allow the press to feed on her personal life like this.

She'd made a bargain. Now she'd live up to it. Those kids needed help, and Erik and his sacred principles weren't getting the job done. But she could. And she would. With his approval or without it.

She turned to her date with a brilliant smile. "Are you ready to go in?"

James returned her smile with something razor sharp that probably photographed well but burned like ice against her bare skin. "By all means," he said.

She took his offered arm but it felt like a snake under her hand--cool, muscular, faintly sinister. They walked slowly into the foyer of the hotel, mounted the curved staircase like a couple of well-trained stage actors and stepped into the ballroom.

Light and heat, expensive perfume and soaring ceilings, deep red wine inside flashing crystal glasses--it all came at Nixie in a fierce, familiar rush. She tossed herself into it without hesitation and the crowd swallowed them whole. The instant it closed behind them James shook his sleeve free of Nixie's touch.

"Are we done here, then?" she asked. Where was the relief? she wondered. Shouldn't she be relieved to be finished with him so soon?

"You wish." He snatched a glass of champagne from a passing waiter and knocked it back with one long swallow. "Christ, *I* wish. But no. Daddy dearest won't be satisfied with a quick photo shoot. Unless I'm well and truly rehabilitated, I'm of no use to a future president." He glanced at the crowd swirling around them, the fanciful swish of ball gowns against the more sober hush of tuxedos. The prominent personalities and powers who wore them. "Judging from the faces I'm seeing, that rehab is costing my father a bundle." He twisted his lips into a smirk. "So no, we're not done here. Not by a long shot."

He grabbed her hand again and shot purposefully through the crowd, towing her behind him.

Erik threw an arm around Mary Jane's shoulders and shepherded her through the swarm of reporters. Her entire body vibrated under his touch, as if she were some kind of human tuning fork in the key of terror. And it didn't ease up when he'd led her up the marble stairs and joined the

Kiss the Girl

crowd of DC luminaries, flitting around the soaring ballroom like rare birds. If anything it got worse.

"Mary Jane?" He bent for a better look at her white, pinched face. "Are you all right?"

She didn't answer. She simply stared ahead, her eyes wide, fixed and dangerously dilated. He didn't think she was even breathing.

"Mary Jane?" He followed her gaze and said, "Ah."

Tyrese Jones stood a dozen feet away, looking like he'd sprung off the pages of GQ or something. Erik didn't know what drug lords paid their accountants these days, but it must be some serious bank because the guy was turned out in what looked like custom tailored Armani. Erik felt a snarl rising to the surface but he squashed it. Maybe things were rocky between him and Nixie right now, but she'd worked hard for this night. He wouldn't be the one to smear the frosting with an on-camera fist fight.

"What's he doing here?" Mary Jane whispered, her lips barely moving.

"Nixie must've asked him."

"Why?" It was one word, but so full of anguish that Erik tightened his arm around her shoulders and pulled her into him, as if protecting her from a physical threat.

"She asked a handful of people from the neighborhood to speak tonight. First person testimonials for the clinic or something. See, there's Mama Mel. And Otto Lyndale--you know, with the huge dog?"

"Yeah." Her voice was faint, and Erik didn't know whether she'd even heard him. She was still staring at Tyrese who was, God help them, staring back at her.

"Hey, look," Erik said, turning her away from the guy. "There's Daryl Johnson."

Mary Jane blinked and focused. "Oh my God, the flasher?"

"Yeah, Nixie has a thing for him."

A ghost of the old Mary Jane surfaced in the smile that tried to curve her mouth. "What kind of thing?"

"Did I never tell you the story of Nixie and the horrible, terrible, no-good, very bad day? God, where to start."

He drew her hand through his arm and started to stroll casually away from Tyrese Jones. "Well, it was the day after you'd been snatched by the Dog crew and Nixie, being Nixie, was worried about you--"

He broke off when Nixie's advisor materialized in front of them, looking for all the world like a trained bear wearing a tux. His scalp glistened with perspiration but he didn't look like he'd been rushing anywhere. He just stood there, a rock in the middle of a stream, ball gowns flowing past him like water. He was everything calm and stoic, except for his eyes. They burned like black flame and Erik knew he wasn't after casual conversation.

"Dr. Larsen," Karl said. "I'm glad I found you. Do you have a minute? There's something I'd like to discuss with you."

Erik glanced down at Mary Jane, who stood in the lee of his arm like a doll. Pretty, blonde, made of plastic. "Sure," he said. "Maybe somewhere quieter?"

"Certainly."

Karl threaded a path through the crowd with an ease Erik had to admire. The man didn't fight for a single step. He simply watched the flow, analyzed it and joined at a precisely chosen spot. Within seconds, they'd landed outside a pair of secluded French doors. Karl opened them with a brisk economy of motion and suddenly, they were all standing in the cool night air, smooth slate stones under their feet, the DC skyline hanging at their backs.

Karl pulled the doors shut behind him, enclosing the three of them on a small balcony, a little oasis of private calm. Mary Jane wilted in visible relief but Erik felt strangely bereft. The ballroom pulsed heat and energy a

Kiss the Girl

few feet away, but he felt cut off. Isolated. Wrong, somehow.

"What can I do for you, Karl?" he asked, stepping away from the railing. He didn't care how absurd it was, he wasn't facing this guy with a two-story drop at his back.

"It's Nixie," he said. "I'm concerned--"

He broke off when the door jerked open and Tyrese Jones stepped onto the balcony.

"I'm sorry," Karl said. "We were hoping to speak privately for a moment. Do you mind?"

Tyrese ignored him, his gazed fixed on Mary Jane. His face matched his tux perfectly, Erik saw with disgust. Exquisitely designed, expertly constructed, no expense spared on materials. But as with Karl, the eyes didn't fit. He stood there like the king of elegant cool but his eyes burned with an anguish Erik didn't want to recognize. It was too close to the emotion that filled Erik's own heart.

But he wasn't in the mood to examine his own heart. He focused on Tyrese instead, and realized with a shock that anguish wasn't all he saw in the other man's eyes.

It was fear, too. A deep, horrible, naked fear, as if he'd found the one woman he needed and had screwed it up beyond redemption. As if he'd have to spend the rest of his life knowing he'd held a gift in his hands and through his own ignorance, fear and stupidity had fucked it all up.

A vicious tremor of recognition shot through Erik, but he shoved it aside. He'd deal with that later. Right now, he had to protect the woman wearing his grandmother's ring.

"Mary Jane," Tyrese said, and put out a hand.

She shook her head and moved backward until she was pressed against the railing. "Oh no," she said, hugging her elbows. "You are *not* allowed to do this. Not here. Not now. Not *ever*. This is *over*." A lock of silvery hair dropped out of the elegant knot at her crown and floated against her cheek.

Erik stepped forward, put a protective hand on Mary Jane's arm. "This isn't the time or place, Tyrese," he said. "Why don't you--"

"Why don't you stay the fuck out of this, Dr. Larsen?" Tyrese said, his tone utterly polite. "This is between me and Mary Jane."

Mary Jane vibrated against Erik's arm, whether from fury or hurt or nerves he couldn't tell. But she glanced up at him and patted the hand on her arm. "It's okay," she said. "I'll handle it." Erik nodded and stepped aside. But not so far that he couldn't knock the crap out of Tyrese if he laid a finger on her.

Mary Jane turned exhausted blue eyes on Tyrese and said, "We're over, Ty. I'm done with all this...drama, okay? So spare me one last scene. I told you before, I've moved on."

"What, with him?" Tyrese snarled the words with elegant disgust and white-hot fury. "You think you're going to be happy with some white-bread doctor? He doesn't know you. He doesn't love you. Not like I do."

"Yeah, that's exactly the point." She laughed, and it was like listening to glass break. "Because you know what your love is like? It's like being stuck in a waiting room for the rest of my life. Waiting for the police to show up at my door telling me you're finally dead. Waiting for you to wake up one day and by some miracle actually love me more than your job, your neighborhood. More than that fucking *anger* you've been cherishing all these years. Waiting for a ring that'll never come, and a life together that'll never start."

She stepped back into Erik's side and he automatically wrapped an arm around her and pulled her close. "Erik loves me like you never did, and that's exactly what I want," she said.

Kiss the Girl

"And you think *I'm* being dramatic." Tyrese shook his head and eased forward, nearly close enough to touch her. Erik's free hand fisted. "Come on, Mary Jane. I just want to talk to you."

"He asked me to marry him," she said softly. "I said yes."

Tyrese dropped back as if he'd taken a blow to the chest, his face going slack with surprise and disbelief. "Like hell you did."

She silently held out her left hand. Erik's ring twinkled there, catching every drop of moonlight and tossing it back into the air with a smug glow.

"Well now, this is an interesting development." Karl spoke from the shadows where he'd melted. Erik started. He'd forgotten the guy was even there. "Is it true?"

Erik's stomach dropped with a sudden burst of insight. This was wrong. Mary Jane wasn't supposed to have his ring. Nobody was supposed to have his ring but Nixie.

Holy Christ, what a mess. He was *in love* with Nixie. Maybe unwillingly. Maybe unwisely. But completely, madly, and irrevocably in love. Had he really thought getting engaged to somebody else could change that?

Well, no. He'd been hoping, but that was different than believing. He glanced at Mary Jane, her ring hand outstretched and defiant, her eyes full of pain and bravado, and knew she didn't really believe it either. Why else would she have insisted on keeping the whole thing quiet? That wasn't normal, was it? Getting engaged and not telling anybody?

But Erik hadn't been overly concerned with details like that at the time. He'd been too busy running from the unpalatable truth in his heart, a truth that had just reared back and kicked him in the teeth at the worst possible moment. He was in love with Nixie and no engagement could change that. It only complicated the shit out of things.

And now judging from the malicious gleam in Karl's eyes, those complications were about to go public. Really, really public. But now wasn't the time to untangle the situation. Maybe getting engaged to Mary Jane had been a mistake--possibly the biggest of his life--but there was no way Erik could abandon her now. Not even for Nixie, though God knew Nixie wouldn't want him to. She understood what love cost, in all its incarnations from friendship on up.

"Of course it's true," Erik said, giving Mary Jane a reassuring squeeze. She was shaking hard enough to loosen her fillings. She looked up at him with grateful eyes and leaned her head against his chest. "That's my grandmother's ring she's wearing. It's been in my family for generations."

"Congratulations," Karl said, smiling at Erik with genuine pleasure.

Tyrese stood as if rooted, all emotion carefully blanked from his face. He offered a hand to Erik. "Congratulations," he said, his voice once again DJ smooth.

Erik smiled grimly and shook the man's hand. Tyrese turned, slipped his hands into his pockets and strolled back into the ballroom as if nothing of consequence had happened. Mary Jane gave a choked sob and turned her face into Erik's lapel. Karl gave him a little finger wave and slipped through the doors, as if discreetly allowing the lady to indulge her emotions.

Right. Erik wasn't fooled. The guy was probably mowing down old ladies and small children so he could go bash Nixie over the head with this, the ultimate proof of Erik's stupidity.

He toyed briefly with the idea of tackling Karl onto the buffet table and punching his lights out, but that would

Kiss the Girl

be self-indulgent and rude. No, responsibilities came first, and right now that meant being the shoulder Mary Jane needed to cry on.

For now he would just pray Nixie would understand. He could beat Karl's smug ass later if absolutely necessary.

God, he hoped it would be necessary.

CHAPTER TWENTY-SEVEN

"Where are we going?" Nixie asked as James towed her across the crowded ballroom. She tried to inject some interest into her tone. She *should* be interested, shouldn't she?

"To the bar," James said. "I need a real drink."

At the bar, he surveyed the array of bottles with a practiced eye. "Give me a bourbon," he said to the bartender. "Rocks."

He tossed back the entire shot in one mouthful, placed the glass precisely on the bar and said, "Another." He glanced at Nixie's lifted brows. "Better make it a double," he told the bartender.

A trickle of alarm seeped into Nixie's stomach, the first thing she'd felt since leaving her own apartment nearly an hour ago.

"This isn't drinking. This is anesthesia," she said. "What are you planning?"

"What am I planning?" He laughed, but it was a harsh, unamused noise. "Me? I don't get to plan, Nixie. I don't get to want. To dream. To follow my goddamn bliss. That shit is for the common folk. Guy like me? Crown prince to a political dynasty? I have *responsibilities*, Nixie. A sacred fucking duty to be a successful, photogenic credit to the family. Anything less, the wrong guy might get elected. There goes the economy. There goes foreign policy. I fall down on the job and the head of every American household is either out of work or getting his ass shot off in one of those countries you're always cleaning up. And it's all my selfish fault." He saluted her with his fresh glass. "See, I'm just like you, Nixie."

Nixie stared at him as he poured fifty bucks worth of bourbon down his throat. *Just like you. I'm just like you, Nixie.* The words rang inside her head, echoed in that vast, cavernous space where her heart used to be.

"Got to be honest with you, though," he went on. "I didn't give two shits about my responsibilities until Daddy dearest made access to my trust fund contingent upon living up to them." He paused to study the empty glass in his hand. "Turns out I dislike being poor more than I dislike being told what to do, when to smile and who to fuck. Another thing we have in common." The smile he gave her was brilliant and charming. "I underestimated you, Nixie. You've got some kind of stainless steel balls. I mean, it's one thing to let my dad pick out my dates. But letting your mother fuck your boyfriend for the press coverage? That's hard core."

"I didn't..." She faltered, her chest constricting. The emptiness at her core shifted, morphed into an unsettling sense of pressure, an urgent restlessness she'd never felt before. She touched one cold hand to her cheek, found it burning.

That awful moment in Kenya reared up from her memory in a rush of disjointed impressions. The frantic creak of ancient bed springs. The musk of sex on stagnant air. Sloan's face, pale and perfect against the sheets. The petty sting of James' betrayal. The vicious slice of her mother's.

Funny how different it all looked now that Nixie's flash-frozen heart wouldn't produce the usual filters of outrage and pain. Details previously content to lurk behind the hurt suddenly thrust themselves forward and demanded notice.

Little things. Like Sloan, whose sexuality had always been more a weapon than a pleasure, moaning her way to a theatrically timed climax. Like Karl, who'd never flinched at using Sloan's body and reputation in service of the cause, allowing Nixie to walk into that scene with the press corps at her back. Karl, who'd never liked James, standing deliberately aside while the flashbulbs strobed.

Yes, Sloan had betrayed her. But Nixie finally saw with a stark clarity that the betrayal hadn't been Sloan's idea, or probably even her inclination.

It had been Karl's.

Her hand drifted to the base of her throat. Her pulse bumped there unevenly, startling evidence that, despite everything she didn't feel, she was still alive.

"I didn't realize--" she started faintly but James cut her off.

"Of course you did." He raised his glass to her in mock salute. "I'm not saying you sold her cheap or anything. I'm sure the payoff was lavish. But don't fuck around with me, Nixie. Not after what we've been through. What we'll go through yet tonight. One child of fame to another? Everything has a price tag. And if you're going to sell your soul, you might as well get your money's worth. God knows I am."

He set aside his glass, an alcoholic film finally dulling the slicing brightness of his eyes. "Now let's get this over with." He snatched up her hand with a grim determination that stopped Nixie's breath in her chest. "Where's Sloan?"

Karl had disappeared, leaving Sloan on one of the small balconies that studded the ballroom. It would do, she thought, pulling open both doors. A frame for the drama she was about to stage. Yes, it would do very nicely.

Kiss the Girl

She snagged a fresh glass of champagne from a passing waiter and arranged herself in the open doorway. If Nixie was even remotely on task, she'd come. If she wasn't, well, Sloan had a lovely view of the entire room. She'd find them.

But no. Not necessary. Here they came now, James scissoring through the crowd, Nixie bobbing in his wake like an unhappy little boat. An ugly flush rode high on his sharp cheek bones and that pretty mouth of his was clamped into a tight, determined line. Sloan smoothed her face into the customary almost-expression her public expected, sipped her champagne and let them come to her. Supplicants to her queen. A nasty little burble of self-disgust mingled in her stomach with the champagne, but it would settle. It always did.

"Well, Nixie and James," she said when they'd stopped in front of her. Completely off the mark, too. No way to get everybody in the picture from there. Christ. Maybe James was an amateur but she expected more from Nixie. She sighed and crossed to the other side of the doorframe, lounged there. Better composition for the photos. "What a surprise."

"Sloan." James bent a dimpled smile on Sloan, but something hard and ugly burned in his eyes as he said, "Good to see you again."

She inclined her head then turned back to Nixie. "Your dress is fabulous," she said. "Bagdley Mischka?"

"Good eye." Nixie gave her a tense smile, then edged in front of her date, as if by putting him behind her shoulder she could forget he was even there. She lowered her voice and leaned in. "Listen, Mom. I've changed my mind, all right? We're not doing this."

"Doing what, baby?" She spoke to Nixie, but let her eyes linger on James. Let them sparkle with scorn and just a hint of sexual knowledge. Of power. He wanted her.

Men did. Even when they hated her, they wanted her. It photographed very well.

"*This*," Nixie said, twirling a finger between the three of them. Her face was very white, the freckles on her nose standing out like splattered ink. "Selling our family for the greater good. No good is this great, Mom. It's not worth it."

"Not worth it?" Sloan stared, nearly choking on the sudden rush of rage lodged in her throat. She'd spent half her life now trying to pay off the cosmic debt she'd incurred when she'd let Archer love her, let him give her a beautiful baby. How could she have known that baby would grow into a woman who would judge her for paying the very debt responsible for her existence?

Sloan forced a tinkling laugh. "I'm sorry, I must have missed the part where *you* paid for anything. But don't mind me. I have a particular gift for doing the, ah, dirty work."

Nixie flinched like the words had been a slap. "I never asked you to--"

"Of course you didn't. You're the messiah, Nixie. The chosen one. How does Karl always put it? The Princess Diana to my Angelina Jolie? You're special and pure. Other people were more than willing to ask on your behalf." Sloan felt nasty. Ugly. She didn't know where the words were coming from, the venom. But she was spilling it all over Nixie and for what? For having the gall to point out that she herself had never sunk to the point of fucking other people's boyfriends for the cause of the week?

"That's not fair." Nixie's lips hardly moved, and her pupils all but eclipsed her irises.

"Fair. Pah." Sloan waved a dismissive hand, finished up with a flick of one careless finger over the curve of Nixie's cheek. "But don't worry, baby. Mama's here. I'll take care of everything." She turned her attention to

Kiss the Girl

James, but Nixie's hand landed on her arm, icy cold against her skin. Sloan blinked at the shock of it.

"No." Nixie's fingers dug in, the first hint of genuine emotion heating that tattle-tale complexion they shared. "Mom, I'm begging you. If you love me, don't do this. Please."

It had never occurred to Nixie, not until those shocking, unplanned words hung in the air between them, that Sloan might not love her. She'd always just assumed. Under all the bad behavior and righteous conviction, surely her mother harbored some kernel of affection for the child she'd cradled in her womb. The child she'd pushed out into the world and taken the trouble to keep relatively close at hand for the next twenty-eight years.

Sloan's face flushed, then went bloodless as she turned deliberately away from Nixie. She looked instead at James. And in that endless moment, Nixie realized the truth.

She had assumed too much.

The knowledge thudded home, directly into the vacuum at her center. It drove the breath from her lungs and everything in her vibrated with the aftershock. Her brain clicked and chugged but simply refused to process this final insult.

That's three, she thought a bit wildly. First Erik, then Karl, now Sloan. Three chances to love me, three *no thank yous* in varying shades of politeness. Three strikes. You're out.

But, miracle of miracles, she was still standing. Okay, her knees were locked and she couldn't feel a damn thing, but standing was standing. She wasn't on her knees. She wasn't dissolved in pitiful tears. Possibly it was because she couldn't move, but whatever. Maybe she was frozen but she wasn't goddamn *broken*. Not yet.

And if the old wives tale about shitty things coming in threes held true--please God let it hold true--then she was safe. She'd paid her cosmic tab and was, for the moment anyway, free and clear.

She pressed her palm to that urgent and expanding *pressure* behind her ribs--so strange--and turned to watch the farce about to play out between James and Sloan.

"What are you doing here, James?" Sloan asked, in full-on, sultry, never-gonna-get-this-back mode. "Daddy trying to rehab your image?"

"I suppose you of all people would recognize an image overhaul in progress."

Sloan let that pass. She arranged a curl in front of her shoulder and sipped at the champagne in her hand.

"That being the case, I'm willing to be guided," James told her.

Sloan cut a look at Nixie, which she returned without expression. Without curiosity.

"Nixie's a bit shaky tonight," Sloan said. "We'll have to take the lead. Are you up for a bit of high drama?"

His eyes glittered with the same bitter fatalism as Sloan's. "Ready when you are."

Sloan didn't hesitate. "You ass," she said, in a calm, ringing tone that cut off the background chatter at the knees. A hush dropped over the crowd and every face-- and every camera-- turned toward the scene Sloan was staging. "You unspeakably crude *ass*. How dare you show your face here?" She emptied her champagne glass onto his tuxedo shirt with a careless flip of the wrist.

James jumped back, dripping, but pitched his voice into the carrying range as well. "Jesus, Sloan. Always with the drama. Grow the fuck up, why don't you?"

Sloan dismissed him with a toss of her head and rounded on Nixie. "And you," she said. "Why, you ungrateful little bitch. You're welcome to him."

Kiss the Girl

Nixie, her back to the room, didn't move. Didn't speak. Certainly didn't chime in with her lines. She simply watched Sloan with a numb fascination. She'd always known her mother was an actor, but she'd never realized the extent of her talent. Never realized before that she was in character every single minute of every single day. She was magnificent.

Sloan leaned in, put her mouth very close to Nixie's ear and said, "I'm lobbing you a softball here, Nixie. I'm the slutty temptress who took advantage of a generally good man in a moment of weakness. Defend him." Her lips curved in her trademark smirk as she leaned back. "You'll want to use your outside voice."

Nixie stared at her, bemused. Sloan arched her brows at the continued silence. "Those kids need the money, Nixie. Now, as James would say, grow the fuck up and earn it."

Grow up, Nixie. Grow the fuck up.

The words were still rattling around Nixie's head when Karl appeared at Sloan's elbow. "I need Nixie."

Sloan cut her eyes toward the crowd of rapt eavesdroppers who were trying valiantly to pretend they weren't listening. "We're kind of in the middle of something here."

"It's important."

She shrugged. "Your call."

"It'll have to do," Karl said and turned to Nixie. "There's something you need to see," he said. "Come with me."

Mary Jane pulled back and swiped a couple fingers under her eyes in the way women did when they were trying to salvage a makeup job. Erik was no expert but he didn't think it was going to help.

"Thanks for doing that," she said, then gave up swiping and just scrubbed at her cheeks with both hands.

"What are friends for?" Erik fished a hanky from his pocket and handed it over. She took it, but instead of mopping up her face, she crumpled it into a tight ball in her fist.

"In our case, I'm starting to think it's being a fake fiancé upon request." She sighed and plunked down on the edge of huge concrete planter squatting in the corner. "You know we're not getting married, right?"

"Yeah, I know."

"Are you in love with Nixie?"

"Yep." Erik tucked his hands in his pockets, amazed at how good it felt to just admit that. "Are you in love with Tyrese?"

Mary Jane shrugged. "A hundred years ago, maybe. Now? I don't know. He's completely wrong for me."

"Yep. Nixie, too. Doesn't seem to matter."

"He works for a *gang*, Erik. He teaches them how to squeeze the maximum potential profit out of their guns and drugs and lord knows what. All the love in the world isn't going to fix that."

"Yeah. I guess not." He poked a finger into her shoulder and said, "Still, he's really good looking. Doesn't that count for something?"

She shook her head and pinched the bridge of her nose. "To think I ever considered getting married to you."

"Hey, I have it on good authority that I'm an excellent catch. You're sure you want out?"

Mary Jane's mouth quirked up in a shadow of her old, sly smile. "Yeah, I'm out. Besides, that thing about you being such an awesome catch? You don't want to believe everything your mother tells you, all right? She's a politician." She twisted the ring off her finger and held it out. Erik took it and tucked it into his pocket. He wondered if he'd still run into Nixie immediately, now that he wasn't trying to propose to Mary Jane.

"At least we didn't make a formal announcement or anything," she said. "Can you imagine how hard it would be to back out of--"

She broke off as the balcony doors burst open. Framed there in the brilliant lights of the ballroom were Karl, Nixie and Missy Jensen of Channel Four news.

CHAPTER TWENTY-EIGHT

Missy poked a microphone in Erik's face and said, "Dr. Larsen! Dr. Riley! I understand congratulations are in order?"

Erik glanced at the crowd of curious onlookers behind the camera, saw Tyrese there and felt his momentary optimism deflate like a day old balloon. He shifted his gaze to Karl--smug, beaming Karl--then to Nixie. Who wasn't smiling. Who wasn't frowning. Who wasn't...*anything*. Something was very wrong with Nixie. He moved toward her, but she pushed a hand toward him, stopped him dead.

"You're engaged?" she asked.

"He is," Karl boomed cheerfully. "Has been, actually."

"A secret engagement?" Missy asked, her smile tickled.

Erik didn't answer. Nixie's eyes hadn't left his, and her gaze had him pinned.

"Is that true?" she asked, her voice low, urgent.

He glanced at Mary Jane whose gaze was fixed on Tyrese. Ah, shit.

"Yes," he said, forcing the words out through lips that wanted to clamp down and keep the lie inside. "I'm...sorry."

Kiss the Girl

"How long?" Nixie heard the words, heard herself speak them, but they were dull and distant over the roar in her ears. Something was happening to her, something terrible. The emptiness inside her chest stretched, strained, and it took both hands on her sternum to force in a thin breath.

She saw Mary Jane shoot to her feet next to Erik, saw her clutch at his sleeve. "Erik, no. You don't have to--"

"How long did you wait?" she asked, cutting through Mary Jane like she didn't exist. She didn't, really. Not for Nixie. Nothing existed for Nixie except Erik and the noise in her head that twisted and rose and reached like a funnel cloud. It fed on the guilt in his eyes, and the horrible pressure inside her grew until it was everything and she was nothing. Until her skin went hot and tight and fragile. "How long did you wait between fucking me and asking another woman to marry you?"

She was dimly aware of the people around them, their nervous eyes, their worried glances. Hands came toward her, touched her elbows, her shoulders, her back, but she shook them off with a fierce shudder and stepped forward. She put her face right into Erik's. Wanted to see the truth of his answer chase itself through his eyes.

"*How long did you wait?*"

"I didn't," he said, and his eyes were stark and honest. "I didn't wait at all. I left you and I went to her."

The roaring in her head died abruptly, leaving behind one awful beat of ominous silence. Then everything in Nixie exploded. The pain layered under the numbness buried under the pure, aching emptiness--it all went up in a molten jet of rage that snapped and roared like fire, leaping and dancing and destroying. Fury spurted into the hollow at her core, filling her, consuming her. It shot along her skin, danced up into her head and turned the air around her hot and dangerous.

Power coursed through her and she gloried in the sharp slap of it. In the sting of coming back to life after so many years of playing dead. Of pretending the insults didn't hurt, the rejections were deserved, the debts of the world were somehow hers to pay.

"Nixie?" Erik reached toward her, his brow creased in concern. A concern that she'd have given the world for an hour ago, but now just fed the beast inside her that devoured pain and turned it into this sparkling, heady rage.

"Don't touch me." She shook off his hand. "You don't get to touch me. I'm not yours, and that's your fault. I offered. Offered you everything. You took it, then gave your ring to somebody else. So don't bother pretending to care now. It's too late. I don't want your concern and I don't want your pity. I don't want you. Not anymore."

And then Karl was beside her, sidling up to her shoulder, touching her elbow, murmuring in her ear.

"Enough, Nixie," he said softly. "Enough. It's time to make your speech, wrap this up and move on."

She switched her focus to Karl, to the small smile hiding in his beard. A small smug smile. She'd pleased him, she realized. She'd finally shoved Erik aside, just as he wanted. Just as he'd planned. She'd *behaved*.

He hooked a hand inside her elbow and drew her into the ballroom. The crowd parted for her as if she were on fire. Maybe she was. Karl didn't seem to notice.

"You'll want James beside you at the podium," he said. "He doesn't need to speak, just be seen in the position of honor next to you. After Sloan's little scene, it'll be enough. You'll want to mention Senator Harper, of course, his invaluable assistance in addressing this shameful problem going unnoticed three miles from the Capitol--"

He went on and on as he steered her toward the podium, kept dropping his words into her ear, one after the other, without waiting to see if she wanted more. Just like

Kiss the Girl

always. The boiling lake of fury inside her sent up a fresh streamer of lava as Nixie arrived at the steps to the stage.

She jerked her arm from Karl's grip mid-sentence, turned her back on his startled face and marched up the steps to the podium. To the microphone. To the avid faces and the expectant hush of a few hundred people who knew something juicy was about to unfold right before their hungry eyes.

Nixie wasn't one to disappoint her public.

"Good evening, everybody." A jagged elation surged through her veins as she grabbed the mic. "First of all, let me just say, you look great. You're all dressed up, you're trading compliments over cocktails, votes over canapés. You've got your checkbooks out and are just waiting for the go-ahead from Senator Harper to write the clinic a nice fat check. And that pleases me. It pleases me beyond words. Because I have it on good authority that when a girl sells her soul, she ought to get her money's worth."

An uncomfortable ripple went through the crowd, a couple hundred people shifting, frowning. Nixie smiled furiously into the blazing lights and plunged ahead.

"So I'm asking myself, has tonight been worth my soul? Don't get me wrong. Helping kids breathe is always a good thing. But I hope like hell it was worth what I've paid for it because I'm all tapped out. I mean, I'm all for saving the children but I don't have a single piece of my soul left to sell for your donor dollars. Do you hear me? I have nothing left for you people. My heart is gone--I gave that to you, Erik."

Every camera in the room swung to Erik but he knew his way around a press corps smackdown. He gave them nothing, his face like granite, his mouth a grim line inside it. She sighed. What had she expected? Nothing was all he had to give. All he *would* give, at least. Hadn't she learned anything this week?

"My family is gone, too," she said. "Karl explained to me just this evening that he'd shun me like the Amish if I didn't give up this ridiculous dream of a personal life. A home. A family. Somebody to love me back for a change. And as for my mother, well."

She paused to glance at Sloan, who stood between Karl and James, eyebrows raised, an enigmatic half-smile curving her lips. "Well, you all know my mother. She's not one to choose family over fame. I learned that tonight. The hard way. Not that I'm throwing stones. Maybe I don't have Sloan's flair for it, but I'm no stranger to renting out my body for a cause. There's a detailed accounting of who I'm wearing tonight in your press packets, as per the lease agreement. But you know what? No matter what I sell, it's not enough. It's not even close to enough and it never will be. So let's just say this right out loud: *Nixie Leighton-Brace is not enough to save the world.* Was that a surprise to everybody, or just me?"

"Enough, Nixie." Karl, his face rigid, marched up the stage steps. "That's enough."

"No. It's not." She turned on him with a savage fierceness that froze him on the last riser. "I've spent my whole life listening to you talk and talk and talk. But it's my turn now, so why don't you just shut up and listen? Besides, I already know your opinion on the subject."

She spun back to the crowd, waved an arm at her fuming advisor. "He'd have me believe I owe it to the universe, based on my tremendous luck in being born *Nixie Leighton-Brace*, to cast myself on the altar of the world's fucked-up-ness and burn. Like that's going to balance the scales somehow. But I've been doing that for twenty-eight years now, and haven't noticed anything getting particularly better. So I'm making a break for it. I'm going to save myself for a change, and I'm going to blow up some really big bridges behind me. So pay attention, all you gossip mongers and bottom feeders. I'm only going to do this once."

She turned back to Karl, to Sloan, to James clustered at the edge of the stage. She found Erik and Mary Jane still framed in the open doors of the balcony where she'd left them. Registered the various states of agitation, condemnation and panic on their faces. Pain sparkled fresh and sharp in her veins. The pain of having disappointed Karl, and the hurt of his loving her name and her image more than who she really was. The pain of having her mother turn away from her one last time. The jagged and bleeding ache of Erik's rejection. She let the beast inside her consume it all and spew it out as rage.

"You can screw off, Karl," she said distinctly. "Go find yourself another messiah because I'm all done trying to love somebody who only cares about what I can do for him. You can have Sloan fuck her way through the United Nations for charity for all I care. She can't hurt with a heart she buried twenty years ago anyway. Can't love, either, can you, Mom? But that's beside the point by now.

"And Erik? I hope you'll be very, very happy in your very, very safe marriage to your very, very nice best friend whom you *do not love*. I hope your cowardice will keep you warm at night. Mary Jane, I'm sorry for all this. Seriously. I don't want to rain on your parade, but what the hell are you doing in this parade anyway? You have such a rare and decent courage, and you deserve somebody who loves you for it.

"But you know what? Whatever. I'm done trying to fix everybody else. I've got enough broken shit of my own to work on. So I'm done with you people. With all of you." She threw out both arms to encompass the whole room. "If you're really committed to children's health care in this country, in this commonwealth, hell, in this *neighborhood*, you'll write us a check anyway. But if you're only here because Senator Harper told you to be here, because you wanted to put on a pretty dress, eat hors d'oeuvres and build up your political capital, then take your money and go home. I don't want it. And I won't sell one damn thing more to get it. I'll find another way."

She shoved the microphone into its cradle, gave the stunned and silent crowd an ironic little bow and sailed off the stage on knees that wanted to buckle.

But not because she was afraid or hurt. She was still hollow, exhausted and empty, but it was a clean empty this time. Fresh. She'd finally purged the poison. She paused in front of Karl, who stared past her as if she didn't exist. She waited for the old guilt to stir, the pain, but everything within her remained still and quiet.

James shook his head. "Stainless steel balls," he said. "I'll give you that. My father's going to crucify you, but damn, what a way to go."

Sloan touched her shoulder, the ends of her hair and shook her head. "Security will take you home," she said. "Backstage."

Nixie slipped through the curtains.

Two hours later, Erik pushed Nixie's doorbell for the ninth time. He hated this doorbell, with its solemn, mournful *bong*. Nixie was many things but she wasn't scored in a minor key.

"She's not home."

He turned, found his mother in her blue bathrobe in the open door of her apartment across the hall. "What are you doing up?" he asked. "It's--" He consulted his watch, winced. "Late."

She dismissed this as the diversionary tactic it was. "You've screwed it up, haven't you? With Nixie."

He scowled. "I haven't screwed anything up. There was nothing to screw up."

"No? Then why are you wearing out her doorbell at 2 a.m.? In your gala tuxedo still?" Her gaze was sharp on his face, and he resisted the urge to scuff his feet. What was he, ten?

"What have you done, Erik?" the Senator asked.

"Nothing, Mom. Jeez."

She rolled her eyes, stepped back from the door and pointed an imperious finger inside. He ducked his head--he *was* ten, powerless against that finger--and walked inside. He plunked himself at her kitchen table while she moved around the room, gathering the makings for a pot of coffee.

"If you want to lie to the press or your friends or yourself, that's one thing. But I'm your mother. I knew you before you knew yourself. You can't lie to me, so stop trying. What did you do?"

"She wanted more from me than I could give, okay?" Something dark and awful inside him strained toward the surface but he strapped it down. "I dented her ego a little, that's all. She'll recover."

She dumped enough grounds in the filter to make a pot of rocket fuel and gave him a look that mixed pity with incredulity. "Nixie Leighton-Brace wanted to date you and you turned her down."

"It was a little more complicated than that."

"Complicated how?"

"I asked Mary Jane to marry me."

"What?" She nearly bobbled the pot of water she was feeding into the machine. She pressed *brew* and turned the full force of her stare upon him. "When? When did you do this remarkably foolish thing?"

He stared at his hands, pushed back against the anger and the fear that had knotted his gut. "Right after I, um, turned Nixie down."

"Did you both have your clothes on when you *turned her down*?"

"Not exactly."

"Oh, Erik."

He hunched his shoulders. "It gets worse. She found out about the engagement at the gala tonight. In front of a lot of people."

"How many people?"

"In person? Couple hundred." He paused, miserable. "I don't know how many people will watch it on TV."

The Senator closed her eyes. "You're my son and I love you, but you're a fool."

The grinding fear that she was right ate at him, had temper snapping up. "I'm a fool? *I'm* a fool? Because I don't want to spend the rest of my life moldering away on the farm while the woman I love loves everybody else in the world first? Sorry, Mom. I saw that one already. I didn't like the ending."

"You're in love with Nixie?"

Erik rubbed his forehead and shut his mouth. Trust his mother to sort through all the really big ammunition and latch onto the tiny, revealing side note. More evidence that Nixie was killing him. Before she'd come along, he'd never have made that kind of tactical error. "I was talking about Dad."

"Don't you dare blame your father for this. He's been gone these ten years and more, and I will not have you--"

The hard, ugly thing inside him snarled and tore free and he said, "I'm not blaming Dad. I'm blaming you."

"Me." She folded her arms and glared at him, more daunting in a bright blue robe than most women were in a power suit.

"Yes, you. What, I'm supposed to blame Dad because you were always leaving? It's somehow Dad's fault that you wanted to be famous more than you wanted to be his wife? That you wanted to take care of everybody else's kids instead of the one you had? That you weren't there for him when he was alive any more than you were there for him when he died?"

Kiss the Girl

She looked at him coolly but her eyes crackled with temper. "I have never spoken a harsh word to you about your father, Erik. I loved you--and him--too much to make that mistake, and I'm not going to make it now. But before you start handing down judgment on me, you might want to ask yourself why you're not passing judgment on him, too."

"On him?" Erik stared at her in disbelief. "For what?"

"For doing exactly what I did--choosing his career over his marriage," she said. "He could have moved to Washington, you know. Kept the family together. But incredibly, he wanted to farm. He didn't care to sacrifice himself on the altar of my ambition any more than I cared to sacrifice myself on the altar of his. In the end, we decided it was better for our marriage--and our son--to live separately." She shrugged. "Is politics really so much worse than farming? Was my dragging you on the campaign trail really more awful than your father making you work the farm?"

"Dad didn't make me do anything. He put my hands in the dirt and taught me to respect life and nurture growth. All you did was put me in front of the cameras every time you needed voters to think you were a good mother."

"I see," she said, her voice jagged and cold as a glacier. She placed a cup of coffee at his elbow with a very precise click. "I'm sorry you feel that way. It wasn't my intention."

"Then what was your intention, Mom? Why else would you put a little kid through the meat grinder of national politics?"

"Maybe I wanted to expose you to the brightest political minds in America. Maybe I also wanted to expose you to the people who most needed those minds working on their behalf. Maybe I wanted you to know what it looks like when you love what you do, when you use what you've been given in service of others. Maybe I wanted passion and fulfillment and ambition to be more than SAT vocabulary words to you, Erik."

Erik stared at the steaming coffee. It looked like tar, and he desperately wished he'd actually drunk some of it. Anything to explain away the sudden twist in his stomach. But no. It wasn't the coffee; it was the truth. The Senator had just eviscerated a life-long grudge with a blast of simple perspective, and the hurt of an abandoned child came oozing out.

"I didn't want any of that, Mom," he forced himself to say. He'd started this thing, he might as well finish it. "I just wanted you."

She shook her head. "No, not me. You wanted a milk and cookies mom, and I wasn't one. I never will be, either, so if that's going to break your heart, you'll have to get over it."

"Mom--"

She cut him off. "I know you resent me for leaving. For leaving your father. For leaving you. For not being there when he--and you--needed me. But staying is as much a choice as leaving. There's no less risk in it, so if you think rejecting a woman like Nixie is going to keep you safe, think again."

She sat down across from him, nudged the sugar bowl his way. "But if that's your choice, make damn sure it *is* your choice. I've watched you turn away from everything I've ever offered you, from girlfriends to law school to political office. If you want to turn away from Nixie too, fine. But don't you dare blame me for your cowardice."

CHAPTER TWENTY-NINE

Cowardice. Erik dumped a spoonful of sugar into his coffee and stirred, his head spinning with a sudden, sickening onslaught of self-knowledge. She was right, of course. He *was* a coward. He'd taken a childhood fear, dressed it up in sensible clothing and passed it off as pragmatism. And it had nearly cost him the one woman who'd ever found her way through the layers of bullshit to his heart.

He set down the spoon and frowned. He didn't take sugar in his coffee. He put aside the mug and scrubbed both hands down his face. "Jesus, Mom. I don't know what I'm doing."

"Do you love her?"

He thought of the fear, the loss, the pain that had defined love his entire life. The exhausting burden and the monstrous cost of it. Then he thought of Nixie and the unimaginable generosity of her heart and he let it all go. The past and all its baggage tumbled away, leaving his heart fresh and clean and whole inside him. And full of Nixie.

"Yes," he said. "I do."

"Then the rest doesn't matter."

A wave of shame broke over him as he remembered the casual brutality with which he'd rejected Nixie's love. The cruelty he'd tried to disguise as honesty. Her cheeks had still been pink from their love-making when he'd deliberately shattered her heart and he would never forget the way she'd summoned up that fragile dignity and asked him to leave, the air around her shimmering with hurt and rage.

He couldn't undo that. He couldn't take it back. He'd dealt out a vicious, indelible blow to the purest, more generous heart he'd ever known, and why? Because he was a coward. Because he was in love with Nixie Leighton-Brace and it scared the shit out of him.

He'd tried to save himself, pledging himself to Mary Jane in a vain attempt to undo that ill-advised leap into love. And Mary Jane, God bless her, had given him that protection when he'd needed it. The space and the time to figure out that he not only couldn't reverse that fateful leap, but he didn't want to. That he would give anything, everything, to undo the damage he'd done. To put Nixie's beautiful heart back together and cherish the gift of it for the rest of his life.

But what if everything he had wasn't enough? A cold shock settled into his stomach and he shook his head.

"I messed up. Mom, I really messed up."

"Then fix it."

"I don't know how."

She smiled at him, a bit crookedly. "Talk to her," she said. "Tell her what's in your heart."

"What if it isn't enough?"

"What if it is? Faint hearts never won jack, boyo."

"I think you may be underestimating the degree to which I've been a total ass."

"I never underestimate the degree to which a man can be a total ass." She smiled, though, and lifted a hand to his cheek. "But you raise a kid, you make a lot of mistakes. And you learn that people who love you can be infinitely forgiving."

Kiss the Girl

He covered her hand with his, pressed it and swallowed hard, past the awkward lump of regret and love blocking his throat.

"And for the record?" she said. "I left a lot behind when I walked away from the farm, but I never left you. Never."

"I know." And he did.

She gave his cheek one last little pat and drew back. "So. What are you going to do about Nixie?"

Erik reached across the table. He took her hand this time and said, "I have an idea, but I'm going to need your help."

Her eyes went round, then filled with an unruly rush of tears that had Erik half out of his chair. "Jeez, Mom, don't cry. I only--"

She waved him back into his seat with an impatient hand. "Oh for goodness sake," she said. "Sit down. I'm allowed a couple of tears when my only child finally asks me to be part of his life." She swiped her sleeve over her eyes, gave the table a brisk pat and said, "Now. Tell me about this plan of yours."

One week later Mary Jane sat savoring the silence of her office. She loved Sunday mornings at the clinic. Doors locked tight until noon, phones routed directly to the answering service. She could brew up a pot of coffee and have a decent shot at actually drinking it before the series of crises that passed for the work day turned it into a pot of hard-boiled sludge.

She didn't love the paperwork she forced herself to do while she drank it, but bills needed paying. And in spite of Nixie's on-air melt-down last weekend--or maybe because of it--the gala had raised enough cash to actually pay them.

She'd made a good dent in both the coffee pot and the mess in her inbox when she heard the door rattle. She froze halfway through her signature. Wanda had a key, as did Erik, but she knew they would both rather drink battery acid than give up a Sunday morning to push paper at the clinic. That was what they paid her the big bucks to handle. What nonprofits considered big bucks, anyway.

Probably a couple of desperate junkies looking to keep Saturday night's party rolling, she thought. She wrapped her hand around the Louisville Slugger she kept beside the filing cabinet for just such emergencies and marched toward the waiting room. The receptionist pen was locked down and bullet proof but the bat was a comforting weight in her hand as she rounded the corner.

And found Ty standing in her lobby.

The breath left her lungs in a whoosh. Her hand went numb on the bat. And her heart, her treacherous, *stupid* heart, sang at the sight of him.

He looked tired, she thought inanely. It was in the set of his shoulders, the tilt of his head. No jaunty charm, no arrogant smirk. He didn't smile at her, and God help her, she sort of missed that I-know-you-want-me-baby grin that made her want to strangle him because she invariably did.

"Hey, Mary Jane," he said. "Brought you something."

She noticed for the first time the woman beside him.

"Jass," she said, and worked up a smile for the pregnant, sullen teenager. "You're starting to show."

"No, I'm smuggling a basketball." Jass rolled her eyes.

"You said you wanted to see her," Ty said. "See the baby. So." He lifted his shoulders. "Here they are."

"Here they are." Mary Jane smiled at Jass. "I'm so glad you came. Come on back. Let's have a look at that baby."

Something moved across Jass' closed face as she cut a questioning glance at Ty, something hopeful and alive and painfully young. He gave her a gentle prod through the door Mary Jane buzzed open.

"I'll wait here," he told her, but kept his eyes on Mary Jane.

Mary Jane nodded and he lowered himself into one of the puke-colored chairs in the empty waiting room. She watched him for a moment--she couldn't help the weakness of drinking him in from a safe distance--then shook it off. She turned to Jass and said, "You ready to meet that baby?"

"Not in person, no."

Mary Jane laughed. "How about just a picture?"

"That'd be cool. I guess."

"This way."

Half an hour later, Mary Jane left Jass with a screen shot of her baby and orders to get dressed and meet her in the receptionist's pen to make her next appointment. She found Ty where she'd left him, his head resting on the chair back, his eyes closed. She let herself into the waiting room and took the seat opposite his. He came awake with barely a ripple.

"So? What's the story?"

"Healthy baby boy," Mary Jane said. "Estimated date of arrival August 22. I'll need to run some standard tests, blood work and such, but everything looks fine." She paused. "Thank you for bringing her in, Ty. It was a good thing to do."

"Yeah, I've been on a roll lately."

"You have?"

"You don't have to sound so surprised."

"Sorry. I just--" She cut herself off. "No, I'm done lying. To you, about you. To myself about you. I *am* surprised. Life shit on you, Ty. I don't dispute that. But you've been shitting right back ever since so yes, the occasional good deed surprises me."

"Yeah. I guess I deserve that. Hell, I deserve a lot more than that from you." He leaned forward, elbows on knees and her heart leapt into her mouth. He made no move to touch her but she drew back anyway. Something shifted in his eyes, but she forced herself to look away. She was finished looking for hope where there was none.

"I'm sorry, MJ," he said. "I really am."

"You are?" Mary Jane narrowed her eyes at him. Better suspicious than gullible. "Why?"

"You were right," he said. "All this time. When they took my license--" He shook his head, started again. "When I *lost* my license, I went a little crazy. I'd worked so hard, MJ. So hard to get myself out of this place. To deserve more than this. I wanted the two thousand dollar suits, the four hundred dollar lunches. I wanted people to look at me and see power. To see somebody important. Somebody who meant something."

"I always saw that, Ty."

"I know. I wanted more."

Her heart--stupid, *stupid*--took the slap. Deserved it, she told herself. Five yards for being an idiot.

"And for a while, I had more," he said. "I had it all-- you, the job, the money, the power. The thrill. God, I loved it."

"I know," she said and the bitterness in her voice shocked her. Was she really still so angry?

"But then I lost it. I wanted to believe somebody took it from me. Because I was young. Because I was smart. Because I was black. Take your pick." He spread his hands. "What I didn't want to believe was that I could be the problem. That my drive for success had somehow disintegrated into an addiction to risk. To playing fast and loose with money that wasn't mine and morals that, unfortunately, were. I wasn't doing anything other people weren't doing, right? Couldn't be wrong if my boss was

Kiss the Girl

okay with it, too, right?" He rubbed the back of his neck. "Well, you know how it played out from there."

"Yeah. I do." And she had the broken heart to prove it, thank you very much. She stood. "So thanks for bringing Jass in. I'll need to see her again in--"

"There's more, MJ. I'm not just here to apologize."

She closed her eyes. More? How much more could she possibly take? "Ty, please. I said everything I had to say at the gala last week. Let's just...not, okay?"

He came to his feet and stuffed his hands into his pockets when she flinched back. "It's not that. I mean, not *just* that. I still love you, MJ. I probably always will. But okay, I've been a jerk and I don't deserve you. I get that. But I'm changing. I'm working hard on changing, MJ. You've got to hear me out."

She put a trembling hand over her eyes. She didn't know if she was trying to block out the sight of him, earnest and nakedly needy, or trying to conceal her own ridiculous tears. Both were good enough reasons to hide. "It's too late, Ty. I'm past that."

"I know," he said. "But I'm not. Don't you want to know how I got in here this morning?"

She dropped her hand, frowned at him. She'd been so relieved about not having to Louisville Slug somebody she'd forgotten to wonder. "How *did* you get in?"

He produced a key from his pocket and held it up.

"Where did you get that?"

"They give them out like candy when you buy the building."

"You bought the building?"

"Yep. Got a really good deal. Apparently, this isn't the best neighborhood."

She rolled her eyes. "Now whose fault is that?"

His grin disappeared and those dark eyes went serious. "Mine, partly. I won't deny it. But I'm working on fixing that."

She folded her arms. "Yeah? You organizing a basketball tournament at the Wash? Donating to the bail-out-your-fellow-gang-bangers fund?"

"Not exactly. I turned my books over to the FBI."

Her knees folded and she landed in the chair she'd just abandoned. "You what?"

He smiled ruefully. "I might not be a model citizen but I'm one hell of a manager. My books are neat, clean and very, very detailed. The paper trail goes right to the top, MJ. Right to some very, very bad men who, as it turns out, the FBI has been looking at for some time."

Mary Jane pressed the heel of her hand to her chest, to the twin jets of hope and fear that spurted there. "Why would you do that?" she asked.

"Besides the immunity from prosecution and the fact that I owed it to every kid in this neighborhood?" He sat down across from her, took her hand. "You, MJ. I did it for you."

A terrifying joy swept over her and she bowed under it. He pressed her cold hand, and the strength, the heat of him washed over her, pulled at her like the sun pulls the planets.

"I was never enough for you before," she whispered. "Why would I be enough now?"

"You were always enough, MJ. More than enough. More than I deserved. But I was too busy pitying myself to see that." He lifted his shoulders. "Then a kid put his gun against your beautiful skin." He brushed a finger against her temple. "There. Right there. That kid pressed a *gun* against your head and I just--"

His voice went unsteady and he cleared his throat. "Well, let's just say I grew up in a fucking hurry. It was time to make some changes. Big ones."

"So you turned over your books to the FBI, and in doing so painted a big old target on your back."

Kiss the Girl

He gave her a grim smile. "Please. I haven't survived in this neighborhood being a fool."

"Yeah, fools don't last long around here. And that's why, when the FBI uses your books to put *everybody but you* in jail, somebody--God, everybody--is going to connect the dots." She swallowed back a choking wave of terror and pulled her hand away from his. "They won't hesitate, Ty. They'll kill you."

"Not if I give them other dots to connect."

She narrowed her eyes. "What does that mean?"

"That deal I made with the feds? It's a little more complicated than I first made out. I'm not getting jail time, but I *am* getting probation and a shit load of community service." He twirled the clinic key absently through his fingers. "Service I was already planning on, but still. It's something. The Dog Crew sees me take a slap, get a record, do my probation. Top it off with Jass' disappearance and--"

"Wait, Jass' *what*?"

"She can't stay here, MJ. You know that. People around here look at her and see a traitor. They look at that baby and see the enemy. And Jass, she looks around and sees nothing but the bastards who killed her lover. Her baby's daddy. Is it such a stretch to think a girl like that might turn a stolen lap top over to the FBI and disappear?"

Mary Jane lifted skeptical brows. "Disappear where exactly?"

"Michigan, I think. Some little town outside Detroit. Bunch of apple orchards or something? I don't know. She has family there. But it's a fresh start and the FBI is willing to get her there clean and quick."

She struggled against the hope trying to sneak onto her face. "It's risky," she said finally. "Really risky."

"I know. But what else can I do? This is my home, MJ. And you're my heart. I won't leave either of you behind, not ever again." He reached out, took her hand. "This is my fresh start, too. Right here."

"Are we talking about me or this building?"

"For now? Let's talk about the building. I have plans for this place. You want to hear them?"

"Your business plan? Yeah, that I'd like to hear."

His smile broke slow and warm over the perfection of his face, and Mary Jane wanted to throw herself into his lap and promise him anything. But she was just old enough, just wise enough, just burned enough, to hold back.

"But beyond the professional?" she said. She slipped her hand free, folded it into her lap. "I don't think so. Not right now."

"I'm a patient man, MJ. I can wait. But for now--" He held out his hand for a shake, all business. "To the future."

She looked hard into his eyes, wondered what she'd find there tomorrow, the day after. She was a fool, she told herself. But she shook his hand.

"To the future."

CHAPTER THIRTY

Nixie slid a perfect omelet from the sauté pan onto a plate and flipped off the burner. She smirked at the stove.

"Played you like a fiddle, *mon ami*."

The stove maintained a stony silence. She almost wished it would start talking to her again. It was all in her head, of course, but even a make-believe fight with a snooty stove would be a nice change of pace from the non-conversations she'd been having with nobody all week.

She sat down at the pretty café table cozied up to the window in her breakfast nook, forked up a fluffy mouthful of rosemary and goat cheese omelet and chewed with a determined enjoyment. She had conquered the damn stove. She had reclaimed her life. She was--

The doorbell rang and she leaped to her feet, her heart pounding into her throat, hope blooming in her chest.

She was goddamn lonely, was what she was.

She raced to the door, flung it open without even checking the peep hole.

"Mom." She didn't bother to disguise her disappointment. What, she really thought Erik was going to turn up at her door one of these days with a bouquet of roses, a ring and a couple tickets to Fiji? After everything she'd said, she was darn lucky anybody rang the bell at all.

Still, it had been barely a week since Sloan had dealt out her final rejection of motherhood. Just because Nixie had other, larger wounds didn't mean this one wasn't still bleeding. "What are you doing here?"

Sloan strolled into the apartment with an assurance that had Nixie backing up automatically to make room. "What, I need an excuse to visit my only child?"

Nixie shut the door and followed her mother into the apartment, the old bitterness welling up, tightening her throat. Nixie seized on it with a shaming gratitude. After the past week, she was used to living with a constant, weeping ache, but at least this was pain from a different source. That was something.

"Last I checked you didn't have a child," Nixie said, taking a savage satisfaction in spewing some of the ugliness inside onto somebody else. "You had a mission and that was plenty for you. Why the sudden desire to play mommy?"

Sloan stopped in the living room, her hands folded in front of her, her eyes alive with a shimmering pain that matched Nixie's own. That small display of honest emotion was enough to startle Nixie into silence but what came next stunned her into utter disorientation.

"I deserve that," Sloan said quietly. "That and more. God knows, after what I've done to you over the years, I have no right to give motherly advice. But your little speech the other night was possibly the bravest, most courageous stand I've ever seen another person take. You *inspired* me, Nixie. We were both just enduring life, but you stood up and said no. You demanded more and now I am, too." She reached one tentative hand into the space between them but it faltered and dropped before she made contact. "I have never been more proud of you. God knows I haven't acted like it, but I do love you. And that's why I'm going to say this to you."

Nixie frowned, caught between the old bitterness and a ridiculous flutter of hope. "Say what?"

"Get dressed."

Nixie squashed the stupid spurt of disappointment. This was Sloan, after all. What had she expected? She waved a hand at her yoga pants and tank top. "I am dressed."

"No, honey, *dressed*. We're going out."

Nixie glanced toward the window, to the bustling streets of DC. Where she ought to be carving out a new life for herself with the freedom she'd paid so dearly for.

A life that wouldn't include Erik. His choice, not hers, no matter what she said. A life that might include Sloan, though not the mother she'd always longed for.

"I'm not ready yet," Nixie said. She looked away, didn't want Sloan to see the fear, the raw hurt that simply wouldn't abate. "I need more time."

Sloan didn't falter this time. She reached out and took Nixie's chin in long, cool fingers, forced her to meet those famous silver eyes. Eyes that held compassion but not a single spark of sympathy.

"No," Sloan said. "No more time. I know something about heart break, Nixie. When your father died, I thought I'd died with him. God knows I wanted to. The grief, my God. It swallowed me whole and I let it. I hid inside that insane sorrow because it was easier to let it define me than to get over it and risk that kind of pain ever again."

Nixie stared at her mother, trying desperately to keep her chin from wobbling. "I can see the wisdom in that," she managed. Please, she thought. Don't let me cry in front of Sloan.

"It wasn't wisdom, Nixie," she said gently. "It was cowardice. And it cost me everything from my self-respect to my precious baby girl."

Tears rushed into Nixie's eyes and she tried to turn away but Sloan held fast.

"Don't misunderstand, Nixie," Sloan said. "I'm not excusing myself. Grief is no justification for what I've done to you. But you need to know that I love you. I have always loved you. But I wasn't brave enough to act on it. I couldn't get out from under the pain you're trapped under right now. The pain I can see in your face."

Nixie stopped struggling, just let her mother touch her cheeks with gentle fingers, brush away the tears that fell there. Because she finally understood. She understood it all. Only now with this great beast of anguish crouching inside her, the one she was terrified would never leave, could she grasp the kind of pain that would drive a woman's heart as far underground as Sloan's. The knowledge didn't erase a life's worth of scarring, but it gave her enough room, just barely enough room for a new perspective. For forgiveness. For putting down some small part of her burden of pain.

She reached up, laid her hands over her mother's and closed her eyes, soaking in the simple comfort of her touch.

Sloan cleared a suspiciously tight-sounding throat. "But I was a coward, Nixie, while you most assuredly are not. There's too much of your father in you for that and you're done hiding now, do you hear me?"

"I'm not hiding," Nixie said, unconvincing even to her own ears.

"You're done pitying yourself, too." Sloan went on as if Nixie hadn't spoken. "The kind of life you're after, the kind you splashed out for last week? It costs, Nixie." Sloan put both hands in Nixie's shoulders and drilled her with an uncompromising gaze. "Now the only question is, are you willing to pay for it?"

Nixie stared into her mother's eyes, into the mingled sternness and compassion she found there. Into the bottomless love she'd been looking for all her life.

She sighed. "Yeah, all right," she said. "No point wasting a good scene, I guess."

Kiss the Girl

Sloan smiled. "There's my girl. Now go get dressed. I want to show you something." She paused. "Some make up wouldn't kill you, either."

The cab that dropped them at the clinic didn't linger. If it hadn't been Sloan Leighton doing the asking, Nixie doubted the guy would've ventured into Anacostia at all. As it was, he shot away from the curb like he'd been fired from a cannon.

Nixie wished like hell she was with him.

"It's Sunday," she said. "The clinic's closed until noon. Can we please go home now?"

"No," Sloan said, tucking a hand into Nixie's elbow and hauling her toward the alley. "You need to see this."

"For the last time, see *what*?"

Sloan tapped a few buttons on her cell phone. "We're here," she said and flipped the phone shut. Nixie frowned at her.

"Who was--"

The clinic's rear door swung open. "Come on in," Mary Jane said. "They're just starting."

Sloan hustled Nixie into the narrow hallway, a finger to her lips as they followed Mary Jane toward the front of the building.

"Starting what?" Nixie asked, but nobody answered. They moved into the receptionist's pen where Tyrese sat twisting idly in Wanda's chair. Nixie blinked at him in surprise. He nodded at her then turned back to the scene unfolding in the waiting room.

Nixie followed his gaze to the rows of ugly chairs, and her heart took a hard thump when she saw Erik sitting there with his mother and Missy Jensen from Channel Four News.

She didn't think, didn't blink, didn't breathe. She couldn't tear her eyes away from him, the planes of his face, the warm wheat of his hair, that super-hero jaw of his. Those lightning strike eyes. Those strong, square hands on the knees of his jeans. Everything in her rose up and yearned toward him.

I am an idiot, she thought. I'm an idiot and my heart has a death wish. But she didn't look away.

Sloan's hand found hers, and Nixie gripped it with desperate strength. "Mom, what is this?" she asked.

"Just listen, okay? Listen to him. Give him a chance."

Mary Jane took her other hand, squeezed it and gave her an encouraging smile. Nixie resigned herself to living through whatever the next ten minutes would hold and turned her attention to the waiting room.

"So Erik," Missy said, camera man hovering behind her shoulder, "you're a pretty private guy."

Erik nodded. "I grew up on the campaign trail. I learned early on to guard what's private or find it on the front page of The Post."

"I think it's fair to say you've done an excellent job. Most people have no idea you're Senator Larsen's son, nor that you share a cause."

"Children's health, yes." He smiled but his eyes stayed serious. "Part of keeping my private life private means not playing the mommy card every time I want or need some attention, even when it's for a good cause."

"And yet we're here today because you and your mother have co-authored a bill that would provide funding to expand neighborhood clinics like this one. After so many years of refusing to let your mother get involved with your professional life, why the sudden change of heart?"

"Change of heart. Funny you should use that phrase." Erik paused. "I did have a change of heart. And I owe somebody an explanation for that." He swiveled in the chair, shaded his eyes with the flat of his hand and squinted toward the receptionist's pen. "Nixie? Will you come out here please?"

"What?" Her eyes flew to Sloan's, wide and panicked. "You dragged me out of my apartment to get humiliated on live TV *again*?"

"Now Nixie--"

"Oh no. I am *so* not going out there." She yanked her hands free of the women on either side of her and headed for the rear hallway. Mary Jane and Sloan were fast on those short little legs, though, and tougher than they looked. The next thing Nixie knew, she was standing in the blinding glare of the spotlight.

"Nixie," Erik rose to stand in front of her. "I have something to say to you."

"And you feel like you should say it in front of a TV audience?"

"I hurt you in front of all those people, it only seems fair that I should fix it in front of them, too."

"Of course," she muttered. "God forbid any small humiliation in my life should play out behind closed doors."

"That's just it. That's what this is all about. I'm done pushing the women I love away because they have the guts to live bigger lives than I do. I'm done closing doors. I'm finally ready to open them up."

She stared at him, her stupid, hopeful heart jammed in her throat. "What does that mean?"

"It means I've finally pulled my head out of my ass and asked my mom for her help keeping the clinic open. It means I, of my own free will, called up Missy Jensen--a card carrying member of the press corps, as you know-- and asked her for this interview." He hesitated, then pushed ahead. "It means I love you, Nixie and I'm ready to do whatever it takes to be with you."

"You love me." Her head felt like a kaleidoscope, with shattered bits of pain and joy and doubt twirling around in a pretty but incomprehensible pattern. "Since when?"

He lifted his shoulders in a rueful shrug. "Probably since your dive into that trash heap in Mattie Getz-Strunk's front yard." He frowned. "Maybe sooner. But for sure by the time Daryl Johnson offered you a hit off the Bounce blower."

"I see." The kaleidoscope went a few degrees brighter as a big chunk of hope dropped into the mix tumbling around in her head. "Definitely before you proposed to Mary Jane, then."

He had the grace to look chagrined. "That was actually *why* I proposed to Mary Jane."

She frowned. "Okay, now you've lost me."

Wry humor mixed with the naked vulnerability in his eyes and Nixie's heart hammered. "I was afraid, Nixie. I was afraid of what loving you would cost me. I was afraid of always being second in your heart when there's no room left in mine for anything but you. The whole world loves you. How could I compete?"

"Oh, sure." Nixie nodded sagely. "Because love is definitely a competition."

He smiled at her. "And I'm a bad loser." His gaze softened and he rocked forward as if to take a step toward her but caught himself at the last second. "Marrying Mary Jane seemed like the ideal solution. We love each other in exactly the same way to exactly the same degree. We'd have a nice comfortable life together. A win-win solution, I thought. Except--"

He broke off and looked at her very directly. Another chunk of hope and a big scoop of joy joined the wild tumble in her heart but she forced a cool tone. "Except?"

"Except then I'm a coward. Because it was never about your fame, or the press, or your travel schedule, Nixie. I rejected you because I was afraid."

"Afraid of what?"

Kiss the Girl

"That you'd make a fool of me."

The cool fell away and Nixie gasped. "I would *never--*"

He cut her off. "That I'd love you too much. More than you'd love me, and the whole world would sneer at me for not leaving. Exactly the way I sneered at my father for not leaving my mother."

She stared at him, riveted by the sight of this incredibly private man confess so baldly to vulnerability. And not quietly, either. No, he'd gone for the grand gesture, confessing in front of her, their parents, their friends and anybody else who happened to be watching Channel Four.

"But I'm no coward, Nixie," he said. "I love you, and I will for the rest of my life if you'll let me." He clenched his hands in his pockets. "If it's not too late."

Nixie forgot about the camera. She forgot about Missy Jensen, forgot about their audience of thousands. Joy and love booted doubt right out of the kaleidoscope and projected a riot of light and color and hope and love onto her mended heart. A smile bloomed on her face, and he held out a hand to her in silent question. She ignored the hand, and with a little cry, threw herself into his arms. When he caught her they were both laughing.

The Senator cleared her throat and turned to Missy Jensen. "So. Maybe now is a good time to bring out Mary Jane Riley, Erik's partner in the clinic, and Tyrese Jones, our neighborhood liaison. He owns the building and has some interesting plans for expanding the clinic to include a day care and a community center."

Missy and her camera turned dutifully to the Senator while Nixie showered Erik's face and neck with dozens of tiny kisses, strung together with a lot of *I love you*s, a few *you jerk*s and a half-dozen *how could you be so stupid*s.

He laughed. "I love the way you talk while you kiss."

She drew back, a little embarrassed. "I do that?"

"All the time."

"Should I apologize?"

"I'll let you know when I'm bored."

She punched his arm. "Jerk."

He laughed and kissed her full on the mouth. "You're the only woman I've ever met I want to talk to as much as I want to kiss, Nixie. I'd marry you for that alone. The rest is a bonus."

She went still. "Was that a marriage proposal?"

His eyes stayed on hers, very blue, very direct. "I'm naked here, Nixie. Yours to take or leave."

She smiled. "I'll take it."

EPILOGUE

The bride wore white. A strapless, hand-beaded Monique Lhuillier of ivory silk, to be exact, sewn onto her body mere minutes before she walked down the aisle. With white satin peep-toe pumps on her feet, a matching white ribbon in her hair, and an armload of pure white roses, she was demure innocence itself.

Except for her hair. Her hair glowed in the candle light like wildfire, and a ribbon of the same deep copper encircled her waist and flowed down the back of her gown like a sunset on the water. The look she shared with her groom danced with laughter and passion as the music swelled, carrying her up the aisle to his side.

He held his hand out for her as she approached and she took it without hesitation. She plaited her fingers into his and promised without doubt or reservation to be a true and faithful partner until death did them part. To love him with all the strength and courage she could muster. To honor him and cherish him and be thankful for the undeserved gift of his love, now and always.

And when he kissed her, the entire world shattered into a cacophony of cheers, applause and popping flashbulbs. It was better, Sloan thought wonderingly, than winning an Oscar. Though she had the same man to thank for both.

She gazed at the man whose hand she held, her new husband. The first man since Archer who'd looked at her and seen more than sex appeal, who'd seen something deep and true and vulnerable. The man who'd asked her to play a grandmother, had directed her to an Oscar in the role, then given her ready made grandchildren when he married her.

She smiled radiantly into the front rows of the church, at the family she and Lars Von Heller had brought together. His son and daughter, their families. Nixie and Erik. The Senator, Tyrese and Mary Jane. She grinned fondly at Nixie, who blew her a watery kiss, and at Erik, who handed his wife a hanky and rolled his eyes at Sloan. Nixie had bawled through Tyrese and Mary Jane's wedding last year, as well as hers and Erik's the year before that. Sloan wouldn't wonder if Erik had hankies in every pocket. He took wonderful care of her baby.

Lars squeezed her hand and Sloan leaned into his dear, solid bulk. A new sense of peace washed over her, a lovely stillness deep in her center where she used to have only static and the manic drive to keep moving. She smiled, then she laughed. She didn't worry about wrinkles anymore, nor about drooping this or sagging that. She was calm at her very heart and when the music swelled again, she sailed down the aisle and into her new life safe in the knowledge that she was loved. She was known from the bones out, and she was loved.

Nixie sopped at her face with Erik's last dry hanky and sighed happily as Sloan and Lars exited the church to thunderous applause. Erik's hands rested on her shoulders and she leaned into him, grateful as always for his quiet support. No matter where she went or what she did, she was always *home* when she was with him. She covered his hands with hers.

Kiss the Girl

"That was definitely my mother's best wedding," she said. "At least the best one I ever attended."

Erik laughed. "I have a feeling it'll be the last one, too."

"Yeah, I think Lars is here to stay." She swiped one last tear away and offered Erik his hanky back.

"Uh, no. Thanks. Put it with the others."

Nixie shrugged and dropped the crumpled linen into her purse. Her cell phone buzzed quietly from the depths, and Erik lifted a brow. "One of your stars need a little hand-holding?"

"Maybe." Nixie shrugged. Karl's departure had left one hell of a void at Leighton-Brace Charitable Giving but Nixie had refused to let it crumble. Maybe she'd retired her own spotlight, but she'd spent years learning how to aim one. And as it turned out, there were a hell of a lot of stars with a yen to do good who respected her expertise on such things. She'd filled Karl's behind-the-camera shoes handily, and with some compassion for the talent to boot. It was, she felt, pretty darn win/win. "But I'm not giving it." She checked the readout on her phone. "Grand Punk Master Jam is being rerouted to the Leighton-Brace Charitable Giving switchboard as we speak. We have a very competent office manager who I'm sure can see to whatever he needs while well-digging in Somalia."

"I'm sure she can," Mary Jane said from the pew behind them. "But I'm still pissed you stole Wanda from us like that."

Nixie smiled. Karl had been a ruthless mastermind, but he had nothing on *Nixie Leighton-Brace* when it came to staffing her empire. "Oh, come on. You know Wanda wanted a job that didn't require regular evenings."

Mary Jane frowned darkly. "You seduced her with access to people like Grand Punk Master Jam."

Tyrese slung an arm around his wife's shoulders. "Maybe she wanted a job where she didn't have to look at

Daryl Johnson's package every time he came in for a flu shot."

Mary Jane shrugged. "Yeah. Maybe."

"Hey, look," Erik said, pointing. "Is that Dame Judi Dench?"

Mary Jane's shoulders hunched. "Why can't your mother have normal friends?" she asked Nixie.

"My bad," Erik said. "It's Helen Mirren. I get them mixed up."

She glared at Erik. "Very funny. You think you can tap into my celebrity phobia and I'll forget about Wanda? I don't think so. I'm--"

"Kristen Stewart and Rob Pattinson are back by the baptismal font." Nixie pointed toward the vestibule of the church. Mary Jane shuddered and grabbed her husband's hand.

"Okay, we'll fight over Wanda later," she said and disappeared.

The Senator leaned forward. "So *are* you rounding up any new talent while you're here in L.A.?" she asked. "I loved the Southeast Asian junket you put together for Sandra Bullock last year. I pushed a sweat shop bill through the Senate thanks to that trip."

Nixie smiled. "I've been meaning to tell you how much I like that bill."

"Thanks." She sighed and glanced at Erik. "Probably the last bill I'll write, you know. Before my retirement."

"I know," Nixie said, smothering a smile.

"Before I turn my office over to some brash young person ready to take their turn at the wheel of national politics."

"Mmmm." Nixie nodded solemnly.

"Enough with the hinting, okay, Mom?" Erik said. "How many times do we have to have this conversation? I'm not going to run for your office. Why would I? I'm a

Kiss the Girl

surgeon, and all my humanitarian impulses are dealt with at home." He gave Nixie a fond squeeze.

"Lucky you," the Senator said sweetly.

Erik smiled. "I married well."

"Well, of course you did. I picked her out, didn't I?" The Senator rolled her eyes. "As it happens, however, I wasn't asking you to run for my Senate seat."

"No?" Erik lifted a skeptical brow.

"No." She smiled. "I was asking Nixie."

He swung around to stare at Nixie, who stared at the Senator. "I've been meaning to mention it for some time now, Nixie," she said. "The work you do with Leighton-Brace is wonderful, don't misunderstand me. We need all the orphanages you can convince celebrities to build. But the circumstances that created the need for orphanages in the first place still exist." She held up one finger, a professor at the podium. "*Until* you start changing the laws. Then you're changing the world."

Nixie stared at her, struck. "I never wanted to change the world," she said.

Erik laughed. "But you do. Every day. You have kind of a thing for it." He looked back and forth between his mother and his wife. "Senator Leighton-Brace," he said. "I like it."

Nixie liked it, too.

About the Author

Some years ago, Golden Heart Award winner Susan Sey gave up the glamorous world of software training to pursue a high-powered career in diaper changing. Two children and millions of diapers later, she decided to branch out and started writing novels during nap time. The kids eventually gave up their naps, so now she writes when she's supposed to be doing the laundry. She currently resides in St. Paul, Minnesota, with her wonderful husband, their charming children and a very tall pile of dirty clothes.

For more about Susan or her books, feel free to visit her website (www.susansey.com) where you'll also find links to her Twitter and Facebook pages, and the occasional deleted scene or bonus chapter. Which have usually been deleted for very good reasons but still.

Printed in Great Britain
by Amazon.co.uk, Ltd.,
Marston Gate.

Punkie Night

A Custom of Hinton St George

By
Charles Bird

Illustrated by
Mike Fenton-Wilkinson

Acknowledgments

Copyright © Text: Charles Bird

Copyright © Illustrations & Design:
Mike Fenton-Wilkinson

This edition first published 2007 by
Punkie Publishing

The publication of this storybook has
been assisted by a grant from the
Hinton St George Reading Room Trust.
All profits from sales will go to the
Punkie Night Committee
for use in perpetuating the tradition of
Punkie Night.

ISBN 978-0-9555577-0-5

Printed by
Creeds The Printers, Broadoak, Bridport, Dorset DT6 5NL

It was a dark and windy evening in late October in the days long before cars and electricity.

Outside you could see neither moon nor stars.
Inside the cottages were lit only by candles.

The menfolk of the Somerset village of Hinton St George had gone earlier in the day to the fair at Chiselborough.

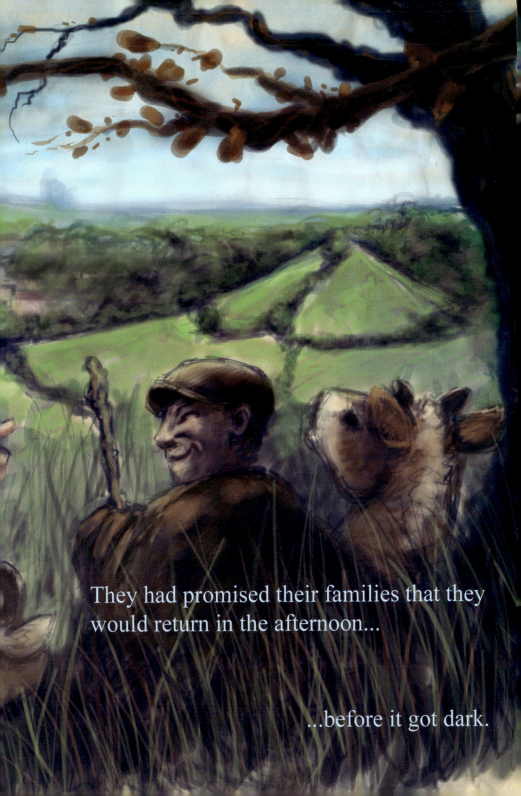

They had promised their families that they would return in the afternoon...

...before it got dark.

At the fair the men of Hinton bought and sold farm animals, fruit, vegetables and eggs.

In fact they were having such a good time and drinking so much cider that they did not notice how late it was.

Soon it grew dark and now it was difficult for them to walk the four miles back to their houses and families in Hinton.

Some of them even had to lie down in the fields to sleep off the effects of the cider.

Back in Hinton the wives and families became worried and were wondering what could have happened to their menfolk. They decided that they had better go out and look for them.
But how would they see in the dark?

They had a few candles but as soon as they took them outside they were blown out by the wind!
And some of them were frightened to venture out in the dark.

The problem was solved by a cunning vegetable. Planted in the fields nearby were mangolds (a kind of mangel-wurzel or large turnip used as cattle feed).

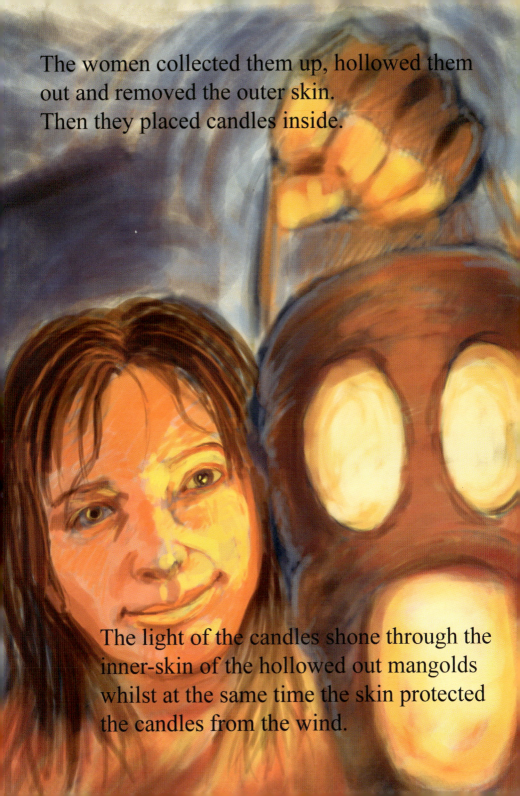

The women collected them up, hollowed them out and removed the outer skin.
Then they placed candles inside.

The light of the candles shone through the inner-skin of the hollowed out mangolds whilst at the same time the skin protected the candles from the wind.

Then the women set off with their lanterns on the road to Chiselborough to find their menfolk and bring them safely home.

It must have been a strange and frightening sight for the Hinton men when they saw coming towards them across the countryside what looked like a row of glowing eerie faces!

Some of them ran off thinking the lights were ghosts or witches come to haunt them or even will 'o' the wisps, which the locals call Punkies.

Eventually the women rounded up their menfolk and escorted them back to Hinton holding up their Punkie lanterns to light the way home.

Let us hope that the men had bought some ribbons or fairings for their wives and sweethearts so they could give them as presents for being rescued in the dark!

Ever since that time it has been the custom in Hinton St George to hold late in October a Punkie night when the children of the village take part in a procession carrying their Punkie lanterns.

A Punkie King and Queen are chosen to lead the procession and everyone sings:

It's Punkie night tonight
It's Punkie night tonight
Give us a candle, give us a light
It's Punkie night tonight

It's Punkie night tonight
It's Punkie night tonight
Adam and Eve wouldn't believe
It's Punkie night tonight

Historical Note

(With thanks to Joan Farris for her help in compiling this note)

No-one knows quite when the first Punkie Night took place but the tradition of celebrating it dates back beyond living memory. Other villages in the area, including Chiselborough itself, also have Punkie Night celebrations.

An account of Punkie Nights is given in 'The Folklore of Somerset' by Kingsley Palmer, (B.T. Batsford, 1976, pages 105-7).

It may well be that Punkie Night is connected with the ancient Celtic festival of Samain when the death of the old year was commemorated and bonfires lit to regenerate the earth. This occurred at the end of October and became All Hallows Eve (or Halloween as it is now called) after the arrival of Christianity when ghosts and witches were thought to ride out at midnight.

There may be a connection between the ghosts of Halloween and 'Punkies'. The Halloween ghosts were said to be the souls of unburied people. In her book 'Somerset Dialect' by Ruth Tongue, (The Folklore Society, 1965), she derives the word 'Punkie' from the north Somerset name for the little dancing lights of marsh gas seen on the Somerset levels. These lights were known as 'spunkies' and were thought to be the souls of unbaptised babies.

Whatever the connection between Punkie Night and Halloween, one can imagine the time of year around Halloween would have been considered especially dangerous for those walking abroad at night because of the presence of witches.

That may explain why the womenfolk were worried about their men being out in the dark and why Punkie lanterns were designed with faces to ward off evil spirits.

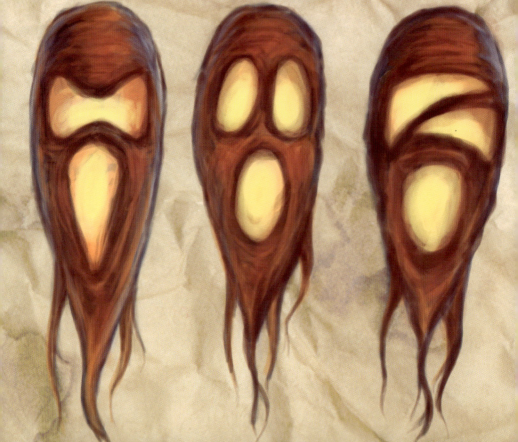

The line in the Punkie Night song 'Adam and Eve wouldn't believe', is difficult to explain. Is it just doggerel or does it have some meaning?

One possible explanation is that it refers to the coat of arms of the Poulett family which shows, as supporters, a wild man and a wild woman not unlike Adam and Eve.

There is also an alternative stanza in the song of more obvious meaning;

'Give us a candle, give us a light
If 'ee don't we'll give 'ee a fright'

How to Prepare a Punkie Lantern

(By Brian Cornelius who took over from the late Douglas Gillard in keeping the Punkie Night tradition alive in Hinton St George)

The preparation of a mangold or similar is as follows:
Firstly, the mangold has to be washed. Then the top or the bottom is cut off to make a lid, (which is removed to fit a candle when necessary). A hole about the size of a finger is made in the lid for air to keep the candle alight.

The mangold or similar vegetable is then hollowed out using items of kitchen cutlery, (knives, spoons etc. and plenty of patience) to form a shell leaving the outer wall thin enough to let the light shine through but thick enough to stop the mangold collapsing.

The outer coloured skin of the mangold is then marked out with a suitable face, pattern or image where the candlelight is to shine through.

The outer skin is then gradually removed to form the pattern with the only hole on the lid. If other holes are made then the candle may blow out much easier and on a windy night it is not easy to light matches to relight the candle.

The final stage is to make a handle (using wire or string), to carry the lantern without burning yourself with heat from the candle but with enough heat to keep your hands warm on a cold evening!

Mangolds are becoming increasingly difficult to come by and Punkie lanterns are often made using pumpkins.

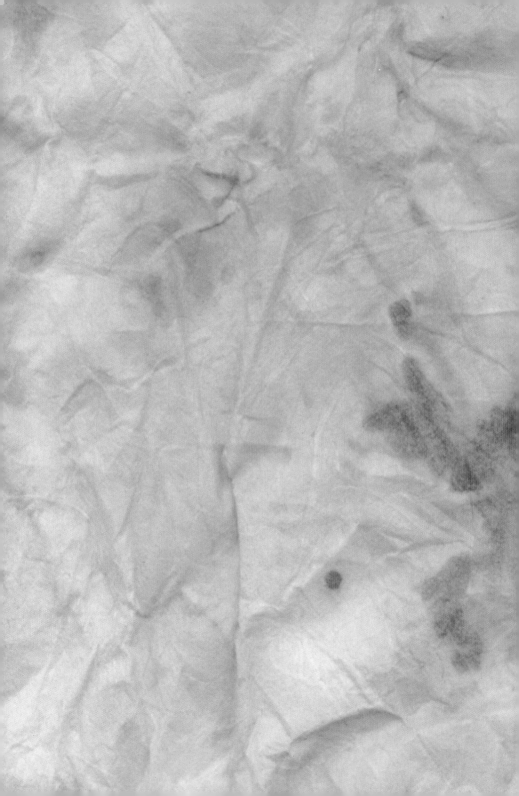